"Now, I see you two were living like kings.

"Here I was picturing you suffering in some hovel in the middle of nowhere. Instead, I find you living in a luxurious villa above the most gorgeous harbor I've ever seen."

Kings. Her word choice smothered Nic's amusement. Had she used the word deliberately? Had his friend given up all Nic's secrets?

"How can you afford a place like this? You guys were always looking for investors for your business. It seems to me that anyone who had enough money to own this villa could have financed the entire project."

A little of his tension fell away, but only a little. She didn't know the truth yet. But when she did…

Tell her. Tell her who you are.

Wise words. Pity he couldn't bring himself to follow his own advice. He'd been hiding his true identity from her for too long. She'd be devastated when she learned how much he'd lied about. Yet it was only a matter of a week before the media found out he was wife-hunting and he went from obscure scientist to international news item. She would know soon enough. And hopefully when that happened she would appreciate that they'd kept their relationship quiet.

Because if he was to be king, she couldn't be his wife.

is part ohield!

A ROYAL
BABY SURPRISE

BY
CAT SCHIELD

Published in Great Britain 2015
by Mills & Boon, an imprint of Harlequin (UK) Limited,
Eton House, 18-24 Paradise Road, Richmond, Surrey, TW9 1SR

© 2015 Catherine Schield

ISBN: 978-0-263-25274-3

51-0815

Harlequin (UK) Limited's policy is to use papers that are natural, renewable and recyclable products and made from wood grown in sustainable forests. The logging and manufacturing processes conform to the legal environmental regulations of the country of origin.

Printed and bound in Spain
by CPI, Barcelona

Cat Schield has been reading and writing romance since high school. Although she graduated from college with a BA in business, her idea of a perfect career was writing books for Mills & Boon. And now, after winning the Romance Writers of America 2010 Golden Heart® Award for series contemporary romance, that dream has come true. Cat lives in Minnesota with her daughter, Emily, and their Burmese cat. When she's not writing sexy, romantic stories for Mills & Boon® Desire™, she can be found sailing with friends on the St Croix River, or in more exotic locales, like the Caribbean and Europe. She loves to hear from readers. Find her at www.catschield.net. Follow her on Twitter: @catschield.

To the 2008 Ionian Islands Crew:
Erik, Sonia, Charie, Renee, Jean and Val

One

Above the sound of the breeze blowing through the cedar trees that dotted the island hillside, Nic Alessandro heard the scuff of a footstep on flagstone and knew he wasn't alone on the terrace.

"So this is where you've been hiding." Brooke Davis's voice was like his favorite vodka: smoky and smooth, with a sexy, implied bite. And she went to his head just as swiftly.

Already suffering from a well-deserved hangover, Nick was further jolted by her unexpected arrival on this out-of-the-way Greek island. But he couldn't let himself be glad to see her. The future he'd once planned to have with her was impossible. His older brother, Gabriel, had married a woman incapable of having children, meaning he would have no son to inherit the throne of Sherdana, the European nation their family had ruled for hundreds of years. Now, as next in line to the throne, it was up to Nic to find a wife that the laws of his country would accept as the future mother of the royal line. As an American, Brooke didn't fit the bill.

"Is this the rustic cabin on the side of a mountain you told me about?" she asked. "The one you said I'd hate because it had no running water and no indoor toilets?"

Nic detected the strain she tried to hide beneath her teasing tone. What was she doing here? Had her brother Glen sent her to talk Nic into returning to California? He couldn't believe she'd come on her own after the way he'd broken things off.

"Here I was picturing you suffering in some hovel in the middle of nowhere. Instead, I find you living in a luxurious villa above the most gorgeous harbor I've ever seen."

Her voice came from the side of the terrace that led down to the beach, so she must have arrived by boat. Walking up the hundred and fifty steps hadn't winded her a bit. She loved to work out. It was what kept her lithe body in perfect shape.

What had he been thinking when he'd finally surrendered to the powerful attraction he'd hidden from her for the past five years? He shouldn't have been so quick to assume that his royal duty to Sherdana ended the minute Gabriel had gotten engaged to Lady Olivia Darcy.

"You're probably wondering how I found you."

Nic opened his eyes and watched Brooke saunter across the terrace. She wore a white, high-waisted cotton blouse and faded denim shorts with a ragged hem. The gray scarf wound around her neck was one of her favorites.

Everything she passed she touched: the back of the lounge chair, the concrete wall that bordered the terrace, the terra-cotta pots and the herbs and flowers they held. As her fingertips drifted along the fuchsia petals of a bougainvillea, Nic envied the flower she caressed.

At this hour of the morning, the sun was behind the villa, warming the front garden. On winter days he would have taken coffee to the side patio and made the most of the sunshine. In late July, he preferred the back terrace where he could enjoy the view of the town of Kioni across the harbor. The wind off the Ionian Sea kept the humidity at bay, making this a pleasant spot to linger most of the morning.

"I'm guessing Glen sent you."

She looked pained by his assumption. "No, it was my idea to come."

A double blow. She hadn't accepted the end of their relationship, and Glen didn't want him back working on the rocket after the explosion that had killed a member of their team. An explosion caused when the fuel system Nic had been working on malfunctioned. When the *Griffin* had blown up, his dream of privatizing space travel had gone up in smoke with it. He'd retreated from California in defeat, only to discover that he was now facing royal obligations back in Sherdana.

"You brought him here two years ago for a boys' weekend after a successful test firing. He came back with horror stories of long hikes in the mountains and an abundance of wildlife. I realize now those hikes involved stairs leading down to a private beach and the wildlife was in the bars in town. Shame on you two. I actually felt sorry for him."

Nic rubbed his hand across the stubble around his mouth, hiding a brief smile. They'd certainly had her going.

"Now I see you two were living like kings."

Kings. Her word choice smothered Nic's amusement. Had she used the word deliberately? Had Glen given up all Nic's secrets?

"How can you afford a place like this? You guys were always looking for investors. It seems to me that anyone who had enough money to own this villa could have financed the entire project."

A little of his tension fell away, but only a little. She didn't know the truth yet. And when she did find out…

Tell her. Tell her who you are.

Wise words. Pity he couldn't bring himself to follow his own advice. He'd been hiding his true identity from her for too long. She'd be devastated when she learned how much he'd lied about. Yet, it was only a matter of a week before the media found out he was wife-hunting and he went from obscure scientist to international news item. She would know soon enough. And hopefully when that happened she would appreciate that they'd kept their brief relationship quiet.

She believed herself in love with a man who didn't exist. A man of duty, honor and integrity. They were principles that he'd been raised to embrace, but they'd been sadly lacking the moment he'd pulled Brooke into his arms and kissed her that first time.

"My brothers and I own it," he said, wishing so many things could be different.

Brooke's very stillness suggested the calm before the storm. "I see."

That was it? No explosion? No ranting? "What do you see?"

"That we have a lot to talk about."

He didn't want to talk. He wanted to pull her into his arms and make love to her until they were both too exhausted to speak. "I've already said everything I intend to." He shouldn't have phrased that like a challenge. She was as tenacious as a terrier when she got her teeth into something.

"Don't give me that. You owe me some answers."

"Fine." He owed her more than that. "What do you want to know?"

"You have brothers?"

"Two. We're triplets."

"You never talked about your family. Why is that?"

"There's not much to say."

"Here's where we disagree."

She stepped closer. Vanilla and honey enveloped him, overpowering the scent of cypress and the odor of brine carried on the light morning breeze. With her finger she eased his dark sunglasses down his nose and captured his gaze. Her delicate brows pulled together in a frown.

He braced himself against the pitch and roll of emotions as her green-gray eyes scoured his face. He should tell her to go away, but he was so damned glad to see her that the words wouldn't come. Instead, he growled like a cranky dog that wasn't sure whether to bite or beg to be petted.

"You look like hell."

"I'm fine." Disgusted by his suddenly hoarse voice, he knocked her hand aside and slid his sunglasses back into place.

She, on the other hand, looked gorgeous. Rambunctious red hair, streaked with dark honey, framed her oval face and cascaded over her shoulders. Her pale, unblemished skin, arresting dimples and gently curving cheekbones made for the sort of loveliness any man could lose his head over. A wayward curl tickled his skin as she leaned over him. Shifting his gaze, he took the strand between two fingers and toyed with it.

"What have you been doing all alone in your fancy villa?" she asked.

"If you must know, I'm working."

"On your tan maybe." She sniffed him and wrinkled her slender nose. "Or a hangover. Your eyes are bloodshot."

"I've been working late."

"Riiight." She drew the word out doubtfully. "I'll make some coffee. It looks like you could use some."

Safe behind his dark glasses, he watched her go, captivated by the gentle sway of her denim-clad rear and her long legs. Satin smooth skin stretched over lean muscles, honed by yoga and running. His pulse purred as he recalled those strong, shapely legs wrapped around his hips.

Despite the cool morning air, his body heated. An hour ago, he'd opened his eyes, feeling as he had most of the past few mornings: queasy, depressed and distraught over the accident that had occurred during a test firing of their prototype rocket ship.

Brooke's arrival on this sleepy, Greek island was like being awakened from a drugged sleep by an air horn.

"Someone must be taking care of you," she said a short time later, bringing the smell of bitter black coffee with her when she returned. "The coffeepot was filled with grounds and water. All I had to do was turn it on."

Nic's nostrils flared eagerly as he inhaled the robust aroma. The scent alone was enough to bring him back to life.

She sat down on the lounge beside his and cradled her mug between both hands. She took a tentative sip and made a face. "Ugh. I forgot how strong you like it."

He grunted and willed the liquid to cool a little more so he could drain his cup and start on a second. It crossed his mind that coping with Brooke while a strong jolt of stimulant rushed through his veins was foolhardy at best. She riled him up admirably all by herself, making the mix of caffeine and being alone with her a lethal combination.

"So, am I interrupting a romantic weekend?"

Luckily he hadn't taken another sip, or the stuff might have come straight out his nose. His fingers clenched around the mug. When they began to cramp, he ground his teeth and relaxed his grip.

"Probably not," she continued when he didn't answer. "Or you'd be working harder to get rid of me."

Damn her for showing up while his guard was down. Temptation rode him like a demon every time she was near.

But he couldn't have her. She mustn't know how much he wanted her. He'd barely summoned the strength to break things off a month ago. But now that he was alone with her on this island, her big misty-green eyes watching his every mood, would his willpower hold out?

Silence stretched between them. He heard the creak of wood as she settled back on the lounge. He set the empty cup on his chest and closed his eyes once more. Having her here brought him a sense of peace he had no right to feel. He wanted to reach out and lace his fingers with hers but didn't dare to.

"I can see why you and your brothers bought this place. I could sit here for days and stare at the view."

Nic snorted softly. Brooke had never been one to sit anywhere and stare at anything. She was a whirling dervish of energy and enthusiasm.

"I can't believe how blue the water is. And the town is so quaint. I can't wait to go exploring."

Exploring? Nic needed to figure out how to get her on a plane back to America as soon as possible before he gave in to temptation. Given her knack for leading with her emotions, reasoning with her wouldn't work. Threats wouldn't work, either. The best technique for dealing with Brooke was to let her have her way and that absolutely couldn't happen this time. Or ever again, for that matter.

When she broke the silence, the waver in her voice betrayed worry. "When are you coming back?"

"I'm not."

"You can't mean that." She paused, offering him the opportunity to take back what he'd said. When he didn't, her face took on a troubled expression. "You do mean that. What about *Griffin*? What about the team? You can't just give it all up."

"Someone died because of a flaw in a system I designed—"

She gripped his forearm. "Glen was the one pushing for the test. He didn't listen when you told him it wasn't ready. He's the one to blame."

"Walter died." He enunciated the words, letting her hear his grief. "It was my fault."

"So that's it? You are giving up because something went wrong? You expect me to accept that you're throwing away your life's work? To do what?"

He had no answer. What the hell was he going to do in Sherdana besides get married and produce an heir? He had no interest in helping run the country. That was Gabriel's job. And his other brother Christian had his businesses and investments to occupy him. All Nic wanted to do, all he'd ever wanted to do, was build rockets that would someday carry people into space. With that possibility extinguished, his life stretched before him, empty and filled with regret.

"There's something else going on." She tightened her grip on his arm. "Don't insult my intelligence by denying it."

Nic patted her hand. "I would never do that, Dr. Davis." A less intelligent woman wouldn't have captivated him so completely, no matter how beautiful. Brooke's combination of sex appeal and brains had delivered a fatal one-two punch. "How many doctorates do you have now, anyway?"

"Only two." She jerked her hand from beneath his, reacting to his placating tone. "And don't change the subject." Despite her annoyance, a huge yawn practically dislocated her jaw as she glared at him.

"You're tired." Showing concern for her welfare might encourage her, but he couldn't help it.

"I've been on planes since yesterday sometime. Do you know how long it takes to get here?" She closed her eyes. "About twenty hours. And I couldn't sleep on the flight over."

"Why?"

A deep breath pushed her small, pert breasts tight against her sleeveless white cotton blouse.

"Because I was worried about you, that's why."

The admission was a cop-out. It was fourth on her list of reasons why she'd flown six thousand miles to talk to him in person rather than breaking her news over the phone.

But she wasn't prepared to blurt out that she was eight weeks pregnant within the first ten minutes of arriving.

She had a lot of questions about why he'd broken off their three-month relationship four weeks earlier. Questions she hadn't asked at first because she'd been too hurt to wonder why he'd dropped her when things between them had been so perfect. Then the fatal accident had happened with *Griffin*. Nic had left California and she'd never received closure.

"I don't need your concern," he said.

"Of course you don't." She crammed all the skepticism she could muster into her tone to keep from revealing how much his rebuff stung. "That's why you look like week-old roadkill."

Although his expression didn't change, his voice reflected amusement. "Nice image."

She surveyed his disheveled state, the circles beneath his eyes, their utter lack of vitality. The thick black stubble on his cheeks made her wonder how long it had been since he'd shaved. No matter how hard he worked, she'd never seen his golden-brown eyes so flat and lifeless. He really did look like death warmed over.

"Brooke, why did you really come here?"

Her ready excuse died on her lips. He'd believe that she'd come here to convince him to return to the project. It would be safe to argue on behalf of her brother. But where Nic was concerned, she hadn't played it safe for five years.

He deserved the truth. So, she selected item number three on her list of why she'd chased after him.

"You disappeared without saying goodbye." Once she better understood what had spooked him, Brooke would confess the number one reason she'd followed him to Ithaca. "When you didn't answer any of my phone calls or respond to my emails, I decided to come find you." She gathered a fortifying breath before plunging into deep water. "I want to know the real reason why things ended between us."

Nic tunneled his fingers into his shaggy black hair, a sure sign he was disturbed. "I told you—"

"That I was too distracting." She glared at him. Nic was her polar opposite. Always so serious, he never let go like other people. He held himself apart from the fun. She'd treated his solemnity as a challenge. And after years of escalating flirtation, she'd discovered he wasn't as in control as he appeared. "You weren't getting enough work done."

She exhaled in exasperation. For five months he'd stopped working on the weekends she'd visited and spent that entire time focused on her. All that attention had been heady and addictive. Brooke hadn't anticipated that he might wake up one morning and go back to his workaholic ways. "I don't get it. We were fantastic together. You were happy."

Nic's mouth tightened into a grim line. "It was fun. But you were all in and I wasn't."

Brooke bit her lip and considered what he said for an awkward, silent minute. "You broke up with me because I told you I loved you?" At the time she hadn't worried about confessing her feelings. After all, she was pretty sure he suspected she'd been falling for him for five years. "Did you ever intend to give us a chance?"

"I thought it was better to end it rather than to let things drag out. I was wrong to let things get so involved between us."

"Why didn't you tell me this in the first place?"

"I thought it would be easier on you if you believed I'd chosen work over you."

"Instead of being truthful and admitting I wasn't the one."

This wasn't how she'd expected this conversation to go. Deep in her heart she'd believed Nic was comfortable with how fast their relationship had progressed. She'd been friends with him long enough to know he didn't squander his time away from the *Griffin* project. This led her to believe she mattered to him. How could she have been so wrong?

Conflicting evidence tugged her thoughts this way and that. Usually she considered less and acted more, but being pregnant meant her actions impacted more than just her. She needed a little time to figure out how to approach Nic about her situation.

"I guess my optimistic nature got the better of me again." She lightened her tone to hide the deep ache centered in her chest.

"Brooke—"

"Don't." She held up both hands to forestall whatever he'd planned to say. "Why don't we not talk about this anymore while you give me a tour of your palatial estate."

"It's not palatial." His thick black eyebrows drew together in a grim frown.

"It is to a girl who grew up in a three-bedroom, fifteen hundred square-foot house."

Nic's only reply was a grunt. He got to his feet and gestured for her to precede him. Before entering the house, Brooke kicked off her sandals. The cool limestone tile soothed her tired feet as she slipped past him. Little brush fires ignited along her bare arm where it came into contact with his hair-roughened skin.

"This is the combination living-dining room and kitchen," he said, adopting the tour guide persona he used when escorting potential *Griffin* investors.

She took in the enormous abstract paintings of red, yellow, blue and green that occupied the wall behind the white slip-covered couches. To her left, in the L-shaped kitchen, there was a large glass table with eight black chairs, offering a contrast amongst the white cabinets and stainless appliances. The space had an informal feel that invited relaxation.

"The white furniture and walls are a little stark for my taste," she said. "But it works with the paintings. They're wonderful. Who did them?"

"My sister."

He had a sister, too? "I'd like to meet her." Even as Brooke spoke the words, she knew that would never happen. Nic had made it perfectly clear he didn't want her in his life. She had a decision to make in the next day or so. It's why she'd come here. She needed his help to determine how the rest of her life would play out. "Did Glen know about your family?"

"Yes."

That hurt. The two men had always been as tight as brothers, but she never expected that Glen would keep secrets from her.

"Tell me about your brothers." She didn't know what to make of all these revelations.

"We're triplets. I'm the middle one. "

"Two brothers and a sister," she murmured.

Who was Nic Alessandro? At the moment he looked nothing like the overworked rocket scientist she'd known for years. Although a bit wrinkled and worse for wear, his khaki shorts and white short-sleeved shirt had turned him into an ad for Armani's summer collection. In fact, his expensive sunglasses and elegant clothes transformed him from an absentminded scientist into your basic, run-of-the-mill European playboy. The makeover shifted him further out of reach.

"Is there anyone else I should know about?" Despite her best efforts to keep her tone neutral, her voice had an edge. "Like a wife?"

"No wife."

Brooke almost smiled at his dark tone. Once upon a time she'd taken great delight in teasing him, and it should have been easy to fall back into that kind of interaction. Unfortunately, the first time he'd kissed her, she'd crossed into a deeply serious place where his rejection had the power to bruise and batter her heart.

"Who takes care of all this when you're not here?" Keeping the conversation casual was the only way to keep sadness from overwhelming her.

"We have a caretaker who lives in town. She comes in once a week to clean when we're not in residence, more often when we are. She also cooks for us, and her husband maintains the gardens and the boat, and fixes whatever needs repairing in the house."

Brooke looked over her shoulder at the outdoor terrace with its informal wood dining table and canvas chairs. A set of three steps led down to another terrace with more lounge chairs. Potted herbs lined the three-foot-high walls, softening all the concrete.

"What's upstairs?"

Nic stood in the middle of the living room, his arms crossed, a large, immovable object. "Bedrooms."

"One I can use?" she asked in a small voice.

A muscle twitched in his jaw. "There are a number of delightful hotels in town."

"You'd turn me out?" Something flared in his eyes that

brought her hope back to life. Maybe she hadn't yet heard the complete explanation for why he'd broken off their relationship. She faked a sniffle. "You can't really be so mean as to send me in search of a hotel when you have so much room here."

Nic growled. "I'll show you where you can shower and grab some sleep before you head home."

Although it stung that he was so eager to get rid of her, she'd departed California suspecting he wouldn't welcome her intrusion.

"Then, I can stay?"

"For the moment."

Mutely, she followed him back out through the open French doors and onto the terrace. He made a beeline toward the duffel bag she'd dropped beside the stairs that lead up from the beach.

"I can't get over how beautiful it is here."

"Most people are probably more familiar with the islands in the Aegean," he said, picking up her bag. "Mykonos, Santorini, Rhodes."

"I imagine there's a lot more tourists there."

"Quite a few. Kioni attracts a number of sailors during the summer as well as some people wanting to hike and enjoy a quieter island experience, but we're not overrun. Come on, the guesthouse is over there." He led the way along the terrace to a separate building.

"You should take me sightseeing."

"No. You are going to rest and then we're going to find you a flight home."

Brooke rolled her eyes at Nic's words and decided to take the fact that he kept trying to be rid of her as a challenge. "My return ticket is for a flight a week from now."

"Don't you have a lot to do to prepare for your students at Berkeley?"

"I don't have the job yet." Though Brooke held a position at UC Santa Cruz, teaching Italian studies at Berkeley had been a dream of hers since her sophomore year in college. And then she and Nic had begun a relationship. Soon the distance from San Francisco to the Mojave Desert had become an impediment to what she wanted: a life with Nic.

He shot her a sharp look.

She shrugged. "The interview got postponed again."

"To when?"

"Not for a few weeks yet."

In truth she wasn't sure when it was. There'd been some scheduling conflicts with the head of the department. He'd already canceled two meetings with her in the past month. Not knowing how many people were up for the position she wanted gnawed at her confidence. Few shared her research credentials, but a great many had more experience in the classroom than she did.

And before Nic had abruptly dumped her, she'd begun thinking she wanted to be closer to where he lived and worked. Seeing him only on the weekends wasn't enough. So she'd interviewed for a position at UCLA and been offered a teaching job starting in the fall. The weekend Nic had come up to Santa Cruz to break up with her, she'd been preparing for a very different conversation. One where she told him she was moving to LA. Only he'd beaten her to the punch and she'd decided to put the Berkeley job back on the table.

"Are you sure?" Nic questioned. "It's July. I can't believe they want to put off their decision too much longer."

She frowned at him, butterflies hatching in her stomach as she realized the risk she'd taken by flying here when she should be waiting by the phone in California. "Yes, I'm sure."

"Because I couldn't live with myself if you lost your dream job because you stayed here imagining I'm going to change my mind about us."

Had she been wrong about his initial reaction to her arrival? Had she so badly wanted him to be glad to see her that she'd imagined the delight in his gaze? It wouldn't be the first time she'd jumped to the wrong conclusion where a man's behavior was concerned. And Nic was a master at keeping his thoughts and emotions hidden.

"Don't worry about my dream job," she countered. "It will still be there when I get back."

She hoped.

When they arrived at the small guesthouse, Nic pushed open the door and set her luggage inside. "There's a private bathroom and a great view of Kioni. You should be comfortable here." Neither his impassive expression nor his neutral tone gave anything away. "Relax. Sleep. I'm sure you're exhausted from your travels. Breakfast will be waiting when you're ready."

"I'm not really hungry." Between morning sickness and anxiety, her appetite had fled. "And no matter how tired I am, you know I can't sleep when the sun is up. Why don't we go into town and you can show me around."

"You should rest."

His tone warned her not to argue. The wall he'd erected between them upset her. She wanted to tear it down with kisses and tears and impassioned pleas for him to change his mind about breaking up. But a big emotional scene would only cause him to retreat. She needed to appeal to that big logical brain of his.

"I've come a long way to find you. And talk."

"Later." He scowled at her to forestall any further discussion.

The determined set of his mouth told her she would get nowhere until he was ready to listen. She nodded, reluctant to provoke Nic into further impatience. She wanted him in a calm, agreeable state of mind when she imparted her dramatic news.

Left alone, Brooke took a quick shower in the white, marble bathroom and dressed in a tribal-print maxi dress of cool cotton. There was enough of a breeze blowing in through the open windows to dry her hair, but she didn't want to give Nic too much time to plan his strategy for getting her to leave. She decided to braid the damp strands rather than leave them loose. The last time they'd made love a little over a month ago, he'd shown a great appreciation for the disarray of her long, curly tresses, but now it seemed better to approach him logically and for that she needed to be restrained, not flirty.

Unfortunately, the mirror over the dresser reflected a woman in love, with wide eyes and a slightly unfocused gaze. Her mouth had a rosy fullness and her cheeks were pink. She doubted that this would go over well with Nic.

And after what he'd told her about his reasons for breaking up, Brooke was certain her pregnancy news would be unwelcome, too.

She hadn't given much thought to what came after she told Nic the news. Maybe she was afraid to face more rejection. What if he wanted nothing further to do with her? He'd said he wasn't returning to California. Would the news that he was going to be a father change his plans?

Brooke slid her feet into sandals, but paused before leaving the room. Talking with Nic about her Berkeley interview reminded her she hadn't checked her messages since leaving San Francisco. She dug her cell phone out of the side pocket of her duffel bag and tried to turn it on, but the battery had died. Time ticked away as she dug out her charger and searched for the adapter she'd borrowed. Then there were the minutes it took for the phone to charge enough to come back to life. By the time the display lit up and showed she'd missed a dozen calls, Brooke crackled with impatience.

Her heart sank as she listened to the messages. Her

Berkeley interview had been rescheduled for 10 a.m. three days from now. This considerably shortened the amount of time Brooke had to tell Nic she was pregnant and figure out what form her future relationship with him would take. A quick check of flight schedules revealed that it would be daunting, but doable.

Brooke tossed the phone onto the middle of the bed and took several deep breaths until the tightness in her throat eased. After a few more deep breaths, the urge to throw herself onto the mattress and scream into a pillow subsided, too. Everything would work out just fine. Somehow it always did.

Applying a bright smile to her face, she strolled along the terrace. But as she stepped into the living room of the main house, the absolute quiet told her something was awry. A quick check confirmed her suspicions, but what clinched it was the car missing from the driveway.

Nic had vanished.

Two

Nic had switched from Greek coffee to beer by the time Brooke showed up in Kioni, the village rising from the harbor to cling to the side of Ithaca's rocky hills. From the shade beneath the taverna's white awning, he squinted against the bright sunlight sparkling off the cerulean water and watched his thirty-four-foot cruiser pull alongside the quay. Three Greek men, each wearing broad smiles, converged to issue instructions and help Brooke settle the boat. Although the distance prevented Nic from hearing their conversation, from Brooke's animated gestures and the men's cheerful faces, he guessed she was chattering away and doing what she did best: charming men.

"You're not drinking them as fast today."

Nic switched his attention to the voluptuous, dark-haired, dark-eyed waitress standing at his side. Natasa had waited on him all but one of the past ten days he'd been on the island. She picked up his half-full bottle, which he'd been nursing for the past hour.

"I'm not as thirsty."

Since arriving on Ithaca, Nic had been keeping himself anesthetized with boredom and beer. The combination was barely enough to keep his demons at bay. Before Brooke's arrival he'd given himself a week or so before he had to make peace with his failures and accept his fate. Now it was all coming to a head faster than he could handle.

Natasa gave him a smoky look and set her hand on her hip. "Perhaps you need some company."

Nic hadn't seen her flirt with any of the other men that came to the taverna, only him. He figured she knew who he was and suspected that had prompted her offer. Acid churned in his gut. Being treated like a personality rather than a person was something he hadn't had to endure in America. He hadn't had to be on his guard and question everyone's motives.

"I get off in two hours," she continued. "I would be happy to join you then."

Natasa had made him a similar proposition last night at closing time. Nic had been moderately drunk, but not enough to wish to share the bed with this woman, no matter how attractive she was. His carefree bachelor days had ended a month ago with Gabriel's marriage. Soon every woman he glanced at twice would become fodder for news stories.

It was worse for him being in Europe than living in America. In California he was an anonymous scientist trying to build a rocket ship. On this side of the Atlantic, he was known as Prince Nicolas, second in line to the throne of Sherdana. Avoiding reporters and paparazzi and being wary of helpful strangers had become a routine part of his life. That's why he and his brothers had chosen Ithaca as a retreat. Homer had described the island as "good for goats" but it gave the Alessandro brothers an escape from their hectic world.

Not that Nic was a fool. He knew his "anonymity" on this sleepy island was tenuous at best. But he and his brothers maintained a low profile, and the locals generously pretended the Sherdanian royals were like any other part-time inhabitants.

"I'm afraid I'm already due for some company," Nic said, nodding toward the harbor.

When the boat was snugly tied, three tanned hands extended to help Brooke onto the quay. She seemed to hesitate before accepting the hands of the two men nearest to her and offering the third man an engaging smile.

Natasa shielded her eyes as she gazed in the same direction Nic was looking. "Isn't that your boat?" Her keen black eyes narrowed as she glanced at him for confirmation.

"Yes."

"And the girl?"

"She's staying with me for a few days." Until the words left his lips he hadn't realized he'd changed his mind about putting her on a plane home as soon as humanly possible. Keeping her around was a mistake, but he was feeling battered and raw. Her company was the balm his psyche needed. He just needed to keep her at arm's length.

Natasa sniffed and tossed her head. Then, without another word, she turned to go. Nic gave a mental shrug. He'd retreated to Ithaca to come to grips with his future, not to tumble into some local's bed. He liked his own company. In fact, most days, he preferred it. Why didn't people understand that and leave him alone?

Reality smacked Nic right between the eyes. Soon enough he'd never be left alone again. Returning to Sherdana meant not only a return to duty, but also a complete loss of privacy and peace. Long, solitary hours in his workshop would be a thing of the past. His father and brothers would ensure that his calendar was packed with meetings, speeches and public appearances. He'd been absent for ten years, five years of studying and another five working with Glen on the *Griffin* project.

Now that he was returning home for good, his family would expect him to get up to speed on a variety of political, economic and environmental issues affecting the country. He would be surrounded by advisors, besieged by demands for decisions and sought after for his opinions.

Balls and state dinners with visiting foreign dignitaries would replace basketball tournaments and pig roasts with the team of specialists that he'd assembled to help build the *Griffin* rocket ship. Then there would be the selection of his bride. Once his mother finished narrowing the field of marriage prospects—women his brother had already rejected—Nic would have to choose whom he would spend the rest of his life with. And he wouldn't be allowed to dawdle over his decision because the succession needed to be secured by the birth of a royal heir.

The burden of what lay ahead of him sat on Nic's shoulders like a sack of cement. Was it any wonder he'd kept Brooke in the dark about his true identity all these years? He would have liked to continue pretending that he was just an ordinary man instead of a royal prince in serious trouble of doing the wrong thing with the right woman. But she'd never agree to back off unless she knew his whole story.

In disgruntled admiration, Nic followed Brooke's progress as she made her way around the horseshoe-shaped harbor. Since he'd left the house, she'd changed into an earth-toned sundress and accessorized with chunky bracelets and a peace sign necklace. Her red hair lay in a braided rope across her left shoulder. The breeze that frolicked through the streets teased the strands around her face that weren't long enough to be restricted by the braid.

Gulls jeered as they swooped past her. She appeared

oblivious to their taunts, focused as she was on scanning the quay. The hem of the sundress brushed her calves as she walked. The thin spaghetti straps were too narrow to hide a bra so he knew she was at least partially bare beneath the dress. Speculating on just how bare renewed the pounding in his head despite the aspirin he'd taken earlier.

She neared the taverna. Nic wasn't sure she'd spotted him yet. Eight restaurants edged the water. This particular taverna was Nic's favorite. He'd sampled enough of the menu in the years since they'd bought the villa to be able to make recommendations. The waitstaff always kept the cold beer coming while he took in the view of the vivid blue harbor, a welcome change from the beige and russet California desert where he'd spent the past six years.

For entertainment he liked to watch the comings and goings of the sailboats chartered by vacationers. The captains often wrestled with the difficulties presented by Mediterranean mooring, the docking technique where the anchor was dropped forty feet into the harbor and then the boat was backed up against the cement quay. Only an hour ago he'd been witness to what could go wrong when you had twenty boats snugged in side by side. One departing boat had lifted its anchor, catching its neighbor's as it went, only to at last drop that anchor across the lines belonging to the boat on the other side, hopelessly tangling the two boats. To Nic's amusement, much shouting and gesturing had accompanied the maneuver.

His earlier question about whether Brooke had spotted him was answered as she wove through the tables, aiming straight for him.

"Where did you get the keys to the boat?" he quizzed as she plopped a big canvas purse on the table and sat down with a whoosh of breath.

"Elena showed up shortly after you left. She fed me breakfast and told me where to find them. She's very nice.

And had flattering things to say about you. I think you're her favorite triplet."

Nic wondered what else Elena had said. Had the housekeeper divulged the rest of his secret?

"I doubt that very much. She's always been partial to Christian. He's the youngest. And the one all the ladies love."

"Why is that?"

"He's not as serious as Gabriel or me."

"What does he do?"

"He buys companies and takes them apart so he can sell off the pieces."

"And Gabriel?"

"He runs the family business." Not the truth, but not exactly a lie.

"And your sister paints."

"Ariana."

"And you build rocket ships. Sounds like you're all successful."

Not all of them. With the failure of his life's work, he certainly wasn't feeling particularly successful at the moment.

"I hope you don't mind, but I used your computer to print out some forms I needed to sign."

Even while on vacation the Alessandro triplets were often working on a project or a deal and having a state-of-the-art computer as well as a combination printer and scanner often came in handy.

"You figured out how to turn it on?"

As brilliant as she was when it came to learning languages or analyzing Italian literature, Brooke was technically challenged. She'd handwritten most of her first thesis until Nic had taken her to buy a laptop. He'd then lost an entire weekend to teaching her the ins and outs of the word-processing software as well as an app that enabled her to organize her research for easy reference.

"Ha-ha. I'm not as inept as you think I am."

"That's not saying much."

She pulled a face at him. "You had about forty unopened emails from the team. Why haven't you answered any of their questions?"

Nic shifted his gaze to the harbor and watched an inbound sailboat. "As I explained to you earlier, I'm done."

"How can you walk away from your team and all the hard work they've put in on the project?"

Why didn't she understand? Even if it wasn't his duty to return to Sherdana, Nic couldn't let go of the fact that his faulty design had destroyed the rocket and resulted in a man's death. Besides, Glen was the heart of the project. He would carry on in Nic's absence.

"Glen will find a new engineer," Nic said. "Work will continue."

The rocket's destruction had hastened the inevitable. Nic had known he couldn't stay in California forever. It was only a matter of time before responsibility to his country would have forced him to return home.

"But you were the brains behind the new fuel delivery system."

And his life's work had resulted in a complete disaster. "They have my notes."

"But—"

"Leave it alone." He kept his voice low, but the sharp snap of the words silenced her. An uneasy tension descended between them. "Are you hungry? If you like eggplant, the moussaka is very good."

She pressed her lips together, but Nic could see she wanted to argue with him further. Instead, she asked, "So, what are you going to do?"

"My family is going through a hard time right now. I'm going home."

"For how long?"

"For good."

"Wow."

The shaky breath she released was a punch to his gut. A week ago he'd left California as soon as the initial investigation of the accident concluded. He hadn't spoken to her before getting on a plane. His emotions were too raw. And he'd had no idea how to say goodbye.

"I wish I could make you understand, but I can't."

"You're afraid."

Nic eyed Brooke. Her perceptiveness where he was concerned had always made him wary of letting her get too close. Maybe telling her the truth would be a mistake. Giving her access to his life would increase his connection to her, and keeping his distance would become that much harder.

"Of hurting more people, yes."

She would assume he meant another scientist like Walter Parry, the man who'd died. But Nic was thinking about his family and her brother. And most of all her. When Gabriel's engagement had been announced, Nic had felt a loosening of the ties that bound him to Sherdana, raising them with Gabriel's twin two-year-old daughters, Brittany and Katrina, who'd come to live with Gabriel after their fashion model mother had died a month earlier. They were illegitimate and the only children Gabriel would ever have.

Lady Olivia's infertility—and Gabriel's decision to make her his wife—meant Nic and Christian were no longer free to marry whomever they wished. Or, in Christian's case, to continue enjoying his playboy lifestyle and never marry at all.

Nic cursed the circumstances that had turned his life upside down and sucked him back into a world that couldn't include Brooke. If he'd been a simple scientist, he wouldn't have to resist the invitation in her eyes. Nic shoved away the traitorous thought. It was pointless to dwell on what could never be.

"I can't believe you're really going to give it all up," she said. "You and my brother were excited about the future. The pair of you would get so caught up in a new discovery you wouldn't have noticed if a tornado swept the lab away. You love being a scientist."

"I do, but…" In the three weeks since the rocket had blown up, he'd lost confidence in his abilities. Yet his passion continued to burn. The opposing forces were slowly tearing him apart.

"What are you going to do when you go home?"

"My brothers are interested in luring technology-based companies into the country. They want me to be their technical consultant."

He tried to inject some enthusiasm into his voice and failed. While he agreed with Gabriel that Sherdana's economy would benefit from an influx of such businesses, he wasn't excited about his role in the process. His whole life he'd been actively engaged in creating technologies that would shape the future. The idea of promoting someone else's vision depressed him.

"Sooo," she dragged the word out, "you're never coming back to California?"

"No."

"If this is about the rocket…"

"It's not."

"I don't understand what's going on with you." She looked more than puzzled. She looked worried. "It's not like you to give up."

Nic knew she deserved a full explanation, but once she found out he'd been keeping a huge secret from her all these years she was going to be furious. "There's a little something about me you don't know."

"Oh, I think there's more than a little something."

He ignored her sarcasm. "It's complicated."

"It's okay. As you pointed out earlier, I have two doctorates. I can understand complicated."

"Very well. I'm not an ordinary scientist." He lowered his voice, wishing he'd had this conversation with her at the villa. "I'm Prince Nicolas Alessandro, second in line to the throne of Sherdana."

"A prince? Like a real prince?" Her misty-green eyes blurred and she shook her head as if to rid her brain of his admission. "I don't get it. You sound as American as I do."

"I went to college in Boston. In order to fit in, I eliminated my accent." Nic leaned forward, glad that there was a table between them. He longed to pull her into his arms and kiss away her unhappiness. That was something he could never again do. "My country is Sherdana. It's a small kingdom tucked between France and Italy."

"How small?"

"A little less than two thousand square kilometers with a population of just over four hundred thousand. We're mostly known for our—"

"Wines." She slapped her palm on the table. His beer rattled against the hard surface. "Now I remember why the name is so familiar. Glen had bottles of Sherdanian wine at one of his recent parties."

Nic remembered that evening without pleasure. "It was his way of sending me a message. He wanted me to tell you the truth."

She stared at Nic with dawning horror. "You jerk. I've known you for five years. And you've kept this huge thing from me the whole time? What did you think I was going to do with the information? Sell you out to the press? Torment you with Disney references? Well, that I would have done, but you're a prince—you could have handled that."

Nic waited for her rant to wind down, but she was on a roll and wasn't going to be stopped until she had her say.

"I thought we were friends." Below the irritation in her voice, she sounded as if her heart was breaking. "Why didn't you tell me any of this?"

"I've concealed my identity for a lot of years. It's a hard habit to break."

"Concealed it from strangers, coworkers, acquaintances." The breath she needed to take wasn't available. "How long has my brother known? Probably since you met. You two are as close as brothers." She shut her eyes. "Imagine how I feel, Nic. You've been lying to me as long as I've known you."

"Glen said—"

"Glen?" She pinned him with a look of such fury that a lesser man would have thrown himself at her feet to grovel for forgiveness. "My brother did not tell you to lie to me."

No. Nic had decided to do that all on his own. "He told me you'd never leave it alone if you knew."

"Are you kidding me?" Her eyes widened in dismay. "You were worried that I'd come on even stronger if I knew you were a prince? Is that how low your opinion is of me?"

"No. That's not what I meant—"

"I came here looking for scientist Nic," she reminded him. "That's the man I thought I knew. Who I've—"

"Brooke, stop." Nic badly needed to cut off her declaration.

"—fallen in love with."

Pain, hot and bright, sliced into his chest. "Damn it. I never wanted that." Which was his greatest lie to date.

"Was that how you felt before or after we became intimate?"

"Both." Hoping to distract her, he said, "Do you have any idea how irresistible you are?"

"Is that supposed to make me feel better?"

"It's supposed to explain why I started a relationship with you six months ago after I'd successfully withstood the attraction between us for the last five years."

"Why did you fight it?" She frowned "What happened between us was amazing and real."

His breath exploded from his lungs in a curse. "A month ago we had this conversation. I thought you understood."

"A month ago you claimed your work was the most important thing in your life. Now I find out you never had deep feelings for me and didn't mean to mislead me about where our relationship was heading. But I've always been of the opinion that a woman should react to how a man behaves, not what he says, and you acted like a very happy man when we were together."

"I was happy. But I was wrong to give you the impression I could offer you any kind of future."

"Because you don't care about me?"

"Because I have to go home."

Her brows drew together. "You didn't think I would go with you?"

"You have a life in California. Family. Friends. A career."

"So instead of asking me what I wanted, you made the decision for me."

"Except I can't ask." His frustration was no less acute than hers. "A month ago my older brother made a decision that affects not only my life, but the future of Sherdana."

"What sort of decision?"

"He married a woman who can never have children."

Brooke stared at him in mystified silence for a long moment before saying, "That's very sad, but what does it have to do with you?"

"It's now up to me to get married and make sure the Alessandro royal blood line is continued."

"You're going to marry?" She sat back, her hands falling from the table onto her lap.

"So that I can produce an heir. I'm second in line to the throne. It's my duty."

Her expression flattened into blank shock for several seconds as she absorbed his declaration. He'd never seen her dumbfounded. Usually she had a snappy retort for everything. Her quick mind processed at speeds that constantly amazed him.

"Your younger brother can't do it?"

The grim smile he offered her conveyed every bit of his displeasure. "I'm quite certain mother intends to see that we are both married before the year is out."

"It is a truth universally acknowledged," she quoted, "that a single man in possession of a good fortune, must be in want of a wife." She stared at the taverna's logo printed in blue on the white place mat as if the answers to the universe were written there in code. "And I'm not the one you want."

"It isn't that simple." He gripped his beer in both hands to keep from reaching out and offering her comfort. "In order for my child to be eligible to ascend Sherdana's throne someday, the constitution requires that his mother has to be either a Sherdana citizen or a member of Europe's aristocracy."

"And I'm just an ordinary girl from California with two doctorates." The corners of her mouth quivered in a weak attempt at a smile. "I get it."

Three

Beneath the grapevines woven through the taverna's roof beams, the afternoon heat pressed in on Brooke. Light-headed and slightly ill, she didn't realize how much she'd set her hopes on Nic's returning to California and giving their relationship another try until he crushed her dreams with his confession. Her fingers fanned over her still-flat abdomen and the child that grew there. Not once since she'd learned she was pregnant had she considered raising this child utterly on her own. Nic had always been there for her. First as her brother's friend. Then her friend. And finally as her lover.

When she'd strayed from her topic during the writing of her second thesis he'd spent hours on the phone talking her through her research and her arguments. He'd gone with her to buy both her cars. He always shared his dessert with her when they went out to dinner even though she knew it drove him crazy that she never ordered her own. And in a dozen little ways, he stayed present in her life even though physically they lived miles apart.

For an instant she recalled the last time she and Nic had made love. She'd gazed deep into his eyes and glimpsed her future. During their time together, their lovemaking had been in turn fast, hot, slow and achingly sweet. But on their last night in particular, they'd both been swept away by urgent intensity. Yet there'd been a single look suspended between one breath and the next that held her transfixed. In that instant, an important connection had been made between them and she'd been forever changed.

But now…

A prince.

The conversion from distracted, overworked scientist to intense, sexy aristocrat had been apparent when she'd arrived this morning. At first she'd ascribed the change to his European-style clothing, but now she understood he'd been transformed in a far more elemental manner.

A month ago he'd given her a speech about how he needed to refocus on *Griffin*, and that meant he had to stop seeing her. She'd been frustrated by the setback, but figured it was only a matter of time until he figured out they were meant to be together. When he'd left California in the wake of the accident, the bond had stretched and thinned, but it had held. Awareness of Nic had hummed across that psychic filament. Although compelled to track him down and investigate if her instincts were correct, she'd decided to give him some space to process the accident before she followed him. Her pregnancy had made finding him much more urgent.

But what good was the bond between them when the reality was he was a prince who needed to find a wife so he could father children that would one day rule his country?

And what about her own child? This was no longer a simple matter of being pregnant with Nic's baby. She was carrying the illegitimate child of a prince. For a moment the taverna spun sickeningly around her. Telling Nic he was going to be a father had become that much more complicated.

Somehow she found the strength of will to summon a wry smile. "Besides, you and I both know I'm not princess material."

"You'd hate it," Nic told her in somber tones. To her relief he'd taken her self-deprecating humor at face value. "All the restrictions on how you dressed and behaved."

"Being polite to people instead of setting them straight." He was right. She'd hate it. "The endless parties to attend where I had to smile until my face hurt. I'm so not the type."

The litany leached away her optimism. With hope reaching dangerously low levels, she cursed the expansive hollowness inside her. Nothing had felt the same since she'd stepped onto this island. It wasn't just Nic's fancy clothes, expensive villa and the whole prince thing. He was different. And more unreachable than ever.

How am I supposed to live without you?

The question lodged in her throat. She concentrated on breathing evenly to keep the tears at bay.

"Are you okay?"

Her pulse spiked at his concerned frown. In moments like these he surprised her by being attuned to her mood. And keeping track of how she was feeling was no small task. Her family often teased her about being a drama girl. She enjoyed life to the fullest, reveling in each success and taking disappointments as world-ending. As she'd gotten older, she'd learned to temper her big emotions and act on impulse less frequently.

Except where Nic was concerned. Common sense told her if she'd behave more sensibly, Nic might be more receptive to her. But everything about him aroused her passion and sent her into sensory overload.

"Brooke?"

Unable to verbalize the emotions raging through her, she avoided looking at Nic and found the perfect distraction in a waitress's hard stare. The woman had been watching from the kitchen doorway ever since Brooke had sat down. "I don't think that waitress likes me," Brooke commented, indicating the curvaceous brunette. "Did I interrupt something between you two?"

"Natasa? Don't be ridiculous."

His impatient dismissal raised Brooke's spirits slightly. She already knew Nic wasn't the sort to engage in casual encounters. Her five-year pursuit of him had demonstrated that he wasn't ruled by his body's urges.

"She's awfully pretty and hasn't taken her eye off you since I sat down."

"Do you want something to eat?" Nic signaled Natasa and she came over.

"Another beer for me," he told the waitress. "What are you drinking?" He looked to Brooke.

"Water."

"And an order of *taramosalata*."

"What is that?" Brooke quizzed, her gaze following the generous sway of Natasa's hips as she wound her way back toward the kitchen.

"A spread made from fish roe. You'll like it."

You'll like it.

Did he realize the impact those words had on her nerve endings?

It's what he'd said to her their first night together. To her amazement, once he'd stopped resisting her flirtatious banter and taken the lead, she'd been overcome by his authoritative manner and had surrendered to his every whim. Her skin tingled, remembering the sweep of his fingers across the sensitized planes of her body. He'd made love to her with a thoroughness she'd never known. Not one inch of her body had gone unclaimed by him and she'd let it all happen. Her smile had blazed undiminished for five months until he'd driven up to San Francisco for *the talk*.

Natasa returned with their drinks. She gave Brooke a quick once-over, plunked two bottles on the table and shot Nic a hard look he didn't notice. Brooke grinned as Nic reached for her bottled water and broke the seal without being asked. He didn't know it, but this was just one of the things that had become a ritual with them. During the past five years, Brooke had repeatedly asked him to do her small favors and Nic had obliged, grumbling all the while about her inability to do the simplest tasks. He'd never figured out that each time he helped her, he became a little more invested in their relationship.

Six months ago all her subtle efforts had brought results. After a successful test firing of the *Griffin's* ignition system, the team had been celebrating in Glen's backyard. Nic had been animated, electrified. She'd been a moth to his flame, basking in his warm smiles and affectionate touches. At the end of the evening he'd meshed their fingers together and drawn her to the privacy of the front porch where he'd kissed her silly.

Lying sleepless in her bed that night she'd relived the mind-blowing kiss over and over and wondered what she'd done to finally break through Nic's resistance. She hadn't been able to pinpoint anything, nor did she think that day's success had been the trigger. The team had enjoyed several triumphs in the previous few months. In the end Brooke had decided her years of flirting had finally begun to reach him.

After that night, she'd noticed a subtle difference in the way Nic behaved toward her and began to hope that he might have finally figured out she was the one for him.

Brooke increased the frequency of her weekend visits to the Mojave Desert airport, where the *Griffin* team had their offices. Despite the increased urgency to finish the rocket and get it ready for a test launch, Nic had made time for quiet dinners. Afterward, they'd often talked late into the night. After two months, he'd taken things to the next level. He'd shared not just his body with her, but his dreams and desires, as well. At the time, she'd thought she was getting to know the real Nic. Now she realized how much he'd kept from her.

With fresh eyes, Brooke regarded her brother's best friend and saw only a stranger. In his stylish clothes and expensive shades he looked every inch a rich European. She contemplated the arrogant tilt of his head, the utter command of his presence as he watched her. Why had she never picked up on it earlier?

Because his English was flawlessly Americanized. Because he went to work every day in ordinary jeans and T-shirts. Granted, he filled out his commonplace clothes in an extraordinary manner, but nothing about his impressive pecs and washboard abs screamed aristocracy. She'd always assumed he rarely let off steam with his fellow scientists because he was preoccupied with work.

Now she realized he'd been brought up with different expectations placed upon him than people in her orbit. A picture formed in her mind. Nic, tall and proud, his broad shoulders filling out a form-fitting tuxedo, a red sash across his chest from shoulder to hip. He looked regal. Larger than life. Completely out of reach.

Brooke had always believed that people didn't regret the things they did, only the things they didn't. She liked to believe she was richer for every experience she'd had, good or bad. Would she have given her heart to Nic if she'd known who he was from the beginning? Yes. Brief as it had been, she cherished every moment of their time together.

While logic enabled her to rationalize why she couldn't marry him, her heart prevented her from walking away without a backward glance. And she suspected he wasn't thrilled to be sacrificing himself so that his family could continue to reign. As devastating as it was to think she'd have to give up on a future with Nic, wanting to be with him was a yearning she couldn't shake off.

"I'm going to ask you a question," she announced abruptly, her gaze drilling through his bland expression. "And I expect the truth this time."

Nic's beer bottle hung between the table and his lips. "I suppose I owe you that."

"You're darned right you do." She ignored the brief flare of amusement in his eyes. "I want to know the real reason you broke up with me."

"I've already explained the reason. We have no future. I have to go home and I have to marry." He stared at the harbor behind her, his expression chiseled in granite.

She'd obviously phrased her question wrong. "And if your brother hadn't married someone who couldn't have children? Would you have broken things off?"

What she really wanted to know was if he loved her, but she wasn't sure he'd pondered how deep his feelings for her ran. Also, a month ago he'd apparently accepted that he had to marry someone else and it wasn't his nature to dwell on impossibilities.

"It's a simple question," she prompted as the silence stretched. He surely hated being put on the spot like this, but she couldn't move on until she knew.

His chest rose and fell on a huge sigh as he met her gaze with heavy lidded eyes. Something flickered within those bronze-colored depths. Something that made her stomach contract and her spirits soar.

She'd journeyed to Ithaca to tell him about the baby, but also because she couldn't bear to let him go. Now she understood that she had to. But not yet. She had two days before she had to return to the States. Two days to say goodbye. All she needed was a sign from Nic that he hadn't wanted to give her up.

"No." He spoke the word like a curse. "We'd still be together."

The instant the words left his lips, Nic wished he'd maintained the lies. Brooke's eyes kindled with satisfaction and her body relaxed. She resembled a contented cat. He'd seen the look many times and knew it meant trouble.

"I think we should spend the time between now and when you leave *together*." She gave the last word a specific emphasis that he couldn't misinterpret.

Nic shook his head, vigorously rejecting her suggestion. "That's not fair to you." *Duty. Honor. Integrity.* He repeated the words like a prayer. "I won't take advantage of you that way."

Brooke leaned forward, her gaze sharpening. "Has it ever occurred to you that I like it when you take advantage of me?"

The world beyond their table blurred until it was only him and her and the intense emotional connection that had clicked into place the first time they'd made love, a connection that couldn't be severed.

"I never noticed." His attempt to banter with her so that she'd adopt a less serious mood fell flat.

Her determination gained momentum. "Tell me you don't want to spend your last days of freedom with me."

Every molecule that made up his body screamed at him to agree. "It's not that I don't want to. I shouldn't." He spoke quickly to prevent her from arguing with him. "Ever since finding out I had to return home and get married, I promised myself I wouldn't touch you again."

"That's just silly." She gave him a wicked smile. "You like touching me."

In the time he'd known her, he'd learned just how powerful that smile could be. It had whittled away at his willpower until he'd done the one thing he knew he shouldn't. He'd fallen hard.

Duty. Honor. Integrity. The lament filled his mind. If only Brooke didn't make it so damned hard to do the right thing.

She got up from her chair and stepped into his space.

He tipped his head back and assessed her determined expression. His heart shuddered as she put her palms flat on his shoulders and settled herself on his lap. Even though Nic had braced himself for the arousing pressure of her firm rear on his thighs, it took every bit of concentration he possessed to put his hands behind his back, safely out of range of her tempting curves. What sort of hell had he let himself fall into?

"What do you think you're doing?"

"Are you all right?" she asked, tracing her fingertips across his furrowed brow.

God, she was a tempting lapful.

"I'm fine."

"You don't look fine."

"I'm great, and you didn't answer my question." He pulled her spicy scent into his lungs and held it there. He longed to bury his face in her neck and imprint her upon his senses. "What are you doing on my lap?"

"Demonstrating that you want me as much as I want you."

He hated himself for hoping she'd continue the demonstration until he couldn't catch his breath. Making love to her was amazing. He'd never been with anyone who matched him the way she did. Anticipation gnawed on him like a puppy with a stolen shoe.

"I assure you I want you a great deal more." How he kept his voice so clinical, Nic would never know.

"Then you'll let me stay on the island for the next few days?"

She knew him better than anyone and once she'd discovered his weakness where she was concerned, she'd pressed her advantage at every opportunity. Before they'd made love, she'd slipped past his defenses like a ninja. Now they'd been intimate and he didn't doubt that she would exploit his passion to get her way.

"I left California without saying goodbye because leaving you was so damned hard." When he'd broken off things a month ago, he'd been lucky to escape before her shock at his announcement wore off. Ending their relationship was one of the hardest things he'd ever done. If she'd begged him to stay, he wasn't sure if he could have done the right thing by Sherdana. "Nothing good will come of putting off the inevitable."

"The way you disappeared left me feeling anxious and out of sorts. I understood that we'd broken up, but what I didn't get was how you could take off without saying anything. You should have explained your circumstances. I could have processed the situation and gotten closure. That's what I need now. A few days to say goodbye properly."

"And by properly you mean…?"

Her serious expression dissolved into one of unabashed mischief. "A few days of incredible sex and unbridled passion should do it."

How could any man resist such an offer? Visions of her flat on her back with his hands skimming along her soft, delectable curves rose to torture him. A smile and a frown played tug-of-war on his face. But this was not the time to stop listening to the voice inside his head that reminded him he had to give her up. The smartest thing would be to avoid making more memories that would haunt him the rest of his life.

"Don't you think it would be better if we didn't let ourselves indulge in something that has no future?"

"I'm not going to pretend we have a future. I'm going to cherish every moment of our time together with the knowledge that in the end we'll say goodbye forever." She slid her fingers into his hair. Her thumbs traced the outline of his ears. "I can see you need more convincing, so I'm going to kiss you."

He drank in the scent of honey and vanilla rising off her skin, knowing she tasted as good as she smelled. Her generous lips, rosy and bare of lipstick, parted in anticipation of the promised kiss. Nothing would make him happier than to spend the rest of his life enjoying the curve and texture of her lips. The way she sighed as he kissed her. The soft hitch in her breath as he grazed her lower lip with his teeth.

A tremor transmitted her agitation to him. He longed to inspire more such trembling. To revisit her most ticklish spots, the erogenous zones that made her moan. With erotic impulses twisting his nerves into knots, Nic snagged her gaze. Silver flecks ringed her irises, growing brighter as she stared at his mouth. His pulse thundered in his ears as the moment stretched without a kiss coming anywhere near his lips.

"Damn it, Brooke."

He would not scoop the wayward strand of hair behind her tiny ear and let his knuckles linger against her flushed cheek. He refused to tug on her braid and coax her lips close enough to drift over his.

"What's the matter, Nic?" Her fingers explored his eyebrows and tested his lashes.

Duty. Honor. Integrity. The litany was starting to lose its potency.

"In less than a week I'll never see you again." He locked his hands together behind his back. Tremors began in his arm muscles.

"I know." She switched her attention to his mouth. Her long, red lashes cast delicate shadows on her cheeks.

Heat surged into his face. Hell, heat filled every nook and cranny of his body. Especially where her heart-shaped rear end rested. How could she help but notice his aroused state?

"We'd only be prolonging the inevitable," he reminded her, unsure why he was holding out when he wanted so badly to agree to her mad scheme.

"I need this. I need you." She stroked her thumb against his lower lip. "An hour. A day. A week. I'll take whatever I can get."

Nic counted his heartbeats to avoid focusing on the emotions raging through him. The need to crush her in his arms would overwhelm him any second. Denying himself her compassion and understanding in the days following the accident hadn't been easy, but at the time he'd known that he had to return to Sherdana. Just because Brooke now knew what was going on didn't give him permission to stop acting honorably.

He wasn't prepared for the air she blew in his ear. His body jerked in surprise, and he sucked in a sharp breath. "Stop that."

"You didn't like it?" Laughter gave her voice a husky quality.

"You know perfectly well I did," he murmured hoarsely. "Our food is going to be here any second. Perhaps you should return to your own seat."

"I'm here for a kiss and a kiss is what I'm going to get." She was enjoying this far too much. And, damn it, so was he.

With a fatalistic sigh, Nic accepted that he'd let himself

be drawn too far into her game to turn back. As much as he wanted to savor the expressions flitting across her face, he stared at the fishing boats bobbing near the cement seawall. Alert to her slightest movement, he felt the tingle on his cheek an instant before her lips grazed his skin.

"Let's stop all the foreplay, shall we," he finally said.

"Oh, all right. Spoilsport. I was enjoying having you at my mercy. But if you insist."

Lightning danced in her eyes. She secured his face between her hands and grazed her lips across his.

"Again." His voice was half demand, half plea. He hardened his will and inserted steel into his tone. "And this time put a little effort into it."

"Whatever you say."

He let his lashes drop as her mouth drifted over his again. This time she applied more pressure, a little more technique. As kisses went, it was pretty chaste, but her little hum of pleasure tipped his world on its axis. And when she nibbled on his lip, murmuring in Italian, desire incinerated his resistance.

"Benedette le voci tante ch'io chiamando il nome de mia donna ò sparte, e i sospiri, et le lagrime, e 'l desio."

How was he supposed to resist a woman with a PhD in Italian literature? Although he knew what she'd said, he wanted to hear her speak the words again.

"Translation?"

"And blessed be all of the poetry I scattered, calling out my lady's name, and all the sighs, and tears, and the passion."

"Italian love poetry?" he groused, amused in spite of the lust raking him with claws dipped in the sweetest aphrodisiac.

"It seemed appropriate." Her fingers splaying over his rapidly beating heart, she swooped in for one last kiss before getting to her feet. "I think I made my point." With a satisfied smirk, she returned to her chair.

"What point?"

"That we both could use closure."

Over the course of the kiss he'd grasped what she wanted to do, but he'd worked diligently over the past month to come to grips with living without her and couldn't imagine reopening himself to the loss all over again. And she'd just demonstrated he'd never survive a few days let alone a week in her company. He'd be lucky if he made it past the next hours. No. She had to go. And go soon. Because if she didn't, he'd give in and make love to her. And that would be disastrous.

"I got my closure a month ago when I broke things off," he lied. "But I understand that I've sprung a lot of information on you today that you'll want to assimilate. Stay for a couple days."

"As friends?" She sounded defeated.

"It's for the best."

Four

The discussion before lunch dampened Brooke's spirits and left her in a thoughtful mood as she ate her way through a plate of moussaka, and followed that up with yogurt and honey for dessert. Nic, never one for small talk, seemed content with the silence, but he watched her through half-lidded eyes.

Telling him she was pregnant had just become a lot more complicated. As had her decision regarding the teaching position at Berkeley. Before Nic had broken it off with her a month ago she'd been confident that he was her future and she'd chosen him over her ideal job. When he left she should have returned to her original career path, but finding out that she was pregnant had created a whole new group of variables.

Gone was her fantasy that once Nic heard he was going to be a father, he would return to California and they would live happily ever after as a family. Since that wasn't going to happen, the Berkeley job was back on the table. Brooke wished she could summon up the enthusiasm she'd once felt at the possibility of teaching there.

And then there were the challenges that came with being a single mom. If she moved back to L.A. she would be close to her parents and they would be thrilled to help.

Thanks to Nic's revelations she was a bundle of indecisiveness. They returned to Nic's car for the ride back to the villa. He told her he would have Elena's husband, Thasos, return the boat later. As the car swept along the narrow road circling Kioni's tranquil bay, Brooke felt her anxiety rise and fall with each curve.

From this vantage point, halfway up the side of the scrubby hills that made up the island's landscape, she could see beyond the harbor to the azure water of the Ionian Sea. Glen had described Ithaca as a pile of rocks with scrubby brush growing here and there, but he'd done the picturesque landscape a disservice.

"We'll be to my house in ten minutes." Nic pointed toward a spot on the hill where a bit of white was visible among the green hillside.

In the short time she'd been here, Brooke had fallen in love with Nic's villa. It made her curious about the rest of his family and the life they lived in Sherdana. Did they live in a palace? She tried to picture Nic growing up in a fussy, formal place with hundreds of rooms and dozens of servants.

As the villa disappeared from view around another bend, Brooke glanced over her shoulder and estimated the distance back to the village. Two or three miles. The car turned off the main road and rolled down a long driveway that angled toward the edge of the cliff. When first the extensive gardens and then the house came into view, she caught her breath.

"This is beautiful," she murmured, certain her compliment wasn't effusive enough. "I didn't see this side of the house earlier."

"Gabriel found the place. We bought it for our eighteenth birthday. I'm afraid I haven't used it much."

Built on a hillside overlooking the bay, the home was actually a couple buildings connected together by terraces and paths. Surrounded by cypress and olive trees, the stucco buildings with the terra-cotta tile roofs sprawled on the hillside, their gardens spread around them like skirts.

The nearby hills had been planted with cosmos, heather and other native flowering plants to maintain a natural look. A cluster of small terra-cotta pots, containing bright pink and lavender flowers greeted visitors at the door. A large clay urn had been tipped on its side in the center of the grouping to give the display some height and contrast.

Nic stopped the car. Shutting off the engine, he turned to face her, one hand resting on the seat behind her head. The light breeze blew a strand of hair across her face. Before Brooke could deal with it, Nic's fingers drifted along her cheek and pushed it behind her ear. She half shut her eyes against the delight that surged in her. Her stomach turned a cartwheel as she spied the thoughtful half smile curving his lips. Nic's smile was like drinking brandy. It warmed her insides and stimulated her senses.

"Maybe tomorrow I can show you the windmills," he said, his gaze drifting over her face. The fondness in his eyes make her chest tighten.

"Sure." Her voice had developed a disconcerting croak. She cleared her throat. "I'd like that."

She let out an enormous yawn while Nic was unlocking the front door. He raised his eyebrows and she clapped her hand over her mouth.

"I see you didn't take my advice earlier about getting some sleep."

"I was too wound up. Now I'm having trouble keeping my eyes open. Feel like joining me for a nap?"

Only a minute widening of his eyes betrayed Nic's reaction to her offer. "From what you've told me I have a bunch of emails to answer. I'll catch up with you before dinner."

All too familiar with Nic's substantial willpower, Brooke retreated to the terrace where she'd first found him. In the harbor a hundred feet below, the water was an incredible cerulean blue, the color accentuated by the tile roofs of the houses that lined the wharf and scaled the steep verdant green hills cupping the horseshoe-shaped harbor.

She rested her hands on the stone wall and pondered the nature of fate. Before she'd met Nic, she'd been pursued by any number of men who were ready to do what it took to win her affection. But instead of falling for one of them, she'd chosen a man who was far more interested in his rocket ship than her. All the while, she'd hoped that maybe his enthusiasm for his work could somehow translate into passion for her.

The explosive chemistry between her and Nic had seemed like a foundation they could build a relationship on. The way he'd dropped his guard and given her a glimpse of his emotions had left her breathless with hope that maybe his big-brother act had been his way of protecting his heart. Thanks to all her previous romantic escapades that Glen was only too happy to bring up over and over, Nic had regarded her as a bit of a loose cannon when it came to love.

Brooke turned her back on the view. She had a lot to think about. Following Nic to this island had proven way more interesting and enlightening than she'd expected.

While she'd only been his best friend's little sister, it hurt that neither man trusted her with the truth. She didn't blame Glen for keeping Nic's confidences. Her brother wouldn't have been the amazing man he'd been without his honorable side. But she could, and did, blame Nic for keeping her in the dark.

For five years he'd kept some enormous secrets from her. That knowledge stung. But now she had a secret of her own. Given what she now knew about Nic, what was her best course of action?

Despite her exhaustion after being awake for twenty-four hours, she paced, the sound of her sandals slapping against the stone of the terrace breaking the tranquil silence. Seeing Nic, kissing him and finding out that he was not the hardworking scientist she'd always known but a prince of some country she'd only heard of in passing, had her thoughts in a frenetic whirl.

And then there was the big question of the day. The one she'd been avoiding for the past hour. Was she going to tell Nic about her pregnancy?

In the wake of all she'd learned, was it fair to tell him he was going to be a father? He couldn't marry her even if he'd wanted to. Nor would they be living on the same continent. Being the prince of a small European country meant he would be under the keenest scrutiny. Would he even want to acknowledge an illegitimate child? Yet was it fair to deny him the opportunity to make that decision?

Her best friend, Theresa, would help her answer some of these questions. She was the most sensible and grounded person in Brooke's life. Brooke went down to the guesthouse, retrieved her phone from the bed where she'd left it and dialed Theresa's number.

"Well, it's about time you called me back," Theresa started, sounding more like Brooke's mother than her best friend. "I've left you, like, four messages."

Brooke tried to shrug away the tension in her shoulders, but that was hard when she was braced against an onslaught of lecturing. "Five, actually. I'm sorry I didn't call sooner—"

"You know I'm just worried about you. The last time we talked, you were going to get your brother to tell you where Nic had gone."

"I did that."

"So where is he?"

"About two miles down the road from the most gorgeous Greek town you've ever seen."

"And you know this Greek town is so gorgeous because…?" Theresa's voice held a hint of alarm.

"I've seen it."

"Brooke, no."

"Yep."

A long pause followed. Brooke almost wished she was there to watch her best friend's expression fluctuate from annoyed to incredulous and back again.

"What about the Berkeley interview?"

"It's in three days."

"Are you going to make it back in time?"

In truth she wasn't sure she wanted to. The idea of raising a baby by herself scared her. She wanted to be close to family and that meant living in LA. "That's my intention."

"What was Nic's reaction when you showed up?"

"He was pretty surprised to see me."

"And when you told him about the baby?"

Panic and longing surged through her in confusing, conflicting waves. Twenty-four hours earlier, coming to find him had felt necessary instead of reckless or impulsive. And in hindsight, it had been foolishly optimistic. She'd been convinced Nic would return to California with her once he knew he was going to be a father.

"I haven't yet."

"What are you waiting for?"

Brooke fell back on the bed and stared at the ceiling. "Things got a little complicated after I got here."

"Did you sleep with him again?"

"No." She paused to smile. "Not yet."

"Brooke, you are my best friend and I want nothing but the best for you," Theresa began in overly patient tones. "But you need to realize if he wanted to be with you he would."

"It's not as simple as that." Or was it? Hadn't Nic chosen duty to his country over her? Once again Brooke pictured Nic in formal attire, standing between two other men who looked just like him. Beside them were two thrones where an older couple wearing crowns sat in regal splendor. "But he cares about me. It's just that he's in a complicated situation. And I couldn't tell him over the phone that I'm pregnant."

"Okay. I'll give you that." Theresa was making an effort to be positive and supportive, but clearly she didn't believe that Brooke's actions were wise. "But you chased him all the way to Greece. And now you haven't told him. So what's wrong?"

"What makes you think anything is wrong?"

"Gee, I don't know. We've been best friends since third grade. I think I can tell when something's bothering you. What's going on?" Theresa's voice softened. "Is he doing okay?"

As long as the two girls had known each other, Theresa never understood Brooke's restless longing for the drama of romance. The thrill of flirting. The heart-pounding excitement of falling in love. Married to a man she'd dated since college, Theresa was completely and happily settled. Safe with a reliable husband. And although Theresa would never say it out loud, Brooke always felt as if her friend judged her because she wanted more.

"Physically yes, unless you count hungover. He looked terrible when I showed up this morning."

"So, he's really taking the accident hard."

"Of course he is. He and Glen have been obsessed with

this dream of theirs for five long years. And as you said, he blames himself for what happened." Brooke's breath came out in a ragged sigh as her reaction to what she'd learned finally caught up with her. "He's not coming back."

"Sure he is. If anyone can convince him to not give up it's you."

"I can't. There's a bunch of other things going on."

"What kind of other things?"

"Turns out there are problems at home and he has to go back and marry someone."

"What?" Theresa screeched. "He's engaged?"

"Not yet, but he will be soon."

"Soon? How soon? Does he have a girlfriend he's going to propose to? Is that why he broke your heart?"

"No." Brooke knew she wasn't being clear, but was having a hard time explaining what she still struggled to grasp. "Nothing so simple. Theresa, he's a prince."

Silence. "I'm sorry, a what?"

"A prince." Her reaction was beginning to settle in. Brooke swiped away a sudden rush of tears as her ears picked up nothing but the hiss of air through the phone's speaker. "Are you still there?"

"Yes, I'm here, but this damned international call has gone wonky. Can you repeat what you said."

"Nic is a prince. He's second in line to the throne of a small European country called Sherdana."

Her breath evened out as she waited out her best friend's stupefaction. It wouldn't last long. Theresa was one of the most pragmatic people she knew. It was part of what kept them friends for so long. Opposites attract. Theresa needed Brooke's particular variety of crazy to shake up her life, and Brooke relied on Theresa's common sense to keep her grounded.

"You're kidding me, right? This whole phone call is some sort of setup for one of those wacky reality shows

where people get punked or filmed doing stupid things."
She paused and waited for Brooke to fill in an affirmative.
When Brooke remained silent Theresa sighed and said,
"Okay, you'd better give it to me from the top."

Nic sat in the small den off the living room, his laptop on the love seat beside him, his thoughts lingering on
Brooke and her crazy notion that they should say goodbye and gain closure by spending the next few days in bed
together. Had he done a good enough job convincing her
that wasn't going to happen when he desperately wanted
to make love to her again? During their five months together, she'd learned all she had to do was crook a finger
and he was happy to abandon his work in favor of spending hours in her arms. Nic growled as he pondered his
susceptibility to her abundant charms. He was fighting a
battle with himself and with her. In a few hours she would
return, refreshed and ready for the next skirmish and he'd
better have his defenses reinforced.

With a snort of disgust, Nic turned on the computer in
the den and cued up his email. She'd claimed there were
dozens of unanswered emails, but the inbox was empty. It
took him fifteen minutes to find them among the folders
where he shunted the messages he didn't wish to delete
and restore the settings to the way he liked them. Brooke
was a disaster when it came to anything involving technology. Glen had found his sister's deficiency funny and
endearing. Nic just found it exasperating. Like so many
other things about her.

She was always late. In fact, her sense of time was so
skewed that if he needed her to be somewhere, he usually
built in a cushion of thirty minutes. Then there was her inability to say no to anyone. This usually led to her getting
involved in something she needed to be bailed out of. Like
at *Griffin*'s annual team picnic when she'd agreed to take

all the kids for a nature hike and then got lost. It had taken Nic and Glen, plus a half-dozen concerned parents, to find them. Of course, the kids all thought it was the best adventure they'd ever been on. Brooke had kept them calm and focused, never letting them know how much trouble they were in. Later, when he'd scolded her for worrying everyone, she'd simply shrugged her shoulders and pointed out that nothing bad had happened. She just didn't think about the consequences of her actions. And that drove him crazy.

As crazy as the way she leveraged her lean, toned body to incite his baser instincts. Whenever she took a weekend break from school and came to visit, he found it impossible to concentrate on the *Griffin* project. She hung out in his office, alternating between cajoling and pouting until he paid attention to her. Most days he held out because eventually she'd grow tired of the game and let him get back to work. Unfortunately before that happened, he had to endure her flirtatious hugs and seemingly innocent body brushes. Usually by the time she headed back to San Francisco on Sunday afternoon, he was aroused, off schedule and in a savage mood.

His phone rang. Gabriel. The first in line to the throne sounded relaxed and a touch smug as he passed along the message Nic had been dreading.

"Mother is sending the jet to pick you up the day after tomorrow and wants to know what time you can be at the airport."

"What's so urgent? I thought I had over a week until your wedding."

"She has a series of parties and events leading up to the big day that you and Christian will be expected to attend. From what I understand she has compiled quite a list of potential brides for you two to fight over."

And so it began. Nic's thoughts turned toward the woman napping in the guesthouse. His heart wrenched at the thought of being parted from her so soon after reconnecting. She would be disappointed to find out their time would be cut short, but he had warned her.

"Are any of these women...?" What was he trying to ask? Without meeting any of them, he'd already decided they were unacceptable. None of them were Brooke.

"Beautiful? Smart? Wealthy? What?"

"Am I going to *like* any of them?" As soon as the question was out Nic felt foolish.

"I'm sure you're going to like all of them. You just have to figure out which one you can see yourself spending the rest of your life with." Gabriel's words and tone were matter-of-fact.

"Is that how you felt when you first started poring over the candidates?"

Gabriel paused before answering. "Not exactly. I had Olivia in mind from the first."

"But you spent a year considering and meeting possible matches. Why do that if you already knew who you wanted?"

"Two reasons. Because Mother would not have accepted that I had already met the perfect girl and at the time only my subconscious realized Olivia was the one."

Nic wished he was having this conversation face-to-face because his brother's expression would provide clues mere words lacked. "You've lost me."

"As I worked my way through the list, I realized I compared each woman I met to Olivia."

"She was your ideal."

"She was the one I wanted."

The conviction throbbing in Gabriel's low voice spurred Nic to envy his brother for the first time since they were kids. Before Nic had discovered his passion for science and engineering, he'd wondered what contribution he could make to the country. Gabriel would rule. All Christian cared about was having fun and shirking responsibility. Nic had wanted to have a positive effect on the world. A lofty ambition for an eight-year-old.

Gabriel continued speaking, "Only I resented my duty to marry and didn't know how perfect Olivia was for me. Even when I proposed to her I was blind to my heart's true desire. Thank goodness my instincts weren't hampered by my hardheadedness."

"At what point did you figure out you'd selected the perfect woman?"

"The night my girls came to stay at the palace. Olivia took them under her wing and zealously guarded them from anyone she believed might upset them. Me included." He chuckled. "And she never wavered in her love for them, not even when she thought I was still in love with their mother."

"And speaking of Karina and Bethany, how are your girls?"

"Growing more beautiful and more terrifying by the week. Thank goodness they adore Olivia or they'd be terrorizing the palace staff a lot more than they do. Somehow she guides their energy into positive channels and makes the whole process look effortless. No one else can manage them without being ready to pull their hair out."

"Not even Mother?"

"At first, but now they realize she is too fond of them to scold. Father indulges their appetite for sweets and Ariana has shown them every good hiding place the palace has to offer."

"It's not called the terrible twos for nothing."

"You'll see soon enough. I'll have the plane pick you up tomorrow around noon."

"Fine." That should give him time to make sure Brooke was safely on a plane heading for home.

"See that you're there on time."

"Where else would I be? I have nowhere to go but home."

Nic ended the call with a weary sigh and mulled what Gabriel had said about his search for a wife. That his brother had settled on the perfect woman before his quest had even begun didn't lessen Nic's unease over what was to come. Already his mind and body had chosen the woman for him. She was currently stretched out on the bed in the guesthouse. If he was anything like Gabriel, he was going to have an impossible time finding anyone who could match her perfect imperfection.

Several hours later, he was opening a bottle of Sherdana's best Pinot Negro to let it breathe when Brooke sailed into the living room. She'd changed clothes again. The tail of her pastel tied-dyed kimono fluttered behind her as she walked, exposing a mint-green crocheted tank and the ruffled hem of her leg-baring floral shorts.

A light breeze swept in from the terrace and plucked at her dark copper curls. She'd loosened her hair from its braid and it flowed in rich waves over her shoulders and down her back. She stroked a lock away from her lips. He caught himself staring at her and shifted his attention back to the wine.

How often in the past five years had he longed to sink his fingers into her tempestuous red locks and lose himself in the chaotic tangle? He'd imagined the texture would feel like the finest Chinese silk sliding along his bare chest. He'd been right.

Nic extended a glass of wine toward her. She shook her head.

"Something nonalcoholic if you have it."

He found a container of orange juice and poured her a glass. She sipped at it, her eyes smiling at him over the edge of the glass. Expecting a whole new round of verbal fencing, Nic was surprised when she said, "You mentioned that your sister paints here. Could I see her studio?"

"Sure."

He led the way onto the terrace and around the villa in the opposite direction of the guesthouse. A small building with broad windows facing north sat on a little rise overlooking the harbor mouth. Nic unlocked the door and gestured for Brooke to go inside.

"Oh, these are all wonderful," she said the minute she walked in.

Though Brooke was always generous with her praise, Nic thought she was going a little overboard in talking about Ariana's work. Nic was proud of what his sister had accomplished with her paintings but didn't really get her modern style. She had often accused him of being stuck in the Middle Ages in terms of his taste. Brooke, on the other hand, seemed to get exactly what his sister was trying to do.

He enjoyed watching her stroll through his sister's art studio and study each canvas in turn, treating every painting like a masterpiece. By the time Brooke returned to where he stood just inside the door, her delighted grin had Nic smiling, as well. The next time he saw Ariana, he would be sure to tell her what an accomplished artist she was.

"I never looked at Ariana's art that way before," Nic said as he relocked the studio and escorted Brooke back toward the main house. "Thank you for opening my eyes."

She looked caught off guard by his compliment. "You're welcome."

At that moment Nic realized how rarely he'd ever offered Brooke any encouragement or a reason to believe he appreciated her. How had she stayed so relentlessly positive as he'd thrown one obstacle after another in her path? All she'd ever asked was for him to like her and treat her with civility. Was it her fault that she agitated his emotions and incited his hormones?

"What are you thinking about?" she asked as they stepped back into the main house. She gathered her hair into a twist and secured it into a topknot.

"Regrets. I spent so much time keeping you at bay."

Again he'd startled her. "You did, but to be fair, I am a little overwhelming."

"And very distracting. I had a hard time concentrating when you were around."

She narrowed her eyes. "Why are you being so nice to me all of a sudden?"

"I had a call from my brother while you were resting and I have to leave for Sherdana the day after tomorrow."

"So soon?" Her lips curved downward.

Nic wanted to put his arms around her, but it would do neither of them any good to deepen their connection when the time to part was so near. "Apparently my mother has planned several events she'd like me to attend in the next week, culminating in Gabriel and Olivia's wedding."

"But I thought they were already married."

"They are. Actually…" Nic stared out the window at Kioni in the distance. "He brought her to Ithaca for a surprise wedding ceremony."

"That's very romantic."

"And unlike Gabriel to put his desires before the needs of the country. But he's crazy about Olivia and couldn't bear to live without her."

Something about Brooke's silence caught his attention. She was staring at the floor lost in thought. "So why are they getting married again?"

"The crown prince's wedding is pretty momentous and my parents decided it was better to have a second ceremony than to rob the citizens of the celebration. There will be parties every night leading up to the big event, both at the palace and venues around our capital city of Carone."

"Tell me about the parties at the palace. They must be formal affairs." Brooke's smile bloomed. "Do you have to dance?"

"Only when I can't avoid it."

"So you know how."

"It's part of every prince's training," he intoned, mimicking his dance teacher's severe manner. "I don't have Gabriel's technique or Christian's flair, but I don't step on my partner's toes anymore."

"After dinner tonight you are going to dance with me." She held up a hand when he began to protest. "Don't argue. I remember on three separate occasions when you told me you had no idea how to dance."

"No," he corrected her. "I told you I don't dance. There's a difference."

"Semantics."

"Very well." He knew that taking her in his arms and swaying with her to soft music would lead to trouble. But he could teach her a Sherdanian country dance. The movements were energetic and the only touching required was hand to hand. "After dinner."

"So what are we having that smells so delicious?"

"Elena left us lamb stew and salad for dinner."

Brooke drifted to the stove where a pot simmered on a low flame. "I don't know how I can be hungry after all we ate for lunch, but suddenly I'm starved."

Something about the way she said the word made him grind his teeth. She was hungry for food, but the groan in her voice made him hungry for something else entirely. Directing her toward the refrigerator where Elena had put the salad, he spooned the stew into bowls and tried not to remember Brooke beneath him in bed, her red hair fanned across his pillow, lips curved in lazy satisfaction.

"Can I help?"

He handed her a bowl and a basket of bread, almost pushing it at her in an effort to keep her at bay.

She walked toward the table. "I love the bread here in Greece. That and the desserts. I could live on them."

"I hope you like the stew, as well. Elena is an excellent cook."

"I'm sure it's wonderful."

Nic's housekeeper had set the table earlier so there was little left to do but sit down and enjoy the meal. The patch of late afternoon sunlight on the tile floor had advanced a good three feet by the time they finished eating. Following his example, Brooke had torn pieces of the fresh-baked bread and dipped them into the stew. He'd lost count how many times her tongue came out to catch a crumb on her lip or a spot of gravy at the corner of her mouth.

For dessert Elena had left baklava, a sticky, sweet concoction made of stacked sheets of phyllo dough spread with butter, sugar, nuts and honey. He couldn't wait to watch Brooke suck the sticky honey from her fingers.

And she didn't disappoint him.

"What's so funny?" she demanded, her tongue darting out to clean the corner of her mouth.

Nic banked a groan and sipped his wine. "I'm trying to remember the last time I enjoyed a pan of baklava this much."

"You haven't had any."

He imagined drizzling honey on her skin and following the trail with his tongue. The bees in Greece made thick sweet honey he couldn't get enough of. Against her skin it would be heaven. The arousal that had taunted him all through the meal now exploded with fierce determination. Nic sat back in his chair all too aware of the tightness in his pants and the need clawing at him.

"You've enjoyed it enough for both of us."

"It was delicious." Cutting another piece, she held it out. "Sure you don't want some?"

The question was innocent enough, but the light in her gray-green eyes as she peered at him from beneath her lashes was anything but. Avoiding her gaze, he shook his head.

"As much as I'm enjoying your attempt to seduce me, I'm afraid my intentions toward you haven't changed."

"We'll see." Resolve replaced flirtation in her eyes. She sat back and assessed him. "I still have two nights and a day to dishonor you."

Eager to avoid further banter, he cleared the plates from the table and busied himself putting away the remnants of the stew.

"I can hear what you're thinking," Brooke murmured, following him to the sink. "You're thinking it took me five years to wear you down the first time." She set the pan of baklava on the counter and swept a finger over a patch of honey. "But have you considered that I know a little bit more about what turns you on after all the nights we spent together?"

Out of the corner of his eye Nic watched, his mouth dry, as she stuck her finger into her mouth, closed her eyes in rapt delight and licked off the honey. She was killing him.

"Two nights and a day, Nic." She said again. "Hours and hours of glorious, delirious pleasure as we explore every inch of each other and get lost in deep slow kisses."

But he wasn't free to have the sort of fun Brooke suggested. And one way or another, he intended to make her understand.

"And then what?" he demanded, his voice more curt than he'd intended.

She blinked. "What do you mean?"

"What happens after the fun?" While hot water ran into the sink, he propped his hip against the counter and crossed his arms. "Have you thought about what happens when we leave this island and go our separate ways?"

Her shoulders sagged. "I head back to California and my dream job."

"And I start looking for a wife." To his surprise, he'd managed to get the last word in.

Deciding to capitalize on his advantage, he scrounged up the CD with Sherdanian folk music Ariana had given him for his birthday several years earlier. As the first notes filled the air, he extended his hand in Brooke's direction. "Get over here. It's time for you to learn a traditional Sherdanian country dance."

Five

Nic woke to the smell of coffee and tickle of something in his ear. He reached up to brush away the irritation and heard a soft chuckle. The mattress behind him dipped. His eyes flew open as a hand drifted over his shoulder and a pair of lips slid into the erogenous zone behind his earlobe.

"You sleep like the dead," Brooke murmured. "I have been taking advantage of you for the last fifteen minutes."

"I doubt that." But oh, the idea that she might have hastened his body's awakening.

"Don't be so sure." She sounded awfully damned confident as she snuggled onto the bed behind him, a thin sheet the only barrier between them as she traced the curve of his backside with her knee, running it down along the back of his thigh. As if this caress wasn't provocative enough, she wiggled her pelvis against his butt, aligning her delicious curves against his back from heel to shoulders. "I know you're not wearing any underwear."

"You're guessing."

"Am not." Her palm drifted along his arm, riding the curve of his biceps. Her touch wasn't sexual; she was more like a sculptor admiring a fine marble statue. "I peeked."

He couldn't even gather enough breath to object. What the hell was she doing to him? Reminded of her threat the night before, Nic knew that letting her get her fill of touching him would only lead to further frustration on his part and more boldness on hers. Yet, he couldn't prevent his curiosity from seeing how far she intended to go.

"How long have you been awake?" he asked as her fingers stole up his neck and into his hair. He closed his eyes and savored the soothing caress.

"A couple hours. I went for a swim, started the coffee and grew bored with my own company, so I decided it was time to wake you. How am I doing?"

Brat.

"I'm fully awake," he growled. "Thank you. Now, why don't you run along and fix breakfast while I take a shower."

"Want some company?"

Her mouth opened in a wet kiss on his shoulder. Nic bit back a curse. The swirl of her tongue on his skin caused his hips to twitch. The erection he'd been trying to ignore grew painfully hard.

"Didn't we come to an understanding last night about this being a bad idea?"

"That was your opinion," she corrected. "I think we wasted a perfectly lovely night dancing around your living room when we could have set fire to this big bed of yours."

"Set fire?" Amusement momentarily clouded his desire to roll her beneath him and make her come over and over. She had the damnedest knack for tickling his funny bone.

"Set fire. Tear up the sheets."

He shifted onto his back so he could see her face. Bare of makeup, lips soft with invitation, eyes shadowed by long reddish lashes, her beauty stopped his breath. He cupped her pale cheek in his palm while his heart contracted in remorse. For five months he'd savored the notion of spending the rest of his life with her. He'd claimed her body and given her his heart. At the time, with Gabriel's wedding to Olivia fast approaching and the future of Sherdana safely in their hands, Nic believed he could at last have the life he wanted with the woman who made him happy. It wasn't fair that circumstances had interfered with his plans for the future, but that's the way it was.

His hand fell away from her soft skin. "You know we can't do this."

"Damn it, Nic."

The next thing he knew, she'd straddled him. Astonished by her swift attack and trapped between her strong, supple thighs, Nic reached for the pillow behind his head and dug his fingers in. The challenge in her green-gray gaze helped him maintain control—barely. She settled her hot center firmly over his erection and smirked as his hips lifted off the mattress to meet her part way. She obviously intended to push him past his limits. To incite him to act. He clenched his teeth and held himself immobile.

She put her palms on his chest and leaned forward. "I'm sad and I hate feeling this way. I want to be blissfully happy for just a little while. To forget about the future and just live in the moment."

Where she touched him, he burned. The curtain of her hair swung forward. Still damp from her swim, it brushed against his cheek. He gathered a handful and gently tugged.

"It's not that I don't want that, too," he began and stopped. She couldn't know that what he felt for her went way beyond physical attraction. "I just can't see where that's going to be good for either of us."

Her hands stalked from his chest to his stomach. His muscles twitched in reaction to her touch, betraying him.

He grit his teeth and focused on something less tantalizing than the slender thighs bracketing his hips or the heat of her burning into him through layers of cotton. Unfortunately with her current position, she dominated his field of vision.

"Is that my shirt?"

The last time he'd seen the white button-down, she'd been driving away from his house after they spent the night together. In his eagerness to get her naked the evening before, he'd torn the delicate fabric of her blouse and rendered the garment unwearable. Today, where her damp hair touched the fabric, transparent patches bloomed on her shoulder and chest.

"It is. Every time I wear it I think about you and the nights we spent together."

Nic gripped the bed sheets, endeavoring to stay true to his word and keep his hands off her. Even if his position didn't lend itself to a series of casual affairs, leaving a trail of broken hearts in his wake was not his style. On the other hand, he didn't need the sort of complication a romance with Brooke would bring to his life right now. But since yesterday afternoon he'd become obsessed with all the ways he could touch her without using his hands, and since she'd arrived, he hadn't brooded over the accident for more than five minutes.

"Tell me about the women who are dying to become your princess," she said in a tone as dry as the California desert near the airport test facility. "Are they all beautiful and rich?"

"Do you really want to talk about this?"

"Not really." Her fingers tickled up his sides toward his armpits.

In an effort to stop her before she made him squirm, Nic snagged her wrists and rolled her over. She ended up beneath him, her legs tangled in the sheets. Now that she was trapped in a web of her own making, this was his chance to escape. He should have immediately shifted away from her and put a safe distance between them, but her expression took on a look of such vulnerability that he was transfixed. Pressed chest to groin, they stared at each other.

"Touch me," she whispered, digging her fingers into his biceps.

He flexed his spine, driving his hips tight into hers. She shifted beneath him, rubbing her body against his in a tension-filled rhythm. A groan ripped from his throat as her heat called to him. Today she smelled like pink grapefruit, stimulating with a sweet bitterness. His mouth watered.

"I promised I wouldn't."

"Then, kiss me. You didn't promise not to do that."

That would be following the letter of the law instead of the intent. "You should have been a lawyer," he groused, surrendering to what they both wanted.

His lips lowered to hers. She opened for him like a rose on a warm summer afternoon. He kept the pace slow, concentrating on her mouth while ruthlessly suppressing the urgent thrumming in his groin. Her heart beat in time with his until Nic wasn't sure where he left off and she began. Time was suspended. The room fell away. There was only the softness of her skin beneath his lips, her soft sighs and the growing tension in his body.

This deviation from his intention wouldn't benefit either of them, but he'd grown sick to death of thinking in terms of what he couldn't do, what didn't work, what he stood to lose. He wanted to take joy in this moment and put the future on hold. Brooke had offered him a gift with no strings attached. He would face a lifetime of limits and restrictions soon enough. Why not go wild for a few minutes? Enjoy this exhilarating, vivacious woman who brought joy and laughter into his stolid existence. Who confounded him with her sassy attitude and liberated his emotions. For five years he'd fought against falling for her, afraid if he let her in he might one day have to leave her.

And he'd been right. No sooner had he risked his heart than he'd been forced to make a terrible choice.

"See, that wasn't so hard," she murmured as he broke off the kiss to trail his lips down her neck to the madly beating pulse in her throat.

"I've never met anyone like you. No one knocks me off my game faster."

"It's my dazzling personality."

"It's your damned stubbornness. If Berkeley doesn't work out, you could always teach seminars to salesmen on the art of not taking no for an answer."

Her rock hard nipples burned his chest through the thin cloth, branding him with each impassioned breath she took.

"Unbutton your shirt."

She hesitated at his demand as if unsure what his change of mind might mean. After a long moment, she raised her hands and slipped the first button free. As the top curve of her breast came into view, he lowered his head and tasted her skin. Her gasp made him smile. What he intended to do next would render her breathless.

"Another."

She obliged. He nudged into the ever-widening V, grazing her sensitive skin with the stubble on his chin. A shudder captured her. Nic smiled.

"Keep going."

She unbuttoned the next two buttons in rapid succession, but held on to the edges of the shirt, keeping the material closed. Sensing what he wanted, she peered at him from beneath her lashes. Nic eyed the pink tone in her cheeks.

"Spread the shirt open. I want to look at you."

"Nic, this is—" She broke off as he nudged the material off one breast.

"Not what you had in mind?" His tongue circled her tight nipple.

"It's exactly what I want." She arched her back, her fingers tightening convulsively. "I feel…"

"Tell me," he urged, eager to hear what effect his mouth was having on her body. He flicked his tongue across her nipple. She jerked in surprise. "I want to know everything. What do you like? What drives you wild?"

At last she unclenched her fingers and spread the shirt wide. Now it was Nic's turn to suck in his breath. She was beautiful. Breathtaking. Perfect. Her small round breasts, topped with dark pink nipples, were a perfect fit in his palm. Pity his mouth would be the only part of him to enjoy all that silky skin. And yet, as he pulled one bud into his mouth and sucked, perhaps that wasn't so bad after all.

She was mewling with gratifying abandon by the time he finished with one breast and moved to the other.

The situation was swiftly disintegrating. Nic felt his control slipping. Heaving a sigh, he caught the edges of her shirt and pulled them together, hiding her gorgeous breasts from his greedy eyes.

"You're stopping?" She sounded appalled. "But things were just starting to get interesting."

His muscles clenched at her frustrated wail. He levered himself out of bed and kept his eyes averted from her. He'd survived temptation once. He wasn't sure he could do it twice.

"You still don't get it, do you? I can't offer you anything beyond this bed."

"I know."

She rolled onto her side, her gaze steady on him. Accusations darted like deer through her gray-green eyes. Anger surged in his chest. Damn her for coming here and littering the clear path to his future with enticement and regret. He retreated to the bathroom. Just before closing the door, he shot a last glance in her direction. She had propped her head on her hand and lay watching him through half-closed lids.

She'd left the edges of her shirt unfastened and the three-inch gap gave him an eye-popping view of the curve of her right breast, almost to the nipple. Aphrodite in all her glory could not have appealed to him more than Brooke's slim form in his bed.

Nic shut the bathroom door with more force than necessary and started the shower. A cold shower, he decided.

As she heard the water start, Brooke exhaled raggedly and rolled onto her back. The empty bed mocked her. Frustration bubbled in her chest and rose into her throat, building into a shriek. She clamped her teeth to prevent any sound from escaping, but it was an effort to hold so much emotion in. So she grabbed one of Nic's pillows and covered her face in it to prevent him from hearing her shrill curses.

Once the tantrum had passed, she lay with her nose buried in the cool cotton, absorbing Nic's scent and reliving the moment when his control had broken. Heat wafted off her skin in surging waves, the source the smoking hot place between her thighs that pulsed and throbbed with frustrated longing. The man had a gift for turning her world upside down.

He only had to give her the slightest bit of encouragement and she went all in. How many times since she'd first discovered she had feelings for him had he crushed her hopes by deflecting her overtures or chased her away when she'd tried to get him to take a break from a problem so he could gain some perspective on it?

Not for the first time an ache built in her chest. What had started out as a whim, a crush, a foolish game had escalated into something she couldn't break free from.

Her mother, Theresa, even Glen, had warned her she was better off with a man who appreciated her. But she hadn't wanted to hear the good advice from her friends and family. And for a while things had been perfect.

The way she'd felt about him the first time he'd kissed her six months ago was nothing compared to the growing connection she felt now. Each day in his presence it grew stronger. How was she supposed to just let him go and move forward? To raise this child on her own? To spend the rest of her life without him? Panic assailed her, causing dark spots in her vision and making it hard to draw a full breath for several minutes.

She rode the paralyzing fear until her emotions calmed. Able to think rationally again, Brooke was mortified by how badly she wanted to cling to Nic and beg him to give up his responsibilities and be with her. Once upon a time she'd prided herself on being an independent woman, capable of living abroad for a year in Italy while she worked on her doctoral thesis on Italian literature. She might make decisions based on emotion rather than logic, but she ruled her finances with a miser's tight fist and had a knack for avoiding bad relationships.

These days she was a rickety ladder of vulnerability and loose screws. What else could explain why she'd charged a fifteen-hundred-dollar airplane ticket on her credit card to chase after a man who'd vanished from her life without even a goodbye? If she'd picked up the phone and delivered her news about the pregnancy she could have saved herself a bucketful of heartache and said to hell with closure.

Brooke sat up and buttoned Nic's shirt once more. A sudden bout of nausea caught her off guard. If the positive pregnancy test result had seemed surreal, here was tangible proof that her body was irrevocably changed. Brooke slipped off the bed and fled the room, afraid Nic would exit the bathroom and catch her looking green and out of sorts, then demand to know what was wrong with her.

On her way to the guesthouse, she snagged a bit of bread and a bottle of water. Once there, she nibbled at the crust, put the chilled bottle to her warm forehead and willed her stomach to settle down. As the nausea subsided, Brooke's confidence ebbed away, as well.

In twenty-four hours Nic was heading home to find a wife. He would be forever lost to her. Maybe she should give up this madness today and run back to California.

Because she still hadn't done what she'd come here to do: tell Nic she was pregnant.

And yet, on the heels of all she'd learned, did it make sense to burden him with the news that his illegitimate child would be living far from him in California? He was returning home to find a bride and start a family. His future wife wouldn't be happy to find out Nic had already gotten another woman pregnant.

Then, too, he'd proven himself an honorable man. It would tear him apart to know he wouldn't be a part of his child's life? What if he demanded partial custody? Was she going to spend the next eighteen years shuffling their child across the Atlantic Ocean so that he or she could know Nic? And what about the scandal this would mean for the royal family? Maybe in America no one thought twice when celebrities had children without being married, but that wouldn't sit well where European nobility were concerned.

Yet morally was it right to keep the information from him? It would certainly be easier on her. Nic had turned his back on Glen and their dream of getting *Griffin* off the ground. Brooke knew she could count on her brother to keep her secret. Her life going forward would be quiet and routine. She would teach at Berkeley or UCLA and throw herself into raising her child. No one would ever know that she'd had a brief affair with a European prince.

Both options had their positives and negatives. And it was early in her pregnancy. So many things could go wrong in the first trimester. She could take another month to decide. The discovery that she was pregnant was only a week old. Maybe if she gave the situation some more thought she could arrive at a decision that she could live with.

Knowing that avoiding a decision was not the best answer, she dressed in black shorts and a white T-shirt. Maybe she would take a hike to the windmills a little later. Although her stomach wasn't back to normal, she had to act as if nothing was wrong.

Half an hour after her encounter with Nic, she returned to the house and found him standing in the kitchen drinking coffee. He was staring out the window as Brooke drew near and when she saw the expression on his face, all the energy drained from her body.

"Don't." Her throat contracted before she could finish.

He swiveled his head in her direction. His gaze was hollow. "Don't what?"

Hearing his tight, unhappy tone, frustration replaced anxiety. Brooke stamped her foot. "Don't regret what just happened."

"Brooke, you don't understand—"

"Don't," she interrupted, despair clutching at her chest. She didn't need to be psychic to know what ran through Nic's mind. "Don't you dare spew platitudes at me. I've known you too long."

"You don't know me at all."

And whose fault was that? She sucked in a breath. Harsh words gathered in her head. She squeezed her eyes shut, moderated her tone. "I wish we had time to change that."

The umber eyes that turned in her direction were a

stark landscape of cynicism and regret. "But we don't."
Although he pushed her away with his words, the muscle
jumping in his jaw proclaimed he wasn't happy to do so.
His agonized expression matched the pain throbbing in
his voice. "My family needs me."

I need you. Your child needs you.

But all of a sudden she knew she wasn't going to put
that burden on him. What he felt for her wasn't casual. She
was finding it hard to let go. He was going through something similar. But they each had their ways of coping and
she should respect that.

Brooke retreated to the opposite side of the room and
picked up her sandals. The silence in the house went un-
broken for several moments while she reorganized her
emotions and set aside her disappointment.

"Are these okay for a hike up to the windmills?" she
asked, indicating the footwear. "I'm afraid I don't have
anything more sturdy."

"They should be fine." He assessed her feet. "There's
a well-defined path up to get there."

"Great."

His brow creased at her flat tone. "Are you okay?"

"Fine. Just feeling a little off all of a sudden. Nothing
breakfast won't cure."

Brooke was glad that Elena picked that moment to enter
the house with bags of groceries. It kept her and Nic from
plunging back into heated waters. With Elena bustling
around the kitchen they had little need to exchange more
than a few words over a meal of eggs and pastries.

An hour later, they were heading to the windmill. The
paved road that led from the town past Nic's villa gave out
two miles farther. Ahead was the narrow path cluttered
with large rocks and tree roots that led to the three windmills she'd seen on arriving at Ithaca. Nic set a moderate
pace through the irregular terrain, forcing Brooke to focus

on where she stepped, and silence filled the space between them. For once she was grateful for the lack of conversation because she had too many conflicting thoughts circling her mind.

"There are a number of windmills on Ithaca," Nic began as the brush lining the path ahead of them gave way to a flat, rocky expanse. Brooke was glad for her sunglasses as they emerged from the vegetation onto the rocky plateau.

Before them lay the three disused windmills. Twenty feet in diameter, thirty feet tall, their squat, round shapes stood sentinel over all the boats coming and going from the harbor. Their walls once would have been whitewashed, but years of wind and weather had scoured the brick, returning it to shades of gray and tan.

Nic headed toward the structures, his words drifting back to her on the strong breeze. "Corn and wheat would come from all over the islands to be ground here because of the constant winds in this area."

In the lee of the squat towers, Nic gestured to direct her attention through a curved doorway into the windmill's interior. "As you can see, the 1953 earthquake caused the grinding wheel and shaft to break and tumble to the bottom."

"Fascinating." But her attention was only half on the scene before her. A moment earlier she'd stumbled when her toe caught on a half-buried rock and he'd caught her arm to steady her. His hand had not yet fallen away. "Thank you for bringing me here. The view is amazing. I can see why you enjoy coming to the island."

"After this we should take the boat to Vathay and have lunch." He was obviously hoping that by keeping busy they could avoid a repeat of the morning's events.

Brooke wasn't sure she could spend a fun-filled afternoon with him while her heart was in the process of shattering. For the first time since her interest in him had sparked, she was bereft of hope. Even after he'd broken things off a month ago, she hadn't really believed it was over. This morning, she'd finally faced up to reality.

Nic was going to marry someone else and build a life with that person.

"If you don't mind," Brooke said, "I think I'd rather just hang out on the terrace and do a little reading. But you go ahead and do whatever it is you've been doing before I got here."

He frowned, obviously unsure what to make of her abrupt about-face. "If that's what you want to do."

"It is." The words sounded heavy.

"Very well."

For the next fifteen minutes, he inundated her with facts about the area, the aftereffects of the 1953 earthquake and other interesting tidbits about the island. Brooke responded with nods and polite smiles when he paused to see if she was listening. Eventually, he ran out of things to say and they headed back down the path. They had to walk single file until they reached the road. Once they got there they strode side by side without speaking. When Nic's villa was less than a mile away, to Brooke's surprise, it was Nic who broke the silence.

"About this morning."

"Please don't," Brooke murmured, expelling her breath in a weary sigh.

"I was wrong to kiss you," he continued, either not hearing her protest or ignoring it. "I'm sending you mixed messages and that isn't fair."

"It was my fault. I shouldn't have intruded on your sleep and thrown myself at you. Most men would have taken advantage of the situation. You showed great restraint."

"Nevertheless." His frown indicated he wasn't happy she'd taken the blame. "I haven't been fair to you. If I'd told you from the start who I really was, you'd never have developed feelings for me."

Brooke couldn't believe what she was hearing. She'd chased this man for five years, teased him, flattered him, poured her heart out to him and received nothing in return until six months ago when he'd kissed her. *He'd* kissed *her*. She hadn't plunked herself onto his lap and tormented him the way she'd done the day before. In fact, she hadn't even flirted with him that night. He'd been the one to draw her away from Glen's party and kiss her senseless.

"I never meant to hurt you."

"You haven't." She wasn't upset with him. She was disappointed in herself. How could she have been such a fool for so long? "If I hurt right now it's because I didn't listen when you told me over and over that we weren't right for each other. I created my own troubles. Your conscience should be clear."

She walked faster, needing some space from Nic. He matched her stride for stride.

"Is this some sort of ploy—?"

She erupted in exasperation. "Get over yourself already. I'm done." She gestured broadly with her arms as her temper flared. "You've convinced me that it's stupid to keep holding on for something that can never be. So, congratulations, I'm never going to ask you for anything ever again."

Her anger wasn't reasonable, but at that moment it was the only way to cope with her deep sadness. She couldn't cry, not yet, so she took refuge in ferocity. This was a side of her she'd never let Nic see. She always kept things light and fun around him. Even when she showed him her temper, it was followed by a quicksilver smile.

Right now she had no lightness inside her, only shadow.

Nic caught her arm to slow her as she surged forward. "I don't want us to end like this."

She was not going to say nice things so he could ease his

conscience about her. "End like what? Me being upset with you? How do you think I felt a month ago when you told me that sleeping together had been the wrong thing to do?"

"I was wrong not to tell you the truth about what was really going on." The intense light in his eyes seared through her defenses. "I'm sorry."

Unbidden, sympathy rose in her. Brooke cast it aside. She didn't want to accept that he was as much a victim of circumstances as she. With a vigorous shake of her head she pulled free and began walking once again.

"What happened isn't fair to either one of us," he called after her. "Don't you think if I could choose you I would?"

She swung around and walked backward as she spoke. "The trouble is, you didn't choose me. Nothing is really forcing you to go home and make this huge sacrifice for your country. This is your decision. You feel honor bound. It's who you are. It's why I love you. But don't blame circumstances or your family's expectations for the choice you are making."

Leaving him standing in the middle of the road, Brooke ran the rest of the way back to the villa.

Six

Nic lay on his back, forearm thrown over his eyes. Moonlight streamed into his room like a searchlight, but he couldn't be bothered to close the shutters. A soft breeze trailed across his bare chest, teasing him with the memory of Brooke's fingers tantalizing his skin this morning.

The regret he'd been trying unsuccessfully to contain for the past twelve hours pounded him as relentlessly as the Ionian Sea against the cliff below the villa. Any sensible man would have taken Brooke to bed rather than inflict on her a long sightseeing adventure to busted-up windmills. Instead he'd rejected her not once but twice this morning, and then disregarded the pain he'd caused.

She'd eaten lunch by herself on the terrace and barely spoken to him during dinner. When she did speak, her tone had been stiff. He didn't blame her for being upset. Any apology he might make would've been way too little and far too late. But he'd been relieved when she'd escaped as soon as the dishes had been piled in the sink.

He gusted out an impatient breath and sat up. Sleeping without the benefit of too much alcohol had been hard enough before Brooke arrived. Knowing she slept thirty feet away made unconsciousness completely impossible. Hell. It used to be that if he couldn't sleep, he would work. That outlet was lost to him now. Still, he hadn't yet looked at the forty emails restored to his inbox. Maybe a few hours of technical questions would take his mind off his problems.

Padding barefoot downstairs, he stopped short as he neared the bottom, his skin tingling in awareness that he wasn't alone.

Beyond the open French doors, the full moon slanted a stripe of ethereal white across the harbor's smooth surface and reached into the living room to touch the couch. Beside the shaft of moonlight, a dark shadow huddled, an ink spot on the pristine fabric.

Brooke.

His breath lodged in his throat and her name came out of him in a hoarse whisper. His body went into full alert. This was bad. Very bad. A late-night encounter with her was more temptation than he was prepared to handle.

"How come you're not in bed?" he demanded, stepping onto the limestone tile. He took two steps toward the couch, his impulses getting the upper hand. He'd come close enough to smell vanilla and hear her unsteady breathing. He set one hand on his hip and rubbed the back of his neck with the other.

"I couldn't sleep." Her voice emerged from shadow, low and passionless with a slight waver. "I haven't been able to stop thinking about what I said to you earlier. You're doing the right thing where your family and country are concerned."

"This whole thing is my fault. You came a long way

not knowing who I was or what my family has been going through."

If circumstances were different…

But it wasn't fair to patronize her with meaningless platitudes. Circumstances were exactly what they were and he'd made his decision based on what he'd been taught to do.

"Still, I shouldn't have hit you with a guilt trip."

"You didn't." Nic took another two steps and stopped. His breath hissed through clenched teeth. What was he doing? The longing to gather her into his arms and comfort her stunned him with its power. His body ached to feel her soft body melt against him. Madness.

"I just wanted you to choose me for once."

Her words slammed into his gut and rocked him backward. He'd been a first-class bastard where she was concerned. How many times had he rebuffed her when all she wanted was to help him work through a problem? So what if her methods sounded illogical and ineffective? She'd been right the time she'd badgered him into playing miniature golf with her when he was busy trying to solve a difficult technical problem. On the fourth hole the solution had popped into his head with no prompting. Had he bothered to thank her before rushing back to his workroom at the hangar and burying himself in the project once more?

And now, it was too late to make everything up to her.

"You should head back to bed. You have a long flight back to California tomorrow."

Her shadow moved as she shook her head. "I'm not going home tomorrow."

"Where are you going?"

"I don't know yet. I have a few weeks before I have to be back at UC Santa Cruz. I thought maybe I'd head to Rome and meet up with some friends."

"What about your Berkeley interview?"

"It's the day after tomorrow."

"But you said it was in a few weeks."

"It was rescheduled."

"Why didn't you tell me?" Annoyance flared, banishing all thoughts of comforting her.

"I thought if you knew, you'd put me on a plane right away and I wanted these two days with you."

Two days during which they'd argued and he'd done nothing but push her away. Irritation welled.

"But why aren't you going right home for the interview? Teaching at Berkeley is all you've talked about since I've known you."

Her temper sparked in response to his scolding. "Plans change. It's just not the right time for me to take the position."

"Are you giving up something as important as Berkeley because of me?"

"Seems foolish, doesn't it?" she countered without a trace of bitterness.

Nic clenched his fists. She was going to be so much better without him.

And he was going to be so much worse.

"You should take your own advice about going to bed," she told him. "Sounds like your mother planned a grueling week for you. It will be better if you're well rested."

Nic had the distinct impression he'd just been dismissed. His lips twitched. He could always count on Brooke to do the last thing he expected. After her assault on his willpower this morning, he'd been lying awake half expecting her to launch another all-out attack tonight.

From the way he'd been with her this morning, she had to know he was having a harder and harder time resisting her. Resisting what he wanted more than anything. With each beat of his heart, the idea of taking her back upstairs and tumbling her into his bed seemed less like a huge mistake and more like the right thing to do.

Walk away.

"What are you going to do?" he asked, knowing that prolonging this conversation was the height of idiocy. It would only make going back to bed alone that much harder.

"Sit here."

"I won't be able to sleep knowing you're down here in the dark."

A small smile filled her voice as she said, "You've never had trouble putting me out of your mind before."

If she only knew. "You weren't sitting on my couch in your pajamas before."

Her sigh was barely audible over the blood thundering in his ears.

"Good night." Calling himself every sort of fool, he headed back upstairs. Leaving his bedroom door open in a halfhearted invitation, he fell onto the mattress. Hands behind his head, eyes on the ceiling, he strained to hear footfalls on the stairs. The house was completely silent except for the breeze stirring the curtains on either side of his window.

His nerves stretched and twisted, but she didn't appear. He caught himself glancing at the doorway, expecting her silhouette. As the minutes ticked by, Nic forced his eyes shut, but he couldn't quiet his mind and the past two days played through his thoughts with unrelenting starkness.

With a heated curse, he rolled off the bed and stalked downstairs. It didn't surprise him to find her exactly where he'd left her.

"You are the most stubborn woman I've ever known," he complained. "I don't know what the hell you expect from me."

Even his mother had given up trying to keep him in Sherdana when his heart belonged in an airplane hangar in the Mojave Dessert. But for years Brooke had relentlessly pushed herself into his life until he couldn't celebrate achievements or face failures without thinking about her.

"My expectations are all in the past," she said, pushing to her feet.

And that's what was eating him alive.

They stared at each other in motionless silence until Brooke heaved a huge sigh. The dramatic rise and fall of her chest snagged Nic's attention. The tank top she wore scooped low in front, offering him the tiniest hint of cleavage. Recalling the way her breasts had tasted this morning, he repressed a groan.

"Brooke."

"Don't." She started past him. Nic caught her wrist. At his touch, she stilled. "I thought I was pretty clear this afternoon when I said that I've given up on you."

"Crystal clear." Nic cupped her face, his fingers sliding into the silky strands of russet near her ear.

"Then what are you doing?"

"Wishing you didn't have to."

He brought his mouth down to hers, catching her lips in a searing kiss that held nothing back. She stiffened, her body bracing to recoil. He couldn't let that happen. Not now. Not when he'd stopped being principled and noble. Not when he wanted her with a hunger that ate at him like acid.

Taking a tighter grip on her wrist, he slowly levered it behind her back, compelling her hips forward until her pelvis brushed against the jut of his erection. The contact made him moan. He deepened the kiss, sweeping his tongue forward to taste her. Her lips parted for him. A soft whimper escaped her throat as she writhed in his grasp, but whether she fought to escape or move closer he couldn't be sure.

"I want you," he murmured, setting his mouth on her throat and sucking gently.

Her body trembled, but her muscles remained tense. Labored, uneven breaths pushed her breasts against his bare chest.

"Damn you, Nic." It was in her voice, in the way she tilted her head to allow him better access to her neck. She was furious and aroused. "It's too late for you to change your mind."

"It's too late when I say it is." He released her wrist and cupped her small, round butt in his palm. The cotton pajama bottoms bunched as he gave a light squeeze.

She gasped, set both hands on his chest and shoved. It was like a kitten batting at a mastiff. "This isn't fair."

"Fair?" He growled the word. "Do you want to talk about fair? You've tormented me for five years. Strutting around the hangar in your barely there denim shorts. Coming to peer over my shoulder and letting your hair tickle my skin. How hard do you think it was for me to keep from pulling you into my lap and putting my hands all over you?"

"You never…" She arched back and stared up into his face. "I had no idea."

"I made sure you didn't. But it wasn't easy." He wrapped his fingers around her red curls and gave a gentle but firm tug. "And it wasn't fun."

Brooke was electrified by Nic's admission; the twinge in her scalp when he pulled her hair merely enhanced her already overstimulated nerves. She welcomed the discomfort. The fleeting pain chased the last vestiges of self-pity from her mind and grounded her in the moment.

Taking her silence and stillness as surrender, Nic bent to kiss her again, but Brooke turned aside at the last minute. Even though this was what she'd wanted when she'd bought her plane ticket, she wasn't the same woman who'd gotten on the plane in San Francisco.

Nic wasn't deterred by her evasion. He kissed his way across her cheek and seized her earlobe between his teeth. Her knees wavered as his unsteady breath filled her ear. Meanwhile, his hands moved over her back, gliding beneath her tank top to find her hot skin and trace each bump of her spine.

"What's wrong?" he murmured as his lips investigated the hollow made by her collarbone.

"You want me to give in." He was doing whatever it took to make her putty in his hand. "Just like you used to want me to leave you alone. It's always about what you want."

She felt as much as heard his sigh. His hands left her body and bracketed his hips. He regarded her solemnly.

"I thought this was what we both wanted."

A breeze puffed in from the terrace, chilling Brooke. Where a second earlier the room had been dark, moonlight now poured over the tiled floor and bathed Nic's splendid torso in a white glow. Her mouth went dry as her gaze traced the rise and fall of his pecs and abs, the perfect ratio of broad shoulders to narrow hips. Although still in shadow, the planes of his face seemed more chiseled, his jaw sharper.

Her pulse began to slam harder, throbbing in her wrist, her throat and between her thighs. She found his eyes in the dimness, fell beneath the hypnotic power of his gaze. A rushing filled her ears, the incessant movement of a stream as it surges past boulders and fallen trees, unstoppable. Once upon a time, she'd been like that, full of purpose and joy. Then she'd let her doubts bottle her up.

Was she really going to stand here being annoyed with him and waste another second of the limited time she had left bemoaning the cards fate had dealt?

She held out her hand to Nic. He linked his fingers with hers and drew her toward the stairs. Without saying a word they entered his bedroom and came together in a slow, effortless dance of hands, lips and tongue. Pajamas landed on the floor and Brooke stretched out on Nic's king-size bed, his strong body pressing her hard into the mattress as they kissed and explored.

Words were lost to Brooke as Nic's fingertips rode her rib cage to the undersides of her breasts. She couldn't remember ever feeling so heavy and so light at the same time. Arching her spine, she pushed her nipples against his palms. Stars burst behind her eyelids as he circled the hard buds, making them ache with pleasure before at long last drawing one then the other into his hot mouth.

The sensations snapping along her nerves made Brooke quiver and gasp. She was hungry for Nic to touch her more intimately, but her senses had gone fuzzy, her body languid. His hand rode upward along her inner thigh with torturous precision and she followed its progress with breaths growing ever more faint. By the time his finger dipped into her wet heat, her lungs had forgotten how to function. She lay with her eyes closed, her head spinning as he filled her first with one, then two fingers, stretching her, finding the spot that caused her hips to jerk and the first shuddering moan to escape her throat.

And then he replaced his hand with his mouth and adored her with tongue and teeth. Sliding his hands beneath her butt, he lifted her against the press and retreat of his kiss. She tried to squirm, to escape the tongue that drove her relentlessly toward pleasure so acute it hurt, but Nic dug his fingers into her skin and held her captive. Mewling, Brooke surrendered to the slow, tantalizing rise of ecstasy.

Nic hadn't made love to her like this the first time they were together. Five years of anticipation had made their lovemaking passionate and impatient. Nic had satisfied her three times that night, his large body surging into hers, filling her completely. She'd come with desperate cries, unable to articulate the incandescent heights to which he'd lifted her.

But the rush upward had been followed by only a brief respite to catch her breath and savor the afterglow. Nic had proven insatiable that night and when at last they'd spent the last of their passion, she'd fallen into a deep, dreamless slumber.

This was different. As if recognizing this was their last time together, he made love to her with his eyes first and then his hands. Languid sweeps of his lips across her skin soothed her soul and set her skin aflame. Words of appreciation and praise poured over her while his fingers reverently grazed the lines of her body.

By the time he slipped on a condom and settled between her thighs, Brooke wasn't sure where she ended and he began. He moved slowly into her, easing in just the head of his erection, giving her time she didn't need to adjust to him.

Tipping her hips as he began his second thrust, she ensured that his forward progress didn't end until he was fully seated inside her. He groaned and buried his face in her neck. She dug her fingernails into his back, reveling in the fullness of his possession. For a long moment neither of them moved. Brooke filled her lungs with the spicy tang of his aftershave and the musk of their lovemaking. She closed her eyes to memorize the feel of his powerful body as he began moving.

Measured and deliberate, Nic rocked against her, thrusting in and out while pleasure built. He kissed her hard, his tongue plunging to tangle with hers. Their hips came together with increased urgency. Brooke let her teeth glide along Nic's neck. He bucked hard against her when she nipped at his skin. The thrust rapped her womb where their child grew and sent her spiraling toward climax. She must have clenched around him because suddenly Nic picked up the pace. Together they climbed, hands pleasuring, bodies striving for closeness. Brooke came first, Nic's name on her lips. He drove into her more urgently and reached orgasm moments later.

His strong body shook with the intensity of his release and a hoarse cry spilled out of him. What followed was the deepest, most emotionally charged kiss he'd ever given her. Brooke clung to him while her body pulsed with aftershocks and surrendered to the tempest raging in Nic. If she'd thought their lovemaking had forever branded her as his, the kiss, tender one moment, joyous the next, stole the heart right out of her body.

"Incredible." He buried his face in her neck, his breath heavy and uneven, body limp and powerless.

Brooke wrapped her arms around his shoulders, marveling that this formidable man had been reduced to overcooked noodles in her arms. Grinning, she stroked the bumpy length of his spine and ran her nails through his hair in a soothing caress.

"Am I too heavy?" he murmured, lips moving against her shoulder as he spoke.

"A little, but I don't want you to move just yet." She was afraid any shift would disrupt this moment of perfect harmony.

"Good. I like it just where I am."

They stayed that way for a long time. Legs entwined, his breath soft and steady on her neck, his fingers playing idly in her tangled curls. Brooke couldn't recall if she'd ever enjoyed being so utterly still before. She didn't want to talk or to think. Only to be.

But as with all things, change is inevitable. Nic heaved a mighty sigh and rolled away from her to dispose of the condom and pull a sheet over their cooling bodies. The breeze had shifted direction and the air that had seemed dense and sultry an hour earlier was swept away.

With her head pillowed on his shoulder and Nic's fingers absently gliding across the small of her back, the lethargy she'd experienced earlier didn't return.

"I can feel you thinking," Nic said, his eyes closed, a half smile curving his lips.

"That's illogical."

His chest moved up and down with his sigh. "If I was in a logical frame of mind, I wouldn't be lying naked with you in my arms."

"I suppose not."

"What's on your mind?"

Not wanting to share her true thoughts, she said the first thing that popped into her head. "If you must know I was thinking about getting a cat when I get home."

"Really?" He sounded genuinely surprised. "I thought Glen said you guys grew up with dogs."

"We did, but dogs are so needy and some of my days can go really long with classes and office hours. I think a cat would be a wiser choice."

"I like cats."

"You do?" She couldn't imagine Nic owning anything that needed regular feeding or care. "Wouldn't a snake be a more suitable pet for you?"

"A snake?"

"Sure, something you only had to feed once a week." She chuckled when he growled at her.

"No snakes." He yawned. "A cat. Definitely."

Brooke could tell by the sleepiness of his voice that she was losing him. "But a cat is going to jump on your worktable and knock things off. It's going to wake you in the middle of the night wanting to be petted and yowling at you for attention. They ignore you when you give them commands and never come when they're called."

Nic cracked open one eye and smirked at her. "Yeah, a cat. They're definitely my favorite kind of nuisance."

It took Brooke a couple seconds to realize he had connected her behavior to what she'd just said about cats. In retaliation, she poked him hard in the ribs and he located the ticklish spot behind her knees that had her squirming. It didn't take long for their good-natured tussling to spark another round of lovemaking.

Much later, while Nic's breathing deepened into sleep, Brooke lay awake in the predawn stillness and tried to keep her thoughts from rushing into the future. The hours she had with him grew shorter every second. So instead of sleeping, as the sky grew lighter, Brooke lost herself in Nic's snug embrace, savored the way his warmth seeped through her skin and awaited the day.

The nausea that had plagued her the day before began as the sun peeked over the horizon and gilded the window ledge. She breathed through the first wave and sagged with relief when her stomach settled down. Remembering how the previous morning had gone, Brooke knew she had to get back to her room. Nic might not be the most observant of men, but even he'd be hard-pressed not to notice if she was throwing up in his bathroom.

Last night while in the grip of insomnia, she'd decided not to tell him she was pregnant. If he hadn't made love to her with such all-consuming emotion, she might have accepted that they could go back to being friends, affectionate but disconnected by distance and circumstances. But now she realized that they had to make a clean break of it. It would be best for both of them if he didn't know the truth.

Before her stomach began to pitch and roll again, Brooke untangled herself from Nic's embrace and eased from his bed. Her head spun sickeningly as she got to her feet and snatched up her pajamas. Naked, the soft cotton pressed to her mouth, she raced from the room and down the stairs.

If Elena was shocked to see her streak by, Brooke never knew because her focus was fixed on crossing the twenty feet of terrace to the guesthouse and reaching the bathroom in the nick of time. Panting in the aftermath, she splashed cold water on her face and waited to see if the nausea had passed. When it appeared the worst was over, Brooke climbed into the shower.

She was dressed and repacking her suitcase when a soft knock sounded. Heart jumping, she eased the door open, expecting to see Nic standing there, and was surprised to see Elena bearing a tray with a teapot and a plate of bread and assorted preserves.

"Ginger tea is good for nausea," she announced, slipping the tray onto the dresser. "I understand you are leaving for Sherdana today."

"Nic is going. I'm heading for Italy." But her plan to visit friends in Rome had lost its appeal. More than anything she wanted to head home to family and friends and start the process of healing in their comforting embrace.

Elena's eyes narrowed. "You let me know if you need anything before you leave."

Seven

Awaking to an empty bed hadn't been the best start to Nic's day, but he reasoned he might as well get used to disappointment because he wouldn't ever wake to Brooke's smile again. The sun was high by the time Nic finished his shower and headed to the first floor. Elena was dusting the already immaculate furniture. She shot him an intensely unhappy look as he poured himself a cup of coffee and he wondered at her barely veiled hostility.

"Have you seen Brooke this morning?" he asked, carrying his cup to the terrace doorway and peering in the direction of the guesthouse. The trip to Kefalonia's airport would take forty-five minutes by boat and another hour over land. They would need to leave soon.

"She has eaten breakfast and had some last minute packing to do."

"Is Thasos ready with the boat?"

Elena nodded. "She is a nice girl. You shouldn't let her go to Italy by herself."

"She is going to visit friends," he explained to the housekeeper, while guilt nibbled at the edges of his conscience. "She knows her way around. She lived in Rome and Florence for a year."

"You should take her home."

Nic was startled by Elena's remark. He'd been thinking the same thing all morning. Unfortunately that wasn't possible. Reality dictated he should distance himself from Brooke as soon as possible, but the thought of letting her go off by herself disturbed him.

If she didn't get on a plane bound for California, he would spend the next two weeks worrying about her traveling alone in Europe instead of focusing on the issues at home and the necessity of finding a wife. Nor did he have time to escort her to the gate and satisfy himself that she was heading to San Francisco. He was expected back in Sherdana this afternoon.

Nic's chest tightened. He was doing a terrible job of lying to himself. In truth he wasn't ready to say goodbye. It was selfish and stupid.

"I need to make a phone call," Nic told Elena. "Will you let Brooke know we'll be leaving in ten minutes?"

Calling himself every sort of idiot, Nic dialed Gabriel. When he answered, Nic got right to the point. "I'm bringing someone home with me. She's come a long way to see me and I don't feel right leaving her alone in Greece."

"She?" Gabriel echoed, not quite able to keep curiosity out of his voice. "Is this going to cause problems?"

Nic knew exactly what Gabriel meant and decided not to sugarcoat it. "That's not my intention. She's Glen's sister. I think I've mentioned her a few times."

"The one who drives you crazy?" Gabriel sounded intrigued.

"The interfering one who flew here to convince me to come back to the *Griffin* project."

"Just the project?"

"What's that supposed to mean?" Nic didn't intend to be defensive, but with last night's events still reverberating across his emotions, he wasn't in the best shape to fence with a diplomat as savvy as Gabriel. "She's Glen's little sister."

"And you talk about her more than any woman you've ever known."

"I know what you're getting at, but it's not an issue. Things got a little complicated between us recently, but everything is sorted out."

"Complicated how?"

"I didn't tell her who I was until she came here looking for me and that upset her. I shouldn't have left her in the dark. We've been...friends...for a long time."

"Why didn't you tell her?"

Nic rubbed his temples where an ache had begun. "I know this is going to be hard for you to understand but I liked being an ordinary scientist, anonymously doing the work I'm really good at."

"You're right. I don't understand. I grew up knowing I belonged to the country. You never did like being in the spotlight. So you didn't tell her you're a prince. Do you think she would have looked at you differently if she'd known all along?"

"Brooke values a person for how they behave not who they are or what they have."

Gabriel laughed. "She sounds like your sort of girl. I can't wait to meet her."

"Honestly, it's not like that." He didn't want his brother giving the wrong idea to their parents. "She understands my situation."

"She knows that you're coming home to find a bride? And she wants to accompany you anyway?"

"I haven't spoken with her this morning." Not exactly a

lie. "She doesn't know I'm bringing her with me to Sherdana yet."

"Well, this should make for an interesting family dinner," Gabriel said. "I'll make sure there's a place set at the table for her beside Mother."

And before Nic could protest that arrangement, Gabriel hung up. Nic debated calling him back, but decided it would only exacerbate his brother's suspicions about Brooke. Playing it cool and calm around his family would be the best way to handle any and all speculation.

Grabbing his bag from his bedroom, Nic made his way toward the steps that Brooke had used to access the terrace two days ago. They led down the steep hillside in a zigzag that ended at a private dock. Brooke had already arrived at the boat and was settled onto the seat opposite the pilot's chair. The smile she offered Nic was bright if a little ragged around the edges.

Thasos started the engine as soon as Nic stepped aboard and quickly untied the mooring ropes. Nic settled into the bench seat at the back of the boat and watched Brooke pretend not to be interested in him. He knew the signs. He'd spent years giving her the impression he was oblivious to her presence. Yet how could he be? She lit up every room she entered. Her personality set the very air to buzzing. Sitting still was probably the hardest thing she did. Yet when her brain engaged, she could get lost in a book or her writing for hours.

They'd shared many companionable afternoons while she was working on her second doctorate. Not surprisingly, she enjoyed sitting cross-legged on the couch in his workroom, tapping away at her computer keyboard or with her nose buried in a book. If he managed to accomplish any work on the weekends she visited, it was a miracle. Most of the time, he'd pretended to be productive while he watched her surreptitiously.

Forty-five minutes after leaving Ithaca, the boat maneuvered into an open space at the Fiskardo quay. A car would be waiting to carry them on the thirty-one-kilometer journey to the airport outside Kefalonia's capital, Argostoli. If traffic was good, they would get there in a little less than an hour.

Thasos carried their bags to the waiting car and with a jaunty wave turned back to the boat. As soon as he'd driven out of sight, Nic turned to Brooke.

"I don't feel comfortable heading home to Sherdana and leaving you on your own."

"Good Lord, Nic." She shot him a dry look. "I'm perfectly capable of taking care of myself."

"I agree. It's just that with everything that has happened in the last few days—"

"Stop right there." All trace of amusement vanished from her tone as she interrupted him. "After everything that's happened…? I am not some delicate flower that has been crushed by disappointment."

"Nevertheless. I'm not going to leave you stranded in Greece. You are coming home with me."

After five years of teasing and cajoling, bullying and begging, Brooke thought she had Nic all figured out. He preferred working in solitude, hated drama and rarely veered from a goal once he'd set his mind to something. But this announcement left her floundering. Had she ever really known him at all?

"What do you mean you're taking me home with you?" The notion thrilled and terrified her.

"Exactly what I said." Nic's jaw was set in uncompromising lines. "You will fly with me to Sherdana and from there I will make sure you get a flight back to California."

The knot in Brooke's stomach didn't ease with his clarification. "I assure you I'm perfectly capable of getting a

flight home from Greece." With morning sickness plagu-
ing her, she'd given up the idea of a summer holiday in
Italy. She wanted to be surrounded by familiar things and
her favorite people. Maybe she'd spend a week in LA visiting her parents.

"Don't make this difficult on yourself."

"Isn't that what I should be saying to you?" Seeing he
didn't comprehend her meaning, Brooke clarified. "Have
you considered what happens when we land? How fast can
you get me on a plane to the States? In the meantime are
you planning on leaving me waiting at the airport? Putting me up in a hotel? Or perhaps you think I'd be more
comfortable at the palace?"

Expecting her sarcasm to be lost on him the way it usually was, Brooke was stunned by his matter-of-fact retort.

"My brother said he'll make sure the staff sets an extra
place for you at dinner next to my mother." Lighthearted
mischief lit his eyes as her mouth dropped open.

"I can't have dinner with your family." Her throat
clenched around a lump of panic.

"Why not?"

"I have nothing to wear."

"You look perfect to me."

With lids half-closed, his gaze roamed over her body,
setting off a chain reaction of longing and need. The July
morning had gone from warm to hot as the sun had crested
the horizon and Brooke had dressed accordingly in a loose-
fitting blue-and-white cotton peasant dress with a thigh-
baring hem and a plunging neckline. The look was fine
for traveling from one Greek Island to another or catching a short flight to Rome, London or anywhere else she
could snag a connection home to California. But to go to
Sherdana and be introduced to Nic's family?

"Why are you really bringing me along?"

"Because I'm not ready to let you go." As light as a

feather, he slid his forefinger along her jaw. It fell away when it reached her chin. "Not yet."

But let her go he would. Her skin tingled where he'd touched her. Brooke saw the regret in his eyes and her heart jerked. Heat kindled in her midsection as she recalled what had taken place between them the night before, but desire tangled with anxiety and sadness. How was she supposed to just walk away?

She jammed her balled fists behind her to hide their shaking and estimated she had half an hour to talk him out of his madness. "Have you considered how unhappy your parents are going to be if you show up with some strange girl in tow?"

"You're not a strange girl. You're Glen's sister."

"And how are you going to explain what I was doing on the island with you?"

"I've already contacted Gabriel and briefed him."

Briefed him with the truth or a diplomatic runaround? "You don't think anyone is going to be suspicious about the nature of our relationship?

"Why would they be? I've spoken of you often to my family. They know you're Glen's annoying baby sister whom I've known for the last five years."

Seeing his wicked smile, she relaxed a little. "Okay, maybe we can do this. After all, Glen knows us better than anyone and he has no idea anything changed between us." If they could fool Glen, they could keep his family from guessing the true nature of their relationship.

"He knows."

Brooke shook her head. "Impossible." Her mind raced over every conversation she'd had with her brother in the past month. "He hasn't said a word."

"He had plenty to say to me," Nic replied in a tight voice, and Brooke suddenly had no trouble imagining how that conversation had gone.

Glen was the best older brother a girl could have. Born eighteen months before her, he'd never minded when she'd tagged after him and his buddies. The guys had accepted her as one of them and taught her how to surf and water-ski. She'd grown up half tomboy, half girly-girl. They'd all had a great time until Glen graduated high school two years early and headed off to MIT where he'd met Nic.

"The morning after we were together," Nic continued, "your brother cornered me in the lab and threatened to send me up strapped to the rocket if I hurt you."

"No wonder you got out of town so fast after breaking things off with me." Her words were meant to be funny, but when Nic grimaced, she realized her insensitivity. He'd actually left not long after the rocket blew up. "I'm sorry." She looked down at her hands. "I shouldn't have said that."

Nic set his fingers beneath her chin and adjusted the angle of her head until their eyes met. "I'd like to show you my country."

And then what? She received the royal treatment and another goodbye? Already her heart was behaving rashly. She'd opened herself to heartache when she'd surrendered to one last night in his arms. To linger meant parting from him would be that much harder. Did she have no self-control? No self-respect? Hadn't she already learned several difficult lessons?

The need in his gaze echoed the longing in her heart. "Sure," she murmured, surrendering to what they both wanted. "Why not."

"Then that's settled."

An hour later, Nic led her onto a luxurious private plane and guided her into a comfortable leather seat beside the window. With his warm, solid presence bolstering her confidence, Brooke buckled her seat belt and listened to the jet's engine rev. As the plane began to taxi, her chest compressed. Try as she might, she couldn't shake the notion that she should have refused Nic's invitation and just gone home to California.

The instant he'd set foot on the plane his demeanor had changed. Tension rode his broad shoulders and he seemed more distant than ever, his bearing more formal, his expression set into aloof lines. Before leaving Ithaca he'd donned a pair of light beige dress pants and a pale blue dress shirt that set off his tanned skin. On the seat opposite him, he'd placed a beige blazer that bore a blue pocket square. Brooke stared at the oddity.

Nic in stylish clothes. And a coordinating pocket square.

He'd always been sexy, handsome and confident, but he now wore a mantle of überwealthy, ultrasophistication. Ensconced in the luxurious plane, his big hands linked loosely in his lap, he looked utterly confident, poised and…regal. For the first time she truly accepted that Nic was no longer the rocket scientist she knew. Nor was he the ardent lover of last night. Swallowed by helplessness, Brooke stared straight ahead unsure who he'd become.

Maybe leaving him behind in Sherdana was going to be easier than she realized. This Nic wasn't the man she'd fallen in love with. A shiver raced up her spine as his hand covered hers and squeezed gently. Obviously, her heart had no problem with the changes in Nic's appearance. Her pulse fluttered and skipped along just as foolishly as ever.

"Are you okay?" he asked.

Did she explain how his transformation bothered her? To what end? He could never be hers. He belonged to a nation.

"This is quite a plane." Feeling out of place sitting beside such an aristocratic dreamboat on his multimillion-dollar aircraft, Brooke babbled the first thought that entered her head. "Is it yours?"

"If by 'yours' you are asking if it belongs to Sherdana's royal family, then yes."

"Well, that's pretty convenient for you, I guess." She mustered a wry grin. "I suppose the press knows the plane pretty well and that your arrival won't exactly be a state secret."

"Your point?"

"Aside from the fact that we're trying to maintain a low profile on our whole relationship thing, I'm dressed like someone's poor relation. The press is bound to be curious about me. Please can I stay on the plane after you get off until the coast is clear?"

He looked ready to protest, but shook his head and sighed. "If you wish. I'll arrange for someone to meet you at the hangar. That way there won't be any press asking questions you don't want to answer."

It hit Brooke what some of those questions might be and her brain grew sluggish. She'd spent most of her life with her nose buried in books. Glen was the sibling who relished the spotlight. He didn't freeze up in front of large crowds, but put people at ease with his charismatic charm and dazzled them with his intelligence. Numerous times she'd stood back during press events and marveled at his confidence. Not even the difficult questions fired at him after the rocket blew up had rattled him. He'd demonstrated the perfect blend of sadness and determination.

"As for clothes," Nic continued, "I'm sure either my sister, Ariana, or Olivia, Gabriel's wife, will be able to lend you some things."

Brooke would be borrowing clothes from princesses. This wasn't an ordinary family he was taking her home to meet. His mother was a queen. His father was a king. Nic was a prince. What the hell was she doing? She clutched at the armrests, suddenly unable to breathe.

The whirr and clunk of landing gear being locked into place startled her. They were minutes from landing. Nothing about this trip was working out the way she'd planned.

She'd stepped onto the plane in San Francisc thinking she would fly to Greece, tell him about the baby and bring Nic back with her so they could be one big happy family.

The full impact of her foolishness now hit her like a mace. Even if Nic were madly in love with her, he couldn't offer her anything permanent. In fact, he was so far out of her league that they could be living on separate planets.

"I need to know details about your family so I'm prepared," she blurted out, her stomach flipping as the plane lost altitude.

"Sure. Where would you like to start?"

So many questions whirled in her mind that it took her a moment to prioritize them. "Your parents. How do I address them?"

Eight

Nic emerged from the plane and hesitated before descending the stairs to the tarmac. In a tight knot, thirty feet away, a dozen reporters held up cameras and microphones all focused on him. He approached the assembled crowd— the prodigal son returning to the bosom of his family— and answered several questions before heading toward the black Mercedes that awaited him.

Although he'd known it was the sensible thing to do, separating from Brooke even for a short period of time didn't feel right. It wasn't as if he expected her to run off and hop a plane back to California. Enough security surrounded the royal aircraft hangar that she wouldn't get five feet from the plane before she was stopped and questioned.

No, it was more the sense that by traveling separately to the palace, he was acknowledging that there was something to hide. And yet, wasn't there? During the car ride to the airport when she'd asked him why he wanted her to come home with him, he'd told her the truth. He wasn't ready to let her go. The answer had distressed her.

Last night she'd accused him of always demanding things be his way. Now, once again he was acting selfishly.

Nic passed the crowd of reporters without another glance. A familiar figure stood beside the car's rear door. Stewart Barnes, Gabriel's private secretary, offered a smile and a nod as Nic approached.

"Good afternoon, Your Highness. I hope you had a good flight from Greece." The secretary's keen blue eyes darted toward the plane. "Prince Gabriel mentioned you were bringing someone with you. Did she change her mind?"

"No. She's just a little skittish about public appearances. Could you arrange a car to pick her up at the hangar?"

If Stewart was surprised that Nic was sneaking a girl into the country, his expression didn't show it. "Of course." He bowed and opened the car door.

Because the car windows were tinted, Nic had no idea anyone besides the driver was in the vehicle. Therefore, when he spotted Gabriel sitting in the backseat and grinning at him, Nic was overcome by an unexpected rush of joy.

"Good heavens, what are you doing here?" Nic embraced his brother as Stewart closed the door, encasing the princes in privacy.

"It's been three years since you've come home and you have to ask? I've missed you."

The genuine thrum of affection in Gabriel's voice caught Nic off guard. As tight as the triplets had been as children, once on their divergent paths, circumstances and distance had caused them to drift apart. Nic hadn't realized how much he'd missed his older brother until this moment.

"I've missed you, too." The car began to move as Nic asked after the youngest of the three brothers. "How's Christian?"

"Unpredictable as always. Right now he's in Switzerland talking to a company that might be interested in bringing a nanotechnology manufacturing plant here."

"That's wonderful." Nic couldn't help but wonder at the timing of Christian's absence given the series of events his mother had designed for the purpose of finding brides for her sons. "When is he due back?"

"In time for the wedding or Mother will skin him alive."

"And the rest of the parties and receptions?"

Gabriel laughed. "All eyes will be on you."

Nic marveled at the change in his earnest brother. Although young Gabriel had been as full of curiosity and mischief as Nic and Christian, somewhere around his tenth birthday it had hit him that the leadership of the country would one day be his. Almost overnight, while his inquisitive nature had remained, he'd become overly serious and all too responsible.

"You're different," Nic observed. "I don't remember the last time you were this…"

"Happy?" Gabriel's eyes glinted. "It's called wedded bliss. You should try it."

A woman had done this to Gabriel? "I'm looking forward to meeting your wife."

"And speaking of fair women, what happened to your Brooke?"

"She's not my Brooke." Nic heard gravel in his voice and moderated his tone. "And she's staying in the plane until it's taxied into the hangar."

"Your idea or hers?"

"Hers. She was concerned that she wasn't dressed properly and wanted to maintain a low profile."

Gabriel's eyes widened in feigned shock. "What was she wearing that she was so unpresentable?"

"I don't know. Some sort of cotton dress. She thought she looked like someone's poor relation."

"Did she?"

Nic thought she looked carefree and sexy. "Not at all, but what do I know about women's fashion?"

The two men fell to talking about recent events including the incident where the vengeful aunt of Gabriel's twin daughters had infiltrated the palace intending to stop him from marrying Olivia.

"And you have no idea where she's gone?" Nic quizzed, amazed how much chaos one woman had created.

"Interpol has interviewed her former employer and visited her flat in Milan, but for now she's on the run."

As the car entered the palace grounds, Nic's mind circled back to the woman he'd left at the airport. "Have you told anyone besides Stewart that I brought Brooke with me?"

"Olivia and her secretary, Libby, know. They are prepared to take charge of her as soon as she arrives."

"Thank you." Nic was relieved that Brooke would be taken care of.

"Oh, and Mother is expecting you in the blue drawing room for tea. She has an hour blocked out for you to view the first round of potential wives. Stewart interviewed several secretary candidates for you. Their résumés will be waiting in your room. Look them over and let Stewart know which you'd like to meet."

"A secretary?"

"Now that you're back, we've packed your agenda with meetings and appearances. You'll need someone to keep you on schedule."

Nic's head spun. "Damn," he muttered. "It feels as if I never left."

Gabriel clapped him on the shoulder. "It's good to have you back."

From the backseat of a luxurious Mercedes, Brooke clutched her worn travel bag and watched the town of

Carone slip past. In the many years she'd known Nic, which she'd spent alternately being ignored and rejected, she'd never once been as angry with him as she was at this moment.

What had he been thinking to bring her to Sherdana? She didn't belong here. She didn't fit into his world the way he'd fit into hers. No doctorate degrees could prepare her for the pitfalls of palace life. She'd be dining with his family. What fork did she use? She would stand out as the uncouth American accustomed to eating burgers and fries with her fingers. Brooke frowned as she considered how many of her favorite foods didn't require a knife and fork. Pizza. Tacos. Pulled pork sandwiches.

And what if she couldn't get a flight out in the next day or two? As Nic's guest, would she be expected to attend any of the parties his mother had arranged? Were they the sort of parties where people danced? Nic had already shown her a dance specific to the country. They'd laughed over her inability to master the simplest of steps. She'd never imagined a time when she'd be expected to perform them.

And the biggest worry of all: What if someone discovered she was pregnant? Now that morning sickness was hitting her hard, what excuse could she make to explain away the nausea?

Brooke gawked like any tourist as the car swung through a gate and the palace appeared. Nic had grown up here. The chasm between them widened even further. It was one thing to rationalize that her brother's business partner was in reality the prince of a small European country. It was another to see for herself.

During her year abroad in Italy she'd been fortunate enough to be invited to several palaces. A few of the older volumes of Italian literature she'd used in her doctoral thesis had been housed in private collections and she'd been lucky enough to be allowed the opportunity to study them. But those residences had been far less grand and much smaller than the enormous palace she was heading toward right now.

The car followed a circular driveway around a massive fountain and drew up in front of the palace's wide double doors. Surprise held Brooke in place. Given her stealthy transfer from the royal private plane to this car, she'd half-expected to be dropped off at the servants' back entrance.

A man in a dark blue suit stepped forward and opened the car door. Brooke stared at the palace doors, unable to make her legs work. One of the tall doors moved, opening enough to let a slim woman in a burgundy suit slip through. Still unsure of her circumstances, Brooke waited as the woman approached.

"Dr. Davis?" She had a lovely soft voice and a British accent. "I'm Libby Marshall, Princess Olivia's private secretary."

"Nice to meet you." Brooke still hadn't budged from the car. "Nic didn't mention he intended to bring me here when we left his villa this morning so I'm not really sure about all this."

The princess's secretary smiled. "Don't worry, all has been arranged. Princess Olivia is looking forward to meeting you. Armando will take your bag. If you will follow me."

If she hadn't flown hundreds of miles in a private jet, Brooke might have been giddy at the thought that a princess was looking forward to meeting her. Instead, it was just one more in a series of surreal experiences.

Brooke slipped from the car and let herself gawk at the sheer size of the palace. Her escort moved like someone who knew better than to keep people waiting and had disappeared through the tall doors by the time Brook surrendered her meager possessions to Armando. She trotted to catch up, but slowed as soon as she stepped inside.

The palace was everything she'd expected. Thirty feet before her a black-and-white marble floor ended in a wide staircase covered in royal-blue carpet. The stairs were wide enough to let an SUV pass. They were split into two sections. The first flight ascended to a landing that then split into separate stairs that continued their climb to the second floor.

She envisioned dozens of women dressed in ball gowns of every color, gliding down that staircase, hands trailing along the polished banister, all coming to meet Nic as he stood, formally dressed, on the polished marble at the bottom of the stairs awaiting them. His gaze would run along the line of women, his expression stern and unyielding as he searched for his perfect bride.

Brooke saw herself bringing up the rear. She was late and the borrowed dress she wore would be too long. As she descended, her heel would catch on her hem. Two steps from the bottom, she'd trip, but there would be no Nic to catch her. He was surrounded by five women each vying for his attention. Without him to save her, she would make a grab for the banister and miss.

Flashes would explode in her eyes like fireworks as dozens of press cameras captured her ignominy at a hundred frames per second.

"Dr. Davis?" Libby peered at her in concern. "Is something amiss?"

Brooke shook herself out of the horrifying daydream and swallowed the lump that had appeared in her throat. "Call me Brooke. This is—" Her gaze roved around the space as maids bustled past with vases of flowers and two well-dressed gentlemen strode by carrying briefcases and speaking in low tones. "Really big. And very beautiful," she rushed to add.

"Come. Princess Olivia is in her office."

Normally nervous energy would have prompted Brooke to chatter uncontrollably. But as she followed Libby past the stairs and into a corridor, she was too overwhelmed. They walked past half a dozen rooms and took a couple more turns. In seconds, her sense of direction had completely failed her.

"You really know your way around." She'd lost the battle with her nerves. "How long have you worked in the palace?"

"A few months. I arrived with Princess Olivia."

"Be honest. How long did it take until you no longer got lost?"

Libby shot a wry smile over her shoulder. "Three weeks."

"I'm only expecting to be here a couple days. I don't suppose there's a map or something."

"I'm afraid not. And I was under the impression that you'd be with us until after the wedding."

Brooke stumbled as she caught the edge of her sandal on the marble floor. "That's not what Nic and I agreed to." But in fact, she wasn't sure if they'd discussed the length of her stay. It certainly couldn't stretch to include a royal wedding.

"I could be mistaken," Libby told her, turning into an open doorway.

The office into which Brooke stepped was decorated in feminine shades of cream and peach, but the functional layout spoke of productivity. On her entrance, a stunning blonde looked up from her laptop and smiled.

"You must be Dr. Davis," the woman exclaimed, rising to greet her. She held out a manicured hand. "Lovely to meet you. I'm Olivia Alessandro."

"It's nice to meet you, as well." The urge to curtsy overwhelmed Brooke and only the knowledge that she'd fall flat on her face if she tried kept her from acting like an idiot. "Your Highness."

"Oh, please call me Olivia. You're Nic's friend and that makes you like family."

It was impossible not to relax beneath Olivia's warm smile. "Please call me Brooke. I have to tell you that I'm a little overwhelmed to be here. This morning I was on a Greek island with no real destination in mind. And then Nic informs me that he intends to bring me to Sherdana."

"Something tells me he didn't plan much in advance, either." The way Olivia shook her head gave Brooke the impression that the future queen of Sherdana believed strongly in preparation and organization.

"Your secretary mentioned something about me staying until after your wedding," Brooke said, perching on the edge of the cream brocade chair Olivia gestured her into. "But I think it would be better if I caught a flight to California as soon as possible."

"I'm sure that could be arranged, but couldn't you stay for a while and see a little of the country? Gabriel and I have plans to tour some of the vineyards in a couple days and it would be lovely if you and Nic could join us."

"As nice as that sounds…" Brooke trailed off. Never before had she hesitated to speak her mind, but being blunt with Nic's sister-in-law seemed the wrong thing to do. "I'm just worried about overstaying my welcome."

"Nonsense."

Brooke tried again. "I got the impression from Nic that his mother had arranged quite a few events in the next week or so that he's expected to attend. I wouldn't want to distract Nic from what he needs to do."

Olivia looked surprised. "You know why he came home?"

"He needs to get married so there can be…" It suddenly occurred to Brooke that the woman who was supposed to produce Sherdana's next generation of heirs but couldn't was seated across from her.

"It's okay." Olivia's smile was a study in tranquility. "I've made peace with what happened to me. And I consider myself the luckiest woman alive that Gabriel wanted to marry me even though I wasn't the best choice for the country."

"I think you're the perfect princess. Sherdana is damned lucky to have you." Brooke grimaced at her less than eloquent language. "Sorry. I have a tendency to be blunt even when I'm trying not to."

"Don't be sorry. It was a lovely compliment and I like your directness. I can't wait for you to meet Ariana. She has a knack for speaking her mind, as well."

"I saw her artwork at the villa. She's very talented. I'm looking forward to talking with her about it."

"She's been vacationing with friends in Monaco for a few days and is expected home late tonight. She's very excited that you've come to visit. When I spoke with her earlier today, she told me she'd met your brother when he and Nic stayed at the villa."

That was something else Glen had neglected to mention. Brooke intended to have a long chat with her brother when she returned to California.

"And now, I expect you would like to go to your room and get settled. Dinner will be served at seven. If you need anything let a maid know and she can get it for you."

Brooke gave a shaky laugh. "Like a whole new wardrobe? I'm afraid I packed to visit a Greek island. Casual things." She imagined showing up to dinner in her tribal print maxi and winced. "I really don't have anything I could wear to dine in a palace."

"Oh." Olivia nodded. "I should have realized that from the little Gabriel told me. It looks like you and I are the same size, I'll send some things down for you to choose from."

Unsure whether to be horrified or grateful, Brooke could see protesting was foolish so she thanked Olivia. Then she followed a maid through the palace in a journey from the royal family's private wing to the rooms set aside for guest use. After five minutes of walking Brooke knew she'd never find her way back to Olivia's office and hoped someone would be sent to fetch her for dinner. If her presence in the palace was forgotten and she starved to death, how long would it take before her body was discovered? She lost count how many doors they passed before the maid stopped and gestured for Brooke to enter a room.

"Thank you."

The instant Brooke stepped into the bedroom she'd been given, she fell instantly in love. The wallpaper was a gold-and-white floral design while the curtains and bedding were a pale blue-green that made her think of an Ameraucana chicken egg. In addition to a bed and a writing desk, the room held a settee and a small table flanked by chairs against the wall between two enormous windows. The room had enough furniture to comfortably seat the students in her class on Italian Renaissance poetry.

On the bench at the foot of her bed sat her well-worn luggage. To say it looked shabby amongst the opulent furnishings was an understatement.

"Can I unpack that for you, Dr. Davis?" The maid who'd brought Brooke here had followed her into the room.

"I've been traveling for quite a few days already and most of what's in here is dirty."

Brooke sensed that she would scandalize the maid by inquiring if there was a laundry machine she could use.

"I'll sort through everything and have it back to you by evening."

Brooke dug through the bag and pulled out her toiletries

and the notebook she always kept close by to write down the things that popped into her head. Her mother was fond of saying you never knew when inspiration would strike and some of Brooke's best ideas came when she was in the shower or grabbing a bite to eat.

Once the maid had left, Brooke picked up her cell phone and checked the time in California. At four o'clock in Sherdana it would be 7 a.m. in LA. Theresa would be halfway to work. Brooke dialed.

When Theresa answered, Brooke said, "Guess where I am now…"

Nic hadn't been in the palace more than fifteen minutes before his mother's private secretary tracked him down in the billiards room where he and Gabriel were drinking Scotch and catching up. The room had four enormous paintings depicting pivotal scenes in Sherdana's history, including the ratification of the 1749 constitution that was creating such chaos in Nic's personal life.

"Good afternoon, Your Highnesses." A petite woman in her midfifties stood just inside the door with her hands clasped at her waist.

Gwen had come to work for the queen as her personal assistant not long before the three princes had been born and more often than not, regarded the triplets as errant children rather than remarkable men.

"Hello, Gweny."

"None of that."

Nic crossed the room to kiss her cheek. "I missed you."

Her gaze grew even sterner, although a hint of softness developed near the edges of her lips. "You missed tea."

"I needed something a little stronger." Nic held up his mostly empty crystal tumbler.

"The queen expected you to attend her as soon as you arrived in the palace. She's in the rose garden. You'd better go immediately." Gwen's tone was a whip, driving him from the room.

Knowing better than to dawdle, Nic went straight outside and found his mother in her favorite part of the garden. Thanks to the queen's unwavering devotion, the half-acre flourished with a mixture of difficult-to-find antique rose varieties as well as some that had been recently engineered to produce an unusual color or enhanced fragrance.

"It's about time you got around to saying hello," the queen declared, peering at him from beneath the wide brim of her sun hat.

"Good afternoon, Mother." Nic kissed the cheek his mother offered him and fell into step beside her. He didn't bother to offer her an explanation of what he'd been doing. She had no tolerance for excuses. "The roses look beautiful."

"I understand you brought a girl home with you. She's the sister of your California friend." She paused only briefly before continuing, obviously not expecting Nic to confirm what she'd said. "What is your relationship to her?"

"We're friends."

"Don't treat me like an idiot. I need to know if she's going to present a problem."

"No." At least not to anyone but him.

"Does she understand that you have come home to find a wife?"

"She does. It's not an issue. She's planning on heading home after the wedding."

"I understand you are taking her along with Gabriel and Olivia on a trip to the vineyards?"

"Gabriel mentioned something about it, but I haven't spoken with Brooke."

"I don't think it's a good idea that you get any more involved with this girl than you already are."

"We're not involved," Nic assured her.

"Is she in love with you?" Nic waited too long to answer and his mother made a disgusted sound. "Do you love her?"

"It doesn't matter how we feel about each other," Nic said, his voice tense and impatient. "I know my duty to Sherdana and nothing will get in the way of that." From his conversation with Gabriel, Nic knew she hadn't gone this hard at Christian. Why was Nic alone feeling the pressure to marry? Christian was just as much a prince of Sherdana. His son could just as easily rule. "I assume you have several matrimonial candidates for me to consider."

"I've sent their dossiers to your room in the visitors' wing. Did Gabriel mention the problem in your suite earlier today? Apparently your bathtub overflowed and flooded the room."

"Gabriel thought it might have been the twins although no one caught them at it."

His mother shook her head. "I don't know why we're paying a nanny if the girl can't keep track of them."

"From what I understand they are a handful."

"There are only two of them. I had three of you to contend with." His mother took Nic's hand in hers and squeezed hard. "It's good to have you home." She blinked rapidly a few times and released her grip on him. "Now, run along and look over the files I sent to your room. I expect you to share your thoughts with me after dinner tonight."

"Of course." He bent and kissed her cheek again. "First I'm off to see Father. I understand he has a ten-minute gap in his schedule shortly before five."

After reconnecting briefly with his father, Nic headed to the room he'd been given until his suite could be dried out. The oddity of the incident left him shaking his head.

How could a pair of two-year-old girls be as much trouble as everyone said?

As his mother had promised, a pile of dossiers had been left on the desk. Shrugging out of his blazer, Nic picked up the stack and counted. There were eight. He had twenty minutes before the tailor arrived to measure him for a whole new wardrobe. The clothes he'd traveled in today had belonged to Christian, as had most of what he'd worn the past ten days. Of the three brothers, Christian spent the most time at the Greek villa.

Nic settled into a chair in front of the unlit fireplace and selected a file at random. The photo clipped to the inside showed a stunning brunette with vivacious blue eyes and full lips. She was the twenty-five-year-old daughter of an Italian count, had gotten her MBA at Harvard and now worked for a global conglomerate headquartered in Paris. She spoke four languages and was admired for being fashionable as well as active on the charity circuit. In short, she was perfect.

He dropped the file onto the floor at his feet and opened the next one. This one was a blonde. Again beautiful. British born. The sister of a viscount. A human rights lawyer.

The next. Brunette. Pretty with big brown eyes and an alluring smile. A local girl. Her family owned the largest winery in Sherdana. She played cello for the Vienna Philharmonic.

Then another blonde. Bewitching green eyes. Daughter of a Danish baron. A model and television personality.

On and on. Each woman strikingly beautiful, accomplished and with a flawless pedigree.

Nic felt like a prize bull.

Replaying the conversation with his mother, he recognized he shouldn't have ignored Brooke's concerns that their relationship would come under scrutiny. He'd deliberately underestimated his mother's perceptiveness. But he didn't regret bringing Brooke to meet his family.

What he wasn't so happy about, however, was how little time they would have together in the days between now and her eventual departure. Being forced by propriety to keep his distance would be much more difficult now that he'd opened the door to what could have been if only he wasn't bound to his country.

At the same moment he threw the last folder onto the floor, a knock sounded on his door. Calling permission to enter, Nic got to his feet and scooped up the dossiers, depositing them back on the desk before turning to face the tailor and his small army of assistants who were to dress Nic.

While the suits he tried on were marked and pinned, Nic fell to thinking about Brooke. He hadn't seen her since leaving the plane and wondered how she'd coped in the hours they'd been apart. Despite the nervousness she'd shown during the flight, he suspected she'd figured out a way to charm everyone she'd encountered. He knew she was supposed to meet with Gabriel's wife right away and wondered how that had gone.

He was eager to meet Olivia. He already knew she was beautiful, intelligent and a strong crusader for children's health and welfare. The citizens loved her and after the drama surrounding her emergency hysterectomy and her subsequent secret elopement with Gabriel so did the media. But Nic was fascinated by how she'd caused such drastic changes in his brother.

The tailor finished his preliminary work and departed. Alone once more, Nic dressed for dinner. Family evenings were for the most part casual and Nic left his room wearing navy slacks and a crisp white shirt he'd purchased at a department store in California. His fashionable younger brother would be appalled that Nic was dressing *off the rack*. Nic was smiling at the thought as he joined Gabriel and his new bride in the family's private drawing room.

"You've made my brother a very happy man," Nic told Olivia, kissing her cheek in greeting. "I haven't seen him smile this much since we were children."

From her location snuggled beneath her husband's possessive arm, the blonde stared up at Gabriel with eyes filled with such love that a knot formed in Nic's gut. At that instant, any lingering resentment he'd felt at the uncomfortable position Gabriel's choice had put him in vanished. His brother deserved to be happy. The responsibility of the country would one day rest on Gabriel's shoulders and being married to the woman he loved would make his burden lighter.

This drew Nic's thoughts back to the dossiers in his room. He was glad there hadn't been a redhead among them. Brooke was a singular marvel in his mind. Marrying a woman with similar hair color was out of the question. He couldn't spend the rest of his life wishing his wife's red hair framed a different face.

Brooke hadn't made an appearance by the time Nic's parents entered the drawing room and he wondered for one brief moment if she'd let her anxiety get the better of her. He was seconds away from sending a maid to check on her when the door opened and Brooke stumbled in, unsteady in heels that appeared too large for her.

She wore a long-sleeved, gold, lace dress that flattered her curves, but conflicted with her usual carefree style. She wasn't wearing her usual long necklace that drew attention to the swell of her breasts, and she'd left her collection of bracelets behind. The look was sophisticated, elegant and formal, except for her hair, which spiraled and bounced around her shoulders like a living thing.

"Dr. Davis, welcome." Gabriel and Olivia had approached her while Nic stood there gaping at her transformation.

"I'm so sorry I'm late," Brooke was saying as he finally approached. "I only meant to close my eyes for fifteen minutes. Then next thing I know it's six thirty. Thank heavens I showered before I sacked out. Of course this is what happens to my hair when I just let it go. If I'd had a few more minutes, I could have done something to it but I had such a hard time deciding which dress to wear. They were all so beautiful."

"You look lovely." Olivia gave her a warm smile and drew her arm through Brooke's in a show of affection and support. "Why don't I introduce you to Gabriel and Nic's parents."

"You mean the king and queen?" Brooke whispered, her gaze shooting to the couple enjoying a predinner cocktail. They appeared to be ignoring the knot of young people.

"They are eager to meet you," Gabriel said.

Brooke's lips quirked in a wry smile. "That's sweet of you to say." She took a clumsy step and smiled apologetically at Olivia. "I'm usually less awkward than this."

"The shoes are a little large for you," Olivia said, giving the gold laser-cut pumps a critical look. "I didn't realize your feet were so much smaller than mine. Perhaps you have something of your own that would fit better? I could send a maid to fetch something."

"Are you kidding me?" Brooke retorted, her voice feverish as she took her next step with more deliberation and improved grace. "These are *Louboutin glass slippers*. I'm Cinderella."

Gabriel waited a beat before following his wife. He caught Nic's eye and smirked. "I like her."

"So do I," Nic replied, his voice low and subdued.

Not that it should have mattered to Nic, but his brother's words sent gratitude and relief rushing into his chest. It was good to know he had at least two people in the palace, Gabriel and Olivia, who would understand how wretched doing the right thing could feel.

"It's very nice to meet you," Brooke was saying to his parents as Nic and Gabriel caught up to the women. "Thank you for letting me stay at the palace for a few days."

Nic felt the impact of his mother's gaze as he drew up beside Brooke. He set his palm on her back and through her dress felt the tension quivering in her muscles.

"We are happy to have you," Nic's father said, his broad smile genuine.

When it came to matters affecting his country, the king was a mighty warrior defending his realm from all threats social, economic and diplomatic. However, he was a teddy bear when it came to his wife and children. But the queen ruled her family with an iron fist in a velvet glove. All four of her children knew the strength of her will and respected it. In exchange she allowed them the opportunity to figure out their place in the world.

This meant Nic had been allowed to attend university in the United States and stay there living his dream of space travel until Sherdana had needed him to come home. But while he'd appreciated his ten years of freedom from responsibility, it made his return that much harder.

"Very happy," the queen echoed. "I understand, Miss Davis, that you are the sister of the man Nic has been working with for the last five years."

"Yes, my brother is in charge of the *Griffin* project."

"Perhaps you will join me for breakfast tomorrow. I'd like to hear more about the project Nic has been working on with your brother."

"I would be happy to have breakfast with you."

"Wonderful. Is eight o'clock too early for you?"

"Not at all. Unlike Nic, I'm an early riser."

Nic knew she'd meant the jab for him. It was an old joke between them on the mornings when he'd worked late into the night and then crashed on the couch in his workroom. But he could see at once that his mother was wondering how Brooke knew what time Nic got out of bed in the morning.

Even without glancing toward his brother, Gabriel's amusement was apparent. Nic kept his own expression bland as he met his mother's steely gaze.

Olivia saved the moment from further awkwardness. "And after breakfast perhaps you could come to the stables and watch the twins take a riding lesson. They are showing great promise as equestrians. Do you ride, Brooke?"

"I did when I was younger, but school has kept me far too busy in recent years."

"Brooke has two doctorates," Nic interjected smoothly. "She teaches Italian language and literature at the University of California, Santa Cruz."

"You're young to have accomplished that much," Gabriel said.

Brooke nodded. "I graduated high school with two years of college credits and spent the next ten years immersed in academia. After my brother went off to college my parents hosted a girl from Italy. She stayed with us a year and by the time she went home, I was fluent in Italian and learning to read it, as well."

Olivia spoke up. "Have you spent much time in Italy?"

"While I was working on my second doctorate, I spent a year in Florence and Rome. Before that my mother and I would visit for a week or two during the summer depending on her deadlines. She writes for television and has penned a mystery series set in sixteenth-century Venice that does very well." Talking about her mother's accomplishments had relaxed Brooke. Her eyes sparkled with pride.

This relaxed Nic as well, but as the family made their way toward the dining room, the queen pulled him aside.

"Lovely girl, your Miss Davis."

"Actually it's Dr. Davis." Although he had a feeling his mother already knew that and had spoken incorrectly to get a rise out of her son. And since Nic had already denied that he and Brooke were anything but friends, why did his mother put the emphasis on *your*? "I'm glad you like her."

"Did you look at the files I gave you?"

"Yes. Any one of them would be a fine princess." He couldn't bring himself to use the word *wife* yet. "You and your team did a fine job of choosing candidates that lined up with my needs."

"Yes we did. Now, let's see if you can do an equally fine job choosing a wife."

Nine

At her first dinner with Nic's family, Brooke sat beside Nic on the king's left hand and ate little. Part of the reason she'd been late to dinner was another bout of nausea that struck her shortly after she'd risen. So much for morning sickness. Brooke wasn't sure why it was called that when it seemed to strike her at random times throughout the day.

"You're not eating," Nic murmured, the first words he'd spoken directly to her since the meal had begun.

"I'm dining with royalty," she muttered back. "My stomach is in knots."

"They're just people."

"Important people." Wealthy, sophisticated, intelligent people. "Normally I wouldn't get unsettled by this sort of thing, but this is your family and I want them to like me."

"I assure you they do."

"Sure." Brooke resisted the urge to roll her eyes. His mother had been observing her through most of the meal, making each swallow of the delicious salmon more trial than pleasure. Brooke sensed that the queen had a long list of questions she wanted to ask, starting with: When are you going home? Not that Brooke blamed her. Nic's mother had plans for her son. Plans that she must perceive as being threatened by an uncouth redhead who regarded Nic with adoring eyes.

Despite the fact that the meal was a relaxed family affair and not the formal ordeal Brooke had feared, by the time the dessert course concluded, she was more than ready to escape. She was relieved, therefore, when Gabriel and Olivia offered her a quick tour of the public areas of the palace before escorting her back to her room.

Strolling the hall of portraits, Brooke realized the extent of Sherdana's history. Some of the paintings dated back to the late fifteenth century. Thanks to all those years when she'd accompanied her mother to Italy and helped her re-search the Italian Renaissance period, Brooke had developed a love of history that partially explained why she'd chosen the same time period for her second doctorate.

"I imagine you have a library with books on Sherdana's history," she said to Gabriel as he and Olivia led the way to the ballroom.

"An extensive one. We'll make that our next stop."

A half an hour later the trio arrived at Brooke's door. She was feeling a touch giddy at the idea that she could return to the library the next day and check out the collection more thoroughly. The vast amount of books contained in the two-story room was an academic's dream come true. She could probably spend an entire year in Sherdana's palace library and never need to leave.

"Thank you for the tour."

"You are very welcome," Olivia said. "If you need anything else tonight, let one of the maids know. There is always someone on call."

Brooke bid the prince and princess good-night and entered her room. As she did, she noticed the store of crackers she'd nibbled on prior to dinner had been replenished. With a grateful sigh, Brooke grabbed a handful and went to the wardrobe. As the maid had promised earlier, her clothes had been laundered and returned. Brooke grinned as she slipped off her borrowed shoes, guessing the staff wasn't accustomed to washing ragged denim shorts and cotton peasant blouses. Regardless, they'd done a marvelous job. Her clothes looked brand-new.

A knock sounded on her door. Brooke's pulse kicked up. Could Nic have come by to wish her good-night? But it wasn't her handsome prince in the hall. Instead, her visitor was a beautiful, tall girl with long chocolate-brown hair and a welcoming smile.

"I'm Ariana." Behind Nic's sister were two maids loaded down with six shoe boxes and four overstuffed garment bags.

"Brooke Davis."

"I know that." Ariana laughed. "Even if the palace wasn't buzzing about the girl Nic brought home, I would have recognized you from the pictures Glen emailed me from time to time. He's very proud of you."

"You and Glen email?" Earlier Brooke had learned that Nic's sister had met Glen in Greece, but an ongoing correspondence was something else entirely. "I thought you'd just met the one time."

"Yeees." She drew the word out. "But it was *quite* a meeting."

Brooke didn't know what to make of the other girl's innuendo and made a note to question Glen about Nic's sister.

"Olivia told me her shoes were too big for you, so I brought you a few pairs of mine," Ariana said, indicating the maids behind her. "They should fit you better—and I included some dresses, as well. That's one of Olivia's, isn't it?"

Brooke couldn't figure out what about the gold lace could possibly have caused Ariana to wrinkle her nose. "Nothing I brought with me is suitable for palace wear. I had no plans to come here with Nic."

For a moment Ariana's eyes narrowed in the same sharp expression of assessment her mother had aimed at Brooke all evening. At last the princess smiled. "Well, I'm glad you did."

"So am I." And for the first time in eight hours, Brooke meant it. "I've really been looking forward to meeting you. I thought your artwork at the villa was amazing."

"Then you'd be the first." With a self-deprecating hair flip, Ariana slipped her arm through Brooke's and drew her into the bedroom.

"What do you mean?" Brooke let herself be led. From the way Nic had talked about his sister and from studying Ariana's art, Brooke felt as if she and the younger woman might be kindred spirits. "Your use of color gave the paintings such energy and depth."

Ariana's eyebrows drew together. "You're serious." She sounded surprised and more than a little hopeful.

"Very." Brooke didn't understand the princess's reaction. "I did my undergrad work in visual and critical studies."

"My family doesn't understand what I paint. They see it all as random splashes of color on canvas."

"I'm sure it's just that they are accustomed to a more traditional style of painting. Have you ever had your work exhibited anywhere?"

"No." A laugh bubbled out of her. "I paint for myself."

"Of course. But if you're ever interested in getting an expert's opinion, I have a friend in San Francisco who runs a gallery. He likes finding new talent. I took some pictures of your work. With your permission I could send him the photos."

"I've never thought…" Ariana shook her head in bemusement. "I guess this is the moment every artist faces at some point. Do I take a chance and risk failing or play it safe and never know if I'm any good."

"Oh, you're good," Brooke assured her. "But art is very subjective and not everyone is going to like what you do."

"I guess I've already faced my worst critics. My family. So why not see what your friend thinks."

"Wonderful, I'll send him the pictures tomorrow morning."

"And in the meantime—" Ariana gestured toward the wardrobe "—show me what you brought from home and let's see if I have anything that will appeal to you."

Brooke suspected the stylish princess wouldn't be at all impressed with the limited contents of her closet, but she knew her fine speech about art being subjective would be hypocritical if she couldn't back it up with action. For what was fashion but wearable art and even though Brooke's wardrobe wasn't suitable for a palace, it worked perfectly in her academic world.

The maids who'd entered behind Ariana deposited their burdens on Brooke's bed. If the princess had brought anything like what she was wearing—a sophisticated but fun plum dress with gold circles embroidered around the neckline and dotted over the skirt—Brooke braced herself to be wowed.

"It feels like every day is Christmas around here," Brooke said as dress after gorgeous dress came free of the garment bags. The variety of colors and styles dazzled Brooke. Of course, with her skin tone, Ariana could wear just about anything.

When the maids finished, Brooke pulled out her own dresses, shorts, skirts and her favorite kimono. Ariana narrowed her eyes in thought and surveyed each item.

"You have a great eye for color and know exactly what suits you."

Coming from the princess, this was a huge compliment. Ariana wasn't at all what Brooke imagined a princess would be like. She was warm and approachable. Not at all stuffy or formal. Brooke warmed to her quickly, feeling as if they had known each other for years instead of minutes.

"In California I blend in dressed like this." Brooke slipped into the tie-dyed kimono. It looked odd over the gold lace dress she'd borrowed from Olivia. "Here I stick out like a sore thumb."

"Hardly a sore thumb, although definitely a stand out. No matter how you dress, your unique hair color will keep you from being a wallflower. No wonder my brother finds you irresistible."

Brooke felt Ariana's comment like a blow. "We're just friends," she explained in a rush, but her cheeks heated as the princess arched one slim eyebrow.

"But he talks about you all the time and he brought you to meet us."

"It's not what you're thinking. I went to the island to convince him to return to California. To Glen and the *Griffin* project. And when he was summoned back here sooner than expected, he didn't want to leave me alone in Greece."

"He must be in love with you. He's never brought a woman home before."

Brooke relaxed a little. "That's because the love of his life wouldn't fit inside an airplane." Seeing she had confused Ariana, Brooke explained. "As long as I've known him, Nic has been committed to the rocket he and my brother hope will one day carry people into space. There's been no room for an emotional connection with any woman."

"And yet here you are."

"Until a few days ago I didn't know he was a prince or that he needs to marry a citizen of the country or an aristocrat so his children can rule some day. Obviously I'm neither."

"He wouldn't have kept something like that from you unless he was worried about hurting you."

"That much is true." Here Brooke hesitated, unsure how much to explain. In the end, she decided to trust Ariana. "I've had a crush on him for years. When I showed up on Ithaca, he told me everything. He didn't want me to hope for a future we could never have together."

"Did it work? Did you stop hoping?"

"I'd be crazy if I didn't."

Like her brothers, Ariana had her father's warm brown eyes flecked with gold, but she'd inherited the intensity of her gaze from her mother. "But you two have been intimate."

Hating to lie, Brooke pretended she hadn't heard the soft question. Instead she chose a dress at random and announced, "I love this."

Luckily her selection was a flirty emerald-green dress that she could see herself wearing. Brooke held it against her body. As she looked at her reflection, she noticed the dress had no tags, but Brooke doubted it had ever been worn.

"I'll take your nonanswer as an affirmative." Ariana's musical laughter filled the room. "Try on the dress." While Brooke obeyed her, the princess continued, "I'm sorry if I was blunt and please don't be embarrassed." The gold bracelets on her slender wrists chimed. "My brothers are very hard for the opposite sex to resist. Thank goodness Gabriel and Nic are honorable and not ones to take advantage. Christian is like a child in a toy store wanting everything he sees."

And getting it, too, Brooke guessed. "Please don't tell

anyone about Nic and me. It's over and I wouldn't want to cause any needless problems."

Ariana nodded. "That dress is amazing on you."

The empire bodice cupped her breasts, the fabric ending in a narrow band of a darker green ribbon. From there, the layers of chiffon material flowed over her hips, the hem ending just above her knee. Brooke stared at herself in the mirror as Ariana guided her feet into strappy black sandals.

"It brings out the green in your eyes."

"I feel like a princess." Brooke laughed. "I guess I should because it's a dress fit for a princess. You."

Next, Ariana urged Brooke into a hot-pink sheath with a V-shaped neckline and bands of fabric that crisscrossed diagonally to create an interesting and figure-slimming pattern. It had a sophisticated, elegant vibe that Brooke wasn't sure she could pull off.

"I understand you are having breakfast with my mother tomorrow. This will be perfect, and I think you should pair it with these."

Ariana grabbed a box and pulled out a pair of white suede and black velvet lace ankle boots that were amazing, Brooke waved her hands in protest. "I can't. Those are just too much."

"You must wear them or the outfit will not be complete."

At Ariana's relentless urging, Brooke slipped her feet into the boots and faced the mirror, accepting immediately that she'd lost the battle. "I never imagined I could look like this."

Ariana's eyebrows lifted in surprise. "Why not? You are very beautiful."

"But not refined and effortless like you and Olivia."

With a very unladylike snort, Ariana rolled her eyes. "This is just how I appear here in the palace. When I go to Ithaca, I assure you, I'm so different you'd never recognize me."

"Do you spend a lot of time on the island?"

"Not as much as I'd like. It's an escape. I go to paint. To forget about the responsibilities of being a princess."

"I imagine there's a lot that keeps you busy."

"It's less now that Olivia is here." Ariana selected five more dresses and put them into Olivia's wardrobe with three more pairs of shoes. "That will do for now, but you will need a long dress for a party we must attend the day after tomorrow. It's the prime minister's birthday."

"Are you sure I will be going?"

"Absolutely. The event is always deadly dull and having you along will make the whole thing bearable."

While the maids returned the rest of the dresses to the garment bags, Ariana squeezed Brooke's shoulder. "I am sorry you and Nic cannot see where things might lead between you. I think you would make him very happy."

"Actually, I drive him crazy."

"Good. He has always been too serious. He needs a little crazy in his life." And with that, Ariana said good-night and left Brooke to her thoughts.

The corridors of the visitors' wing were quiet as Nic made his way back to his temporary quarters. The tranquility would vanish over the next few days as guests began to arrive for the week of festivities leading up to the royal wedding. The conversation he'd had with his parents after dinner had highlighted their expectations for him. The women in the dossiers had been invited to the palace. He was to get to know each of them and make his selection.

As he'd listened to his mother, Nic realized he'd been in America too long. Although he'd grown up in a world where marriages sometimes were arranged, he'd grown accustomed to the notion of dating freely without any expectation that it might end in marriage.

He'd almost reached his suite when the door to the room

beside his opened and two maids emerged carrying garment bags. Their appearance could only mean he had company next door. It hadn't occurred to Nic that Brooke had been placed on this floor, much less in the room beside his, and his suspicion was confirmed when his sister came out of the room a few seconds later.

"Nic!" She raced across the few feet that separated them and threw herself into his arms. "How good that you're home."

She smelled of the light floral perfume he'd sent her the previous Christmas. He'd asked Brooke to help him pick out the perfume because he'd sensed the two women were a lot alike. Seeing his sister's good mood upon leaving Brooke, he knew he'd been right.

"I'm happy to be here."

Ariana pushed back until she could see his expression, and then clicked her tongue. "No you're not. You'd much rather be in California playing with your rocket."

"I'm done with that." The accident and Gabriel's marriage had seen to that.

"It's not like you to give up."

Her remark sent a wave of anger rushing through him. The emotion was so sharp and so immediate that he could do nothing more than stand frozen in astonishment. The loss of *Griffin*. His obligation to give up his dream and come home to marry a woman he didn't love. None of it was of his choosing.

But without this call to duty, would he have stayed in California and started over? The accident had been a disaster and his confidence was in shreds. Was that why he wasn't fighting his fate or figuring out a way around the laws that were in place so he could choose whom he married?

"Nic?"

As quickly as it had risen, his rage subsided. He shook

himself in the numb aftermath. "Sorry. I'm just tired. It's been a long day. And I didn't give up." He gave her nose an affectionate tweak the way he used to when she was an adorable toddler and he an oh-so-knowing big brother of ten. "I was called home to do my duty."

Ariana winced. "You're right. I'm sorry." Her contrite expression vanished with her next breath. "I met Brooke tonight. She's wonderful."

He was starting to wish his siblings would find something about Brooke to criticize. It was going to be hell bidding her goodbye and it would have been easier on him if they behaved as if falling for her was a huge error in his judgment.

"I'm glad you think so."

"If you're going to visit her, you might want to hurry. I think she was getting ready for bed."

For a second Nic wasn't sure if he should take his sister's statement at face value or if she was trying to get a reaction out of him. He decided it was the latter.

"This is my room." He indicated the door to his left. "I didn't know where she was staying in the palace."

"Why are you in the visitors' wing?"

"Something about my room flooding."

She gave him an incredulous look. "Who told you that?"

"Gabriel." Nic was starting to suspect something might be up. "Why?"

"Because I stopped by your suite earlier and it looked fine to me." She smirked. "I think our brother is trying to play matchmaker. You and Brooke all alone in the visitors' wing with no one to know if you snuck into each other's rooms. Very romantic."

"Damn it." Now he had another dilemma facing him. Confront Gabriel and return to his suite in the family wing or pretend he and Ariana never had this conversation and do what his heart wanted but his brain protested against.

"Honestly, stop being so noble." It was as if Ariana had read his mind. "Gabriel followed his heart. I think he wants the same for you."

"And then who will produce the legitimate heirs to ascend the throne?"

His sister shrugged. "There's always Christian. He isn't in love with anyone. Let him be the sacrificial lamb."

Nic hugged his sister and kissed the top of her head. "You are the best sister in the world."

"So are you going to choose Brooke?"

"You know I can't and you know why."

With a huge sigh, Ariana pushed him away. "You are too honorable for your own good."

"I know how this whole thing is making me feel. I can't do that to Christian." He paused and looked down at her. "Or to you."

"Me?"

"Have you considered what would happen if both Christian and I failed to produce a son? The whole burden shifts to your shoulders."

Ariana obviously hadn't considered this. Even though the constitution wouldn't allow her to rule as queen, she was still a direct descendant of the ruling king and that meant her son could one day succeed.

"Okay, I see your point, but I think it's terrible that you and Brooke can't be together."

"So do I."

Nic watched as his sister retreated down the corridor. For several heartbeats he stood with his hand on the doorknob to his room, willing himself to open the door and step inside, while Ariana's words rang in his head. *Brooke was getting ready for bed.* They were isolated in this wing of the palace. He could spend the night with her and sneak out before anyone discovered them. But how many times could he tell himself this was their last time together? Just that morning he'd been on the verge of saying goodbye.

He pushed open the door to his room, but didn't step across the threshold. He'd invited Brooke to Sherdana; it would only be polite to stop by and find out how her day had gone. If he stood in the hall, they could have a quick conversation without fear that either of them would be overcome with passion. That decided, Nic strode over and rapped on Brooke's door. If he'd expected her to answer his summons looking disheveled and adorable in her pajamas, he was doomed to disappointment.

The stylish creature that stood before him was nothing like the Brooke he'd grown accustomed to. Even the dress she'd worn at dinner tonight, as beautiful as she'd looked in it, hadn't stretched his perception of her as much as this strapless pale pink ball gown that turned her into a Disney princess.

Obviously enjoying herself, Brooke twirled twice and then paused for his opinion. "What do you think?"

"That's quite a dress."

She laughed, a bright silvery sound he hadn't heard since before the day he'd put an end to their fledgling romance. His heart lifted at her joy.

"I never imagined dressing like a princess would be so much fun."

His gut clenched at her words. She didn't mean them the way they'd sounded. The last thing she'd ever do was pick on him for rejecting her as unsuitable. Brooke wasn't the sort to play games or come at a problem sideways. It was one of the things he appreciated about her.

But that didn't stop regret from choking him.

"You look incredibly beautiful."

She shot him a flirtatious grin. "Aw, you're just saying that because it's true. Ariana brought the dress. I simply had to try it on since I'll never get the chance to wear it in public."

"Why not?"

"We both know the answer to that."

She drew him into the room and closed the door. Her actions had a dangerous effect on Nic's libido. He really hadn't come to her suite to make love to her, but it wouldn't take more than another one of her delicious smiles for him to snatch her into his arms and carry her to the bed.

"I don't think I follow you," Nic said, crossing his arms over his chest, his gaze tracking her every move as she enjoyed her reflection. He caught himself smiling as she shifted from side to side to make the skirt swish.

"Your mother and I are having breakfast tomorrow. I'm certain she's going to politely but firmly give me the heave-ho."

"She'd never be that rude."

"Of course not. But she can't be happy that her son brought home some inappropriate girl when he's supposed to be focused on selecting a bride."

"You're not inappropriate."

"I am where your future is concerned." Brooke reached for the dress's side zipper and gave Nic a stern look. "Turn around. I need to get out of this dress."

Blood pounded in his ears. "You are aware that I've seen you naked many, many times."

"That was before I was staying beneath your parents' roof. I think it would be rude of us to take advantage of their hospitality by getting swept up in a passionate moment. Don't you?" She set her hands on her hips. "So, turn around."

"My not watching you strip out of your clothes isn't going to prevent us from getting swept up in a passionate moment. I have memorized every inch of your gorgeous body."

"Turn around." Although her color was high, her firm tone deterred further argument.

At last Nic did as she'd asked. For several minutes the only sound in the room was the slide and crinkle of fabric as she undressed and the harsh rasp of his breath. He berated himself for acquiescing. If she was going to return to California in a few days, they were fools not to steal every moment they could to be together.

Bursting with conviction, Nic started to turn back around. "Brooke, we should..." He didn't finish because she gave him a sharp shove toward the door.

"No we shouldn't."

"One kiss." The irony of his demand wasn't lost on Nic. How many times had she teased, tormented and begged for any little bit of attention from him over the years? Time after time he'd refused her. "I missed waking up with you this morning."

"Whose fault was that?"

"Mine." It was all his fault. The five years when they could have been together if he hadn't been so obsessively focused on work. The way he'd hurt her because he'd chosen duty to his country over her. The emotional intimacy he couldn't give her because he was afraid his heart would break if he opened up.

"One kiss." He was pleading now.

"Fine. But you need to be in the hall with your hands behind your back."

A muscle ticked in his cheek. If she wanted to be in control, he would do his best to let that happen. "Agreed," he said and stepped out of her room.

Given the way he'd yielded to her conditions, Nic expected more demands from her.

"Close your eyes. I can't do this with you glaring at me."

In perfect stillness she waited him out. At last Nic let his lashes drift down. Years of working toward a single possibly unattainable goal would have been impossible without a great deal of fortitude, but Nic had recently discovered a shortage of patience where Brooke was concerned.

"Dear Nic." Her fingertips swept into his hair and tugged his head downward until their lips met.

Sweetness.

The tenderness of her kiss sent his heartbeat into overdrive. The desire previously driving through his body eased beneath her gentle touch. For the first time he acknowledged what existed between them wasn't born out of passion alone, but had its origins in something far deeper and lasting. A sigh fluttered in his chest as she lifted her lips from his and grazed them across his cheek.

"Good night, sweet prince."

Before he'd recovered enough to open his eyes, she was gone.

Ten

Thanks to Ariana's help with her wardrobe, Brooke had gone to bed feeling confident about her breakfast meeting with the queen. However, when she woke at dawn plagued by the increasingly familiar nausea, she plodded through her morning routine, burdened by anxiety.

By the time she'd swept her straightened hair into a smooth French roll, Brooke had consumed half a package of crackers in an effort to calm her roiling stomach. It seemed to be working because by the time she finished applying mascara and lipstick, she was feeling like her old self.

A maid appeared promptly at ten minutes to eight and Brooke dredged up her polite interview face as she followed her downstairs and into the garden. The girl pointed to a grassy path that curved past flowerbeds overflowing with shades of pink and purple. Brooke's destination— a white gazebo overlooking a small pond—appeared to be about fifty feet away. As she neared the structure, she noted that the queen had already arrived and was seated at the table placed in the center of the space. Rose-patterned china and crystal goblets were carefully arranged on a white tablecloth. The whole display reminded Brooke of a storybook tea party.

"Good morning, Your Majesty," Brooke said cheerfully as she neared.

The queen turned her attention from the electronic tablet in her hand and her keen gaze swept over Brooke, lingering for a long moment on the low boots. Brooke withstood the queen's assessment in silence, wondering if custom required her to curtsy.

"Hello, Dr. Davis. Don't you look lovely. Please sit down."

Noticing the change from last night in the way the queen addressed her, Brooke perched on the edge of a mint-green damask chair and dropped her napkin on her lap. Two maids stood by to wait on them. Brooke accepted a glass of orange juice and a cup of very dark coffee lightened with cream which she sipped until her stomach gurgled quietly. To cover the noise, Brooke began to speak.

"Your garden is beautiful." Ariana had offered Brooke several safe subjects on which to converse. "I understand you have several rare varieties of roses."

"Are you interested in gardening?" the queen asked, offering a polite smile. A diplomat's smile.

Brooke's whole digestive track picked that moment to complain. She pinched her lips tight in response. After a second she took a deep breath. "I love flowers, but I don't have much of a green thumb."

"I suppose you've been busy earning your two doctorates. That's quite impressive for someone your age." Most people thought it was impressive, period, but it made sense that the queen of a country would be hard to impress. "And now you teach at a university."

"Italian language and literature."

"Olivia tells me you've traveled around Italy quite a bit."

"As well as France, Austria and Switzerland. I love this part of the world."

"Have you ever wanted to live in Europe?"

At that moment Brooke wished she'd never agreed to come. Nic's mother obviously regarded her as an intruder, or worse, an opportunist. Should she explain that she understood Nic was off-limits? She couldn't imagine that was the sort of polite conversation one made with the elegant queen of Sherdana.

"I love California. I did my undergraduate work in New York City." Brooke knit her fingers together in her lap lest she surrender to the urge to play with her silverware. "I couldn't wait to get back home."

"Home is a wonderful place to be. Are you hungry?" The queen gestured to the maids and one of them lifted the lid off the serving dish. "Crepes are my weakness," the queen said. "There are also omelets made with spinach and mushrooms or the chef would be happy to prepare something else if you'd prefer."

"I don't want to be any trouble." The crepes looked marvelous. Some were filled with strawberries, others with something creamy and covered in apples or...

"Pears roasted in butter and honey over crepes filled with ricotta cheese," the queen said, her eyes softening for the first time in Brooke's company.

If Brooke hadn't been so queasy, she could have easily eaten her way through half a dozen of the thin fluffy pancakes. As it was, she took one of each kind and nibbled at them.

"Olivia tells me you spoke of leaving in the next few days," the queen remarked in her delightfully accented English. "But when I spoke with Nicolas last night, he wishes you to remain through the wedding." She tucked into her breakfast with relish, obviously enjoying herself. "I think my son believes himself in love with you."

Brooke's coffee cup rattled against the saucer as she set it down too abruptly. Her stomach seized and suddenly eating the crepes didn't strike her as the smartest idea. The queen's words repeated themselves several times in Brooke's head. *He believes himself in love with you.* Not *he's in love with you.* Brooke recognized the difference. In high school and college she'd believed herself in love any number of times. Then she'd met Nic and began the discovery of what love truly was.

"I'm sorry, but you're wrong." Brooke put her napkin to her lips as her body flushed hot. It wasn't embarrassment or guilt, but her system reacting to stress and being pregnant. "Nic knows his mind like no man I've ever met. His heart belongs to this country and his family."

The queen sighed. "And you are in love with him."

The edges of Brooke's vision darkened. What was Nic's mother trying to establish? Already Brooke had accepted that she and Nic had no future. She knew he would never give his mother any cause to believe otherwise so she guessed the queen's protective instincts were kicking in. She understood. In a little more than seven months she would have her own child to keep from harm. Heaven help anyone who got in her way.

"He's my brother's best friend..." Brooke said, her voice trailing off. "I've known Nic for years. Did I once want something more? Yes. But that was before I knew who he was and what was expected of him."

"Are you trying to tell me you didn't know he was a prince?"

Brooke held still beneath the queen's penetrating regard. The older woman's face became difficult to stay focused on. Brooke wanted nothing more than to lie down until the spinning stopped.

"I didn't know until a few days ago. He left California without a word after the accident. I tracked him down to Ithaca because he wouldn't return my phone calls or emails. I was worried about how he was coping in the aftermath." She hoped the queen was satisfied with her reason for following Nic to Greece and would refrain from probing further.

The queen nodded. "The rocket ship was very important to him. But it's gone and he needs to put it behind him." Her tone was matter-of-fact as she dismissed her son's driving passion.

"He can't just put it behind him. He feels responsible for the death of one of his fellow scientists." Brooke endured a sharp pinch of sadness that Nic's mother didn't understand this about her son. "Walter hadn't been with the team long, but he worked closely with Nic. I think part of the reason why Nic was so willing to come home and let you marry him off was because he felt as if he'd failed Walter and Glen and even you and the king. I think the reason he worked so hard was to justify being away from Sherdana. He spent every day proving that his work would benefit future generations, driving himself beyond exhaustion in order to contribute something amazing to the world. So that his absence from you had meaning."

Brooke didn't realize she'd gotten to her feet until the gazebo began to sway around her. She clamped a hand over her mouth as the unsettled feeling in her stomach increased. She couldn't throw up. Not now. Not here. Sweat broke out on her body. She was about to ruin Ariana's gorgeous dress in an inglorious way the palace would be talking about for weeks. Brooke blinked and gulped air to regain her equilibrium. But she was too hot. Too dizzy.

"I have to…" *Go.* She didn't belong here. She'd been unbearably rude to Nic's mother, who was the queen of a nation. But she could no longer tell in which direction lay escape.

"Dr. Davis, are you all right?" The queen sounded very far away.

Brooke tried to focus on the queen's voice but she stumbled. Abruptly a wood column was beneath her fingers and she clutched the rough surface like a lifeline as darkness rushed up to claim her.

Nic exploded through the green salon's French doors and raced toward the gazebo as soon as Brooke stood and began to weave like a drunken woman. For the past fifteen minutes he'd been positioned by the windows that overlooked the garden so he could observe the exchange between his mother and Brooke and step in if things appeared as if they were going badly. Like Brooke, he'd expected his mother to diplomatically encourage her to leave as soon as possible and he was worried that Brooke might say something she'd immediately regret. Never could he have predicted that he'd be just in time to catch Brooke's limp body before it hit the gazebo floor.

"What happened?"

For once his mother looked utterly confounded. "She was going on and on about you and the rocket and then she turned bright pink and collapsed."

Nic scooped Brooke into his arms and headed toward the palace. Whereas she'd been flushed a moment earlier, her skin was now deathly pale. He entered the green salon and crossed the room in several ground-eating strides. His heart hammered harder in his chest each time he glanced down at Brooke's unconscious face. What was wrong with her? As far as he recalled she'd been sick a mere handful of times and it had certainly never been this drastic. A cold. Sinus infection. Once a bad case of food poisoning.

He didn't realize his mother had followed him until he

pushed open the door to Brooke's suite and carried her to the bed.

"Is there something wrong with her that caused her to pass out?" the queen demanded, sitting on the bed to feel Brooke's skin. "She's clammy."

"She's perfectly healthy." He pulled out his phone, unsure if this was a true emergency. "She was anxious about coming here, but seemed all right at dinner last night. What did you say to her at breakfast? She seemed agitated before she passed out."

"You were watching us?"

"I was worried about how you two would get along. Seems I was right to be."

"I merely told her that I thought you believed yourself in love with her."

Nic closed his eyes briefly and shook his head. "What would possess you to tell her that?"

"I needed her to understand that what was between you wasn't real."

"How would you know? You barely know her and I haven't been around for ten years so you scarcely know me, either."

His mother looked shocked. "You are my son. I raised you."

With effort, Nic reeled in his temper. "None of this is helping Brooke. She hasn't awakened yet. I think she needs a doctor."

He was texting Gabriel when a single word from his mother stopped him.

"Wait."

"Why?"

She pointed at a package of crackers on the nightstand. "How long has she been eating these?"

"I have no idea." And what did it matter? "Do you think there's something wrong with them?"

"No, but when I was pregnant I used to eat crackers to fight nausea." His mother looked thoughtful. "She barely ate any of her dinner last night and she was picking at breakfast today. Pregnancy could explain her fainting spell."

"Pregnant?" Nic shook his head to clear the sudden rushing in his ears. "Impossible."

"Impossible because you haven't been intimate or because you thought you were being careful."

The blunt question shocked him for a moment before comprehension struck. Of course his mother knew he'd been involved with Brooke. They hadn't kept their relationship secret and no doubt Ariana had mentioned that he was seeing someone in California.

"We've been very careful."

"Then perhaps she has someone else in her life."

Nic glared at his mother. "There's no one else."

The queen pressed her lips together and didn't argue further. "I suggest we wait for her to come around and ask her. If there's something more serious going on, we can call the doctor then." His mother stood and smoothed her skirt. "I'll give you some privacy. Please let me know how she's doing when she wakes."

And with that, the queen left and Nic was alone with Brooke.

Pregnant.

With his child. The thought of it filled him with warmth. But all too quickly questions formed. Had she realized it yet? She wasn't showing and he guessed that she was between five and eight weeks along. Was that too early for her to suspect? Yet she'd obviously been queasy and had to wonder why.

Brooke began to stir and Nic went to sit beside her. She blinked and slowly focused on him.

"What happened?"

"You passed out."

"Damn." She rubbed her eyes. "I yelled at your mother. She must hate me."

"She doesn't." He skimmed his knuckles against her cheek. "What's going on with you? I've never known you to be sick."

She avoided his gaze. "Nothing, I'm just really overwrought and I think my blood sugar is low because I was too nervous to eat much at dinner."

"Is that why you were eating these?" He picked up the crackers and held them before her.

"Whenever my stomach gets upset, I eat crackers to absorb the acid." Her words made sense, but something about her tone told him she wasn't giving him full disclosure.

"My mother told me she used to eat crackers when she was pregnant," he said. "She claimed it helped with nausea."

Brooke's body tensed. "I've heard that before. I think if you keep something bland in your stomach it settles it."

Nic's irritation was growing by the second. Brooke was a terrible liar because she believed in being honest. So much so it had gotten her into trouble a number of times. Her behavior while answering his questions demonstrated that while she hadn't actually said anything false, she was keeping things from him.

"Are you pregnant?"

"We've been careful."

"That didn't answer my question." He leaned down and grabbed her chin, pinning her with his gaze. "Are you pregnant?"

"Yes." Her voice came out small and unsure.

He sat back with a muffled curse. "Why didn't you tell me?"

"That was the plan when I came to Ithaca." She pushed into a sitting position and retreated away from him as far as the headboard would allow. "I couldn't tell you something like that over the phone, but then I showed up and you were so unhappy to see me." She wrapped her arms around herself and stared at her shoes. "And then you announce that you are a prince and you need to get married so your country could have an heir and that your wife needed to be an aristocrat or a citizen of Sherdana."

"So you were planning on leaving without ever telling me?" Outrage gave his voice a sharp edge.

"Don't say it like that. You made a choice to come back here and do the honorable thing. I made a decision that would save you from regret."

"But to never see my child?"

She put her hands over the lower half of her face and closed her eyes. After a long moment she spoke. "Don't you think I considered that? But I knew you would have other children, hopefully lots of them."

Her every word slashed his heart into ribbons. The woman he loved was having his child and he'd been days away from never knowing the truth. "Well, there's no question of you going home now."

"What? You can't make that decision for me. My job, friends and family are in California. That's where I belong. Just like you belong here in Sherdana with your family and your future *wife*."

She was crazy if she thought he was just going to let her vanish out of his life. "You belong with me just like I belong with you and our child."

"Maybe if you were the ordinary scientist I first fell in love with, but you are a prince with responsibilities that are bigger than both of us combined. Do the right thing and let me go. It's the only thing that makes sense."

"I refuse to accept that." Nic got to his feet and stared down at her. Where a moment earlier she'd seemed fragile and lost, her passionate determination to do what she perceived as the honorable thing gave her the look of a Valkyrie. "Get some rest. We will talk at length later."

Nic should have gone straight to his mother to deliver the confirmation of Brooke's condition as he'd promised, but found he needed some privacy to absorb what he'd just learned. He headed to his suite in the royal wing, curious to see if it was in the condition Gabriel had said. But just as Ariana had said, there was no leak.

The rooms that had been his growing up couldn't feel any less familiar than if he'd never seen them before. The past ten years of his life, first living in Boston, then California, felt much more real to him than the first twenty-two being Sherdana's prince. But that had been the case before he'd found out Brooke was pregnant. If he put aside duty and engaged in an honest conversation with himself, he'd accept that he no longer felt connected to his birth country. Yet his failure in the Mojave Desert meant that California was no longer a welcoming destination, either.

Never had he felt so conflicted about his future path. No matter what direction he chose, he was destined to leave disappointment and regret in his wake. Staying in Sherdana and marrying a suitable bride would require him to give up the woman he loved and abandon his child. But if he chose to make a life with Brooke could he convince her that he would never regret turning his back on his country when he knew it would always haunt him? And what would he do in California without the *Griffin* to work on? Teach at a university? He frowned.

When an hour of self-reflection passed without a clear solution presenting itself, Nic left his suite and sought his mother. He found her and his father in the king's private office deep in discussion.

"Well?" the king demanded, his eyes reflecting disappointment. He was seated behind a large mahogany desk that had been a gift from the king of Spain back in the early eighteenth century. "Is Dr. Davis pregnant?"

"Yes." Nic refused to feel like a chastised teenager. "And the child is mine." This last he directed to his mother, who sat on one of the burgundy sofas in the office's sitting area.

She was in the process of pouring a cup of tea and sent a pained look to her husband. "It seems as if none of my grandchildren are going to be legitimate."

"I won't apologize for what happened," he told his parents. "And I won't shirk my responsibility to Brooke."

"What does that mean?" his father said, his deep voice charged with warning.

"I don't have all the details worked out yet."

"You're not planning to marry her."

"It would take both of us to be on board for that to happen and at this point she's determined to return to California alone."

"You must let her," his mother said. "We will make sure she and the child are well taken of, but news of this must not get out. You need to marry and produce children that can one day succeed Gabriel."

The press of duty had never felt more overwhelming. Nic wanted to struggle free of the smothering net of responsibility that his parents cast over him.

"And what about Christian?" Nic asked, his heart burning with bitterness. "Will he not be expected to do the same?"

"Of course." The king nodded. "We are calling on both of you."

And with that, Nic accepted that one decision had been made for him.

Embarrassment and remorse kept Brooke from venturing out of her room the rest of the day. She put her pajamas back on, pulled the curtains closed and huddled in bed. A maid brought her lunch, which she barely touched, and when Ariana poked her head in the room sometime in the late afternoon, Brooke pretended to be sleeping.

She couldn't hide like this forever. For one thing it wasn't her style to avoid problems, and she really wouldn't shake the despair gnawing at her until she apologized to the queen for her outburst.

Around five she roused and phoned Theresa, needing to pour her heart out to someone who was one hundred percent on her side. Unfortunately, the call rolled to voice mail and Brooke hung up without leaving a message. This was her problem to solve and the sooner she faced the music, the better.

A maid came by around six and found Brooke dressed in her tribal print maxi dress and sandals. Wearing her own clothes was like wrapping herself in a little piece of home. She didn't fit into Nic's world and trying to appear as if she did had been silly. Better to face the queen's displeasure as her authentic self, a woman who knew her own mind and was determined to do what was best for her and for Nic.

"Princess Olivia sent me to ask if you felt well enough to have dinner with her in half an hour," the maid said.

"Tell her yes."

When Brooke entered Prince Gabriel and Prince Olivia's private suite thirty minutes later, she wasn't surprised to discover Olivia had heard all about the morning's events. Up until now the princess had seemed like an ally, but would that continue? Brooke regarded Olivia warily as the princess indicated a spot on the gold couch. Brooke sat down while Olivia poured a cup of something that smelled like peppermint from a silver tea set.

The princess's kindness brought tears to Brooke's eyes. "How badly have I messed everything up?"

Olivia's eyes grew thoughtful. "Your pregnancy has

created quite a stir as you can imagine, but you shouldn't feel responsible. I doubt either you or Nic planned this."

"I don't mean that. I mean how mad is the queen that I yelled at her?"

"I didn't hear anything about that." Olivia's lips twitched and her eyes glinted with merriment. "What happened?"

"It's a bit of a blur. She said something dismissive about Nic needing to forget about the rocket and I straight up lost it." Brooke cradled the teacup, hoping the warmth would penetrate her icy fingers. "I started ranting about how he worked so hard because he wanted to justify his being away from his country for so long." Brooke shook her head as her heart contracted in shame. "It's none of my business, I shouldn't have said anything."

"You were defending the man you love. I think the queen understands."

"You didn't see her face." Brooke squinted and tried to summon a memory of the queen's reaction, but all she recalled was the garden pitching around her and the descent into darkness. "I was so rude."

"You are being too hard on yourself," Olivia said. "No wonder you and Nic get along so well. You're both such honorable people."

"I don't feel very honorable at the moment. But I'd like to change that. I made arrangements for a flight leaving the day after tomorrow at nine in the morning. I could use some help getting to the airport."

"You can't really mean to leave."

"You can't possibly think it's a good idea for me to stay. The longer I'm here the more likely it will leak that I'm pregnant. Better if I disappear from Sherdana so Nic can move forward with his life."

"What makes you think he's just going to let you go? When faced with the same choice, Gabriel fought for me.

Nic is no less an Alessandro and I don't think he's any less in love."

Olivia's words provoked many questions as Brooke realized that the princess had been confronted by a similar choice of whether to marry her prince when doing so put the future line of Alessandros at risk. But as much as curiosity nipped at her, Brooke feared asking would insult the princess.

"I think Gabriel is more of a romantic than Nic," Brooke said. "Your husband's heart led him to choose you and he will never question whether he made the right decision. Nic approaches matters with logic, listing the pros and cons, assigning values so he can rank what's most important. I think he takes after his mother in that respect."

Olivia's beautiful blue eyes clouded. "You know him well so I will just have to accept that you're right, but I hope for your sake that you're wrong."

Eleven

Both Olivia and Ariana had ganged up on Brooke and convinced her to go to the prime minister's birthday party the next evening. As it was her last night in Sherdana—she was due to fly out the next morning—the princesses were opposed to her spending any more time alone. Their concern was a balm to Brooke's battered spirit and because Ariana had tapped into her contacts in the fashion world and found Brooke the perfect Jean-Louis Scherrer gown to wear, she'd caved with barely a whimper.

Trailing into the party behind the crown prince and princess with Ariana beside her for support, Brooke experienced a sense of wonder that made her glad she'd come. The gown Ariana had found for her had the empire waist Brooke loved and a free flowing skirt. With every stride, the skirt's bright gold lining flashed and showed off the most perfect pair of Manolo Blahnik shoes with tasseled straps. The bodice was crusted with bronze beading that made her think of Moroccan embellishment and the gown's material was a subdued orange, gold and pink paisley pattern that exhibited Brooke's bohemian style.

After meeting the prime minister and wishing him a happy birthday, Brooke relaxed enough to gaze around at the guests. With Ariana at her side, no one seemed overly interested in her. It wasn't that she was ignored. Each person she was introduced to was polite and cordial, but no one seemed overly curious about the stranger from California. Brooke suspected that Ariana's social nature brought all sorts of individuals into her sphere.

Of Nic she saw nothing. The party was crowded with Sherdanian dignitaries and Brooke was determined not to spend the entire evening wondering which of the women Nic might choose to become his wife.

"Do you see what I mean about dull?" Ariana murmured to her an hour into the party. "We've made an appearance. Anytime you're ready to leave, just say the word. A friend of mine owns a club. It's opening night and he'd love to have me show up."

Brooke had been finding the party anything but dull. Unlike Nic, she liked to balance hours of study and research with socializing. People-watching was the best way to get out of her head and the prime minister's party was populated by characters.

"Sure, we can leave, but this isn't as dull as you say."

"I'm sorry, I forget that you are new to all this."

"I suppose you're right. Who is the woman in the black gown and the one over there in blue?" Each of them negotiated the room on the arm of an older gentleman, but Brooke had observed several telling glances passing between them.

"That's Countess Venuto." Ariana indicated the woman wearing blue. "And Renanta Arazzi. Her husband is the minister of trade. The men hate each other."

"Their wives don't share their husbands' antagonism."

"What do you mean?"

"I think they're having an affair." Brooke grinned. "Or they're just about to."

Ariana gasped, obviously shocked. "Tell me how you know."

Brooke spent the next hour explaining her reasoning to Ariana and then commented on several other things she'd picked up, astonishing the princess with her observations and guesses.

"You have an uncanny knack for reading people," Ariana exclaimed. "Gabriel should hire you to sit in on his meetings and advise him on people's motives."

Flattered, Brooke laughed. "I'm trained as an analyst. Whether it's art, literature or people, I guess I just dig until I locate meaning. Just don't ask me about anything having to do with numbers or technology. That's where I fail miserably."

"But that's what makes you and my brother such a perfect pairing. You complement each other."

At the mention of Nic, Brooke's good mood fled. "If only he wasn't a prince and I wasn't an ordinary girl from California." She kept her voice light, but in her chest, her heart thumped dully. "I didn't tell you earlier, but I made arrangements to fly home tomorrow morning."

"You can't leave." Ariana looked distressed. "At least stay through the wedding."

The thought of delaying the inevitable for another week made Brooke shudder. Plus, she hadn't yet been offered the opportunity to apologize to the queen in person and didn't feel right taking advantage of the king and queen's hospitality with that hanging over her. "I can't stay. Coming here in the first place was a mistake."

"But then I'd never have met you and that would have been a tragedy."

Brooke appreciated Ariana's attempt to make her feel

special. "I feel the same way about you. I just wish I'd handled things better." By which she meant the incident with the queen and Nic's discovering that she was pregnant.

She hadn't spoken to him since he'd left her room the day before. She'd dined that night with Olivia and taken both breakfast and lunch in her room. Ariana had joined her for the midday meal, bringing with her the gown Brooke was wearing tonight and reminding her of the promise she'd made to attend the birthday party.

Suddenly the crowd parted and Nic appeared, looking imposing and very princely as he strode through the room. Brooke stared at him in hopeless adoration, still unaccustomed to the effortless aura of power he assumed in his native environment. What was so different about him? He'd always radiated strength and confidence, but he'd been approachable despite his often inherent aloofness. What made him seem so inaccessible now? Was it the arrogant tilt of his head? The way he wore the expensive, custom tuxedo as easily as a T-shirt and jeans? The cool disdain in his burnished gold eyes?

And then he caught sight of her and the possessive glow of his gaze melted the chill from his features. Brooke's heart exploded in her chest and she abandoned Ariana with a quick apology, slipping through the party guests in Nic's direction before she considered what she would say. When she'd drawn to within five feet of him, her path was blocked by a petite brunette in a shimmering black mini.

"Nicolas Alessandro, I heard you returned home." The woman's cultured voice stopped Brooke dead in her tracks.

She turned aside and spotted French doors leading onto a terrace. Moving in that direction with as much haste as she dared, Brooke chastised herself. What had she been thinking? She and Nic couldn't act as friends or even acquaintances at this public event. All eyes were on the returning prince. During her self-imposed incarceration,

she'd pored over the local gossip blogs and read several
news articles speculating on Nic's abrupt return. The
media were having a field day detailing all the women
who'd been invited to the royal wedding the following
week and speculating on who might be the frontrunner to
become the next Sherdanian princess.

Not one of the news sources had mentioned a girl from
California. For that Brooke was grateful, but if she threw
herself at Nic during this party, how long would it be before someone started wondering who she was.

Brooke had about five minutes of solitude on the terrace before she was joined by Olivia.

"Are you all right?" the princess inquired, her concern
bringing tears to Brooke's eyes.

"I almost made a huge mistake out there. I saw Nic and
raced through the crowd to get to him." Her story came
out in uneven bursts as her heart continued to pound er-
ratically. "If someone hadn't beaten me to him, I don't
know what I would have done." Brooke braced herself on
the metal railing as hysterical laughter bubbled up, making her knees wobble. "I am such an idiot."

"Not at all. You are in love. It makes us behave in strange
and mysterious ways."

Brooke loved Olivia's British accent. It made even the
most impossible statements sound plausible. Already calm
was settling back over her.

"I'm so glad I had the chance to get to know you,"
Brooke said. "Ariana, too. Nic is lucky to have you."

"He'd be lucky to have you as well if only you wouldn't
be so eager to rush off."

"I know you mean well." Brooke shook her head. "But
Nic needs me to go."

"What if instead he really needs you to stay? He's been
locked in the library since yesterday morning. His mind
is a hundred miles away from anyone trying to have a

conversation with him. He called Christian and could be heard yelling at him to get home all the way across the palace."

That didn't sound much like the Nic she knew, but then he'd been through a lot in the past month. Was it any surprise that having his entire world turned upside down would cause a crack in his relentless confidence?

"It's my fault," Brooke said, her own confidence returning. "I dropped a huge bomb on him yesterday when I said I was going back to California without consulting him."

"You should speak to him. He wants badly to do right by everyone and it's tearing him apart."

As it had torn Brooke apart, until she'd concluded that Nic would be better off not knowing about her pregnancy. "But I'm leaving in the morning. It will have to be tonight." Brooke considered. "Ariana's friend has a club opening tonight and she wants to go. I'll have her drop me at the palace. If you'll let Nic know, I'll be waiting for him in the library at midnight."

She didn't want him to leave the party early. His mother would expect him to spend the evening getting acquainted with all the available women there. Brooke turned to go, but Olivia stopped her.

"If Nic could marry you, would you accept?"

The princess asked the question with such poignant sincerity that Brooke faced her and answered in kind. "I love him with everything I am. Which is why it's both incredibly simple and impossibly hard to let him go so he can be the prince his family needs him to be."

Olivia wrapped her in a fierce hug and whispered, "If he asks you to stay, please say yes."

Brooke smiled at the beautiful princess without answering and then squared her shoulders and went to find Ariana.

* * *

Trapped in a tedious conversation with one of Christian's former girlfriends, Alexia Le Mans, Nic watched Brooke exit the ballroom for the less populated terrace and was just extricating himself to go after her when Olivia beat him to it. He'd only come to the party tonight in the hopes of seeing Brooke and demanding they have a conversation about the child she carried. He might not be able to marry her, but he'd be damned if the child would disappear out of his life. Nic had seen Gabriel's regret at not knowing his daughters during their first two years and Nic wasn't going to let that happen to him.

Ten minutes after Brooke left the room, she was back, and almost immediately he lost her in the crush. He moved to intercept her, but was stopped three times before he reached where he thought Brooke had been headed.

"Nic."

He turned at Olivia's voice and saw that she and Gabriel were coming up behind him. "I can't talk right now, I'm looking for Brooke."

Olivia exchanged a wordless look with her husband. "Ariana was heading to a club opening and she offered to give Brooke a lift back to the palace. But before she left, she gave me a message for you. She said she'll be waiting to speak to you in the library at midnight."

"Thank you." Nic had no intention of waiting until then to talk with Brooke. "And thank you for all you've done for her."

"No need to thank me," Olivia said, her smile affectionate. "She's lovely and I've enjoyed being her friend."

"Yes," Gabriel added. "Too bad she couldn't become a permanent fixture in the palace. I think she'd make an outstanding princess."

The temptation to say something disrespectful to the future king sizzled in Nic's mind, but he quelled his frustration and thanked Olivia with as much courtesy as he could muster. Bidding them goodbye, Nic headed downstairs to reclaim his car and follow Brooke to the palace.

The drive from the hotel where the prime minister's party had taken place back to the palace only took ten minutes, but Nic discovered Brooke had already disappeared into the visitors' wing by the time he arrived. He'd hoped to catch her before she went upstairs so they could have their conversation someplace that wouldn't invite gossip, but that wasn't going to stop him from tracking her down.

As he knocked on her door, he was a little out of breath from his rush up the stairs to the third floor. Listening to his heart thunder in his chest as he waited for her to answer, he made a note to drink less and exercise more than had been his habit in the past month. But when Brooke answered the door, snatching his breath away as he stared down into her soft gray-green eyes, he knew it wasn't stamina that had caused his heart and lungs to labor, but excitement at being close to her again.

"Nic? What are you doing here?"

"You wanted to talk." He stepped forward, forcing her to retreat into her room. As soon as he cleared the door, he shut it behind him. His hands made short work of his tie and slipped the first buttons of his shirt free. "Let's talk."

Brooke's body immediately began to thrum with arousal at Nic's apparent intent in entering her room. Her lips couldn't form protests as he removed his tuxedo jacket and unfastened his gold cuff links. Those went into his pocket before he set the jacket on a convenient chair while still advancing on her.

"Didn't Olivia tell you midnight in the library?"

"I considered it a suggested time and place." He pulled his shirt free of his pants and went back to work on the buttons. Each one he freed gave her a more evocative glimpse of the impressive chest beneath. "I prefer this one."

The gold shards in Nic's eyes brightened perceivably when his temper was aroused. Because she enjoyed riling him, Brooke had noticed this phenomenon a lot. She could judge the level of his agitation by the degree of the sparkle. At the moment his gaze was almost too intense to meet.

She thought about Olivia's words and wished he'd ask her to stay in Sherdana. No, she didn't. She ached for him to ask her. But he wouldn't. He shouldn't. From the start he'd been right to keep her at bay.

Nic closed the distance between them and swept her into his arms. As he bent her backward, his lips gliding along her temple, Brooke's senses spun.

"Stay in Sherdana a while longer."

He wasn't asking for forever, but every second with him was precious. "I don't belong here."

"Neither do I," he whispered an instant before his lips met hers.

With a moan, she sank her fingers into his thick black hair and held on as he fed off her mouth. Desire lashed at her, setting her pent-up emotions free. She met him kiss for kiss, claiming him as he sought to brand her with his passion.

Both were breathing unevenly when he lifted his lips from hers and captured her gaze. With her heart thundering in her ears, Brooke barely heard his words.

"You and I belong together."

"In another life. As different people. I'd give up everything to be with you," she murmured, the last of her resistance crumbling as he slid his hands down her back and aligned her curves to his granite muscles. "But not here and now."

"Yes to here and now," he growled. "It's tomorrow and

all the days beyond we can't have. Don't deny either of us this last night of happiness."

Brooke surrendered to the flood of longing and the demanding pressure of his arms banded around her body. Tomorrow would come all too soon. She wanted him for as long as possible.

With her face pressed against his bare chest, her ear tuned to the steady beat of his heart, she said, "I love you."

His arms crushed her, preventing any further words. For a long moment his grip stopped her from breathing, and then his hold gentled.

"You are the only woman I'll ever love."

Brooke lifted up on tiptoe and pushed her lips against his. He immediately opened to her and she matched the fierce hunger of his kiss with a desperation she couldn't hide. He loved her.

Working with deliberation that made her ache, he eased down the zipper of her dress, his lips sending a line of fire along her skin as he went. She'd never felt so adored as he unwrapped her body, treating her as if she was a precious gift. By the time his fingers lifted away the exquisite designer gown, exposing all of her, she was quivering uncontrollably.

Nic stripped away the last of her clothes, pushed her to arm's length and stared. Looking at her excited him and that set her blood on fire. She licked her dry lips and his pupils flared, almost vanquishing his gold irises. Her legs trembled. She couldn't take much more without ending up in a heap at his feet.

Without warning he surged back to life, lifting her into his arms and carrying her to the bed. As she floated down to land on the mattress, Brooke's thighs parted in welcome and Nic quickly stripped off the rest of his clothes and covered her with his body. She expected him to surge inside her, such was the intensity of his erection, but instead, he went back to work on her body with lips and hands, driving her to impossible levels of hunger.

At long last, she'd gone light-years past the point of readiness and gathered handfuls of his hair. "I can't wait any longer to have you inside me."

"Are you asking or commanding?" He sucked hard on her neck and she quaked.

"I'm begging." She reached down and found him. Her firm grip wrenched a satisfying moan from his lips. "Please, Nic."

His hands spanned her hips and in one swift thrust he answered her plea. She flexed her spine and accepted his full length while he devoured her impassioned groan. Before she could grow accustomed to the feel of him filling her, Nic rolled them over until she sat astride his hips.

This new position offered a different set of sensations and freed his hands to cruise across her torso at will. She took charge of their lovemaking and began to move. Whispering words of encouragement, he cupped her breasts, kneading and rolling her hard nipples between his fingers to intensify her pleasure.

When she came, it was hard and fast. If she could have lingered in the moment forever, she would have known perfect happiness, but such profound ecstasy wasn't meant to last. And there was a different sort of joy in the lazy aftermath of being so thoroughly loved. As Nic nuzzled his face in the place where her neck met her shoulder, Brooke savored the synchronized beat of their hearts and knew no matter where her body existed, her soul would stay with Nic where it belonged.

Morning brought rain and the distant rumble of thunder. Nic woke to the soft, fragrant sweetness of Brooke's naked body curved against his and held his breath to keep from disturbing the magic of the moment. Last night had been incredible. And it had been goodbye. He'd tasted it in the desperation of her kisses and felt it in the wildness of his need for her.

"What time is it?" she asked, her voice a contented purr.

"A little before seven."

"Oh." She practically sprang out of bed and began to hunt around for her clothes. "I have to go."

Nic sat up, automatically admiring the fluid movement of her nude form as she dressed. "Where are you going?"

"Home. My flight leaves in two hours."

Shock held him motionless and she'd almost reached the door before he caught up with her. If he hadn't barged into her room and spent the night would he have even known she was gone?

"And if I ask you to stay?" He thought he was ready to set her free, but now that the moment had arrived, he was incapable of saying goodbye.

"Don't you mean command?" Her smile was both wicked and sad.

Despite his solemn mood, Nic's lips twitched. "You aren't Sherdanian. I have no way to make you behave."

"And throwing me in the dungeon would create an international scandal that would upset your mother."

"Is that why you're running away? Because you think either I or my family would be bothered by some adverse publicity?"

Her body stiffened. "I'm not running away. I'm returning to California where I live. Just like you are staying in Sherdana where you belong. Besides, the longer I stay the more I risk becoming fodder for the tabloids and that wouldn't do your marriage hunt any favors."

"No. I suppose it wouldn't. But I still don't want you to go."

"And yet I must."

"You're breaking my heart," he said, carrying her hand to his lips and placing her palm against his bare chest.

"I'm breaking *your* heart?" She tugged her hand from beneath his, but his free arm snaked around her, and pulled her resistant body against him. "Do you have any idea how unfair you're being right now?"

He knew and didn't care. Nic tightened his hold, letting his heat seep into her until there was no more resistance. And then he kissed her, long and slow and deep, while in the back of his mind he acknowledged that this would be their final goodbye. By the time he broke away they were both gasping for breath.

Brooke spoke first. "You were right."

"About?" He nuzzled her cheek, feathering provocative kisses along her skin. His teeth grazed her earlobe, making her shudder.

"Starting something that had no future." Her pain and grief tore at him.

"I didn't want there to be regrets between us."

"I don't regret it."

"But you can't help thinking if we'd never been together that leaving would be easier." His arms tightened. "And you might be right. But for the rest of my life I will cherish every second we've spent together." And now he had to be strong enough to let her go. Only knowing that their child would connect them together forever gave him the courage to set her free. "There's no getting you out of my system," he said. "Or my heart."

"I love you." She kissed him one last time. "Now let me go."

Twelve

"You let her go?" Gabriel Alessandro, crown prince of Sherdana, was furious. "What the hell is the matter with you?"

From her seat behind the ornate writing desk, Olivia watched her husband storm around the living room of their suite, her expression a mask of sadness and resignation.

"Why are you yelling at me?" Nic demanded, pointing at Gabriel's princess. "She's the one who arranged to have a car take her to the airport."

It was shortly before lunch and Brooke's flight had departed Carone International over two hours prior. By now she would be over the Atlantic Ocean on her way to New York's JFK airport and her connecting flight to San Francisco.

"It's not my wife's fault that she was leaving in the first place. You were supposed to stop her before she ever got into the car." Gabriel raked his fingers through his hair in a gesture of acute frustration. "Do you realize what you've done?"

"I did what the country required of me."

Silence greeted his declaration, but Nic refused to feel bad that he'd at long last addressed the elephant in the room. He'd let Brooke get away because Gabriel hadn't acted in the country's best interest when he'd married Olivia.

"For the first time in your life," Gabriel shouted back. "How the hell do you think I felt having to carry the burden of responsibility for both you and Christian all these years? Maybe I would have enjoyed being an irresponsible playboy or playing at an impossible dream like building a rocket ship."

"Playing at—"

"Enough." Olivia's sharp tone sliced through the testosterone thickening the air and silenced both men. "Tossing accusations back and forth is not solving our immediate issue."

Gabriel was the first to back down. He turned to his wife and the love that glowed in his gaze made Nic's heart hurt.

"She's right." Gabriel's attention returned to his brother. "I know you were doing amazing things in California and I wish you were still there doing them. I really don't begrudge you any time you've spent chasing your dream."

Nic was seeing a different side of his brother. Never before had Gabriel spoken so eloquently about what he was feeling. The crown prince could speak passionately about issues relating to the country and he had a fine reputation for diplomacy, but he'd always been a closed book with regard to anything of a personal nature.

"I've lost my nerve." Since Gabriel felt comfortable sharing, Nic decided it was only fair to give a little in return. "Since the accident, I am afraid to even think about what went wrong with *Griffin*. Five years of my life went into designing the fuel delivery system that caused the rocket to blow up. I killed someone. There's no coming back from that for me." Nic's voice was thick with regret as he finished, "It's part of the reason I let Brooke go. Her life is in California and there's no place for me there anymore. I belong here where I can make a difference."

"Oh, Nic." Olivia was at his side, her soft hand gentle on his arm. "I'm sorry you are in so much pain. And what happened to your rocket and that man's death are a horrible tragedy, but you can't let that get in the way of your happiness with Brooke."

Gabriel grabbed his other arm and gave him a shake. "And you really don't belong here."

"Yes, I do. The country needs an heir to the throne." But his protest was cut short as Olivia and Gabriel shared a moment of intense nonverbal communication. "What's going on?"

Olivia shifted her gaze to Nic and offered him a sympathetic head tilt. "We can't get into specifics..."

"About what?" There was obviously an important secret being kept from him and Nic didn't like being left out.

The crown prince's lips quirked in a wry smile. "What if as the future leader of your country I order you to return to California, resume work on your rocket ship and marry the mother of your child?"

Nic spent a long moment grappling with his conscience. He'd come to grips with sacrificing his happiness for the sake of the country and although it had torn him apart to let Brooke go, he'd known it was for the greater good of Sherdana and his family.

Now, however, his brother was offering him a way out. No, Nic amended. Gabriel was directing him to forsake his duty and chase his dreams all the way back to California. The walls he'd erected to garrison his misery began to crumble. He sucked in a ragged breath. Permission to marry Brooke and raise their child with her. The chance to complete his dream of space travel. All on a silver platter compliments of his brother. It was too much.

But as he scrutinized Gabriel's confident posture and observed the secret smile that lit Olivia's eyes, he sensed that whatever was going on, these two were well in control of the country's future.

Nic offered Gabriel a low bow, his throat tight. "Naturally, I'd do whatever my crowned prince commands."

On her way to the Mojave Air and Space Port to visit her brother, Brooke took a familiar detour and drove past the house Nic had rented for the past three years. The place looked as deserted as ever. Nic hadn't spent much time there, sometimes not even sleeping in his own bed for days at a stretch because the couch in his workroom was within arm's reach of his project.

Still, when she could get him to take time off, they'd often had fun barbecuing in the backyard or drinking beer on the front porch while they stared at the stars and Nic opened up about what he and Glen hoped one day to accomplish.

Brooke stomped on the accelerator and her Prius picked up speed. Those days were behind her now that Nic was back in Sherdana, but at least she had the memories.

A ten-minute drive through town brought her to the hangar where Glen and his team were working on the new rocket. Brooke hadn't been here since the day Nic had broken off with her and she was surprised how little work had been done. From what Glen had told her, the inflow of cash hadn't dried up after the first *Griffin* had exploded. In fact, the mishap had alerted several new investors who'd promised funding for the project.

Brooke spent several minutes walking around the platform that held the skeleton of the *Griffin II*, her footsteps echoing around the empty hangar. She wasn't accustomed to this level of inactivity and wondered if she'd misunderstood her brother's text, asking her to meet him at the airfield rather than at his house.

As she made her way to the back of the facility where the workrooms and labs were set up, Brooke detected faint strains of music and figured her brother had gotten caught up in something and lost track of time. Except the music wasn't coming from Glen's office, but from Nic's former workroom.

The wave of sorrow that swarmed over her stopped Brooke in her tracks. Someone had obviously been hired to replace Nic on the team and had been given his office. The shock of it made her dizzy, but she quickly rationalized the unsteadiness away. How could she expect forward progress on the rocket without someone taking on the fuel delivery system Nic had abandoned? With the exception of her brother, no one else on the team could match Nic's brilliance or comprehend the intricacies of his design. Someone new would have to be brought in.

Brooke squared her shoulders and continued down the hallway. She might as well introduce herself to Nic's replacement and start to accept the changes that he'd bring to the team.

"Hi," she called over the music as she first knocked, and then pushed open the unlatched door. "I'm Brooke Davis, Glen's…" Her voice trailed away as the tall man in jeans and a black T-shirt turned to greet her.

"Sister," Nic finished for her. "He told me you might be stopping by today."

Brooke's throat tightened. "What are you doing here?"

"I work here." His smile—at once familiar and utterly different from anything she'd seen before—knocked the breath from her lungs.

"I don't understand." She sagged back against the door frame and drank in Nic's presence. His vibrant, imposing presence made it impossible for her to believe he was a hallucination, but she couldn't let herself trust this amazing turn of fortune until she knew what was going on. "I left you in Sherdana. You were going to get married and make Alessandro heirs."

Nic shook his head. "Turns out I was completely wrong for the job."

"How so?" His wry amusement was beginning to reach through her shock. She was starting to thaw out. The ice water that had filled her veins for the past week heated beneath his sizzling regard. "You're not impotent or something, are you?"

He laughed and reached out to snag her wrist, pulling her away from the wall and up against his hard body. "That was not the problem."

"Then what was?" She wrapped her arms around his neck and arched her back until they were aligned from chest to thigh.

"No one wanted me."

"I can't believe that." And she didn't. Not for a single second.

"It's true. Word got around that a spunky redhead had stolen my heart and left me but a shell of a man."

Brooke purred as he bent his head and nuzzled his lips into her neck. "So you've come here to take it back?"

"No. I've come here to sign it over all legal and such."

Fearing she'd misunderstood what he was saying, Brooke remained silent while her mind worked furiously. He'd left Sherdana and resumed his old position on the team. From the way his lips were exploring her neck, she was pretty sure he intended that their physical relationship would get back on track.

"Brooke?" He cupped her face and stared deep into her eyes. "You're awfully quiet."

"I guess I'm not sure what to say."

"You could start by saying yes."

Relief made her giddy. "You haven't asked me a question."

"You're right." And to her absolute delight, he dropped down on one knee and fished a ring out of his pocket. "Brooke Davis, love of my life and mother of my child, will you marry me?"

She set her hands on her hips and shook her head. "If this is about the baby, I assure you I'm not expecting you—"

"Oh, for heaven sakes," came an explosive shout from the hallway behind them. "Just tell the guy yes."

"Yes," she whispered, leaning down to plant her lips on Nic's.

He wrapped his arms around her and shot to his feet, lifting her into the air and spinning her in circles. She laughed, delirious with joy, and hugged him back. When he let her toes touch the floor once more, Glen was there to pound Nic on the back and offer his congratulations.

Amidst this, Nic slipped an enormous diamond ring onto her left hand. She ogled it while Glen played the brother card and threatened Nic with bodily harm if he didn't take good care of her. Then Glen left her and Nic alone so he could fill her in on what had transpired after she'd left.

"Gabriel almost killed me when he heard that you'd left," Nic explained, sitting on his couch and pulling her onto his lap.

She let her head fall onto his shoulder and savored the contentment that wove through her. "He did?"

"Apparently he decided to play matchmaker and wasn't particularly happy that I failed to do my part."

"Matchmaker?"

"He made sure we were in adjoining rooms in the visitors' wing of the palace and enlisted Olivia and Ariana to convince you not to give up on us."

"They did a pretty good job of that," Brooke agreed, thinking about that last night she'd spent with Nic. "In fact, I almost left without seeing you one final time, but both of them convinced me I owed it to us to say goodbye." But there was something she still didn't understand. "And we did. I left and you didn't stop me. You were determined to do the honorable thing and stay in Sherdana and get married. So what's changed?"

"Two things. First, I thought long and hard about what made me happy. Spending the rest of my life with you and my work. But I couldn't marry you without regretting that I'd decided not to step up when my family needed me and I couldn't see returning to the *Griffin* project when my design had caused a man's death."

"And yet you're here," Brooke pointed out.

"I didn't accept I couldn't live without you until I had to start."

"But what about Sherdana and producing an heir?"

"Gabriel released me from duty. Before I left he explained how it had nearly destroyed him to lose Olivia and he refused to let me go through the same sort of pain."

"But what about an heir for the throne?"

"I guess it's up to Christian."

"And you don't feel bad that he has to carry the full burden of the country's future on his shoulders?" Brooke arched her eyebrow at Nic's poor attempt to conceal a grin.

"If he had to choose between the woman of his dreams and duty to Sherdana, I'd feel horrible." Nic brushed Brooke's hair aside and kissed his way down her neck. "But he's never dated any woman long enough to fall in love and it's time he let someone in."

"Et benedetto il primo dolce affanno ch'i' ebbi ad esser con Amor congiunto."

Nic translated, "And blessed be the first sweet agony I suffered when I found myself bound to Love." He grazed his lips against Brooke's, making her sigh in pleasure. "I only hope the woman who finally breaks through to Christian makes him half as happy as you've made me."

Heart singing, Brooke wrapped her arms around Nic's neck and set her forehead against his. His gaze fastened on hers, letting her glimpse his joy and his need for her. For the first time she truly understood the depth of Nic's love for her. He'd made light of his decision to leave Sherdana, but she suspected even though Gabriel had released him from duty, the king and queen hadn't backed either of their sons' actions.

"I haven't begun to make you happy," she promised, tightening her hold.

"You don't say."

"I do say." And she proceeded to demonstrate how she planned to start.

* * * * *

Adam traced his fingers up and down her spine as Melanie leaned into him.

He was drawn back into the memory of having her in his apartment, the way she felt in his arms. Her words from that night came rushing back. *You feel like a dream.*

"I shouldn't have hugged you. It was unprofessional."

"I thought we were taking a break from professional."

She reared her shoulders back and looked him in the eye. "Are you going to let me go?"

"As near as I can tell, you're holding on to me just as tight."

She rolled her eyes—childish from most women, adorable from Melanie. "I'm trying to keep myself upright."

He was certain he'd heard every word she'd said, but her lips were so tempting and pouty that it was hard to grasp details. "Then stop being upright."

Before Melanie knew what was happening, Adam was kissing her. And like a fool, she kissed him right back.

THAT NIGHT
WITH THE CEO

BY
KAREN BOOTH

Published in Great Britain 2015
by Mills & Boon, an imprint of Harlequin (UK) Limited,
Eton House, 18-24 Paradise Road, Richmond, Surrey, TW9 1SR

© 2015 Karen Balcom

ISBN: 978-0-263-25274-3

51-0815

Harlequin (UK) Limited's policy is to use papers that are natural, renewable and recyclable products and made from wood grown in sustainable forests. The logging and manufacturing processes conform to the legal environmental regulations of the country of origin.

Printed and bound in Spain
by CPI, Barcelona

Karen Booth is a Midwestern girl transplanted in the South, raised on '80s music, Judy Blume and the films of John Hughes. She loves to write big-city love stories. When she takes a break from the art of romance, she's teaching her kids about good music, honing her Southern cooking skills or sweet-talking her supersupportive husband into mixing up a cocktail. You can learn more about Karen at www.karenbooth.net.

For Bobbi Ruggiero and Patience Bloom.
We share an unbreakable bond—the sisterhood
that comes from loving John Taylor for more than
thirty years. Now, let's arm wrestle for him.

One

Women had done some nutty things to get to Adam Langford, but Melanie Costello was going for a world record. Adam watched on the security camera as her car pulled through the gate in the most relentless rain he'd seen in the four years since he'd purchased his mountain estate. "I'll be damned," he mumbled, shaking his head.

Thunder boomed.

His dog, Jack, nudged his hand, whimpering.

"I know, buddy. Only a crazy person would drive up here in this weather."

The hair on his arms stood up, but the electricity in the air wasn't from thunderstorms. The anticipation of seeing Melanie for the second time in his life left him off-kilter. She'd done a number on him a year ago, giving him the most consuming night of passion he could remember and then slipping out the door before he awoke. There'd been no goodbye whispered into his ear, no nudge to wake him for a parting kiss. All she'd left behind was a memory he couldn't shake and countless questions, the most pressing of which was whether she'd ever make him feel that alive again.

He hadn't even known her last name until a week ago, not that he hadn't tried like hell to figure it out after she disappeared. No, it had taken a personal nightmare of monstrous proportions—a tabloid scandal that refused to die—to bring Melanie Costello to him. Now she was here to save his ass from the gossip rags, even though he doubted anyone could do that. If any other public relations person had been given this job, he would've found a way out of it, but this was his chance to capture lightning in a bottle. He had no intention of passing that up, even if he also had no intention of letting the lightning know that he remembered her. He wanted to hear her say it. Then he would get his answers.

The doorbell rang and Adam made his way over to the fireplace, jabbing at the smoldering logs. He stood before the flames, staring into them as he polished off his small-batch bourbon. He was needled by guilt, knowing Melanie was standing outside, but she could wait to begin the reformation of his public image. She'd been in such a hurry to leave him alone in his bed. She could sit tight for a few minutes before he'd let her in.

It was just Melanie Costello's luck that she'd end up regretting the best sex of her life. As recently as a week ago, her one night with Adam Langford was her delicious secret, a tingly memory that made her chest flutter whenever she thought about it, and she thought about it a lot. The phone call from Adam's father, Roger—the call that required a confidentiality agreement before they could speak a single word—had put an end to that. Now the flutter in her chest had sunk to her stomach and felt more like an elbow to the ribs.

Melanie parked her rental car in the circular driveway of Adam Langford's sprawling mountain retreat. Tucked away on a huge parcel of land atop a mountain outside Asheville, North Carolina, the rustic manor, complete with tall-peaked roofs and redwood arches, was lit up in spectacular fashion against the darkening night sky. She couldn't have been any more impressed or intimidated.

Cold smacked her in the face as she wrestled her umbrella, her pumps skating over the flagstone driveway. *I'm the only woman boneheaded enough to wear four-inch heels in a monsoon.* She bound her black raincoat against her body, shuffling to a grand sweep of stone stairs. Icy raindrops pelted her feet, the wind whipped, her cheeks burned. Lightning crackled across the sky. The storm was far worse now than it'd been when she'd left the airport, but the most daunting assignment of her public relations career, retooling Adam Langford's public image, required prompt attention.

She scaled the staircase, gripping the rail, juggling her purse and a tote bag weighed down with books on corporate image. She eyed the door expectantly. Surely someone would rush to usher her inside, away from the cold and rain. Someone had opened the gate. Someone had to be waiting.

No welcoming party appeared at the towering wood door, so she rang the bell. Every passing second felt like an eternity as her feet turned to blocks of ice and the cold seeped through her coat. *Don't shiver.* Once she caught a chill, it took her forever to warm up. Imagining the man waiting for her, Adam Langford himself, only made her more certain she'd never stop trembling if she started.

Memories flashed, of one glass of champagne, then two, while watching Adam across a crowded suite at The Park Hotel on Madison Avenue. Perfectly unshaven, he wore a slim-cut gray suit that flaunted his trim physique so well that it had made her want to forget every etiquette lesson she'd ever learned. The party had been the hottest invitation in New York, held to celebrate the launch of Adam's latest venture, AdLab, a software developer. Prodigy, genius, visionary—Adam had been given countless labels since he earned his fortune with the headline-grabbing sale of social media website ChatterBack, all before he graduated summa cum laude from Harvard Business School. Melanie had snagged an invitation hoping to network with potential clients. Instead, she did the last thing she'd ever imagined, going home with the man of the hour, who had one more notable label on his résumé: notorious philanderer.

He'd been so smooth with his approach, building heat with eye contact as he wound his way through the bustling room. By the time he'd reached her, the notion of introductions seemed absurd. Everyone in the room knew who he was. Melanie was a virtual nobody in comparison, so he'd asked for her name, and she'd answered that it was Mel. Nobody called her Mel.

He'd held on to her hand when he shook it, commenting that she was the highlight of the party. She blushed and was immediately sucked into the vortex of Adam Langford, a place where sexy glances and clever quips reigned supreme. The next thing she knew, they were in the back of his limo headed to his penthouse apartment while his hand artfully slid beneath the hem of her dress and his lips roamed the landscape of her neck.

Now that she would again be in the presence of the man who'd electrified her from her pedicure to her last hair follicle, a man from a powerful Manhattan family and who had no lack of money or good looks or mental acumen, she couldn't help but feel queasy. If Adam recognized her, the "absolute discretion" his father had demanded would fly right out the window. There was nothing discreet about having slept with the man whose bad-boy public image she'd been hired to overhaul. Adam's reputation for one-night stands had certainly contributed to the wildfire nature of the tabloid scandal. She shuddered at the thought. Adam was her only one-night stand, ever.

It seemed rude to ring the bell a second time, but she was freezing her butt off. The sooner she and Adam got the first chunk of work done tonight, the sooner she could be in her pj's, warm and toasty under the comforter at her hotel. She pressed the button again, just as the latch clicked.

Adam Langford opened the door, wearing a navy and white plaid shirt, sleeves rolled to the elbows, showing off his muscled forearms. Jeans completed his look, an appealing contrast to the suit she'd last seen him wear. "Ms. Costello, I presume? I'm shocked you made it. Did you pick up a canoe at the airport?" He held the door with one hand while the other raked through his thick chestnut-brown hair.

She laughed nervously. "I upgraded to the fan boat."

Melanie's heart was a jackrabbit thumping against her chest. Adam's steely-blue eyes, edged with absurdly dark lashes, made her feel so exposed, naked. She knew full well that other aspects of his manner could make her feel the same way.

He smirked, welcoming her inside with a nod. "I'm sorry if you had to wait. I had to put my dog in the other room. He'll charge at you if he doesn't know you."

She averted her gaze. There was no way she'd sustain another direct hit from his eyes so soon. She held out her hand to shake his, which was impossibly warm. "Mr. Langford. Nice to see you." She'd stopped short of saying "*meet* you," since that would've been a big fat lie. When she'd accepted this job, she'd rationalized that Adam kept company with countless women. How could he possibly remember all of them? Plus, she'd lopped off her hair and gone from dishwater blond to golden since their tryst.

"Please, call me Adam." He shut the door, mercifully cutting off the cold. "Did you have any problems finding the place in the rain?"

He'd greeted her with the niceties you reserve for a stranger, and for the first time since he'd opened the door, she felt as though it was okay to breathe. *He doesn't remember me.* Perhaps it was okay to make eye contact again. "Oh, no. No problem at all." The complexity in his eyes held her frozen, stuck in the memory of what it had felt like the first time he looked at her, when he seemed to be saying that she was all he wanted. Those eyes were enough to leave her tongue-tied. "Piece of cake." Apparently they also made her want to lie, as she'd just spent two hours squinting through a foggy windshield and cursing the GPS.

"Please, let me take your coat."

"Oh, yes. Thank you." This wasn't what she'd expected. Adam Langford had enough money to hire an assistant for someone to take her coat. She fumbled with the buttons and turned herself out of it. "No hired help up here in the mountains?"

He hung her coat in a closet and she took that millisecond to smooth her black dress pants and retuck her gray silk blouse. After the long, stressful drive from the airport, she had to be a wreck.

"I have a housekeeper and a cook, but I sent them home hours ago. I wouldn't want them out on the roads."

"I know I'm a few hours late, but we really need to stay on schedule. If we can go over the media plan tonight, we can devote the entire day tomorrow to interview preparation." She reached into her bag and removed the books she'd brought.

He blew out a deep breath and took them, examining

the spines. *"Crafting Your Image in the Corporate World*? You can't be serious. People read this?"

"It's a fabulous book."

"Sounds like a real page-turner." He shook his head. "Let's take this into the living room. I could use a drink."

Adam led her down a far-reaching hall and into a cathedral-like great room with redwood-beamed ceilings. A sprawling sectional and leather chairs made an inviting seating area, softly lit by a dimmed wrought iron chandelier and a blazing fire. Floor-to-ceiling windows spanned the far wall, animated by raindrops pattering the panes against the backdrop of the gray evening sky.

"Your house is stunning. I can see why you'd come here to get away."

"I love New York, but you can't beat the quiet and the mountain air. It's one of the only places I can take a break from work." Adam rubbed his neck, stretching the shirt taut across his athletic chest, showing her a peek of dark chest hair her fingers had once been wonderfully tangled in. "Although apparently, work somehow managed to find me."

Melanie forced a smile. "Don't think of it as work. We're fixing a problem."

"I don't want to insult your profession, but isn't it tiring spending your day worrying about what other people think? Molding public opinion? I'm not sure why you bother. The media says whatever they want to. They couldn't care less about the truth."

"I think of it as fighting fire with fire." She knew that Adam would be a difficult case. He hated the press, which made the persistent nature of what was now known as the Party Princess scandal much worse.

"Frankly, the whole thing seems like a colossal waste of money, and I can only assume that my father is paying you a lot of it."

But you wouldn't want to insult my profession. She pursed her lips. "Your father is paying me well. That should tell you how important this is to him." As annoyed as she was by Adam's diatribe, the retainer from his father was greater than she'd make from her other clients combined this month. Costello Public Relations was growing, but as Adam had alluded to, it was a business built on appearances. That meant a posh office space and an impeccable wardrobe, which did not come cheap.

A bark came from the far side of the kitchen, the door beyond the Sub-Zero fridge.

Adam glanced over his shoulder. "Are you okay with dogs? I put him in the mudroom, but he'd really rather be where the action is."

"Oh, sure." She nodded, placing her things on a side table. "What's your dog's name?" She already knew the answer, and that Adam's dog was a sweet two-hundred-pound hulk—a Mastiff and Great Dane mix.

"His name is Jack. I'll warn you. He's intimidating, but he'll be fine once he gets used to you. The first meeting is always the roughest."

Jack yelped again. Adam opened the door. The dog barreled past him, skidding on the hardwood floors, taking the turn for the great room. Jack thundered toward Melanie.

"Jack! No!" Adam may have yelled at the dog, but he made no other attempt to stop him.

Jack sat back on his haunches and slid into her. Immediately, Melanie had a cold dog nose rooting around in the palm of her hand. Jack whacked his sizable tail against her thigh.

She hadn't bargained on Adam's dog ratting her out by revealing that they shared a past, too. "He's friendly."

Adam narrowed his stare. "That's so strange. He's never done that with anyone he's never met. Ever."

Melanie shrugged, averting her eyes and scratching

behind Jack's ears. "Maybe he senses that I'm a dog person." *Or maybe Jack and I hung out in your kitchen before I left your apartment in the middle of the night.*

The only sound Melanie could hear were Jack's heavy breaths as Adam stepped closer, clearly appraising her. It made her so nervous, she had to say something. "We should get started. It'll probably take me a while to get back to my hotel."

"I'm still not sure how you got up the mountain, but you aren't getting back down it anytime soon." He nodded toward the great room windows. It was raining sideways. "There have been reports of flash floods in the foothills."

"I'm a good driver. It'll be fine." She really was nothing more than a skittish driver. Living in New York meant taxis and town cars. She kept her license valid only for business trips.

"No car can handle a flood. I have room for you to stay. I insist."

Staying was the problem. Every moment she and Adam spent together was another chance for him to remember her, and then she'd have a lot of explaining to do. This might not be a great idea, but she didn't have much choice. She wouldn't get any work done if she was lost at sea. "That would give me one less thing to worry about. Thank you."

"I'll show you to one of the guest rooms."

"I'd prefer we just get to work. Then I can turn in early and we can get a fresh start in the morning." She took a pair of binders from her bag. "Do you have an office where we can work?"

"I was thinking the kitchen. I'll open a bottle of wine. We might as well enjoy ourselves." He strode around the kitchen island and removed wineglasses from the cabinet below.

Melanie lugged her materials to the marble center

island, taking a seat on one of the tall upholstered bar stools. "I shouldn't, but thank you." She flipped open the binders and slid one in front of the seat next to hers.

"You're missing out. Chianti from a small winery in Tuscany. You can't get this wine anywhere except maybe in the winemaker's living room." He cranked on the bottle opener.

Melanie closed her eyes and prayed for strength. Drinking wine with Adam had once led down a road she couldn't revisit. "I'll have a taste." She stopped him at half a glass. "Thank you. That's perfect." The first sip took the edge off, spreading warmth throughout her body—an ill-advised reaction, given her drinking buddy.

Jack wandered by and stopped next to her, plopping his enormous head down on her lap.

No. No. You don't like me. Melanie squirmed, hoping to discourage Jack. No such luck.

Adam set down his glass, his eyebrows drawing together. "I swear, Miss Costello. Something about you is so familiar."

Two

"People say that I have a familiar face." Melanie's voice held a nervous squeak. She turned and practically buried her face in her project binder.

Adam considered himself an expert at deciphering the underlying message in a woman's words, but he was especially fluent in coy deflection. *I can't believe she's going to try to hide this.* "Have you done any work for me?"

She shrugged and scanned her blessed notebook. "I would've remembered that."

Time to turn up the heat. "Have we dated?"

She hesitated. "No. We haven't dated."

To be fair, she might have him on a technicality there. They hadn't *really* been on a date. He scoured his brain for another leading question. "Do I detect an accent?" A slight twang had colored the word *dated*.

She screwed up her lips and sat straighter, still refusing to make eye contact, which was a real shame. Her crystalline blue eyes were lovely—plus, he'd be able to tell if she was being deceitful. "I grew up in Virginia."

"I met a woman from Virginia at a party once. She was a real firecracker. Maybe a little bit crazy. If only I could remember what her name was." He rubbed his chin, took another sip of wine, rounding to the other side of the kitchen island and taking the seat next to hers. Jack hadn't moved, standing sentry at her hip. *That's right, buddy. You know her.*

"I'm sure it's difficult to keep track of all of the people you meet." She pointed to a page titled "Schedule" in his notebook. "So, the interviews…"

He scanned the page, getting lost in a confusion of publication names and details. "No wonder my assistant was panicked this afternoon." He flipped through the pages. "I generally work eighteen-hour days. When exactly am I supposed to find time for this?"

"Your assistant said she'll rearrange your schedule. Most interviews and photo shoots will take place at your home or office. I'll do everything I can to make sure your needs are met."

Right now, his greatest need was to seek comfort in a second bourbon as soon as he'd dispatched the Chianti. Continuing this charade held zero appeal, and her refusal to own up to their past was frustrating as hell. He needed the question that had been hanging over his head for the past year to be answered. How could a woman share an extraordinary night of passion with him and then disappear? Even more important, *why* would she do that?

"For the moment, the biggest interview is with *Metropolitan Style* magazine," she continued. "They're doing a feature on you and your home, so that will entail a photo shoot. I'm bringing in a professional home stager to make sure that the decor is picture-perfect. Jack will need to see a groomer before then, but I'll take care of that."

Adam bristled at the idea of home stagers messing with his apartment, but no one decided what happened with his dog. "Jack hates groomers. You have to hire my guy, and he's always booked weeks out." Of course, his groomer would make himself available whenever Adam needed him, but it was the principle.

"I'll do my best, but if he isn't available, I'll have to hire someone. Jack is important. People love dogs. It will cast you in a more favorable light."

"How did you know I have a dog anyway?"

She cleared her throat. "I asked your assistant."

She had a roundabout answer for everything. He'd never endure an entire weekend of talking in circles. "What if I didn't already have a dog? What would you do then? Rent one?"

"I do whatever is needed to make my clients look good."

"But it's all a lie. Lies catch up with you eventually."

Dropping her pen down onto the notebook, Melanie took a deep breath. She rolled up the sleeves of her silky blouse with a determination that made him wonder if she wanted to flatten him.

"The home stager is a waste of time," he added. "My apartment is perfect."

"We need it to look like a *home* in the photographs, not a bachelor pad."

He saw his chance. She knew what his apartment looked like, but only because he'd seduced her in it. "So I have to get rid of my neon beer sign collection? Those things are everywhere." He hadn't owned one of those since college, but he wouldn't hesitate to fabricate absurdities to get her to spill it.

She twisted her lips. "We can work around that."

He had to up the bachelor-pad ante. "Now, what about the stuffed moose head above the mantel? Does that scream single guy or does that just say that I'm manly?" That was hardly his taste either, and she knew it.

"I don't know." She rubbed her temple. "This isn't really my area of expertise. Can we come back to this later?" Melanie clenched a fist, waves of frustration radiating from her.

"No. I want to get this straightened out now." His mind raced. His goal in sight, he was prepared to crank out crazy ideas for hours. "There are the beer taps in the kitchen, and I need to know if they'll photograph my bedroom. I have a round bed, like in James Bond movies."

"That's ridiculous."

"Why? Lots of men have moose heads and James Bond beds."

"But you don't," she blurted.

The color drained from her face, but that gorgeous mouth of hers was just as rosy pink as he'd remembered. Just thinking about her lips traveling down the centerline of his chest charged every atom in his body. She didn't say another thing, but he swore he could hear her heartbeat, drumming between her heavy breaths.

"How would you know?" he asked, wishing he felt more triumphant at having caught her.

She straightened in her seat, struggling to compose herself. "Uh…"

"I'm waiting."

"Waiting for what, exactly?"

"Waiting to hear the real reason why you know I have a dog and what my apartment looks like. I'm waiting for you to just say it, *Mel*."

Melanie's shoulders drooped under the burden of her own idiocy. Her mother had always been emphatic that a lady never lies. Melanie had already skirted the truth, and she didn't want to be that person. "You remember me."

"Of course I do. Did you honestly think that I wouldn't?"

His disbelief made her want to shrink into nothingness. How could she have been so foolish? "Considering your reputation with women, I figured I was a blip on the map."

"I never forget a woman."

His response might have prompted extreme skepticism if he hadn't said it with such conviction. He hadn't forgotten her. She knew for a fact that she hadn't forgotten him. Of course, there were probably lots of other women he hadn't forgotten, too.

"You changed your hair," he said.

Her pulse chose a tempo like free-form jazz—stopping and starting. He really did notice everything. "Yes, I cut it."

"The color's different. See, I still remember what it looked like splayed across the pillows of my bed." He rose from his seat and stalked back around the kitchen island, refilling his wineglass. Plainly still angry, he didn't offer her more. "Did you really not see a problem with taking this job even though we'd slept together? I'm assuming you didn't reveal that little tidbit to my father. Because if you had, he never would've hired you."

Adam was absolutely right. She'd stepped into a gray area a mile wide, but she needed the payday that came with this job. Her former business partner had crippled her company by leaving and sticking her with an astronomical office lease. The crushing part was that he'd also been her boyfriend—nearly her fiancé—and he'd left because he'd fallen in love with one of their clients.

"I would hope we could be discreet about this. I think it's best if we just acknowledge that it was a one-time thing, keep it between us, and not allow it to affect our working relationship." Mustering a rational string of words calmed her ragged nerves, but only a bit.

"One-time thing? Is that what that was? Because you don't seem like a woman who runs around Manhattan picking up men she doesn't know. Trust me, I meet those women all the time."

Did it bother him that it had been a one-night stand? She wasn't proud of the fact either, but she never imagined it would even faze Adam. "I didn't mean to say it like that."

"What about the contract my father had you sign? The clause about no fraternization between you and the client?"

"Exactly why I thought it best to ignore our past. I need this job and you need to clean up your image. It's a win-win."

"So you need the job. This is about money."

"Yes. I need it. Your father is a very powerful man, and having a recommendation from him could do big things for my company." Why she'd put her entire hand out on the table for him to see was beyond her, but she wasn't going to sugarcoat anything.

"What if I told you that I don't want to do this?"

She swallowed, hard. Adam was doing nothing more than setting up roadblocks, and they were becoming formidable. If he wanted to, he could end her job right then and there, send her packing. All she could do now was make her case. "Look, I understand that you're mad. The scandal is horrible and I didn't make things any better by hoping that you wouldn't recognize me. That was stupid on my part, and I'm sorry. But if you're looking for a reason to go through with this, you don't need to look any further than your dad. He's not just worried about his company and your family's reputation. He's worried about what this will do to your career. He doesn't want your talents to be overshadowed by tabloid stories."

Dead quiet settled on the room. Adam seemed deep in reflection. "I appreciate the apology."

"Thank you for accepting it." Had she finally laid this to rest? She took a deep breath and hoped so.

"And yes, it was incredibly stupid on your part. I'd go so far as to call it harebrained."

There went the instant of newfound calm, just as Melanie's stomach growled so loudly that Adam's eyes grew as large as dinner plates.

"Excuse me," she mumbled, horrified, wrapping one arm around her midsection to muffle the sound.

"Coming up with bad ideas must've made you very hungry."

"Very funny. I'm fine." She shifted in her seat, mad at herself for not owning up to the fact that she would've killed for a day-old doughnut. Her stomach chimed in, as well.

"I can't listen to that anymore," he declared. "It's unsettling." He marched to the fridge and opened it, pulling out a covered glass bowl. "My cook made marinara before I sent her home. It'll take a few minutes to make pasta."

"Let me help." Desperate for the distraction of a new topic, she shot out of her bar stool and walked to the other side of the island. Jack followed in her wake.

"Help with what? Boiling water?" He cast her an incredulous smirk. "Sit."

"Are you talking to me or Jack?"

He cracked half a smile and she felt a little as if *she* might crack. In half. "You. Jack can do whatever he wants."

"Of course." She filed back to her seat and watched as he filled a tall pot with water and placed it on the six-burner cooktop. "Careful or I might have to book you an appearance on the Food Network."

"You should see me make breakfast." He sprinkled salt into the water then placed a saucepan on the stove and lit the flame beneath it. "I could've made you my world-famous scrambled eggs if you hadn't done your Cinderella routine that night and taken off."

The man had no fear of uncomfortable subjects. What was she supposed to say to that?

"Care to comment, Cinderella?"

"I'm sorry." She cleared her throat and picked at her fingernail. "I couldn't stay."

Adam spooned the sauce into the pan, shaking his head. "That's a horrible excuse."

Excuse or not, there was no way she could've stayed. She couldn't bear the rejection of Adam running her off the next morning. She couldn't bear to hear that he'd call her when she knew that he wouldn't. She'd already suffered one soul-crushing brush-off that month, from the guy she'd thought she would marry. The pain of a second would've prompted the question of whether she might make a good nun. "I'm sorry, but it's the truth."

Wisps of steam rose from the pot, and the aroma of tomato sauce filled the air. Adam dropped in a package of fresh pasta and gave it a stir. "All I'm wondering is why you wouldn't stick around when you have that kind of chemistry with someone. At least say goodbye or leave a note. I didn't even know your last name."

When he had the nerve to say it out loud—to be so rational about it—it sounded as if she'd done the most insane thing ever. *Wait. Chemistry?* She'd assumed that what she'd felt was mostly one-sided, a lethal combination of champagne and Mr. Smooth. Regret and embarrassment weighed on her equally. What if she'd stuck around? Would he have said what he was saying now? "Hopefully you can find a way to forgive me."

He narrowed his gaze, eyes locking on hers. "Maybe someday you'll tell me the real reason."

Oh, no, that's not going to happen.

The timer buzzed. Adam gripped the pot handles with a kitchen towel and emptied the contents into the prep sink. Steam rushed up around his face and he blew a strand of hair from his forehead. He slung the towel over his shoulder, capable as could be, adding the noodles to the sauté pan and giving the mixture a toss with a flick of his wrist. The most brilliant man to hit the business world in recent history, the man who'd given her the most exhilarating night of her life, was toiling away in the kitchen. For her.

Adam divided the pasta into two bowls and grated fresh Parmesan on top. He set one bowl before her and filled her wineglass then topped off his own. Tempting smells wafted to her nose, relief from her epic hunger in reach. He took his seat, saddling her with a return of nerves. Now that they were shoulder to shoulder again, she was acutely aware of the specter of Adam Langford.

"Cheers," he said in a tone still more annoyed than cheery. He extended his arm and clinked her glass with his.

"Thank you. This looks incredible." She took a bite. It was far better than her usual Friday night fare, Chinese takeout on the couch. She dabbed at her mouth with the napkin. "This is delicious. Thank you." Quieting her rumbling stomach was wonderful, but they hadn't resolved the greater issue—she still wasn't sure he was willing to let her do her job. "Now that we've talked through things, are we okay to get to work tomorrow? We need to bury the Party Princess scandal."

"Can we put a ban on saying that? No man wants a scandal, but the princess part just makes it worse."

"I know it's awful. That's precisely why I'm here. I can make all of that go away."

"I don't see why we can't just ignore it. Aren't we feeding the fire if we go on the defensive?"

"If we had a year or more, that might work, but with your father's illness, there just isn't that kind of time. I'm so sorry to say that. I really wish that part was for a different reason."

"So you know. The timetable." Adam blew out a deep breath and set down his fork.

Her heart went out to him. She could only imagine what he was going through, about to ascend to the immensely powerful job he'd likely dreamed of since he was a boy, all because his father's cancer was terminal. "Yes. He told me in confidence. I think he needed me to understand just how urgent this is. It's crucial that the board of directors see you in a better light so they'll approve your appointment to CEO. The scandal needs to be a distant memory by the time the succession is formally announced at the company gala. That's only a few weeks away."

"The board of directors. Good luck with that." He shook his head, just as his phone rang. "I'm sorry. I have to take this."

"Of course."

Adam got up from his seat and walked into the living room. Melanie was thankful for a break from persuading him that she could do this. Even if he cooperated, the pressure of turning around public perception in a month was monumental. She wasn't entirely sure she could pull it off. She only knew that she had to.

"I'm so sorry," he said, when he got off the phone. "Problems with the launch of a new app next week."

"Please don't apologize. I understand." Melanie got up and took her dish to the sink. She rinsed it and put it in the dishwasher. "You should finish your dinner. I'm going to grab my suitcase and get some rest. If you could point me in the direction of the guest room."

"Call me old-fashioned, but no woman should have to go out in the rain for a suitcase. I'll do it." He held up a finger, just as she was about to protest. "I insist."

She watched from the doorway as he braved the rain and wind without a jacket. His hair and shirt were soaked by the time he was back inside. He stomped on the entryway rug and combed his fingers through his dripping-wet hair. Her mind flashed to their night together—stepping out of the shower with him, sinking into the softest bath-mat she'd ever felt beneath her feet. He'd raked his hand through his soaked locks, a sultry look in his eyes that said he was ready to claim her again. He'd coiled his arms around her naked waist, pressed his hands into her back, and kissed her neck so delicately that she'd trembled be-neath his touch.

She might faint if she ever saw him toy with his wet hair again.

"Your room is upstairs. Second door on the right."

Adam trailed behind her as she climbed the grand stair-case.

"This one?" she asked, poking her head inside, still a bit light-headed from the memory of the shower.

Adam reached past her and flipped on the light, illumi-nating a bedroom outfitted with a beautifully dressed king bed, a stacked stone fireplace and its own seating area. "I hope this will work." He followed her into the room, placing her suitcase on a luggage stand next to a gorgeous Craftsman-style bureau.

"It's perfect." Melanie turned to face him, his physical presence exercising undue influence on her as he rubbed the closely cropped stubble dotting his jawline. Her brain wasn't sure how to react to his kindness, but her body knew exactly what it thought. The flutter in her chest returned. Heat flooded her, the memory of his fingers tracing the length of her spine while he had her in a bed much like the one she was standing next to. "Thank you for everything. The room. Fetching my suitcase."

"I hate to disappoint you, but I'm not the cad the world thinks I am." He strode past her, stopping in the doorway.

She wasn't sure what Adam was, where exactly the truth lay. Maybe she'd find out this weekend. And maybe she'd never know. "That's good. That will make it a lot easier to show the world the best side of Adam Langford."

A clever smirk crossed his face. "You've seen me naked, so I'd say you're definitely qualified to say which is my best side."

Melanie's brain sputtered. Her cheeks flamed with heat.

"Good night," he said, turning and walking away.

Three

Melanie sat up in bed, half-awake, tugging the butter-soft duvet to her chest. Last night hadn't gone according to plan, but in many ways, it was a relief to have the whole, stupid, ridiculously hot thing out in the open.

It'd taken hours to fall asleep. Adam's reminder that she'd seen him naked had only set her on the course of determining which side was indeed his best. After revisiting their night together…kissing in the limo, unzipping her dress in his living room, peeling the paint off the walls in the shower…she'd decided the front. Definitely the front.

Too bad she could never see him like that again.

She threw back the covers and glanced outside at the open vista of the grounds surrounding the house. A creek rushed along the edge of manicured gardens, threatening to breach its rocky banks. Towering pines framed the view of the Blue Ridge Mountains beyond. It was a new day, storms a distant memory. Time to start fresh.

She retrieved her makeup bag, beelining to the beautifully appointed guest bath—gray granite countertops and silvery glass tile, a soaking tub for two. After a quick shower, she dabbed on foundation and undereye concealer to hide her lack of sleep. A sweep of blush, some eyeliner and a coat of mascara came next. Polished was appropriate, not done-up.

Finishing with a sheer layer of pale peach lip gloss, Melanie rubbed her lips together and popped them to the mirror. She could hear her mother's syrupy Virginia drawl. *You catch more flies with honey than vinegar.* She remembered first hearing that when she was a little girl, only six years old. It was the strongest memory she had of her mother, which also made it the most bittersweet. She and her sisters lost her to a car accident months later.

Melanie ruffled her pixie-cut hair and swept it to the side. Lopping off and dying her hair to exorcise the memory of her lying, cheating ex might have been drastic, but she'd had this crazy idea about renewal. It hadn't really worked. She still hadn't gotten past the fact that she'd thought Josh would propose. She hadn't forgotten that he'd packed up and left with another woman, leaving her to fend for herself. No, she might've looked a little different on the outside, but she was the same Melanie on the inside—hurt some of the time, lonely most of the time, determined not to quit all of the time.

Back in her room, she slipped on a white scoop-neck tee, black cardigan and slim-fitting pair of jeans. She stepped into ballet flats and hurried downstairs, the smell of coffee wafting in from the kitchen. She was invigorated, undaunted, ready to go. And then she saw Adam.

You've got to be kidding me. She'd come downstairs prepared to work, but she hadn't bargained on Adam's bare chest. Or his bare stomach. Or an extra eight hours of scruff along his jaw and the narrow trail of hair below his belly button. More than that, she hadn't bargained on any part of him glistening with sweat.

"Morning." He stood in the kitchen, consulting his phone. "I made coffee. Let me get you a mug." He turned, opened the cabinet and reached for a coffee cup. Gentlemanly behavior, all while showing off the sculpted contours of his shoulders and defined ripples of his back.

Her eyes drifted south, calling into question whether the front really was the best. The way he filled out the rear view of his basketball shorts made a compelling case for the back. Then she remembered what that view looked like without clothes. She was all kinds of conflicted over the best-side verdict.

"Cream? Sugar?" he asked, filling her mug.

"Both, please." She shook her head in an attempt to think straight. "I'll do it."

"Help yourself." He gestured to a small white pitcher and sugar bowl. "Sleep well?"

She spooned the sugar into the mug, gluing her focus to the steaming coffee. "I did, thank you. I'm ready to get started whenever you are. We have a lot of ground to cover today."

"Already got in my workout."

"So I see." She turned, but even a fraction of a second was too long to look at Adam right now. Her eyes darted all over the room, desperate for something undesirable to look at.

"Is something wrong?"

"No. It's just…" Her voice trailed off, betraying her. "You can't put on a shirt?"

"Why? Does it bother you? I can't help the fact that I'm hot." He grabbed her attention with his blazing smile, smoothing his hand over the flat plane of his stomach.

"Excuse me?"

"Hot, as in temperature hot."

Damn him. "It's a little difficult for us to keep things professional when you're traipsing around the house half-dressed."

"I assure you, I have never once traipsed."

"Regardless, isn't it polite to wear a shirt to breakfast?"

"It is. My mother always made me wear one when I was a kid. She also told me to floss every day and wear clean underwear. So I'll be two-for-three today. Nobody's perfect."

He knows what he's doing. He's making me crazy because he can. "Look, we have a ton of work to do. I suggest you grab a shower so we can start."

"It'll go faster if I have someone to scrub my back."

"Adam, please. The contract I signed? No fraternization or interpersonal relations? I take those things very seriously, and I know your dad does, too."

"We both know the only way to enforce that is the honor system." His eyebrows bounced.

"Yeah, well, you need to keep your honor system in your pants."

"Hey, you're the one suggesting showers. Not me."

Melanie exhaled in exasperation. "Things will go smoother today if you cooperate. Why do you have to joke around about everything?"

"Because it's Saturday and I work my ass off all week and I'd much rather read a book or catch a game on TV than practice answers to interview questions and talk about whether or not you think Oprah will like me."

"First off, Oprah said no. Secondly, I know you hate this, but we have to put the scandal to an end." Her phone buzzed. "Excuse me. I should check this." She reached into her pocket. The push notification on her phone did not bring good news. "There's something new in the papers this morning. A reporter got your ex-fiancée to comment on the scandal." She shook her head, feeling a little sorry for Adam. "This is why you need to let me do my job. This can't be what you want."

Adam buried his face in his hand. Jack wandered over and nudged Adam's hip. "Hey, buddy." Adam's voice was tinged in sadness, which seemed odd considering his fondness for his dog. He crouched down and looked Jack in the face, ruffling his ears. "No, that's not what I want."

Adam parked himself on the long leather bench in his walk-in closet and untied his sneakers, cradling his cell phone between his ear and shoulder. His mother answered after a few rings.

"Mom, hi. Is Dad around?"

"Well, hello to you, too. You don't want to talk to me?"

"Of course I want to talk to you, but I was hoping to talk to Dad and see how he's doing." He peeled off his socks and tossed them across the room, connecting with the hamper.

"Your father's fine. I'm screening his calls. Otherwise, he takes work calls all weekend and never gets any rest. He needs his rest."

Dad. Once a workaholic, always a workaholic. "Has he been tired since he got home last night?"

"Yes. Fridays are the worst. I don't know why he continues with this charade of going into LangTel every day."

"I don't know why he does it either."

LangTel was the telecom corporation Adam's father started from the ground up in the seventies. Adam had grown up heir apparent, but once he went to Harvard Business School, he realized that—just like his father and every Langford man before him—he would never be content taking over someone else's empire. He wanted to build his own, which was precisely why he started his first company while he was still in school. It made him his first fortune before the age of twenty-four.

Even so, when his parents had asked him to help run LangTel from behind the scenes after his father first fell ill, he had done his familial duty. At the time, Roger Langford's prognosis was uncertain and they didn't want him to appear "weak" for fear of the company stock plummeting.

It was meant to be a dry run and Adam passed with flying colors, but it was the worst year of his life—preparing to launch his current company while running interference at LangTel. The timing couldn't have been any worse—right on the heels of his fiancée ending their two-year relationship. LangTel had worn a hole in his psyche.

"At some point," Adam continued, "we're going to have to tell the world that his cancer is far worse than anyone realizes. I'm tired of the song and dance."

"I agree, but your father doesn't want to say a word until things have been cleared up for you with, you know, the newspapers."

His mother couldn't bring herself to utter the word *scandal*, and he was thankful for it. At least it had been only photographs that had been leaked and not something worse, like a sex tape. Adam glanced at his Tag Heuer watch, which sat atop the mahogany bureau in the center of the closet. It was nearly nine thirty and Melanie had been clear that she was ready to get to work. "Hey, Mom. Can I put you on speaker?"

"You know I hate that."

"I'm sorry. I just have to get into the shower in a minute." He pressed the speaker icon on his iPhone. He shucked his basketball shorts and boxer briefs and tossed them over his head, but missed the hamper this time. "I'll talk to Dad about it when I'm back in the city. Maybe I can come by on Sunday afternoon after I fly in."

"Be sure you call first. There are still photographers camped outside our building. You might have to sneak in through the service entrance."

Such a pain. It was one thing for him to have to deal with the photographers, quite another for his mother and father to have to do it. "Okay." He grabbed his robe from the end of the bench and slipped it on.

"If you want to stay for dinner, we could invite your sister, too. Your father and I would love that."

"That sounds great. Anna and I can work on Dad, see if we can talk to him some more about working Anna into the succession plan for LangTel. We both know she'll do an incredible job." He no longer talked to his parents about the fact that he didn't want to run LangTel. It was always dismissed as ludicrous. Now his focus was getting his dad to give his sister, Anna, the chance she wanted and deserved.

"Your father would never dream of letting your sister run the company. He wants Anna shopping for a husband, not sitting in a boardroom."

"Why can't she do both?"

"I'm about to lose your father, and now you don't want me to have any grandchildren? You won't have any until you find the right woman, and Lord knows when that will happen."

There she goes. "Look, Mom. I have to go. I have a houseguest and I need to shower." He strode into the bathroom, across the slate tile floor.

"Houseguest?"

He reached into the shower, cranking the faucet handle. "Yes. Melanie Costello, the woman Dad hired to do this futile PR campaign."

"It's not futile. We need to preserve your father's legacy. When he's gone, you'll be the head of this family. It's important that you're seen for your talents, not for the women you run around with."

He sighed. He didn't like that his mom saw him this way, but he also didn't like feeling as if he couldn't make his own damn decisions, bad or not. He'd be thirty-one soon, for God's sake.

"So tell me. Is she pretty?" she asked.

He couldn't help but laugh. "Mom, this isn't a date. It's work. Nothing else." He couldn't tell his mother that he wouldn't mind if this was a date or that he and Melanie had a past. He certainly couldn't tell her how much he loved being around Melanie, even when she got mad. It made her already vibrant blue eyes blaze, which was particularly intoxicating when packaged with gentle curves and those unforgettable lips.

The mirrors in the bathroom began to fog up. "I need to go, Mom. Tell Dad to call me if he has a chance. I'm worried about him."

"I'm worried, too, darling."

Adam said his goodbyes and slid his phone onto the marble vanity. He dropped the robe to the floor and stepped into the spray, willing the hot water to wash away his worry about his father, if only for a moment. His mother wasn't doing well either. He could hear the stress in every word she said.

He lathered shampoo and rinsed it away. However heartbreaking his father's illness, he could do nothing about it except to make his father's final months happy ones. That was much of the reason Adam had agreed to the PR campaign. The final deciding factor he'd kept to himself—the instant he looked up the Costello Public Relations website and saw Melanie's picture, he had to say yes. After a year of wondering who she was, he not only knew the identity of his Cinderella, he'd be working with her.

Adam shut off the water and toweled himself dry before heading back into his walk-in closet, bypassing the custom-made suit he'd worn on the corporate jet into Asheville. Those clothes were made for the city, and he relished a respite from Manhattan and the media microscope. He certainly preferred the uniform of his freer existence in North Carolina—jeans, plaid shirts and work boots. Choosing to dress in exactly that, he headed downstairs to find Melanie, curious how she planned to air his dirty laundry in public.

Four

The inside of Melanie's purse might have resembled a yard sale, but she never forgot where she put something.

"Have you seen my binders? The ones with the interview schedule?" she asked, peeking behind the cushions of the massive sectional in Adam's living room. Nothing.

Adam was tending the fire, a welcome sight even though the rain had cleared up. "Not the binders again. Can't you send that to me in an email? I'll read it off my phone." He stood and brushed the legs of his perfect-fitting jeans. She had a weakness for a man in an impeccably tailored suit, but a close second was a guy dressed exactly as Adam was. Each held its own appeal—in-command businessman and laid-back mountain guy. So of course Adam had to knock both looks out of the park.

"I like paper. I can rely on paper," Melanie said as she headed into the kitchen and tapped the counter. "It's so weird. Did I bring them up to my room?" She went for the stairs, but didn't make it far. Her notebooks sat mangled behind one of the leather club chairs. She scooped them up. "Did you feed these to Jack?"

Adam was tapping away on his phone. "What? No. Did you actually leave those out where he could get them?"

"I assumed they'd be safe on the coffee table."

"Um, no. He's only three. As well trained as he is, he might as well be a puppy. He'll chew on anything if you give him the chance."

She flipped through the notebooks. One had massive teeth holes at the corners, and the binding of the other was twisted. "I hope he enjoyed his snack."

Jack was sound asleep in front of the fire.

"I'd say he's dead-tired after it."

"We should probably concentrate on interview preparation anyway. You're going to need coaching."

"You can't be serious. I'm unflappable." He sat on the couch, running his hand through his touchable head of hair, giving off a waft of his cologne or shampoo or perhaps it was just plain old Adam. Regardless, it made Melanie's head do figure eights.

"Okay then, Mr. Unflappable." She took a seat opposite him. "We'll do a mock interview and see how you do."

"Fine. Good."

Melanie clicked her pen furiously, well acquainted with the techniques writers might use to put Adam on edge. "Mr. Langford, tell me about that night in February with Portia Winfield."

Adam smiled as if they were playing a game. "Okay. I went out, I ran into Portia. We'd met a few months ago at a party. We had a few too many drinks."

"Don't say how much you had to drink. It casts you in an unflattering light."

"Why? It's a free country."

"Never, ever say that it's a free country. It's an excuse to do whatever you want, without regard for the consequences." She ignored the scowl on his face. "Now try again. Tell me about that night in February."

There was deep confusion in Adam's expression. Hopefully that meant he was realizing what a narrow tightrope he had to walk to get past a scandal. "That question is so open-ended, and I already told you the truth. Now I don't even know where to start."

"These journalists are skilled in the art of tripping someone up. They want you to say something embarrassing or break down. They want something juicy. It's your job to control the conversation. Make the scandal exactly what you claim it to be."

"Which is?"

"You tell me." She flipped her pen in her hand, watching him. The gears were turning behind his dappled blue eyes. For someone with an IQ that was reportedly off the charts, this was clearly a puzzle to him.

"I didn't go to the club with her. I just ran into her."

"That makes it sound like you were there to pick up women. Focus on the benign or the positive. Nothing that can be construed as negative."

He pressed his lips together in a thin line. "I'd been working like crazy on a new project and I wanted to blow off some steam."

"I'm sorry, but that won't work either. The work stuff is good, but blowing off steam makes you sound like a man who uses alcohol to have fun."

"Well, of course I do. What's the point, otherwise?" He sank back against the cushions. "You know, I don't think I can do this. My brain doesn't work like this. People ask me a question, I answer it and move on."

"I know this is difficult, but you'll get it. I promise. It's just going to take some honing of your answers."

"Why don't you show me what you mean? If I don't defer to you on this, we'll be sitting here for days."

"Okay. First off, you establish your relationship with Ms. Winfield. Maybe something like, 'I've known Portia Winfield for a few months and we're friends. She's a delightful woman, a great conversationalist.'"

He cocked an eyebrow and smirked. "You do know she's not the sharpest tool in the shed, right?"

"All I said is that she's amusing and can talk a lot."

A flicker of appreciation crossed his face. "Go on."

Melanie deliberated over what to say next, not enjoying the idea of Adam with another woman. Feeling that way was irrational. She had no claim on him, and Adam's reputation suggested that he could have any woman he wanted. Just last year he had a brief romance with actress Julia Keys, right after she'd been deemed the most beautiful woman in the world. Melanie remembered well standing in line at the drugstore, seeing Julia's perfect face on the cover of that magazine, a distinct sense of envy cropping up, knowing that Julia was dating the man Melanie could have for only one night.

"You could say that you two enjoyed a drink together," Melanie said, collecting her thoughts.

"It was more like three and she was well on her way when I got there."

"But it's true that at some point in the evening you enjoyed one drink, right?"

"Sure."

"There you go."

He grinned. "Please. Keep going."

"Here's where I get stuck, because I can't figure out exactly how you two ended up kissing, while the back of her dress was stuck in the waistband of her panties, the famous disappearing panties."

Adam sighed and shook his head in dismay. "Do you have any idea how idiotic this whole story is?"

"You're going to have to paint me a picture, because I really don't."

Adam folded his arms across his chest. "I kissed her, and it was more than a peck on the mouth. That much is true. But I quickly realized how drunk she was. I wasn't about to let it go any further. I had no idea she was mooning half of the bar. She'd just come back from the ladies' room. And I definitely didn't know that anyone was taking pictures with a camera phone."

As the woman who had more than once tucked her skirt into her pantyhose by accident, Melanie knew this was a plausible explanation. "Then what?" Curiosity overtook her, even when the story was making her a bit queasy.

"I told her that I thought it would be a good idea for me to walk her to her car so her driver could take her home. I settled up the tab while she went back to the ladies' room. I walked her outside, but she could hardly walk and was hanging on me. She dropped her phone on the sidewalk, bent over to pick it up, but I still had my arm around her. That's when she showed the entire world her, well, you know..."

"Ah, yes. The hoo-ha that launched a million internet jokes."

"I'm telling you, I had no idea."

"And from that, the world assumes you took her panties off at the bar."

"Of course they do, but that's not what happened. I have no idea what she did with them or why she took them off in the first place. I was trying to be a good guy."

"The reality is that the press loves to catch famous people doing stupid things, but the bad publicity doesn't hurt her like it hurts you. All she does is ride around in a limo all day and go shopping. If anything, this probably makes her more interesting to her fans."

"I never should've bought her a drink. Or kissed her for that matter."

She almost felt sorry for him. He hadn't done anything wrong. It had all gone horribly awry.

"Are you going to tell me what my ex said in the paper about the scandal? I don't think I can read it for myself."

Melanie cringed, knowing how bad it was. If her ex had ever said anything this ugly about her, she'd probably curl into a ball and die. "I don't think we should worry about that. Nothing good will come from it. As far as the PR campaign goes, we're going to have to hope that today was just a slow news day."

"No. I want to know. Tell me." He spoke with clear determination.

"Just remember. You asked." Melanie pulled the article up on her phone, sucking in a deep breath. "She said, and I quote, 'I'd love to say that this surprises me, but it doesn't. Adam has always had a huge weakness for pretty girls. I don't know if Adam is capable of taking any woman seriously. I certainly don't think he's capable of love. I feel sorry for him. I hope someday he can figure out how to be with a woman and finally give of himself.'"

Adam shot up from the couch, marched over to the fireplace and began anxiously jabbing the logs.

"I know you're mad, but setting the house on fire won't solve anything," she said.

"Do you have any idea how hurtful that is? I'm not capable of love? She was my fiancée. We were going to get married and have kids."

Call it an occupational hazard, but Melanie often had to look past clients' hurt feelings over the way they'd been treated by the media. It was far more difficult in Adam's case, because she'd experienced the same rejection. She knew how hard it was to go on, alone, living a life that bore no resemblance to the one you'd thought you'd have.

No wedding bells, no home to make together, no children to love and care for.

"You obviously loved her very much."

"I did. Past tense." He returned to poking at the fire. "The minute she walked out on me, I knew she never really loved me."

Melanie had to wonder if that was true, if he'd known right away that it hadn't really been love. It'd taken her months to figure that out when Josh left, and in many ways, that made the pain far worse. "Why did she break it off? If you don't mind me asking." Her curiosity was too great not to ask.

"She said I was too wrapped up in work." He shrugged and left the fire to blaze away. "If you ask me, I think she was disappointed I didn't want to feed off the Langford family fortune and jet around the world, going to parties. It's ridiculous. I work hard because that's the way I'm built. I don't know any other way."

"There's no shame in working hard."

"Of course not, but I don't get to tell my side of the breakup in the papers. I just have to accept the awful things she said about me."

"I'm sorry. I know it's difficult to have your personal life on display like this."

"I'm not the guy in those pictures. You do realize that, don't you?"

"Unfortunately, that's all people care about."

Adam shook his head in disgust. "The whole thing is so ridiculous. Can't we go back to my plan? Ignoring it?"

"Not if you want Portia Winfield's lady parts to be the first thing people think of when they hear your name."

He groaned and plopped down on the couch again. "Let's keep going."

Melanie closed her notebook and set it on the coffee table. She needed to switch gears for both of their sakes.

"Let's discuss wardrobe. For most of these photo shoots, I'd like you to appear polished, but still casual. We'll do a suit for the business publications, but for the lifestyle magazines, I'm thinking dark jeans and a dress shirt. No tie. I'd love to see you in a lavender shirt. It will bring out your eyes, and women react well to a man who isn't afraid to wear a softer color."

"You have got to be kidding. I wear blue, gray and black. I wouldn't know lavender if it walked up to me and started talking."

"I'm not asking you to pick the color out of a box of crayons. I'm asking you to wear it."

"No lavender. No way."

Melanie pressed her lips together. There were only so many battles she could win. "We'll do blue. A light blue. Nothing too dark. You'll have to wear makeup too, especially for the TV appearances, but you don't need to do anything other than sit there and let them take care of it. It's painless."

"How'd you learn all of this, anyway?"

"Public relations? I studied it in college."

"No. The things about lavender and women liking softer colors."

"Let's just say I grew up in a family that cared a lot about appearances." That may have been underselling it a bit, but she wasn't eager to open up this particular can of worms.

"Oh, yeah? Like what?"

She dismissed it with a wave of her hand. "Trust me, it's boring."

"Look, I need a mental health break after the mock interview and the quote from the paper. Just tell me."

She didn't want to dismiss him, mostly because she hated it when he did the same to her. Maybe the highlights, or lowlights as she referred to them, would be okay.

"Both of my parents were big on appearances, although my mother passed away when I was little, so I don't remember being lectured about it by her." The way Melanie missed her mom wasn't what she imagined to be normal. She'd been so young when she lost her, that it was more like losing a ghost than a real person. "I definitely remember it from my dad."

Adam frowned. "Like what?"

Melanie shrugged, looking down into her lap. She'd told herself many times that she shouldn't allow these memories to make her feel small, but they did. "He'd order me to put on a dress, or try harder with my hair, be more like my sisters. I'm the youngest of four girls and I was a little bookish growing up. They were all into beauty pageants. My mother had won tons of pageants as a girl, but she was stunning. I knew I'd never live up to that."

"Why? You're pretty enough."

She blushed. It was silly, but she enjoyed hearing Adam say she was pretty, or at least pretty enough. "There's more to it than that. You have to walk up on stage and smile perfectly and wave your hand a certain way and follow a million rules that somebody, somewhere, decided were the ways a girl should present herself. I couldn't do it. I couldn't be that plastic girl."

He rubbed the stubble along his jaw. "And yet you chose a profession that involves an awful lot of smoke and mirrors."

She'd never really thought of it that way. "But I can make my own rules when I need to, make my own way. It's creative and strategic. I love that part of my job. It's never dull."

"Did you participate in any beauty pageants, or did you rebel from the beginning?"

A wave of embarrassment hit her, quite a different type of blush from the one she got when Adam had said nice things. "I did one pageant. I actually won it, but that was enough for me."

"Little Miss Virginia? You're from Virginia, right?"

"Yes. Rural Virginia. The mountains. And I can't tell you what my title was or I'll have to kill you. It's far too humiliating."

"Well, now you *have* to tell me. No one gets past me without sharing at least one humiliating story."

She shook her head. "Nope. Sorry. We're discussing business. Let's get back to your wardrobe."

"Come on. We already had to talk about me and the girl who can't keep track of her own undies. And one could argue that this is business. These are your qualifications for being my wardrobe consultant."

"It's dumb."

"What if I say I'll wear a lavender shirt? One time." He held up a single finger for emphasis.

She really did want him to wear lavender. It would make for some great pictures. "Okay. Fine. I was crowned Little Miss Buttermilk. I was five."

Adam snickered. "I can't believe you won the coveted Little Miss Buttermilk title."

Melanie leaned forward and swatted him on the knee. She'd never told any man this stupid, stupid story, not even her ex. "If you must know, I think I largely took it based on the talent portion. I was an excellent tap dancer."

"I have no doubts about that. I've seen your legs, Buttermilk."

Melanie swallowed, hard, and tucked one leg under the other. Had he ever seen her legs—every last inch of them. Adam cleared his throat. Thankfully, Jack got up from his nap and ambled over, providing a logical means of changing the topic.

"Hey, buddy." Adam scratched Jack behind the ears.

"Your parents must've made you do things you didn't want to do when you were a kid."

"It's always been about business. Some kids got base-ball mitts for Christmas from their dad. I got a briefcase." Adam nodded, looking at Jack. "That actually happened, by the way. No lie. I love my dad, though. I really do." That sadness was in his voice again, the one that cropped up whenever he spoke of his father.

"That's why you agreed to let me come. To make your dad happy."

His eyes connected with hers, holding steady for a few, insanely intense moments. "That's a big part of the reason. Of course."

Five

Adam's brain was mush. There was no more gas in the tank. He and Melanie had talked about interviews and wardrobe for hours. They'd delved into the details of his past that they needed to focus on, and the ones they absolutely needed to avoid. She'd lectured him about refraining from flipping the bird to the photographers when they got pushy. He'd done it only once, but he still wasn't sure he could make any promises on that last point.

He rolled his neck, admiring Melanie as she eyed her watch for what had to be the third or fourth time. She was especially lovely in the fading light of day, with a golden pink flush to her cheeks that closely matched the lips he'd never be able to forget. "Do you have somewhere you need to be, Buttermilk?"

"Hey. Are you really going to call me that? Because I kind of hate it."

"Really? Because I kind of love it." It wasn't the nickname that he loved. It was her reaction, the way she got a little riled up but still seemed to enjoy some part of it.

"If you're going to call me that, then at least turn on the TV so we can watch some basketball. My team is playing." She smiled as if she couldn't keep it inside any longer. "Actually, it's our league championship. This is the first year in a really long time that we've been any good."

"Yeah. Of course." He picked up the remote and turned on the TV. "But wait. The NBA championship isn't until June."

"I'm talking college." She shook her head and cast him a glance over her shoulder, a glance that stopped him dead in his tracks. Those blue eyes of hers were magic. Flat-out magic. "March Madness, baby."

He couldn't have fought a smile if he'd wanted to. He loved hearing her say "baby," especially coupled with a sports reference. It was the sexiest damned thing ever. "Your wish is my command." He scanned through the channels until he found her game. "I'm more of an NBA guy than college, but I'm up for anything."

She scooted to the edge of her seat, watching the screen intently as a pair of announcers pontificated about the game, dozens of screaming fans camera-hogging behind them. "The college game is so much better than the pros." She didn't tear her eyes from the TV. "I can't stand to watch a game with a bunch of millionaires standing around, not playing defense."

"Sounds like most of the parties I go to."

"I bet."

He'd hoped he'd get a laugh out of that one, but this seemed to be serious business for Melanie.

"Do you have any beer?" She granted him another glance, smiling sheepishly. "Just seems like we should be drinking beer if we're going to watch this. Plus, I need to take the edge off. If we lose, I might die."

Adam hopped off the couch. "Beer coming up. Stat." He strode into the kitchen, took two beers from the fridge, popped the tops off, grabbed a bag of potato chips from the pantry and returned to the living room.

"Thank you." She gazed up at him, their fingers touching as she took the bottle. Her eyes were as wide as they were deep—he could spend a lifetime unraveling everything behind them. She waved him out of the way, craning her neck. "Can you move? I can't see. It's time for tip-off."

He obliged her request and settled near her, leaving a polite distance, wishing they could sit hip to hip. If he didn't think she'd slug him in the stomach, he would've leaned back with his arm across the back of the couch, hoping she'd settle in and rest her head against his shoulder. What would it be like to have a night with Melanie again? To have her curl into him, kiss him, trail her fingers along his jaw. It was painful to imagine, and yet he didn't want to ignore the visions that ran through his head.

When Melanie had come through his door twenty-four hours ago, he wasn't sure exactly what he'd expected, although he knew what he'd hoped. He'd longed to hear her confess that leaving him in the middle of the night was the most stupid, rash decision she'd ever made, that she hoped he could forgive her, that she wanted a second chance.

She hadn't come close to giving him that. If he were being impartial, he understood her reasons, however disappointing. So instead of another searing-hot liaison, he got to watch basketball and drink beer with her, a woman who was smart and determined and so effortlessly sexy. It could've been worse.

She might've expected that he'd watch the game, too, but he couldn't pass up the chance to study her. It was much like the first time he'd seen her, at the party at The Park Hotel. He'd noticed her because she'd been talking to one of his biggest business rivals. Her musical laugh filtered through the crowded space, rose above the din of chatter, spiking his curiosity. As he trudged his way through dry conversations about investors and start-ups, he struggled to keep his eyes off her. Her entire being came alive when she spoke. She was a beacon in a sea of dullness. Every phony, contrived exchange he'd had that night had left him starved for something real. He hadn't quite bargained on how real their night together would be, or how much it would disappoint him when she left.

He quickly learned that he could read everything happening in the game from her actions. If her team was shooting free throws, her hands flew to her temples, fingers crossed. If they made a fast break, she launched herself off the couch and yelled, "Go! Go!" If the other team had the ball, she groaned, "Guard him!" and "Get the rebound!" ESPN had nothing on Melanie Costello in terms of sports entertainment.

Ninety minutes later, after the roller coaster of Melanie's jubilation and dismay, her team was down by one point, with twelve seconds left. Her resignation was plain during the commercial break. "I should've known it was too good to be true." She turned to him, her long bangs falling across her forehead, making her look so sweet, so vulnerable. "We always find some way to choke."

The disappointment in her voice was almost too much for him to take. If she were his, he wouldn't have hesitated to pull her into a snug embrace. Hell, he would've paid off a referee or two if it meant her team could win and she'd be happy. "You never know. Plenty of time to get off a good shot."

"Yeah, right. That's never going to happen."

The station cut away from commercial back to the game. The announcers speculated as a player for Melanie's team waited to throw the ball inbounds.

Melanie again sprang up from the couch. "I can't even

look." She bounced up and down on her toes, shook her hands at her side as if they'd gone numb. Adam had to admire the appealing shape of her rear view, especially as she nervously wiggled in place. He longed to have his hands on that part of her again, caressing her soft skin, pulling her closer.

The announcer spoke. *Miller inbounds the ball, full-court pass to Williams down in the key. He's double-teamed. Nowhere to go.*

"Oh, no," Melanie blurted.

He kicks it back out to Miller. He hasn't hit a shot all night.

"Just shoot it!" Melanie screamed.

He steps back behind the three-point line. The shot is off. We have the buzzer...and it's good!

Melanie whipped around, her eyes like saucers. "It's good!" She charged at him with open arms, flattening him against the back of the couch. "Oh my God, Adam. We won," she said breathlessly. "You were right." She trembled with excitement.

He reflexively wrapped his arms around her, breathed in the sweet smell of her hair. "So I heard. It's wonderful." *But not as wonderful as this.*

"I'm sorry." She distanced herself a few inches, shaking her head. Now that she was there, he wasn't about to let her go without at least a moment of discussion. "We haven't won the championship since I was a kid."

"Don't be sorry. This is the highlight of my entire weekend." He traced his fingers up and down her spine as she leaned into him, both of them still sitting, but definitely leaning. He was drawn back into the memory of having her in his apartment, the way she felt in his arms, as if these limbs of his were made for nothing other than keeping her close. Her words from that night came rushing back. *You feel like a dream.*

"I shouldn't have hugged you. It was unprofessional."

"I thought we were taking a break from professional."

She reared her shoulders back and looked him in the eye. "Are you going to let me go?"

"As near as I can tell, you're holding on to me just as tight."

She rolled her eyes—childish from most women, adorable from Melanie. "I'm trying to keep myself upright."

He was certain he'd heard every word she'd said, but her lips were so tempting and pouty that it was hard to grasp details. Mostly he wanted this to keep going. "Then stop being upright."

Before Melanie knew what was happening, Adam was kissing her. And like a fool, she kissed him right back.

Melanie had all kinds of resolve until the kiss. Good God… His mouth and hands and his broad, taut frame. He was temptation, served up on a silver platter. He was the fuel to her fire—bodies pressed together, her body weight against his, her lips absolutely starved for more. The fire inside her finally had what it had waited to feed on.

His lips were impossibly gentle, even when there was no mistaking his powerfully male intentions. He wanted her. He was in charge. She felt it in every grasp as his hands slipped under her sweater, cradling her waist, his strong arms effortlessly rolling her to her back. He kissed her cheek, trailing to her jaw and the delicate spot beneath her ear—the spot that made electricity zip along her spine. She arched into him, eyes closed, mind floating in the nether, between the present and her past.

The night she shared with Adam hadn't been a dream. She hadn't built it up in her head—kissing him really was unlike kissing any other man. Sublime, a never-ending moment of pleasure to sink into. He was real. This kiss was real. Perfect. She hadn't spent the past year aimless. She'd spent the past year missing this kiss.

His leg pressed between hers, white-hot friction in just the right place. Adam was the last man to touch her there, to fill her every need. He was the last man she'd wanted like this. It was almost too perfect. Could they start where they left off? Forget the past year? Erase it?

"I've wanted to do this since you walked in the door last night," he mumbled, unbuttoning her blouse. "The minute I saw you again, I had to have you."

She drank in his wonderfully possessive words, his strong hand gliding across her stomach. She had to have him, too. They were on the same page, except he seemed to be reading ahead—everything he did was exactly what she was hoping for. He trailed his finger along the lacy edge of her bra, ever so slightly dipping it beneath the fabric, bringing her skin to life.

But her brain barged into the conversation. *What in the hell are you doing? You can't do this. You need this job. Didn't you spend the past year vowing to never allow a man the chance to destroy your heart and your career in one fell swoop?*

Her body warred with the logic. *But I want him. I've waited a year for him. Nobody would ever have to know.*

But you would know.

Adam's hand was on her back, at her bra strap. *Pop.*

Oh, no. "Adam. Stop. We can't." She expected him to groan in frustration, possibly even push her back in disgust, but he didn't.

"Are you okay? What's wrong?" He cupped the side of her face, washing his thumb over the swell of her cheek.

"I'm sorry. I'm so sorry, but we can't. We can't do this." She shut her eyes, needing a break from the allure of his mouth, especially when his breath was brushing her lips. She had to collect her thoughts. "I never should've let it go this far. It's just that…" She stopped herself. The more she explained, the stupider she would sound. And eventually she would have to admit that if she had her way, if her job didn't mean everything and if she could suspend belief and think for a second that Adam would want her for more than a fling, they'd be upstairs in his bed right now. They would be making memories that put the first night they shared to shame.

"It's just what?" he asked. "Did I do something wrong?"

How could he still be so calm? She was about to frustrate the hell out of him. Surely he had to realize what was happening. She felt him against her leg, hard and ready, and yet he was worried that he'd done something wrong. "I'm sorry. It's just not right."

"I don't understand. Do you have a boyfriend? Because I never would've made a move if I'd known that."

"No, I don't have a boyfriend. This is just wrong. I signed a contract. It would be a mistake."

"A mistake." Adam sat up, distancing himself from her, creating a cold and uncrossable divide. Maybe that was for the best, although it didn't feel like the best. It felt awful. "You really have a way with words when you aren't concerned with the public relations spin, don't you?"

His question left her thinking that he had a way with words as well—his cut her to the core, not so much with *what* he said, but with the way he said it. With little effort, he left her feeling hollowed out. And that put her on the defensive. "I thought you deserved the truth."

"I'm not really sure what I deserve, but right now it feels like I'm being punished for something I can't help."

She got up from the couch, buttoning her blouse. She couldn't believe he was going to use *that* as his excuse. "I'm very sorry about that." She pointed in the general direction of his crotch. "A cold shower might help."

"Cute. Real cute. That's not what I mean."

"Oh. Sorry." Wave after wave of embarrassment battered her. Could she possibly make this any worse? She didn't dare try to make it better. "Look, I'm sorry. I think we should just say good-night and forget this ever happened."

He shook his head, not looking at her. "Whatever you say."

She thought she'd felt hollowed out before, but now it was as if she didn't exist. Wanting to do nothing but hide, she rushed upstairs and closed the guest room door behind her, ducking under the comforter and curling into a ball. Tears came, and she hated that more than anything.

How was she going to do this job? How would this ever work? She couldn't spend day after day coaching Adam through interviews and running interference at photo shoots. She'd never make it, knowing how badly she wanted him, knowing what a horrible idea it was to give in to feelings like that.

She wiped her cheeks, willing the tears to stop. She had to get through this or else she'd fail, and that couldn't happen. She just had to get her act together and find a way to get Adam off her mind. She needed a plan.

Six

Before last night, when was the last time Adam had been turned down? He didn't care to remember, but it sure stung. The fact that it came from Melanie and that he'd waited an entire year for a chance only made it worse. Was he really that far off base about their chemistry? Because she certainly seemed to care a hell of a lot more about her job than about him.

When she pressed against him on the couch, he'd had only one thought—the electricity was back. It jolted every atom of his body. How could that be one-sided? How could two people create that much heat if only one person felt it? How else could she so easily put on the brakes? Something didn't add up, that was for sure.

Melanie clopped down the stairs with her overnight bag in tow. He wished he hadn't noticed how pretty she was in the morning, fresh-faced and lovely, even when wearing a distinct frown.

"I would've gotten that for you if you'd asked," he said, pulling his jacket out of the closet.

"I'm okay to do it myself."

"I'm sure you are." He folded his arms across his chest. Creating a physical barrier made it easier to ignore his deep desire to invite her back upstairs and kiss her as he had last night, only this time with an entirely different, naked, ending.

She drew a deep breath in through her nose, avoiding anything beyond a blip of eye contact. "I need to ask a favor. I just got a notification from the airline that my flight is overbooked. They bumped me."

"And?" He had a strong suspicion about the question that was coming. He just wanted to hear her ask for it.

"I was wondering if there's room on your corporate jet for me to ride along."

"I don't know. Jack really prefers having two seats. He's a big boy."

Melanie dropped her chin, delivering that hot look of admonishment. "Really? Are you really that mad about last night? Because you know as well as I do that it's not a good idea for anything to happen between us. It would be reckless and stupid. It would be a huge mistake."

Adam hadn't planned on prompting that little rant. And would she stop using that damn word—*mistake*? *Well, then.* "Yes, you may join me on the plane back to New York. Of course."

"Oh. Okay. Thank you."

"You're welcome, Buttermilk."

"Did you really just call me that again?"

"It seemed to fit today. Not sure why."

An hour and a half later, they were on board the plane, just the two of them, the pilot and, of course, Jack. Normally, Jack would curl up on the floor at Adam's feet. Sometimes, he'd attempt to climb into his own seat, although that always ended disastrously as he was far too big. Today, he'd parked himself next to Melanie, his head on her lap. *Traitor.*

"Adam, I need to talk to you about something."

Stinging words lingered on Adam's lips. *Oh, really? Something about how you're glad things didn't go any further last night? How we need to remain professional?* "I'm listening." He thumbed through an email on his phone.

"I was thinking that women seem to be your problem, but they could also be your salvation."

"In light of what happened last night, I'd love to know where this is going."

"I thought we agreed we weren't going to talk about last night."

"I didn't agree to anything."

Melanie shook her head as if she couldn't possibly be more frustrated. "One thing I've learned in public relations is that if people have been inundated with a bad image, you can replace it with a more positive image, until eventually they forget the bad."

He looked up from his phone and narrowed his focus. "Like what? Pictures of me volunteering in a soup kitchen? Loading sandbags in a hurricane?"

"No. I was thinking something extremely believable. You. With a woman. Right now, the world thinks you're only capable of meaningless flings, which is the image your parents and the board of directors have such a hard time with."

Adam coughed. If he'd wanted to, he could've gone for the jugular and reminded her that their acquaintance had started out as a one-night stand. As much as the events of last night had scarred his ego, he couldn't do it. He'd never thought of her as a meaningless fling, not even when they'd had only a few hours together. "You want me to start dating classier women."

"Woman. Singular. Basically, you need a girlfriend. A serious one. You need to find a woman and be seen around town together. Ideally, for the next few weeks leading up to the LangTel gala. Then you take her to the party that night, your father makes his announcement about the succession plan, you'll have been in magazines and on talk shows by then. It'll be the unveiling of a brand-new Adam Langford."

He grumbled under his breath. "Great. My debutante ball."

"You know what I mean."

"You're going to find me a new girlfriend?"

"You're going to have to do that part. I do have some criteria for you, though."

Adam slid his phone onto the table next to him and took a sip of club soda, but it felt more like bourbon o'clock. "Can't wait to hear this."

Melanie cleared her throat. "She should be beautiful, of course. You're Adam Langford. No one will believe you're with anyone who isn't stunning."

Jack looked up into her eyes, shot a glance at Adam, and went back to being as close to a lapdog as he could, draping his head across her legs.

"She should be someone who is well-known," Melanie continued. "But she should have a pristine reputation. No more party girls. It should probably be someone who's accustomed to the media microscope. You know as well as anyone how tough that can be to deal with."

"And what do I do with this person?"

"Go out to dinner. Go out for coffee. Take Jack for a walk. You'll just need to let me know ahead of time, so I can leak information to the press."

"I really don't think this is going to work. I'm not good at faking anything. The photographers will see right through it if it isn't real."

Melanie considered him with those blue eyes of hers, the ones he wished he could see looking up at him while she was pinned beneath his body weight, at his mercy. "You might have to get good at faking it."

That was never going to happen. It was already too much work to sit here and talk about another woman. "What happens if I fall in love? After all, I'm hopelessly single and, despite what you might think of me, I don't plan to be that way forever." *Shut up already.*

"Whatever the emotional entanglements are, that's for you to decide."

"Of course." Was this her way of getting rid of him? Pushing him into another woman's arms? If so, she might live to regret it, although he couldn't fathom anyone capturing his imagination the way she had. Perhaps if she were a tinge jealous, it might be enough to make her rethink the wisdom of turning him down.

"Do you have anyone in mind?" Her voice squeaked at the end, as if she'd forced disinterest in the answer.

"I do, actually. I think I know the perfect woman."

The perfect woman. *Great. I can't wait for the perfect woman.*

On paper, Adam finding a fake girlfriend was a beautiful idea, crafted in the middle of the night amid crying jags and brainstorms. It accomplished two very important things—it rounded out Melanie's PR plan, and it created distance between her and Adam. They would be working together a lot. At least if he had to keep his hands to himself, she could do her job and ignore how badly she longed to put her hands all over him.

She glanced at Adam as they rode in his limo on their way back into the city. Her thoughts drifted to what this moment would be like if she and Adam were a couple, if they'd just spent an impossibly romantic weekend at his mountain estate. Surely they'd spent hours making love, hardly ever getting out of bed, except perhaps to tiptoe downstairs for a bite to eat. They'd curled up in front of the fireplace, drifted off to sleep in each other's arms. *Perfect* wouldn't begin to describe it, but *perfect* wasn't reality.

Adam had been on the phone with his father since they landed, discussing LangTel business. She had her own phone call scheduled with Roger Langford tomorrow morning. Would he actually ask her questions about whether or not anything had happened between her and Adam? And what would she say if he did? She'd crossed the line, big-time.

The embarrassment of the scene on the couch Saturday night still ate at her. How could she have gotten so wrapped up in Adam that she hadn't even cared that he'd unbuttoned her blouse? If anything, she'd welcomed it. How could one man have that much influence over her, mind and body? Not even her ex could make her cast aside restraint like that.

Adam said goodbye to his dad and began scrolling through the contacts on his phone. "I was thinking I should get the ball rolling with my new girlfriend. No time like the present."

"Fake girlfriend."

"I told you that I'm not good at faking things. I have to buy into it a little bit or it won't work."

She choked back a sigh of frustration. "Whatever you need to do."

"Just remember," he said, cocking an eyebrow, "it's your fault if I fall in love."

Melanie longed to slap him silly. *Fall in love.* Wouldn't that be the ultimate way for him to get even with her? After all, she hadn't merely left his apartment in the middle of the night. Now she was guilty of losing her moral compass and leaving him with what she'd witnessed as an extra-snug fit in his pants. "As long as you're taking my directives, that's all I care about."

"Here she is." He tapped his phone decisively. "Lovely Julia."

Melanie's stomach turned so sour it was as if she'd downed a gallon of lemon juice. *Julia? Julia Keys?* Was Adam really going to pick an ex-girlfriend and one of the most beautiful women in the history of mankind to be his new fake, but possibly real, girlfriend?

"Julia. It's Adam. How are you, beautiful?"

Beautiful? Melanie sighed. She probably deserved the punishment of listening to this conversation. Desperate for a distraction, she yanked a magazine from her tote bag and began flipping through the pages, imagining they were Adam's very slappable face.

"I hear you're back in New York. I'm hoping we can get together. I have a proposition for you." He leaned back, caressing the black leather seat with his hand.

Was that Julia's effect on him? That merely talking to her made him want to rub things?

"I was hoping I could ask you in person," he said in a voice entirely too sexy for Melanie's liking. "Let's just say that I might have a new role for you. It would involve us spending a lot of time together." He smiled at whatever she said in response.

Melanie pursed her lips, reminding herself that he was doing exactly what she'd asked him to do. *Exactly.* So why was she so pissed off? Oh, right. Because she'd hoped Adam would pick someone pretty and proper and not much else. She certainly hadn't bargained on him picking a woman who exemplified the feminine ideal, nor did she think he would pick someone he might actually fall in love with.

"Would dinner Tuesday night work?" he asked. "I'll have my cook prepare a meal at my place, just so we can talk privately. If you're up for my plan, we can go out for dinner later in the week if your schedule allows." This time, Adam laughed—he practically guffawed—at whatever Julia had said.

Great. She's beautiful, talented, wife material and apparently hilarious. Melanie glared out the window. They were only a block or so from her Gramercy apartment, thank goodness. The end, in sight. She couldn't live through another minute of Adam's phone call. She shoved the magazine in her bag and leaned forward to speak to the driver. "It's right here, on the left."

"Yes, ma'am." The driver pulled up to the curb in front of her brownstone.

She turned to Adam as the driver opened her door.

Adam was nodding and grinning like a damned fool. He put his hand over the receiver on his phone. "Anything else?"

The light filtered through the open door, glinting off his sunglasses. She tried to remind herself that this was the real Adam Langford—the flirt in the expensive car, doing whatever the hell he wanted to. He wasn't boyfriend material. He was a client, end of story.

"That's it. I'll talk to you tomorrow." She scurried out of the car before she could say something foolish, something like, "Please hang up the phone and forget that I ever came up with this stupid fake-girlfriend idea."

Melanie fumbled with her building keys. Why was the car still sitting there? It felt as if Adam's eyes were boring into her back. Finally, the lock turned, she stumbled through the door, and the limo pulled away. She longed for a measure of relief, but all she felt was confused and disappointed.

She trudged up the stairs to her second-floor walk-up. She'd moved in after Josh had dumped her. Even if she didn't miss him, she missed their old apartment. It was quaint and quiet, in the Chelsea neighborhood, with the best spot for reading on a Sunday afternoon, cuddled up on the couch. Luckily, that apartment had gone to a month-to-month rental, or she'd be stuck with that and her office space. The bad news was that they hadn't renewed the apartment lease because they were looking to buy a home, one big enough for a nursery.

Melanie rounded the railing to her door. Her neighbor Owen came down from the third floor, dressed for a run.

"You're back from your trip." He grinned wide and jogged in place, as if to remind her that he was in exceptional shape. Funny how his perfect physique did nothing for her except reassure her that she was out for more than a hot bod. She needed a companion. A partner.

She managed a smile. Owen was harmless, even if the way he kept tabs on her bordered stalker behavior. "Yep. Just now."

"Good to hear it. The building is too quiet without you around. Maybe we can see a movie this weekend."

He dipped his head to make eye contact, but she was nothing if not distracted by the thoughts of Adam whirring through her head—their near miss and the aftermath, the humiliating apology and her plan to keep herself on the straight and narrow.

"Um. Maybe," she answered. "We'll see. I'm in the middle of a huge job right now."

He nodded and smiled reassuringly. "Gotta keep the bills paid."

"You know it." *Understatement of the year, actually.* She unlocked the door to her unit. "I'll let you know if my plans change." With a quick wave, she bid Owen goodbye and let the door close. Exhausted, she leaned against it. Her apartment felt nothing like home today. It really just felt empty.

Seven

Every time Melanie opened the doors at Costello Public Relations, memories smacked her in the face. Time had dulled the pain, but it was still there—the betrayal of the man she'd once loved, the man who'd stuck her with the office lease from hell.

Things had once been perfect in this office, she and Josh working as a team, a devoted support staff around them. The sky was the limit, the future bright. She and Josh went home every night together, tired but satisfied. They were building something, and it felt wonderful.

They had made a vow to spend at least one hour each evening talking about things other than work. That typically made conversation difficult since their entire lives revolved around the business. The easiest thing was to fall into bed and make love. It wasn't fireworks, but it was an extension of their life together, inexorably wound together. They completed each other, or so she had thought.

She'd had no idea that the last eight months of their relationship were a lie. Josh was so good at faking it, so adept at putting up a facade that said everything was peachy keen, when in fact he was sneaking around, meeting another woman, romancing her, taking her to bed.

When she'd suspected that something was going on between Josh and their client, he'd dismissed it as preposterous. The flirtation, the rapport beyond the professional, was all in her head. The next thing she knew, he had a cold and was staying home for the day, when in fact he was emptying his things out of their apartment, hopping a plane to San Francisco and relocating with his new love, his "soul mate." Melanie didn't want it to hurt so bad anymore. It was exhausting.

She hurried past the unmanned reception desk. It'd been months since she'd been able to keep someone on full-time. For now, it was better to run a tight ship, continue to build back the client list and come out on the other side stronger. That was the entire reason she'd done what she probably shouldn't have done and taken this crazy Adam Langford job in the first place.

She sat at her desk, quickly remembering that she hadn't made coffee. She sprang back out of her seat. Once that task was done and she had a steaming-hot cup of courage, she sat down to call Adam's dad, Roger.

"Ms. Costello," Roger's voice boomed over the other line. "To be honest, when I hired you, I was fairly certain that this would be the phone call where I would have to fire you."

Melanie swallowed. "Sir?"

"You know, the first check-in after you'd worked with Adam."

Right. Work. Adam. "The weekend went very well, Mr. Langford, I assure you."

"I hope I can count on you for complete honesty, Ms. Costello. I love my son very much and there's no one I

trust more when it comes to business, but he has a veri-
fiable lack of good judgment when it comes to the fairer
sex. I trust that you kept to our agreement?"

How would she answer this? Find a technicality? She
didn't have a choice. She needed this job and one could
argue that she'd made only one mistake, even if it was a
doozy—kissing Adam on the couch and losing all sense
of time and space. "I stayed away from Adam's bedroom,
if that's what you're asking." That much was the truth, but
guilt still choked her. She'd not only violated the contract
keeping her company in the black, she'd done the thing she
told herself she'd never do—she'd become involved with a
client. Thank goodness she'd had the presence of mind to
stop herself. If Adam's lips had roved any farther, if she'd
taken the chance to caress his bare chest, there would've
been no looking back.

"Forgive me for even asking. It's just important to me
that we keep things aboveboard." Roger cleared his throat.
"I won't keep you, Ms. Costello. I spoke to Adam. He's
very impressed with your work, which isn't quite what I
expected to hear. He fought me hard on hiring a PR person,
although he softened on the idea when your name came
into the mix. As soon as he researched your background,
he said yes. I suppose your reputation preceded you."

Melanie's mind raced. She knew Adam had fought the
public relations campaign—he'd said as much himself.
What he'd failed to mention was that he changed his mind
after he found out she'd been hired. Researched her background… Her picture was front and center on her website
and he'd said that he never forgot a woman, even though
she hadn't anticipated that was his superpower. What went
through his mind when he made the connection?

"Adam told me all about your plan with Julia," Roger
continued. "It's a stroke of pure genius. Mrs. Langford
and I adored her the first time we met her. Their romance

was so short-lived, but maybe they'll see the error of their ways now that they'll be spending time together. Nothing like close quarters to kindle love's flames."

Kindle love's flames? Melanie's stomach churned. How would she make it through the coming weeks without wanting to take a nap on railroad tracks? "The press will eat it up, sir." *Will they ever.*

"Absolutely excellent, Ms. Costello. Looking at Adam's interview schedule, I'd like you to keep me apprised of the *Midnight Hour* appearance. I'd really like for that to happen."

She scribbled herself a note to make yet another call to the *Midnight Hour* producer, knowing the answer was likely still "we'll see." Adam was the right kind of guest for the late-night talk show—in the limelight, a "personality"—but their schedule was booked months in advance. "Yes, sir. I'm on it."

"Well, keep up the good work. I've spoken to my assistant. Your next check is on its way."

Melanie exhaled—money. That and a stellar endorsement from a man as powerful as Roger Langford was the reason she was doing this. Having to aid and abet Adam and Julia was merely the horrific trade-off. "Thank you, sir. I'll keep you posted."

It was only a little past nine thirty when she said goodbye, but she already felt as though she'd been at the office for days. Coffee. More coffee.

The next hour was spent catching up on other clients—a New Jersey real estate agent who wanted to build her profile with the well-heeled of New York society, and a hotshot chef in need of a PR campaign surrounding his nomination for a prestigious cooking award. After finishing her second cup of coffee, she got around to the mail—big, fat bills for her rented office furniture, internet, travel. Even the little things such as office supplies added up. When would every day stop feeling like one step forward, two steps back? She was a fighter and she wouldn't quit, but being a one-woman army was no fun.

The main office line rang. Melanie hated it when this happened, because it meant that she had to pretend to be the receptionist. She'd trained most people to call her cell phone, and many of her clients preferred email for communication, but her sisters still called the office when they needed her to deal with their difficult dad, and of course, new clients often placed a phone call first.

"Costello Public Relations," she answered. "How may I direct your call?"

"Melanie? Is that you?" Adam's warm, familiar voice did peculiar things, sending both excitement and nervousness pumping through her veins. "I hope your receptionist is out on a coffee run. The boss should never answer her own phone."

"I don't mind it every now and then." How she hated hemming her answers. "Did you lose my cell number?"

"I guess I just pressed the number for your office. Would you prefer I call your cell?"

"I want to make sure you can reach me."

"I take it you spoke to my dad?"

"Yes. About an hour ago." She wondered whether she should let him know that his dad had essentially asked whether or not they'd slept together. Surely it wouldn't make Adam feel better about their father-son relationship to know that the distrust when it came to that topic was so deeply ingrained.

"I told him about Julia."

"So I heard. He's very excited."

"Yeah, sorry about that. I suppose I should've warned you. He's thrilled by the prospect of me spending time with Julia. Don't worry, though. I gave credit where credit was due. It's all your brilliant idea."

I'm a veritable mastermind. "Thank you. I appreciate that."

"I wanted to let you know that I've worked everything out with Julia. We had coffee this morning."

"Instead of dinner tonight?" Apparently he just couldn't wait to start spending time with her.

"No. We're still having dinner. That's why I'm calling. I wanted to let you know where we'll be going and what time we'll be there."

"Oh. I see." She steeled herself. This was going to be her reality for the next several weeks, whether she liked it or not. Best to get used to it now.

"That's how this works, right?"

She shook her head to extricate herself from unpleasant thoughts. "Yes. That's right." She grabbed a pen. "Go ahead. I'm listening."

"We'll be at Milano. Reservations are for eight."

Only the most romantic restaurant in the city. "And Julia's publicist is okay with this?"

"Yes. Julia doesn't have another movie coming out for over a year. She'll do anything to stay in the papers, just so producers and directors don't forget about her. She's going to be thirty soon. That's ancient for an actress."

And yet she's still absolutely stunning. "Okay, then. I'll leak this to a few photographers."

"Great. Thanks, Melanie."

"And Adam, please don't…" Her voice cracked, breaking before the words she really wanted to say, which were "do this." "Please don't flip off any photographers."

"Don't you trust me to do the right thing?"

At this point, the person she didn't trust was herself. Her miracle fix for dazzling Roger Langford while making Adam less of a temptation was burning a hole through her stomach. Every time she thought about it, which was every moment since she'd told Adam her idea, it made her uneasy. Something about it was wrong, and she had an inkling as to what it was, but it was no fun to go there. If money and career were extraneous factors rather than center stage, she never would've asked Adam to spend more time with another woman. *Focus on the work.* "It's just a reminder."

Melanie hung up the phone and sat back in her chair, rubbing her now-throbbing forehead. If she was so brilliant, why did she feel like the biggest dummy on the planet?

Adam tapped away at his laptop, trying to fully express his ideas for a new app he wanted his development team to explore, but he was writing in circles. He dropped his elbows onto the desk and ran his hand through his hair. This entire workday had been a waste. He couldn't get his mind off Melanie.

How was he going to make the Julia thing appear real, and if he did, how would that impact his relationship with Melanie? His ego had been bruised in the mountains, but now that he'd had a chance to heal, he had to admire her tenacity, her devotion to doing her job well and aboveboard.

His assistant, Mia, leaned into the doorway of his office. "It's six thirty, Mr. Langford. You're supposed to be picking up Ms. Keys at seven and your car is waiting outside. With traffic, you'll be cutting it close."

"Thanks. Guess I'd better change." *And I need a drink before my first public outing with Julia.*

Adam closed the door to the private bathroom in his office and changed into a fresh shirt. He grabbed his matching suit coat from its hanger on the back of the door, and put on a black-and-gray-striped tie. *Here goes nothing.*

He wasn't nervous about seeing Julia. They'd had coffee and that had gone fine. The truth was that their breakup had been as amicable as could be. After three dates, Julia had grasped his hand in the back of the limo and said, "There's nothing here, is there?"

Adam had been immensely relieved. They liked each other. They could make each other laugh. But there was zero chemistry. On paper, they should have made the perfect couple. In reality, it all fell flat.

His real worry was whether or not they could pull off the charade of a romantic relationship. Surely people would see them together and know that they weren't *really* together.

He had to make it work, however much it contradicted the way he chose to live his life. It was in his own best interest to make the scandal fade away so his father could live his final days knowing for certain that the integrity of the Langford name was intact. It had to work to make Melanie happy, since so much of her job depended on it succeeding. In the end, if he was lucky, it would have one of two effects on her—it would either make her so jealous that she realized that she wanted him, too. Or it would help her see that he was a good man. This would be his audition, his opportunity to show Melanie what he was really made of. Hopefully that opportunity would help him ultimately make Melanie his.

The limo arrived at Julia's new apartment, and after a long twenty minutes of idle chitchat during the ride, they arrived at Milano. As Melanie had promised, a handful of photographers were out front of the restaurant.

"Julia," one of them shouted, "over here."

Cameras flashed as Julia held on to the tips of Adam's fingers. She knew how to work the situation, smiling enough to avoid an unflattering photo, but not enough to appear posed, walking just the right speed so they could get their shot.

One benefit of choosing Julia as his fake girlfriend was that she could take center stage. Even after the media inferno of Adam's scandal, she was still a bigger name. Her face had been plastered across national tabloids for years. Adam managed to hit the grocery store newsstands across the country a few times a year, not that he wanted the attention at all, but Julia was a fixture.

They strolled into the restaurant, dark wood paneling and white tablecloths as far as the eye could see. The gentle clinking of silverware and crystal stemware rose above a soundtrack of smooth jazz. The maître d' spotted them and whisked them to their corner table. Everyone in the restaurant gawked and whispered.

Julia consulted her menu. "So, sweetie." She glanced at him sideways. "What are you thinking about for dinner?" A bright smile crossed her lips and she knocked her head to the side, allowing her wavy brown hair to fall over her shoulders.

Any other man would've been drooling at her feet. Adam felt nothing. "Sweetie?" he whispered. "I don't think you called me that when we were dating."

She traced her finger on the tablecloth in a circle. "If we're playing a part, we have to do it right. We need pet names."

Adam nodded. "Oh. Okay." This would take some getting used to.

The waiter stopped by and took their drink orders—prosecco for Julia, bourbon, neat, for Adam.

He perused the menu again, not hungry for anything more than a good burger. "I guess I'll get the Tuscan rib eye."

Julia raised her eyebrows at him, imploring him to say what he'd forgotten to add.

"I guess I'll get the Tuscan rib eye, honey." He'd practically coughed out the word, a term of affection he'd never used for a woman. He wished he could've saved it for Melanie.

"Sounds great. I'll have the shrimp Caesar salad." Julia closed her menu and flattened her hand on the table. She stared at it, drummed her fingers then shot a look at Adam.

Oh. Right. He took her hand in his, but it felt wrong. This wasn't where he belonged. This wasn't the person he should be with. Of course, the person he wanted to be with, or at least have a chance with, had put him in this situation to start. So maybe it was best to just shut up, continue the charade and hope for the best. The LangTel gala was little more than three weeks away, and Melanie's assignment would be ending. He could try then. Try and possibly get shut down, again, but try he could.

"We should get our stories straight," Julia said once they'd ordered their entrees. "You know, how we got back together. People are going to ask questions. We need to have answers or it won't be believable."

Adam pinched the bridge of his nose. He was creative when it came to software and web applications, not when it came to making up stories. "Why don't you start?"

Julia sat up tall and smiled, an almost wistful look on her face. "I spent some time thinking about it today. I'm thinking that you called me when you heard that I was moving back to New York. Your life was in a shambles, of course. I mean, you'd really hit a low point."

Adam blinked, disbelieving what she said, even when it was the truth. "Uh, yeah. I get it." He shifted in his seat.

"We talked for hours on the phone that night and I agreed, hesitantly, to let you come by my apartment when I got into the city."

"Why hesitantly?"

"Adam, be serious. Of course I'd seen those horrible photos. They were all over the internet. What woman wouldn't be at least a little leery of you?"

His stomach soured. That could be one of Melanie's

doubts, too. She'd seen the worst side of him and been hired to show only the good. "I suppose you're right."

"You brought me flowers, white roses, I'm thinking, as a sign of good intentions."

"I thought white roses were for apologies."

"Well, you did break up with me."

"I thought we mutually decided to break up. And no one is going to believe that I broke up with you. That's absurd." He shook his head. Talk about absurd, this entire conversation was absurd.

"Okay, fine. Red roses. For passion." Julia winked at him flirtatiously.

Adam didn't say a thing. He just took a gulp of his bourbon.

"Sparks flew the minute we saw each other," Julia continued. "We knew that we had to get back together."

Adam leaned forward. "What do we say in a month when we end up breaking up?"

"Oh, the usual." Julia took a ladylike sip of her wine. "Two people devoted to their careers couldn't find a way to make enough time for each other. That's believable, right?"

A slow and steady sigh escaped Adam's lips. "More than you know, honey. More than you know."

Eight

The tabloid photos of Adam and Julia outside the restaurant on their first "fake" date were one thing—painful to look at, but tolerable. The shots of them having coffee a few days later were another thing—an odd ache cropped up in Melanie's chest, but she told herself it was heartburn.

There was hand-holding in the pictures. There were smiles. There were what might be construed as romantic glances. It was enough to make a girl give up all hope, which Melanie had already nearly done, all in the name of saving her business. But today, he was staring at Julia's butt. How much of this would she be able to take?

Fidgeting in her seat in the waiting room at Adam's office, she flipped open the newspaper, forcing herself to look at the photos of Julia and Adam running in Central Park with Jack. They looked so right together—smiling and running. It made her entire body hurt. After all, who smiles on a run? People ridiculously in love, that's who.

Adam and Julia were a perfect match on paper, as beautiful as could be. Adam, in particular, looked drop-dead gorgeous. Every woman in the city was probably gawking at these pictures. His gray Knicks T-shirt was stretched across his chest and stomach, taut enough that she could make out the subtle ripples of his abs. Oh, the kisses she'd bestowed on that magnificent stomach of his. The sensation of her lips on his skin still lingered. And now those abs were as off-limits as an entire cheesecake on a diet.

Hands down, the picture of the post-run stretch was the most painful. Julia, donning skin-tight black leggings and a similarly fitting tank top, was bending over, touching her toes. Adam, being a man, or at least Melanie was sure that would be his excuse, was ogling her butt. Julia had apparently received a free pass on gravity. *I could do five million squats and my behind would never look that good.*

Part of her wanted to take Adam to task over the photo since he was displaying the sort of behavior that had tripped him up in the first place, but the papers thought it was sexy, giving it the headline For His Eyes Only.

This was no way to start her day, not when she was about to spend the next two hours with Adam. Any minute now she'd be called into his office to help direct an online press conference, where he was set to speak with a dozen major business publications from around the globe via webcam. Today wasn't about the scandal. It was about putting the spotlight on Adam's business prowess, all to impress the LangTel board of directors.

She glanced at her watch. Adam was already five minutes behind on the schedule she'd given him. Luckily, she'd anticipated this and had given him the wrong time on purpose, just so that he wouldn't mess up.

"Ms. Costello, Mr. Langford will see you now," Adam's assistant, Mia, said, appearing from a door adjacent to the spacious lobby.

Melanie followed her through the door and down a wide

corridor as a steady stream of employees flowed back and forth from one open workspace to the next. The entire office was abuzz with people, countless staff, an army of Adam's choosing. She couldn't fathom the luxury of that much help.

Mia rapped on a door and opened it for Melanie. Adam's office was easily twice the size of Melanie's apartment—a luxurious yet modern space that was, like Adam, handsome and impressive. He was seated behind a sleek, black desk, phone to his ear, his back turned to her.

"We have the computer and monitors set up for the interviews." Mia pointed to a conference table on the far side of the room.

"Great. Thank you," Melanie whispered, not wanting to disturb Adam. She was taking a seat when he spoke.

"Hi there."

She glanced over at him. The instant their eyes connected, she was in trouble. It sent waves of attraction through her, which given the photos in the paper, only irritated her.

"Hi yourself." She wished she could've hidden the biting tone of her voice, but it was impossible. Her annoyance over him staring at Julia's miraculous butt wasn't going anywhere anytime soon. It would take a blowtorch to remove that image from her head. "This shouldn't last more than ninety minutes." She powered on the computer in front of her. "This has a webcam, right?"

"Of course. This is state of the art. What computer doesn't have a webcam?"

"Sorry. I didn't mean to insult your office equipment."

"You okay? You seem agitated." He grabbed that morning's newspaper off his desk and walked it over to her. "You've seen this, right? This is exactly what you wanted, isn't it? Everybody in the office was talking about it when I got to work. My dad called to tell me he loved it."

Melanie folded her arms across her chest. "Yes, I saw. Well done. Maybe next time don't get caught staring at her butt."

"Is that what this is about? Didn't like seeing that, huh?" Adam grinned like the damned Cheshire cat, taking a seat in the chair next to her. "Are you jealous?"

Melanie narrowed her focus, beyond perturbed by the question. "I'm trying to make you look like less of a womanizer, not more."

"Oh, come on." Adam shook his head, half laughing. "You can't be serious. Any man in the world would've done what I did. Her ass is spectacular. There's no harm in looking."

A heavy sigh left her lips, even when she didn't want him to see how much it bothered her. Did he have to use the word *spectacular*? It felt like a punch in the stomach. "Somehow I knew you would use the guy defense. I swear, men are so predictable sometimes. You see a pretty face and you just can't control yourself."

"Or a particularly attractive derriere, as the case may be." He leaned back in the office chair, arching both of his eyebrows at her, clearly enjoying himself. Mischief sparked in his steely eyes, even more compelling than usual when complemented by his deep blue dress shirt, tailored to flaunt every glorious inch of his chest and shoulders.

"Don't be cute. You have an interview to do in a minute. We can't be talking about this right now."

"Sure we can. They can wait. I want to know why this is bothering you."

"And I don't care to talk about it. You ended up in the newspaper with Julia. That's all I can ask."

The computer screen sprang to life, a grid of a dozen unfamiliar faces. The man in the upper right-hand corner waved. "Hello, Mr. Langford. Ms. Costello. I'll be moderating the chat today. We'll be ready to start in a few minutes."

"Sounds great. We're ready." Melanie neatly arranged her notes and pen.

"Actually, we're going to need about five minutes if that's okay," Adam said.

The moderator looked up from his desk. "Uh, sure, Mr. Langford. Just don't make it any longer than that. The journalists joining us today are all on a tight schedule."

"Don't worry. I won't hold you up." Adam reached over and muted the computer. "I want to know why the photo bothers you so much. Or do I have to remind you that it was your idea to fix me up with Julia?"

She hadn't been in close quarters with Adam like this in a week, and her mind and body were as conflicted as they could be. Everything about his physical presence—his smell, his hair, his hands—made her want to climb inside his shirt, while everything he was saying made her want to clasp her hand over his lips and tell him to shut the hell up. "Please stop reminding me that it was my idea. My brain can only take so much of this at one time."

"So much of what? Work? The photos? Julia?" He picked up a pen and flipped it back and forth in his fingers.

"Let's focus on the interview. You really don't want to know everything going through my head right now."

"Actually, I'd pay good money to know what's going on in that head of yours. We can start with the comment about men being so typical. Is there some jerky guy in your past? I mean, I'd like to think this is all about me, but now I'm wondering if there's something else going on."

She wasn't about to venture into the topic of her ex and her disastrous love life. "There's nothing more going on than me trying to do my job and you putting your special Adam touch on everything. It's like I spend hours setting a table for dinner and you walk by and turn the forks upside down. You thrive on making everything just slightly off-kilter, don't you?"

"Off-kilter?" He cocked an eyebrow. "How about real? I don't like things that are fake and contrived, that's all. I was spending time with Julia, she bent over, her butt is nice to look at, end of story. You don't have to read so much into it."

Then why can't I believe it's as simple as that? Melanie looked up to see the moderator waving at them both furiously. She turned the speakers and microphone back on.

"Mr. Langford. Ms. Costello. We really need to start."

"Yes, of course," Melanie said. "I'm so sorry for the delay."

Adam cleared his throat. "Yes, let's get started." He then began scrawling a note on a piece of paper. He slid it over to Melanie.

If you bent over in that skirt, I'd be happy to stare at your butt, too.

Nine

Adam let himself into his parents' Park Avenue apartment, the place he'd lived as a boy. It was opulently decorated, a bit stuffy for his tastes, but it was still home, crystal chandeliers, button-tufted sofas and all.

"Adam, darling." His mother swept into the foyer wearing her trademark look—black from head to toe with a vibrantly colored scarf around her neck. Adam couldn't remember a time when she'd worn anything much different, even when he was a boy.

"Mom. You look great." He kissed her on both cheeks, noticing that she'd lost more weight. The stress of caring for her ailing husband was taking its toll. "Is Anna here?"

"She's in the powder room. Should be out any second. We're having dinner in fifteen minutes. Margaret's making your favorite, beef Wellington."

"Sounds great. And Dad?" Adam and his mother strolled down the wide hall, shoes clacking on the black-and-white checkerboard marble floors.

"Watching television. He's developed a fondness for college basketball. Funny, since he never watched it before."

Adam had to smile, thinking about Melanie that night in the mountains. Even with the way it had ended, he would give anything to be back there with her right now—just the two of them, alone in that big house, the rest of the world a distant thought.

"Adam. My boy." Roger struggled to get out of his chair, but Adam knew better than to stop him, or worse, offer to help. The man was as stubborn as they came.

Adam hugged his father, who felt frail in his arms but still mustered a strong clap on Adam's back.

"Dad. It's good to see you." Every time he saw his dad, he had to wonder if this time would be the last. The thought was simply too sad to bear. He wanted to believe the doctors, and that Roger still had two or three months to go.

"And under such wonderful auspices, too. I couldn't be any more pleased with the way this public relations campaign has gone. Best money I've spent in years."

"Ms. Costello is very talented. No question about that."

Anna filed into the room. Her long dark hair was pulled back in a high ponytail. Always polished and professional, she wore a charcoal-gray suit and cream-colored blouse, having just come from her job as COO for a company that manufactured women's workout clothes.

Anna gave Adam an uneasy smile. Time with Dad was difficult for her. She was strong and independent, with a solid mind for business, but their father saw her in the context of their family—the only girl, the spitting image of her mother, a prized possession to be shielded from the harsh realities of board meetings and quarterly earnings reports. Roger Langford would never agree to let his little girl run LangTel, however desperate she was for the opportunity.

"Dad," Anna murmured, embracing their father. "You look good. Rosy cheeks and everything."

"That's because I'm happy. Adam and I were just talking about how well the public relations campaign is going. Your mother and I have two of our three children here for dinner. These days, I'm thankful for every little thing that goes my way."

"I actually heard from Aiden," Anna said, referring to their brother, the eldest of the Langford siblings. "He's somewhere in Thailand. I don't know much more than that. It was just a few lines in an email, and it'd been weeks since I'd reached out to him."

Their father shook his head in dismay. "God forbid that boy should call your mother and tell her he's alive."

Their mother's eyes grew sad. "He needs to stop avoiding your father's illness and come home."

"You know that's not going to happen," Adam said.

Aiden wasn't coming back anytime soon, not after the last argument he'd had with their father. No one dared speak of it, but Adam suspected it was about why Aiden was never considered to run LangTel and was left with little more than his personal shares in the company.

Aiden's upbringing was markedly different from Adam and Anna's. Six years older than Adam, Aiden had been sent off to boarding school when Adam was only two and Anna was a baby. Adam still didn't know why he and Anna attended private school in New York instead. He only knew that Aiden got into a lot of trouble at school—big trouble—and that Adam had been treated from a very young age as if he was the first-born. In many ways, it was as if Aiden didn't even exist, or at least not in their father's eyes. It saddened both Anna and Adam that they weren't close with their brother, but Aiden seemed content with keeping his distance.

"Anna, can I get you a drink?" Adam asked.

"Please. I've had a brutal day."

Adam stepped over to the bar in the corner to mix his sister a gin and tonic. She followed.

From the sound of things on the TV, someone had just hit a big shot in the basketball game. "Darn it all." Their father eased back into his seat. "I always miss the big plays."

Their mother consulted her watch. "Dinner should be ready in a few minutes. I'll check with Margaret and see how things are coming."

"You really heard from Aiden?" Adam asked Anna, careful to keep his voice low.

"It wasn't much. It's pretty clear he'd rather catch the plague than come home and face Dad."

"It'd be nice if they'd stop feuding." Adam shook his head, adding a jigger of Hendrick's gin to the glass and topping it off with tonic. "So what's the plan tonight? Are we going to talk to Dad?"

"Honestly, I don't know if I have the strength. If I have to listen to the speech about how I should be looking for a husband and thinking about private school for my unborn children, I might scream. Between Dad and my current job, I feel like I spend my entire life beating my head against a wall."

Adam drew in a deep breath. It was a miracle this subject hadn't given both his sister and him an ulcer. Ironic that they both had what the other wanted—he saw LangTel as a soul-sucking proposition, seeing out someone else's vision instead of his own. How he longed to have options like Anna.

She, on the other hand, would have done anything to become the first female CEO of a major telecom. More than anything, he sensed that she longed to prove herself, and do it on the largest stage imaginable.

Adam patted Anna's back. "I'll go to bat for you. We need to keep trying."

Margaret, the family's longtime cook, appeared in

the family room doorway. "Dinner is ready, Langford children." She smiled wide, looking like a pudgy Mary Poppins. For a moment, Adam could remember exactly what it was like to grow up in this household—every privilege a child could ever want, every expectation a young boy could never shoulder.

After dinner, Adam followed his father into his office, swirling bourbon in a cut-crystal old-fashioned glass. Since the cancer diagnosis, his dad had laid off the liquor. Roger took his place behind the massive mahogany desk, which had once been the prized possession of Adam's grandfather, the second Langford man to make a fortune in business. Even when Adam and his dad were having father-son time, the setup always more closely resembled a meeting.

"Tell me how things are going with Julia. I know you didn't want to talk about it in front of your mother, but you can tell your old man. You know, we actually look forward to seeing your picture in the paper now." He laughed quietly. "That's a big improvement from a month ago."

Adam wasn't convinced it had made things any better, at least not for him personally. Parading around Manhattan with his fake girlfriend made him feel like a human puppet, and for someone who had his own ideas of what he should be doing, that was uncomfortable. He settled into one of the leather club chairs opposite his father's desk. "Dad, I've told you. It isn't real. It was Ms. Costello's idea, remember?"

"I know what I saw in those pictures. You're happy together." Roger collected a handful of envelopes and neatly arranged them on his desk blotter. "Sometimes a man needs to open his eyes to what is already in front of him. You'd be a fool to pass up a woman like Julia."

All Adam could think was that the woman who was

already in front of him was Melanie. And she wanted nothing to do with him, at least not romantically.

"Julia is beautiful and famous, Adam. She's exactly the sort of woman your mother and I would love to see you with. You're a man. She's a woman. I don't see the problem."

The problem is that I don't feel anything when I'm with her. Adam took another sip of bourbon. His father was accustomed to getting what he wanted. Adam wasn't about to deny a dying man, but he wouldn't lie. "I need you and Mom to keep your feet firmly planted on the ground. Unless something drastic happens, there is no Adam and Julia."

"Son, let me ask you this. Do you know what I saw when I looked at you and your sister on the days you were born?"

Adam pursed his lips. "Wrinkly newborns?"

"I saw the future. I saw a boy to carry on my name and my legacy. I saw a girl to give your mother and me grandchildren."

"What about Aiden?"

"I thought I saw the future in him, too, but it turns out that I was wrong."

"Dad, don't say that."

"It's true. I have very few days left on this earth. The only thing I have left is hope that you and your sister and your mother will be okay after I'm gone. I need to know that you will have the lives you want. That means a husband for your sister and a wife for you. That means a roomful of grandchildren at Christmas for your mother." His dad's booming voice softened and wobbled. A single tear rolled down his cheek.

Adam sucked in a deep breath. He'd seen his father cry only once, the day his Grandmother Langford had died.

Adam knew that his dad had a heart as wide as an ocean, even if he could be stern and demanding.

"You can't worry about us like that. We'll be fine. And you have to stop assuming that you won't be around for those things, because you never know."

"I just need you to know that the three of you are the most important thing in the entire world to me. You're my only thought when I wake up in the morning."

Of course, Adam knew that his dad's statement wasn't entirely true. Willing to admit it or not, Roger Langford had an awful lot of ego wrapped up in the future of the corporation he'd built from the ground up.

"Dad, you know we need to talk about Anna and LangTel. You really hurt her feelings at dinner, and I don't understand why you refuse to see what an amazing job she'll do."

"It's not her abilities I question. I put her in charge of organizing the gala, didn't I?"

"That's not the assignment she was hoping for."

"She's a smart girl, but you have to be bulletproof to do my job, and I'm not willing to put my little girl in that position. It's my job to protect her. Call me an old man if you want to, that's just the way I feel."

Adam would've simply grumbled if he weren't so dead set on proving his dad wrong on this point. And it wasn't just selfish reasons that motivated him. There was more to it than his lack of enthusiasm for running LangTel. His sister had grown up in Adam's shadow, and he hated it. She was just as smart as him, maybe even smarter, innovative, quick on her feet. It was just that she'd had the unlucky lot of not being a boy. She was at an unfair disadvantage from the outset.

"Anna is as tough as any man. Maybe tougher. And you know, she helped me a lot when you put me in charge during your surgery and first wave of treatments. I don't understand why you won't give her the chance."

"You said it right there. She helped you. I can see her in a subordinate role. Perhaps she's senior assistant to the CEO or some such. You'll be at the helm, just as you've dreamed about since you were little."

Adam had to say what was on the tip of his tongue. "What if I don't want to run LangTel?"

The look on his dad's face was one of utter horror. "Don't let your sister's wishes cloud the issue. Of course you're going to run LangTel. That has been the plan from the day you were born, and I'm not about to stray from that now. End of discussion."

"Dad, I'm a grown man. I have my own company to run. You, more than anyone, must appreciate that I want to see my own vision come to life. I want to succeed with my own plans, not see out what you had hoped to do, but won't have the chance to." Dead silence rang through the room as Adam realized what he'd said. "Dad, no." He sat forward, placed his hands flat on his father's desk. "I'm sorry. That's not what I meant."

"You think I don't wish we were having this discussion because I was getting ready to retire? Because I do, dammit." He pounded his fist on the desk. "But I'll be gone by then. LangTel is my life's work and your mother's financial security, and you're the person I trust with it. So, like it or not, I need you to accept the fact that you were born to do this job. Period."

Adam sank back in his chair. How could he argue with his dad when he was facing death? He couldn't.

Ten

Most magazine editors were notorious for last-minute changes, and Fiona March, editor in chief of *Metropolitan Style*, was no exception. Adam's cover feature in the weekly magazine was one of the first things Melanie had put in place for the campaign, and it was easily her biggest coup. So when Fiona called her the night before and requested—no, begged—that Julia be present for Adam's interview and photo shoot, Melanie had no choice. Plus, Fiona had decided to conduct the interview herself, something she did only once or twice a year. Melanie had to make it happen.

Great. Can't wait to hang out with Mr. and Ms. Beautiful.

Melanie blew out a breath, staring at the numbers above the elevator door. She considered pushing the alarm. The temptation was so great that her hand twitched. A screeching siren would at least delay her arrival at Adam's penthouse apartment and create a diversion. If she was super lucky, maybe they'd send a hunky fireman to her rescue and she could have a fling with him and forget Adam. Firemen made good boyfriends. They didn't complicate a woman's life, and especially not her career.

Much to her dismay, she hadn't had the nerve to press the red button, and the doors slid open when she reached Adam's apartment. This was her first time here since their night together, and visions were already flashing through her mind. To make matters worse, her stroll down memory lane would be accompanied by her first meeting with Adam's new "love interest," Julia. *Breathe. Breathe.*

The last time she'd been in this room, she was half-undressed, Adam's hands all over her while she frantically unbuttoned his shirt, nearly breaking the zipper on his pants, before embarrassingly stepping on his foot. He'd played it off so sexily, too, sweeping her into his arms and mumbling into her ear, "No more walking for you." A minute later, her hair was splayed across his bed and he was blazing a trail of kisses down her stomach. Just thinking about it created waves of pleasant warmth, followed by emptiness. She'd needed him so badly that night. She'd needed him in the mountain house. What was it about him that elicited that response?

A *Metropolitan Style* photographer was busy capturing the open-plan living room—high ceilings, dark wood floors, cool gray walls, brown leather furniture just as Adam liked it. There were the more feminine touches now—a cashmere throw, decorative candles and objets d'art on the coffee table, all added by the home stager Melanie had hired and to which Adam had protested. The neon beer signs and moose head were indeed fiction.

As much as she wasn't thrilled to meet Julia, she needed to be here to make sure this interview went perfectly. She needed to be here to give Adam the stink-eye if he started down the wrong path with his answers. She scanned the room, catching sight of Adam perched on a tall wooden stool in the corner, Jack at his side.

She hurried over, admiring him in the icy blue shirt she'd convinced him to wear. It wasn't lavender, but at least he was taking direction. He was ridiculously handsome in the lighter color, even when the look on his face was one of distinct misery. "It's okay to smile, you know," she said.

The male makeup artist working on Adam cast Melanie a knowing grin. "I'll be done with him in a minute. I don't think he's enjoying it."

"I just want to get this over with," Adam mumbled as he had concealer applied to the corner of his mouth. "I've had about a dozen important emails in the last five minutes. This is seriously the last thing I have time for right now."

"I made him put down his phone," the makeup artist said. "It was making him wrinkle his forehead, which makes my job pointless."

A vaguely recognizable female voice rang out behind Melanie. "I think he looks perfect. Handsome as ever."

Melanie turned, coming face-to-face with the most stunningly gorgeous nightmare she'd ever seen.

"You must be Melanie. I'm Julia." She held out her hand, flashing the smile that had graced dozens of movie posters. Her shoulder-length brown hair glinted with auburn highlights, her minimalist makeup flawless. And then there was her outfit.

Julia burst out laughing. Her stunning green eyes grew wide with surprise. "Oh my goodness. We're wearing almost exactly the same dress. Neiman Marcus? Last fall?"

If Melanie could've done anything at that moment, she would've gladly taken her chances with the elevator alarm. "Ha. Oh. Wow. Yeah. Funny." *Kill me now. Please.* "Mine is vintage. It belonged to my mother."

"Oh, how wonderful. Even better that you have a story to go along with it." Julia tucked her hair behind her ear.

Julia's voice had a sweet edge that instantly put a person at ease, except Melanie refused to be at ease. She was too busy feeling Adam's eyes on them, knowing he had to be studying how she measured up to the picture-perfect gazelle wearing nearly the same outfit.

"Turn around, so I can get a look at you." Julia looped a circle in the air with her finger.

Melanie's stomach sank when she caught the smirk on Adam's face. This bore far too much resemblance to the things her father used to make her do—twirl around in a fancy dress for the neighbors, look pretty for company. Melanie's sisters were always far better at it than she was, just as Julia was when it came to showing off the sublime lines of her black wool dress.

"I promise you, you aren't missing anything." Melanie internally begged for all attention to be taken away from her. Especially when she was forced to stand next to a woman with four percent body fat and not a single pinch-able inch.

"I'll tell you one thing, you fill out the skirt so much better than I do." Julia perched on the back of Adam's leather sofa.

Melanie would've gasped if she weren't so dumbstruck. *Fill it out?* Any woman would've wondered if Julia was using girl code for *fat*. Melanie knew for certain that she wasn't fat, but she was no waif either. She had curves—real hips, a real butt.

"She does look fantastic in it, doesn't she, Jules?" Adam chimed in.

"Perfection. Makes me think I need to take mine to a tailor." Julia crossed her mile-long legs.

Now Melanie was beyond confused. Julia hadn't meant it as an insult? Maybe it was easy to be generous with compliments when she was always the most beautiful woman in the room, wherever she went.

The elevator into Adam's apartment opened and Fiona March, willowy with short black hair, made her entrance. She was juggling a large designer purse and an oversize bottle of water. "Melanie, so glad you're here already. Sorry I'm late."

Melanie rushed over. Fiona was one of Melanie's most important contacts. "You're never late. You're right on time."

"You're sweet," Fiona answered. "You're also a terrible liar, but so was my third husband and he was fantastic in the sack, so I'll give you the benefit of the doubt."

Melanie laughed, leading Fiona across the room. "Let me introduce you to Adam and Julia."

The three exchanged niceties, but Adam seemed distant, as if something was bothering him. She pulled him aside while the cameraman adjusted the lighting for the photos they would take during the interview.

"Are you okay?" Melanie looked up at him, trying like hell not to get caught up in his eyes.

He cracked half a smile, which was better than most men's full smile. "You're so sweet when you want to be."

I always want to be sweet. My job doesn't always afford me that luxury. "I just want to make sure you're okay. You're my client. I need you to be okay."

"Ah, so that's what you're concerned with. Whether or not your client is going to perform for you today."

"Not exactly. I'm genuinely worried." She pointed at his forehead. "The makeup guy was right. You get this little crinkle between your eyes when you're thinking too much."

Adam rubbed the spot with his fingers, as if to erase it. "I do? No one has ever told me that before."

"Probably from staring at a computer screen all day long. You need to give your eyes a break every now and then." She reached out and grasped his elbow. "Let me know if you need a minute, okay? It's better to take the time to collect yourself now, rather than later. I don't want you to be caught in an uncomfortable situation."

Adam cast his eyes to his arm, where Melanie was holding it so tenderly with her elegant hands. He'd almost forgotten the way her touch brought him to life. Her sweet smell washed over him, her curves in that black dress called to him, reminding him where his hands fit best, the places she loved to be squeezed.

She patted him on the shoulder. "Everything okay?"

He nodded. "Yep."

"You'll do great. Don't worry."

He fought a smile. Even though it didn't seem to go beyond their professional relationship, she cared. Sometimes she cared too much about things, about what other people thought, in particular, but she was passionate, and that was so damn sexy.

It tormented him to see her in this room, in his apartment, knowing the things they'd shared the first time she was here. Those few hours were engraved in his memory. She'd made him laugh, she'd made him growl with desire, she'd made him feel something strong and real, when that had been missing from his life. He'd never had that kind of instant chemistry with anyone, not even with his ex-fiancée, and he'd been deeply in love with her. Logic said that he could have that with Melanie, but it took two to tango, and she'd shown she had no interest in dancing.

He could still remember Melanie's words from their night together, as she wrapped her legs tightly around his waist, her slick heat inviting him inside for the first time. She'd arched her back, rolled her entire body into his, grasped the back of his neck with both hands and murmured in the sexiest voice he'd ever heard, "You feel like a dream." If he closed his eyes, he could still hear her say it, and that made everything in his body grow tight and hot.

Sure, women had lauded Adam with praise, but much of it was meaningless—things about having an amazing apartment or looking hot in his suit or having an air of power and control, whatever that meant. Melanie had chosen a simple line, sweet and almost poetic, that was all about him as a man, the things he could give to her that had nothing to do with money or prestige. His God-given talents.

"Adam," Melanie said.

"Yes?" She was still close enough to pull into his arms and dammit if his hands didn't want to do exactly that.

"Fiona is ready to start the interview."

Adam forced a smile. Showtime. All he could think as he took his place opposite Fiona was that as soon as he was asked about his relationship with Julia, this would all become real, at least to the world. The photos in the tabloids were largely conjecture. This would make it seem authentic, and that made him wish he could stand up and tell everyone but Melanie to leave.

"So, Adam." Fiona leaned forward and placed her hand on his knee. "May I call you Adam?"

"Of course."

She smiled warmly. "Tell me about your rekindled romance with Julia Keys. We've all been seeing you two around town together, and I'm sure our readers would love to know more about the hottest couple in Manhattan."

Okay, then. Right into it. Adam cleared his throat, on edge, torn between what Melanie would want him to say and what he wanted to say in front of Melanie if he had the chance. "What can I say? Julia is a lovely woman and we're having a great time becoming reacquainted." If only he could spout the reality, because what he really wanted to say was, "Well, you see, the truth is that I went from casually dating dozens of women to having a fake girl-friend while pining for a woman who wants me to remain her client."

"Can you tell us about how you got back together?" Fiona asked.

Adam shifted in his seat, tugging at his collar, remembering the script Julia had given him at the restaurant. "Well, I heard that Julia was moving back to New York and I wanted to see her, so I called her." Out of the corner of his eye, he could see Melanie hanging on every word. Was he doing what she wanted? He thought so, but he'd been wrong before. "She agreed to let me come by her new apartment when she arrived in the city. That was the start of it."

"Don't forget about the roses," Julia blurted, stepping forward and placing her hand on Fiona's shoulder. "I'm sorry to interrupt, but I must. You see, Adam is so romantic, and he doesn't give himself credit."

"Tell me more," Fiona said. "Actually, Adam, if it's okay with you, I would love it if Julia joined us for the interview."

Adam shot a look at Melanie, who had her arms folded squarely across her chest. He had no earthly idea what she was thinking. "Perhaps we should ask Ms. Costello."

Melanie nodded. "Sure. Of course. Whatever seems right, Fiona." Her voice wobbled when she spoke. Perhaps this was as nerve-racking for her as it was for Adam.

"Can we get a chair for Ms. Keys, please?" Fiona asked.

Julia perched herself on Adam's chair and draped her arm across his shoulders. "Don't worry about me. I'm just fine like this." She wiggled herself into place against him, making him exponentially more uncomfortable. "So, yes, Adam brought me a dozen roses that night. At first it made me mad, because roses seemed like such a cliché."

Adam wanted to scream. *The damn roses were your*

idea. Instead, he forced himself to watch Julia as if he was captivated by her every word.

Julia shrugged and pressed a kiss to Adam's forehead. "But it was so romantic, I couldn't do anything but tell him that yes, I wanted to get back together with him, too. It's been like a dream ever since."

Except that it wasn't a dream, at all. It was a big, messy lie that he was expected to perpetrate.

Plus, Melanie had called him a dream, and that was the only context in which he ever wanted to think about that word again.

Eleven

Melanie's email and voice mail had become the Julia and Adam show, and she, its unwitting choreographer.

Everyone had questions. *Is it true that they're serious?* How was Melanie supposed to answer that? It appeared so. The photos were heartbreakingly convincing. Even when Melanie was supposed to *know*, deep down, that they weren't really a couple, it looked as if they were. Why else would she get a pit in her stomach every time she saw them in the newspapers together?

Is he finally settling down? His family sure seemed to think so. Roger Langford had called and thanked Melanie again for her supersmart plan. The Langfords had reportedly hosted Julia for dinner and she regaled everyone with her wit and Hollywood stories. Adam's mom had apparently remarked that Julia and Adam would make beautiful babies. Of course they would…not that Melanie could stand to think about it for even a minute.

Will Julia be the woman to tame him? Melanie audibly

snorted when she read that one. Tame Adam Langford. It made him sound like a lion in the circus, when she knew that he was nothing of the sort. Not even when he'd been engaged had Adam allowed himself to be anything less than the person who called the shots.

Her cell phone rang and she was about to chuck it across the room, especially when she saw on the caller ID that it was Adam. Spending the past three hours dwelling on the question of whether or not the relationship between Adam and Julia was real had left her in no mood to converse with the man in question. But she had to answer.

"Adam, hi."

"I'm coming to your office." The sound of car horns blared in the background.

"What? Where are you? When?" Melanie closed her eyes and pinched the bridge of her nose. "Why?"

"Aren't you full of questions? I'm in the car, stuck in traffic, and late for the interview with that tech magazine. We're about a block from your office. I just had my assistant call the writer and tell him to meet me there. It actually works out better for him, anyway."

Melanie surveyed her disastrous desk. The lobby area was fairly tidy, but there was one glaring thing missing—someone manning the actual reception desk. How does someone run a so-called up-and-coming public relations firm with no staff? She had absolutely no idea, only that she had to do it every day.

She scrambled to put on a pot of coffee and arrange a suitable interview space in her reception area for Adam and the writer. The final throw pillow on the sofa had been fluffed when Adam strolled in.

"Sorry. Crazy day," Adam said, hitting a button on his phone and shoving it into his front pocket. He was dressed in impeccable gray flat-front trousers and a black dress shirt with the sleeves rolled up to the elbows, no tie. The dark stubble along his jaw was at its usual perfection. It was a windy day in the city and Adam's hair showed the effects, disheveled and mussed, just so—sexy and enticing, almost like bed head.

She had to clasp her hands together, squeeze them hard, all while gritting her teeth to keep from combing her fingers into the thickest part of his hair, at the top of his head, where it got a little curly when it was wet. It was no wonder he had such a pull on her. Why did he have to be so flawless? Well, he did have one or two flaws, the most glaring of which was his unwillingness to make a serious relationship with a woman a priority.

Adam scanned the reception area. "Where is everyone?"

"Everyone?" She turned, forcing herself to keep from drifting closer to him after catching a whiff of his heady scent.

"Your staff. Receptionist. Assistants. Interns. I had visions of a busy office like mine. Your client list is a mile long."

It used to be a lot longer. When Josh was here. There had been a lot of things when Josh was still there— someone to share the workload, someone to talk to about her problems, someone to hold her at the end of a long day and tell her that everything was going to be all right. Her support system, her safety net, was gone.

If she'd had the strength to put the right spin on the merits of a one-woman operation, she would have, but she'd spent her morning creating spin. Putting a glossy shine on everything she said to Adam was exhausting. It was so much easier to be honest. "It's just me right now. Lean and mean. Makes things a lot simpler."

"Oh. Okay." He seemed skeptical despite the affirmation, furrowing his brow. "But who runs the office? Who buys office supplies and fixes computer problems? And what about things like arranging your travel or organizing your calendar or hell, even the little stuff, like making appointments to get your hair cut or running to the dry cleaners?"

When he had to put it like *that*, it made it all sound impossible, so utterly absurd. "Maybe my life isn't as complicated as yours. I work all day, I go home and sleep. Rinse. Repeat."

"Sounds boring."

It is.

"And a little unfulfilling," he had the nerve to continue.

"It isn't, thank you very much. It also makes it remarkably easy to keep myself out of the tabloids."

Awkward silence hung in the air. "Ouch."

She felt horrible. "I'm sorry. That was out of line."

"Just seems like you'd get a lot more clients, and bigger ones at that, if you had a staff to take care of the little things. You need to delegate if you're going to be successful." He was not about to let this go.

"Follow me. I need to get you guys some coffee. Unless you'd prefer water."

"Definitely coffee. I need the afternoon pick-me-up."

Melanie stalked into the state-of-the-art office kitchenette, twenty times nicer than what she had in her apartment and just as expensive, to finish cobbling together some hospitality, yet another of the many hats she wore. She removed a lacquered tray from the cabinet, spread out a white linen napkin and topped it with a sugar bowl and pitcher of cream. Two teaspoons were added to finish it. "Will you want anything to nibble on? I have a few different kinds of cookies in the pantry. Or I could run down to the bakery and see what they have for pastries."

"See? Like this. You should not be doing this. You're a smart, capable businesswoman and you work hard. You should not be worrying about cookies and pastries for a client."

Did he really see her that way?

He leaned against the black granite counter, his hand close to her hip—so close he could've touched her with little effort if he'd wanted to. "I'm not wrong."

Oh, he was all kinds of wrong, only in that he was a little *too* right. Ideas swirled in her head, of a hot kiss in the break room, his insistent lips on hers. Maybe he'd back her up against the refrigerator with enough force to flatten the back of her hair, maybe even hard enough to make the magnets fall off the door. If that ever happened, he wouldn't hesitate to untuck her blouse and snake his hands along her back. He'd unhook her bra, mold her breasts in his hands. She'd have no choice at that point—she'd have to take off every stitch of his clothes so they could send each other into blissful oblivion. Or she could slam on the brakes, as she had in the mountains, because a tryst with Adam in the kitchen, or anywhere else, would be wrong.

Melanie's eyes fluttered. Her face flushed, her chest burned. She'd have to stick her head in the freezer if she allowed herself any more daydreamy latitude. No more Adam fantasies. Not today.

She filled two mugs emblazoned with Costello Public Relations. What a joke. Her company was hardly custom coffee cup–worthy in its current state. Adam had insinuated as much. "Anything else, Mr. Wizard? Should I be taking notes?"

"Very funny. Mr. Wizard. I'm just giving you a little free advice. I do know what I'm doing, you know." He claimed one of the coffees from the counter and added a splash of cream. "I made my first million out of a dorm room. I know how to grow a company."

"You know how to grow *your* company. We're in two completely different lines of work. Believe me, I know how to grow mine." Sure, she could snag a lot more clients if she didn't have to worry about things like vacuuming the office before meetings. It didn't matter. She simply didn't have the means. She'd have to work more and sleep less until that turned around.

"Okay." Adam headed out of the kitchen and back into the reception area. "We can talk about it later. I'll take you out for a drink after the interview. One of my favorite neighborhood bars is around the corner."

"A drink?" *Just what I need. Liquor to fog up my already questionable resolve.*

"Yes. I know it falls outside the scope of going to work and going home, but I think you'll enjoy yourself. We haven't spent enough time together that wasn't related to work."

"We'll still be talking about work. I think that counts."

"Something tells me we'll get around to other topics."

Other topics. Melanie did not want to discuss her family or her love life. What else was there? The weather? She made a mental note to check the forecast online while Adam did the interview. Maybe she'd brush up on NBA scores, knowing that Adam followed the Knicks. Anything she could launch at him to steer the conversation toward the benign. If he brought up Julia, she wanted to be prepared to change the subject, pronto.

There was a knock at the door and a lanky man opened it. "I think I'm in the right place. I'm looking for Adam Langford."

"Yes, you're in the right place," Melanie answered, smiling and rushing across the room to shake his hand. "Please. Come on in. I made coffee."

Twelve

This was as close Adam could come to taking Melanie out on a date, at least while he was in a fake relationship with another woman. And at least while Melanie was dishing up roadblocks and mixed signals.

He opened the creaky, dark wood door of Flaherty's Pub for her. "Ladies first."

She grimaced, peering into the dimly lit bar. "Something tells me they aren't going to want to make me a mojito in this place."

"Sorry, Buttermilk. Nothing with a sugared rim, either."

She pointed at him accusatorially, pursing her lips, but he caught a fraction of a smile. "You know how I feel about that nickname."

He ushered her ahead. "I do, but the problem is it fits you so perfectly. A little sweet, a little sour. Most of the time I can't think of anything better to call you."

"Adam Langford, you're lucky I need a drink so badly."

His favorite watering hole in Manhattan was dark as

could be—poor lighting, worn mahogany, deep maroon upholstery on the booths. A jukebox predating them both sat at the back. A few regulars were lined up at the bar. They'd probably spent their afternoon knocking back a cold one, preserving the lost art of conversation.

Melanie clutched her purse to her chest. "This isn't what I imagined when you said you'd take me out for a drink."

Adam shook his head, placing his hands on her shoulders. "Relax. Don't you trust me? I've been sneaking in here since I was a teenager. I love it. It's totally different from anywhere else I spend my time. My parents would be appalled if they knew about it."

Jones, the gray-haired bartender, flipped a towel over his shoulder and nodded at Adam. "Look who's here. The prodigal son returns." Jones had long called him that, but he knew little about Adam's background. He never asked, Adam never offered. Coming to Flaherty's was time for throwing darts and leaving everything else behind.

Adam laughed and curved his hand at Melanie's waist. "Come on," he said quietly. As much as she looked out of her element, she did trust his taste enough to follow his lead across the room. Adam shook Jones's hand. "How are you, my man? Business treating you right?"

Jones pushed his black-framed glasses up onto his nose. "I've got every microbrewery in the country trying to get me to sell their beer, but for the most part, I can't complain." He wiped a spot on the bar with a towel. "Where are your manners? Are you going to introduce me to the lovely lady you brought to my fine establishment?"

Adam nodded. One thing he loved about Flaherty's was that nobody gave him a hard time about anything serious. There was no speculation about him or his character. They certainly wouldn't know what was playing out in the tabloids. Jones, especially, was concerned with the sports page and not much else. Here he could be single Adam Langford and he could take Melanie out for a drink. "Yes, of course. This is Melanie Costello. Her office is about a block from here. I'm surprised you two haven't run into each other."

Melanie smiled, seeming to warm to her surroundings. "Probably just on different schedules."

"Jonesy, I need you to make Melanie a very special drink. She loves mojitos. Anything you can get close to that?"

Jones scoffed. "Are you kidding me? I spent two years in Puerto Rico after I was in the military. I make the best mojito ever. My wife grows the mint out at our place in Staten Island."

Melanie saddled up to the bar, perching in a swivel stool and crossing her splendid legs. "That sounds wonderful. Tell me about your wife. How long have you been married?"

"Her name is Sandy. Been married twenty-seven years. Not counting tomorrow, of course." Jones winked at Melanie as he got out a pint glass.

What the hell? "How did I not know you could make a mojito?" Adam asked.

"Maybe because you never ordered one." Jones went to work, muddling mint and sugar in the bottom of a cocktail shaker. "Maybe because you never ordered anything more than a bourbon or a beer. And maybe because lovely Melanie is the first woman you've ever brought in here."

Melanie rested her elbow on the bar and turned back to look at Adam. She flashed her beguiling blue eyes. "The first woman ever. I feel so special."

He knew she was being sarcastic, but he loved bringing out that side of her—the sassy, flirtatious side. It made his entire body tight, especially everything below the belt. He opted not to sit next to her, instead draping his arm across the back of the bar stool. Here, in a place where he could be anonymous, he didn't mind allowing his mind to wander to thoughts of what it would be like to be with Melanie. To have her as his girlfriend, or more.

In that world, he could deal with his other problems in a much better fashion. If he had Melanie, she would understand his work stresses. She would understand at least some of his family stresses because she'd dealt with similar things herself. And damn if she wouldn't be a sight for sore eyes after a long day.

Jones finished up their drinks. "I'll put yours on your tab, Adam. Melanie's is on the house." He again winked at her, which elicited an uncharacteristic giggle.

Adam wasn't shocked by Jones's attempt at flirtation. How could a man not be drawn to Melanie? Aside from her beauty—deep blue eyes and soft pink lips, curves designed to make him lose all sense of direction, and that was only the start—she had something within her that was simply magnetic. There was her staunch independence and her fiery devotion to her work, but she also possessed vulnerability. There was a caring and gentle woman inside, as well.

Melanie stirred her glass, poking at the ice with her straw. "Jones, this is delicious. Absolutely the best I've ever had, and I've had more than my fair share of mojitos."

Adam drank in the vision as Melanie skimmed the corner of her mouth with her tongue and flashed a satisfied grin. He had both feet firmly planted on the ground and still he felt as if he might fall over. "Let's take one of the booths in the corner," he said.

"Keeping her all to yourself?" Jones asked.

"I'm no dummy," Adam replied, taking his drink from the bar.

They settled into the small, half-round booth, Melanie placing her large purse squarely between them.

Damn. He'd been counting on a chance to inch closer. "Talk to me about Costello Public Relations. I want to know how you can run a one-woman shop. And don't tell me you're keeping it lean and mean. I don't buy it."

Melanie cocked her head to the side. "What is so mystifying about the concept? I'm capable. I get stuff done."

"I never said you didn't. I only said that you'd get more done if you had support staff. You must be bringing in enough money. I know how much my dad is paying you and it's substantial."

The sound that came out of Melanie was equal parts frustration and resignation. "Let's just say I'm upside down in my office lease and I'm still paying off the furniture." She shook her head and took another long draw of her mojito. "If you must know, that's the real reason I don't have a staff. I can't afford it. Yet." She planted her finger on the table. "Someday I will."

"Why'd you spend so much money on your office? You had to have had a business plan, a budget for the first few years."

"It was my former business partner's idea."

"So sue her."

She paused before she answered, seeming to calculate what to say. "Sue *him*. And it's not that simple."

"Sure it is. You have to be ruthless when it comes to things like this. It's just business."

"It's not just business." Melanie took a sip of her drink that was so long, he thought she might make it all the way to the bottom. "It's personal. Very personal."

Whatever was very personal was also clearly a sore spot. Maybe she didn't like talking about work after hours. It wasn't his intention to draw her into an unwelcome conversation, especially now that they finally had the chance to go out together, but he had to know.

"I'm listening. Tell me everything."

"I'd rather not talk about it."

He fought disappointment that she still didn't trust him

enough to simply come out with it, but he had to keep trying. "Please don't be afraid to confide in me. I'm only trying to help. No judgments. Just help."

She looked him in the eye, searching, for what he did not know. He took the opportunity to reciprocate, scanning her lovely features, his heart heavy that she was obviously suffering over whatever had happened.

Finally, she sighed and dropped her shoulders. "My business partner was also my boyfriend. I thought he was about to become my fiancé, but I was clueless. He had an affair with one of our clients, while he and I were living together and talking about marriage and children." Her voice wobbled, but her resolve was still evident. "He left with her. For San Francisco. They went into real estate together. And unfortunately, I trusted him and it's only my name on the lease, or anything for that matter. Costello PR is all mine. Sink or swim."

Anger bubbled under Adam's skin. He hadn't been in many fistfights in his life, but he wouldn't hesitate to flatten Melanie's ex, to make him feel a fragment of the pain he'd caused her. "I'm so sorry. Talk about a double whammy."

He was about to reach across the table and take her hand, but she pulled it back, picking up her drink and downing the last of it.

"A triple even," she muttered when she came up for air.

"An affair. With a client…" And there it was. Aside from the contract with his father and her extreme attachment to doing things her way, there was another reason to keep him at arm's length.

"Yes, Adam. An affair. With a client. It looks a little different from the outside, doesn't it? Some people would call it unseemly."

Adam wanted to protest, to say that it wasn't the same because this excuse for a man, her ex, was a coward. And he had to be certifiable. Why would anyone leave her? "The way he went about it, it does. It wouldn't have to be like that. If two people were attracted to each other, they could wait until the working relationship had come to a close and then proceed with romantic intentions."

"But both people would have to be unattached, completely, for real." Something wouldn't allow her to say that she meant Julia. "And both people would have to be capable of commitment. Because I don't do casual. It's not in my DNA."

Did this mean she was interested? And could he do commitment? Could he start out a relationship that way? Usually he eased into that mode, knowing he'd likely never get there, but Melanie deserved far more. "Are you giving me a checklist?"

"Even if I did, it still wouldn't account for *my* checklist, and trust me, mine is a mile long."

Adam's phone beeped with a text. *Dammit.* Just when he was learning the landscape of the epic battle to win over Melanie. "I'm sorry. I should've put it on vibrate."

"It's okay. I understand."

Adam cringed as he read the message from Julia.

I need you at a dinner Saturday. Director in town.

It turned out that the fake relationship benefited Julia more than they'd originally thought it might. She'd landed a gritty role as a mouthy Long Island mob wife, a part her agent said she wouldn't have been considered for before she got serious with a man immersed in controversy. Julia was convinced this was her chance at industry awards.

The text was an unwelcome reminder of what was waiting for him outside Flaherty's—obligations that revolved around other people's needs, all of it keeping him from Melanie, and just when he'd convinced her to open up. She knew so much about him, even the bad things. He didn't know much beyond Little Miss Buttermilk and now, her bastard of an ex.

"Crisis in the office?" she asked.

Adam clicked off his phone and shoved it into his pocket. "Just something that will have to wait." He smiled, relishing his return to conversation with Melanie. "Where were we?"

"Nowhere. I'd like a change of subject." She looked over her shoulder. "Or a turn with the jukebox." She whipped back and dug through her purse. "Shoot. I don't have any change."

"The machine takes quarters. I'll get some from Jones."

"And another drink?" She lifted her glass and shook it at him.

He laughed quietly. He adored her playful side, especially since she didn't show it often.

Melanie slid out from the booth and wound her way to the jukebox. Adam got change and another round of drinks, listening dutifully as Jones informed him that he was a "certifiable idiot" if he did anything less than treat Melanie like a princess and figure out a way to make her his wife. For the moment, he was going for a successful first date.

Adam watched the sway of Melanie's hips as she stood before the jukebox, pushing the button and making the records go by. He would've done anything for the chance to walk up behind her, wrap his arms around her waist and kiss her neck. But even in the place where they could shut out the world, he wasn't sure she'd be amenable.

"About time," she said when he reached her. She plucked the quarters from his hand and plugged the machine, then tapped away at the numbers.

"Don't I get to pick any?" He moved in next to her until they were standing virtually hip to hip. He had several inches of height advantage, even when she was wearing heels. Heels that he couldn't help but notice made her legs look incredible.

She grumbled. "I don't even know if you have good taste in music." She turned to block his access to the number pad controlling the jukebox.

You clever minx. "You've got to be kidding. I have excellent taste in music, and don't forget that I financed this endeavor. I at least deserve a turn."

She punched in another number. "Okay. You can pick one song. But it'd better be good." With a flourish, she stepped back, placing the tips of her graceful fingers on her collarbone.

Give me strength. Adam's head was doing somersaults. When Melanie let down her guard, when she was being sassy and independent and sexy, exactly the way she'd been the night he first met her, he had no logical thought other than getting her into his bed, ASAP. He chose a song with little deliberation, so little that he didn't remember what he'd picked.

"What's your song? I didn't see."

"Um. It's a surprise."

Melanie swirled her drink with the straw. "I could drink about seven of these, but then you'd have to put me in a cab because I would either be asleep or very, very stupid."

"I don't want you to drink that much, but I'm willing to go along with whatever you want tonight."

Melanie cast him a smirk. "You ready to put your money where your mouth is? Because I want to dance."

Adam knew exactly where he wanted to put his mouth, squarely on hers. "This isn't really the place for dancing." Flaherty's customers were accustomed to their feet sticking to the floor. It wasn't exactly the place to bust out a box step.

"Maybe we need to change that." She grabbed his hand and placed it on her hip.

She was lucky his fingers didn't have a mind of their own because her dress had a tie at the hip, and that was precisely where she'd placed his hand. That stretch of cobalt blue knit would be gone in two seconds flat if his hands were in charge.

He took her other hand, wrapped his fingers around hers, bringing her right next to him with a decisive tug. "What if I told you I don't dance?" He led her in a small circle on their impromptu dance floor, sliding his hand to the small of her back. His hand fit perfectly.

"I'd say you're a liar," she muttered, following him in their back-and-forth sway. It was only the slightest of surrenders, but he'd take what he could get. Every last drop.

"The truth is that I really don't like to dance, but I like this. A lot. At least I can have you in my arms."

"Is three minutes long enough? That's how long a song is, right?"

"We put in two dollars. I bought myself a good twenty-four minutes if my math is correct."

"If you play your cards right, I'll stick around that long."

Adam laughed quietly. "You and I are exceptionally good at talking in circles around each other. Neither one of us wants to give in and say what we're really thinking."

Melanie looked up into his eyes, unafraid. "So just tell me, Adam. Tell me what you're thinking." Maybe her bravery was born of the mojitos, but he'd have to match it with his own bravado.

He sucked in a deep breath, steeling himself, hoping this wasn't going to make her put up an even bigger wall between them. The last time he'd been honest about his feelings, she'd done exactly that. "I'm thinking that you're beautiful and smart and sexy and fun to be with. I'm thinking that any man who would walk out on you is a moron. I'm thinking that I might not be much better for spending time with Julia when I could be trying to build something with you."

Her lashes fluttered as she seemed to wrestle with what he'd said. "Wow."

"Too much?"

"Um, no." She shook her head. "I'm just surprised."

"By what part? Surely you know how I feel about you. Surely you know that I'd take a chance with you if I had one."

"And to what end? So we can date for a week or two and you can get bored of me?"

His heart pounded fiercely. If he'd ever been bored with a woman, it was only because she wasn't the complete package. She wasn't like Melanie. "I would never get bored of you. Ever."

"How am I supposed to believe that, Adam? Even when you were engaged, she didn't manage to hold your interest."

Thirteen

Roger Langford was paying Melanie a significant sum of money, but her job description didn't include party-planning duties. She took on the extra work partly because the annual LangTel gala also raised money for charity. The other half of the equation was that all of her work with Adam led up to this one night. It had to be perfect. She would do everything she could to make sure that it was nothing less.

Several minutes late and fighting a monster headache, Melanie rushed into the grand ballroom where the gala was to be held. Anna, Adam's sister, was already there.

Anna smiled and shook Melanie's hand. "Thank you for meeting me and helping out. I'm a fish out of water with this sort of thing." Her long chestnut brown hair, the color exactly like Adam's, was pulled back in a high ponytail. Also like Adam, she was confident, but hers was more reserved than cocky. Her demeanor exuded grace and professionalism.

Melanie placed her bag on a table, wishing she'd taken more pain reliever before she'd left the office. "It's not a problem. I have a fair amount of experience organizing parties. Every now and then I end up doing one for a client."

Just thinking about the gala made the corners of Melanie's mouth draw down. That night would spell the end of working with Adam. He'd go back to his life, she'd go back to hers. As to what that entailed, she wasn't sure. She'd thought once or twice that maybe she and Adam could go out to dinner once her assignment was over, although she wasn't sure how that would work either. Did she have the guts to ask him out on a date? Sitting around and waiting for him to do it would be torture. Not that it would matter. For all she knew, Julia and Adam would be running away together after the party.

The two women walked the opulent space, going through the notes Roger Langford's assistant had given them. Table linens, decor and menu had been decided months ago. It was really Melanie and Anna's job just to discuss how the flow and timing of the party would work, since Roger would be making his big announcement and Adam making the closing comments.

"An hour for cocktails should be sufficient, I think," Melanie said. "I'll make sure the media has an unobtrusive spot to view everything. Your dad gives his speech, which I hope will be short." Her phone rang, but she let it go to voice mail.

Anna let out a breathy laugh that said she didn't find it funny. "Don't bet on that one. My father loves the sound of his own voice."

"I already need to work with Adam on what he's going to say, so I'll coach your dad, as well. If he goes too long, the networks will chop it up for broadcast. There are already enough misperceptions about your family. We don't need to add to them." In her planner, Melanie scribbled down a reminder about the speeches. "After that, Adam takes the stage and addresses everyone, we have a toast and dinner is served."

"The king will have ascended to the throne."

Precisely—Adam's long-awaited chance to take over his father's massive corporation. "It is almost like a coronation, isn't it?"

Anna nodded slowly. "From everything my mother says, my father has been waiting since the moment Adam was born for this to happen." Her voice faltered, but she wasn't choking back tears. As near as Melanie could tell, Anna had extreme command of her emotions. "Of course, we all thought it would happen when my dad retired. We never imagined it would be because he's dying."

Melanie's heart ached for Anna, and for Adam, as well. Watching their father fade away had to be so difficult. Did it make things easier that Roger had opted to keep the severity of his illness a secret, or had that added to the family's burden? Adam didn't always talk about it, but she'd seen how much it weighed on him. "I can only imagine how hard this must be for you." Her phone rang, but she let it go to voice mail again. If only there was more she could say, or something she could do to make it better, but it was an unsolvable problem. They'd be lucky if Roger Langford lived to see another Christmas with his family.

"Thank you," Anna said. "I'm not really sure why my father put me in charge of the final party details, aside from the fact that he felt like he needed to throw me a bone. And I'm a girl. There's that, too."

"Throw you a bone?"

Anna looked up at the ceiling. "I'm surprised Adam hasn't told you, considering how much time you two spend together. I've been lobbying to take Adam's place since before my dad got sick. I'd like to be the one to carry out his vision for LangTel. Unfortunately, my dad's logic is straight out of the 1950s. He only approves of me in business if I'm shopping for a husband while I do it."

Melanie had no idea that the sibling rivalry between Adam and Anna was so intense that they would be at odds over running the company. As much as she wanted Adam to take his rightful position, she sympathized with Anna. "My dad treats me the same way. He's just waiting for me to fail, so that he can tell me that he told me so. Of course, that only makes me want to work harder to prove him wrong."

Anna smirked. "Exactly. Do you have any idea how hard I worked at Harvard to beat Adam's GPA? Just so I could show my dad that I was equally capable?"

"I can only imagine. Your brother is a smart guy. I'm sure his grades were nearly impossible to beat."

"Tough, yes. Impossible, no. I did it, but it wasn't by much."

Melanie's phone rang for the third time. "Somebody really wants to get a hold of me. I'm so sorry."

She held up her finger while Anna mouthed, "No problem."

"Hello? This is Melanie."

"Ms. Costello, this is Beth, one of the producers for the *Midnight Hour*. We've had a last-minute cancellation on tonight's show. One of our guests has fallen ill. Is Adam Langford still available? We'd love to have him if he is."

Melanie glanced at her watch. "What time?"

"Can he be here in an hour for hair and makeup?"

Oh, crap. "Yes. Of course. We'll be there."

Two hours after Adam received the frantic phone call from Melanie, he was ready to walk out in front of the *Midnight Hour* cameras. Almost ready. "I don't know what's wrong with me. I can't stop sweating."

Melanie waved a magazine in front of his face. "You're going to have to find a way to stop. By sheer willpower or something." Judging by the expression on her face, she was as horrified by his physical state as he was.

"Maybe if I'd had more notice." He wished he hadn't sounded so annoyed, but he was still bothered by the things she'd said when they'd gone to Flaherty's a few nights before.

Yes, he'd made mistakes when he was engaged. He knew better now, even if no one seemed to believe him. And Melanie's suggestion that he'd get bored with her was absurd. Part of the reason he was so drawn to her was because he was certain she'd never bore him. Still, he had to admit that she had reason to bring it up. There'd been a time when women went through a revolving door in his life. Her comments weren't completely unfounded.

"Relax," she said, working hard to convey calm. "It's going to be fine."

"You don't understand. I never get nervous. It's an omen or something." Adam ran his hand through his hair.

"Stop messing with your hair. You'll make it look weird."

He groaned under his breath. "Do you realize that I'm about to go on a show that millions of people watch? People who expect guests to be funny and charming and clever." Why had he agreed to do this? This was not what he did. He was always in control. He was always in charge. He didn't allow himself to fall prey to circumstances, but being on this show—the lights, the audience, the host— made him feel as if he was about to do exactly that. "I can't perform on command."

Melanie smirked. "I don't enjoy seeing you uncomfortable, but I do like seeing a chink in the armor every now and then." She firmly placed her hands on his shoulders. "First off, you need to take about ten deep breaths. Second off, you need another shirt. I'm not letting you go on television in the one you're wearing." She strode over to the garment rack in his tiny dressing room and picked out what was supposed to be a backup. "Take off your shirt."

"This is no time for sex."

"Okay, Mr. I Can't Be Funny and Charming on Command. You're going to be fine. Now take off your shirt so we can get you out there."

Adam unbuttoned, distracting himself with the vision of Melanie. Every inch of his body warmed to the idea of doing this with her, taking off clothes, for real. In his fantasy, she did the unbuttoning. Always. How disappointed his body would be when he had to break the news. Melanie didn't take him seriously when it came to romance. Her career and her company were her first priority, and it would be hypocritical to blame her—he'd suffered a broken engagement for the same reason.

Melanie grabbed deodorant from the dressing table and thrust it at him. "This reminds me that we need to decide what you're wearing to the gala. We need something that will look perfect in pictures and on television. We can do it when we go over your speech."

"Uh, okay. Sure."

"Mr. Langford?" The stage manager leaned into the room, clipboard in hand. "Five minutes until you're on." She then seemed to realize the problem. "You have thirty seconds to get that shirt on or I'm going to go into cardiac arrest. Makeup is on their way for touch-ups."

Melanie shook out the shirt and held it for him. "I'll button the front. You do the cuffs."

The makeup woman whizzed into the room. She tucked two tissues into his shirt collar and dabbed at his face with a large cosmetic sponge. "You're sweating," she remarked, pursing her lips. "You need to stop doing that."

"He'll be fine." Melanie cocked her head to the side,

finishing the buttons. "He's so damn handsome, the camera will love him no matter how sweaty he is."

He knew she was just trying to distract him, but his heart felt lighter to hear her say something like that. He couldn't help it.

The makeup woman whisked away the tissues around his collar. "That's as good as it's going to get."

Melanie straightened his shirt, brushing his shoulder. "You say you're nervous, but you're really not. I've had clients who were far more on edge than you. You make it look like a piece of cake."

"If I'm not nervous, it's because of you."

The look she gave him—sweet and kind, edged with skepticism—was enough to make him forget all time and place. "You're going to be great. I know you. You'll knock 'em dead."

When was the last time someone had said something like that to him? "You're amazing. I don't think anyone else would be this patient with me."

"I have complete confidence in you. I never doubt your ability to do anything."

He leaned forward, grasped her elbows and kissed her on the temple. "Thank you."

"You're welcome." She nearly leaned into the kiss, placing the tips of her fingers on his chest. She peered up into his face then shied away with a blush that would've made a rose envious.

The stage manager poked her head into the dressing room. "Mr. Langford. You're on." She led them down the short hall to the stage entrance.

He took a deep breath. If he didn't stop thinking about Melanie, he'd have more than a sex scandal to explain on national TV. He conjured one of his most unpleasant memories in hopes of stemming the tide of blood flow between his legs. "I haven't been this nervous since I ran for class president in sixth grade."

"Oh, please. I'm guessing you were formidable even at eleven years old."

"Are you kidding? It was a disaster." He looked back over his shoulder before he stepped between the gap in the velvet stage drapes. "I lost by a landslide."

Melanie had prepared herself for the worst. What a waste of time.

The instant Adam was out under the studio lights, he turned on his irresistible charm and the entire world fell under his spell, or at least everyone watching in that studio. Melanie knew very well what it was like to get swept up in Adam. The audience never stood a chance.

The host, Billy Danville, didn't hesitate to poke fun, starting the interview by donning a tiara that spelled out "Princess" in glittery rhinestones above his head. "So, Adam. I understand there's been a scandal."

Three weeks ago, Adam wouldn't have been able to take the joke. He would've rolled his eyes in disgust and admonished everyone in that room for caring about the personal life of someone they didn't know.

Not today. Adam didn't flinch. He sat back in his chair, a wry smile on his face. "Has there been a scandal? I've been so wrapped up in college basketball that I hadn't noticed."

The audience laughed. The host laughed. Melanie chuckled a bit as well, but mostly she was in awe of Adam.

"But, seriously," Billy said, thankfully ditching the tiara, "it looks like you've put the scandal behind you. We've all had a chance over the last few weeks to get to know you from the various interviews you've done, which is great. We know now that you're not just a ridiculously handsome tech whiz, but that you also have a fondness for staring at your girlfriend's rear end."

"The great American pastime," Adam countered.

Billy smiled. "Indeed. You know, *just* this morning, I was thinking I should spend more time looking at your girlfriend's rear end."

The crowd erupted again.

"But seriously, tell us about your relationship with Julia Keys," Billy continued. "Things are looking pretty hot and heavy in the newspapers. Are there wedding bells in the future?"

Wedding bells? Melanie held her breath, unsure how Adam would answer, unsure what she *wanted* him to say. With every passing day, his relationship with Julia continued to look real. And that was what she'd wanted, wasn't it? She'd asked him to make it convincing. She'd practically shoved him into Julia's arms.

Adam shifted in his seat. "No. No wedding bells, despite what the tabloids want to speculate about."

"Everything's good, though?"

"Oh, sure. Everything's great. What can I say? Julia is a beautiful, smart and talented woman. Any guy would be lucky to spend time with her." On that topic in particular, Adam seemed as calm as could be.

Billy nodded eagerly. "Of course. I mean, give her my number in case she gives you the heave-ho."

Adam continued to roll with the punches, taking the jokes at his expense, handling every sensitive subject, and there were many, including the things his ex-fiancée had said about his ability to commit, and ultimately, the question of his father's health.

Billy gathered a stack of index cards in his hands. "I hate to bring this up, but there are an awful lot of rumors that your father's illness is much worse than we've been led to believe."

Adam pressed his lips into a thin line. "You know, my dad is receiving excellent medical care. He's in great hands. He's as sharp as a tack, stubborn as a mule, and still goes into the office every day."

All true. All glossing over the reality, the one the Langfords wanted to hide. Adam had learned to handle the tough questions flawlessly.

"And at what point will you be taking over LangTel?" Billy asked, not seeming to notice that Adam hadn't really answered his question.

"If that ever happens, it's still a ways off. I try not to focus on it too much."

"What was it like growing up in the shadow of such a formidable man?"

"You know, if I stand in the shadow of my dad, I'll never measure up. That's something I've come to realize over the years. He wants me to be just like him and we are alike in many ways, but I have to be my own man, as well. I can see where he's coming from, though. If I had a son, I'd probably want the same thing."

By the time Adam was offstage, it felt as though a massive weight had been lifted. His appearance on the *Midnight Hour* had been a triumph. She couldn't have been any more proud.

"Well? I did okay, huh?" he asked. The smile on his face said that he knew very well he'd done far better than okay.

"Spectacular. I couldn't have scripted you any better if I'd wanted to."

"This calls for a celebration."

"Flaherty's? We can't really go anywhere else without you being seen." She strolled down the hall with him to his dressing room.

"We need champagne and Flaherty's is not the spot for that." Adam flashed her a look. "I was thinking my apartment. Just a nightcap. It'll be fun."

Adam's apartment. Champagne. Melanie could see danger signs in her head. He was a temptation when she was mad at him—she couldn't imagine mustering a shred of resolve when she was ready to nominate him for Man of the Year. "It's late. You have work tomorrow, I have work."

"And as far as I'm concerned, we've been working all night. We deserve a break and a celebration. I promise I'll be a perfect gentleman."

"Why do I have a feeling you think you're always a perfect gentleman?"

"I don't need to think it. I am."

Fourteen

Pop. Champagne bubbles fizzed and sparkled as Adam filled two glasses. Maybe it was the high of having aced his appearance on the *Midnight Hour*, but it felt as though every sense was heightened. Or perhaps it was having Melanie in his apartment, alone.

Melanie clinked her glass with his. She sipped her champagne, vivid blue eyes gleaming. The look on her face was so familiar and damning—flirtation, invitation. It only made him want to try, again, even when it could end with her hand squarely in the center of his chest, her supple lips muttering, "I can't."

"You really were spectacular tonight. Truly," she said.

He unbuttoned his shirt cuffs and rolled up the sleeves, feeling as on top of the world as he'd felt in a long time. He'd kicked ass tonight, but more important, he and Melanie had kicked ass together. "Thank you, but it was all your doing. If you hadn't gotten me centered before I went on, I could've easily flopped." He trailed Melanie as she wandered into the living room.

"I knew you were going to be great." She waved off his comment. "I always had complete confidence in you. We might disagree from time to time, but I always know one thing. When you say you're going to do something, you do it."

Whenever life or work got messy, a lot of people's confidence in him seemed to waver—his father, the board of directors, even his own company had been tough on him lately. When it came right down to it, when push came to shove, Melanie had unequivocal faith in him. It was like a universal truth to her, a closely held belief.

She leaned against the frame of one of the tall windows, the city lights bringing out her singular radiance.

"And what if I said that I was going to kiss you?" he asked, acutely aware of his breathing. "Would you believe that, too?"

"Adam. You know that's not what I meant."

"But I want to. That's all I can think about. That's all I've thought about since we went to Flaherty's. And now, looking at you in the moonlight, seeing you in that dress, remembering exactly how well my hand fits in the curve of your back…"

"That sounds like a lot more than a kiss."

"If we do it right, then yes."

She kept her eyes set on the city. "What about Julia?"

"She isn't what I want."

She laughed in a sweet, hushed tone. "I'm going to need more champagne to believe that. You said it yourself tonight. Any man would be a fool not to want to be with her."

He shook his head. "No. I said that any man would be lucky to spend time with her. It's not the same thing."

"You've learned the art of the spin all too well."

He grasped her shoulder, urging her to look at him.

"Please tell me that you know it isn't real. This was your idea. It was all your plan."

She turned and studied his face, as if searching for the answer, when he was already giving her everything exactly as it was. "You said it yourself. You aren't good at pretending. I've seen you two together. It looks real."

"Pictures are only as real as the newspapers want them to be. You should know that better than anyone."

She knocked her head to the side, releasing a wisp of her delicate scent. "I guess."

"Pictures in a newspaper don't make a relationship. You need a connection."

"I know that. I do." She nodded, but her eyes still showed doubt. "It's just that it's so convincing."

He shook his head again. How would he get her to believe? "It's all Julia's doing. I'm only following her cues. She's not the one I want. You are."

Melanie reached out and took his hand. It was as if the earth stopped moving. "Maybe it's the words that are tripping me up. Maybe I need you to show me."

He took the champagne glass from her other hand and set it on the table, never taking his eyes off her. "I've been waiting to show you. All I want to do is show you." He cupped the sides of her face with both hands, cradling it and gazing deeply into her eyes as his fingers caressed the silky skin of her neck. The blood was coursing through his body like a raging river. If there was any justice in the world, he would have her. It was the most basic and undeniable need he'd ever endured. "Let me show you all night long."

Melanie's breath caught when Adam lowered his head and kissed her. His mouth on hers was arresting. There was no mistaking what he wanted. He claimed her, and it electrified her, right down to her toes. She needed him closer and she pressed into him, craving his heat, arching into him, molding her lips to his as their tongues circled.

Weeks of holding back had her about to jump out of her own skin. She wanted to savor every touch, and at the same time nothing was happening fast enough. She frantically unbuttoned his shirt. "Watching you change tonight was torture." She dragged her fingers across the flat plane of his abs, spreading her hands upward to his chest, eagerly crossing the small patch of hair and across to his firm shoulders, pushing the shirt to the floor. Even just having her hands on his skin was heaven. "All I wanted to do was touch you."

"Just being around you is torture. I can't think straight half of the time."

He took her into his arms, holding her tight, the warmth pouring into her from his bare skin. It felt so right. He had her exactly where she was meant to be. It ushered in a war of relief and hunger deep inside her belly. Push and pull. Give and take. Her mind couldn't help but obsess over finally having what she wanted, what she'd spent the past year wishing she hadn't walked out on—Adam.

He kissed her neck with an open mouth, unzipping the back of her dress and tugging it forward, his knuckles grazing her shoulders. It was one of the most expensive items of clothing she owned, and she couldn't have cared less. She let it drop to the floor like a wet towel after a shower, then started on his belt.

He stopped her with his hands. "Not here."

Her chest wobbled, as if someone had plucked a single string of a guitar. Was it his turn to be sensible and sane? Because for once, she wanted them both to be weak at the same time, both of them to give in. No more *shouldn't*. No more *can't*. "Please don't tell me you're turning me down," she said breathlessly, her hands still on his belt buckle.

"Never. I just want you in my bed. I've waited long enough to make love to you. I want it to be perfect."

He took her hand and led her through the living room, down the corridor to his bedroom. "Much better," he muttered, gripping her waist with both hands and easing her back onto the bed. "I need to look at you." Pale moonlight filtered through the windows, casting a glow around him. His eyes raked over her body. "You're so beautiful, I'm having a hard time wrapping my head around it."

She couldn't tear her sights from him either—his chiseled jaw and broad, defined chest called to her in every way. She wanted her hands all over him, his all over her, and then she wanted him inside her.

"Enough looking, Langford. I need you now." Scooting to the edge of the bed, she sat up and rid him of his belt and pants. Every inch of him was rock-hard, especially what was right before her. She eased his boxer briefs past his hips, pressing the heel of her hand to the base and wrapping her fingers around his length.

Adam closed his eyes and groaned, clutching her shoulders then pushing her back onto the bed. He lay down beside her, rolling her to her side and unhooking her bra. He took the puckered skin of her breast into his mouth, sucking her nipple gently as he shimmied her panties down her hips. Goose bumps spread across her skin like a wildfire through the underbrush, anticipation now at a full boil. There was nothing else in the way. Their legs tangled, they bucked their hips against each other. Kisses came hot and fast and everywhere.

"Let me get a condom," Adam said breathlessly, reaching for the bedside table.

"I'll put it on." She wanted every chance she had to touch him.

He handed her the foil pouch. "Have I mentioned that you're perfect?"

"No, you haven't." She pushed him to his back, strad-
dling his thighs, relishing the delight on his face as she
took care of him. "So say it again."

Adam chuckled quietly. "I thought we decided that I
should show you." He pulled her shoulders down to him
and kissed her like he was making up for lost time and lost
opportunities, passionately and deeply. "I need to feel as
close to you as possible."

Melanie lifted her hips and reached between her legs,
taking him in her hand, guiding him inside. In that instant,
it seemed as if neither of them took a breath, him filling
her while she sank down and her body molded around him.
By the time they succumbed to oxygen, they were one, and
there was no having enough of each other.

Kisses came at full tilt as they rocked back and forth in
a perfect rhythm. Pleasure coiled tightly inside her. The
way he swiveled his hips built the pressure at a rate that
her body struggled to keep up with. She knew the release
would have her holding on with both hands. She'd waited
so long for this and it was finally happening. Adam set
every fiber of her being on fire—just like the first time,
except so much better, because she knew him on a deeper
level now. They had history.

Adam rolled Melanie to her side, threading his fingers
through her hair, kissing her softly as he took long, slow
thrusts. She hitched one leg over his hip, bringing him
closer by pressing against his back with her calf.

"You feel so incredible," he said between kisses. He
swept his lips across her jaw, down her neck, stopping at
her breast, which he gathered in his hand and squeezed,
making the already tense skin harden. He licked and
sucked, sending her barreling toward her peak.

His breaths became uneven. Hers were ragged. She was
so close. The dam was about to break. Adam doubled his
efforts, driving harder until she knocked her head back

and gave in to rolling waves of bliss. Light flashed in her mind—a supernova, magnified.

Adam quickly followed, calling out as his body froze before he shuddered with his own release. He pulled her snugly into his arms as their breathing slowed. He kissed her forehead gently, again and again.

Was this real? Was it all a dream? She gave in to the warmth of Adam's body and the tender caress of his unforgettable kisses. For the first time in a long time, everything was not only right—it was real.

"That was incredible," Adam said. "Everything I've waited for."

"Spectacular," she replied, kissing him and running her fingers through his very messy hair.

"I have to say one thing, just so we're clear."

Melanie's heart jumped. What was he going to say? "Yes?"

"You're not going anywhere. I don't want you to leave after what we just shared. I need you to stay the night."

Contentment took hold again—he wanted her to stay. But just as quickly she realized the ramifications. "Are you sure that's a good idea? There could be photographers outside your building. That'd be bad if I'm seen leaving in the morning."

"Then we scope it out. I'm not letting you out of my sights. Tonight, you stay here. With me. The whole night. Deal?"

What was the old saying about going for broke? She'd already done the thing she'd sworn she would never do and it had been so worth it. If something went wrong, she and Adam would deal with it, together. For now, they had each other, and they had the whole night. "Of course I'll stay. The whole night."

Fifteen

Melanie awoke feeling as if she was floating inside a daydream. Did last night really happen? The morning sun beamed through Adam's bedroom windows. She clutched the sheets to her chest. Adam's sheets. Adam's bed.

The distinctive sound of paws on the hardwood floor filtered into the room and Jack appeared. As soon as he spotted her, he rounded to her side of the bed.

"Good morning, buddy." She rolled to her side, facing Jack.

He lowered his head, begging for scratches behind the ear, which she was all too happy to provide.

"Don't you two make an amazing pair," Adam said from behind her.

Melanie looked over her shoulder, drawn to the sleepy warmth of his voice. He knocked the breath right out of her, wearing gray pajama pants loose around his hips, no shirt, holding two coffee cups.

"Good morning." It was impossible to fight her grin—he was too damn sexy.

He set his knee on the bed and leaned down to kiss her forehead. "Morning, beautiful." He handed her a mug. "Cream and one sugar, right?"

She nodded, incredulous. "You remembered." Of the millions of things Adam had crammed in that gorgeous head of his, how he'd managed to remember the way she took her coffee was beyond her.

She blew gently on the coffee and took a small sip, feeling, well, conflicted. Last night had been absolutely glorious, and it had felt so good to finally surrender to him, but there was no question it had been born of a moment of weakness. She'd been so caught up in the moment, so swept away by Adam and weeks of telling herself she couldn't have him.

And she still didn't have him, even if she was fairly certain now that the illusion of Adam and Julia was exactly that, an illusion. He wouldn't have slept with her if Julia was a genuine love interest. The Adam she knew would never do that. The Adam of urban legend might, but that wasn't the real him.

What was first and foremost on her list of concerns was the contract with his father. She'd made a pact with herself to honor the agreement, and she'd broken it. She hated making excuses. She hated the notion of giving herself a free pass or letting anything slide, and yet that was the only way around what she'd done.

"I wish we could spend the morning in bed." Adam placed his coffee cup on the bedside table and crawled under the covers with her. "But I have a ton of meetings, starting at nine. If it was only one or two, I'd move them."

"Meetings." Melanie's heart thundered in her chest. "Oh my God. What time is it?"

"A little after seven. Don't tell me you're late for something this early."

"I have a nine-o'clock, too. But I have to get all the way down to my apartment, shower, change, then get to the office and make coffee. I'll never make it if I don't leave right now." She threw back the covers, quickly realizing she had nothing to cover herself with. She grabbed a pillow and shielded her body, scanning the floor for her bra and panties.

"It's a little late for modesty, Buttermilk. There isn't a square inch of you I didn't reacquaint myself with last night."

"Can you please help me find my underwear?"

He reached to the floor on his side of the bed, producing the garments. "I don't get to keep these as a souvenir?"

She scrambled over and snatched them from his hand. "Very funny." She pinned the pillow to her chest with her chin and tugged on her underwear. She wasn't exactly sure why she didn't want Adam to see her naked right now. Perhaps it was the unforgiving nature of sunlight. Or worse, the unforgiving nature of guilt. "I have to get my dress."

She cast aside the pillow and hurried out to the living room. Adam followed her. Seeing her dress and shoes cast aside on the floor brought back a flood of memories, the way she had felt when he'd rubbed her cheek with his thumb and placed that impossibly soft kiss on her lips, the heat of his hand on the bare skin of her back, the way he filled her so sublimely. It was all so perfect and all so wrong.

"Hold on two seconds," he blurted as she wrestled on her dress. He shook his head, smirking as if she were crazy. "For God's sake, let me do the zipper."

She turned, but that sense of Adam approaching her

from behind, knowing that her stretch of back was exposed to him, sent a zillion goose bumps racing over the surface of her skin.

Zip. He quickly grasped her shoulders and pulled her close, her back to his chest. "Talk to me." He delivered the words straight to her ear in a low, tone that reverberated in her body. "I can tell that you're panicked, and I need to know why. I have a feeling it's about more than a meeting."

Hearing his voice, her body wanted nothing more than to be naked with him all day, especially when his warm breath brushed the tender spot behind her ear. Her brain, however, was waging a counteroffensive, about to force her to blurt something about needing to leave, which meant her poor heart struggled for itself, stuck in the middle. "I just…" She sucked in a deep breath. How many times had she uttered these words? Surely Adam was tired of them. She sure as hell was.

"You just what? You're just worried? That what we did last night was wrong?"

She blew out a deep exhalation. "Yes." There was nothing left to say. He'd boiled it down to its essence.

He turned her around and pulled her into a hug. "I understand." He rubbed her back reassuringly. "Listen, we both know that this isn't ideal, but we have nothing to be ashamed about. I wanted you, you wanted me. It's as simple as that."

"But your dad. The contract."

He only reined her in tighter with his arms. "Don't worry about my dad. He'll never know a thing." He kissed her forehead. "Now, let me walk you downstairs and put you in a cab so you aren't late for your meeting. I'd have had the doorman arrange for a car if I'd known you needed to be out the door so soon."

Melanie reared back her head, shaking it. He was being

so sweet. And so stupid. "What if someone is outside your building? Photographers?"

"I'll call downstairs and make sure the coast is clear. The doormen are extremely efficient at clearing away the riffraff by now."

"You call, but I'll go by myself. It's safer that way." Her stomach wobbled. Sneaking around was so far outside her comfort zone.

"What kind of gentleman would I be if I didn't escort you downstairs?" He scrubbed the scruff along his jaw with his hand. "Tell you what. I'll ride with you down to the lobby. I won't take no for an answer."

Melanie collected her things while Adam made the call. He threw on a sweatshirt and slid his feet into a pair of running shoes, leaving the laces untied. They stepped onto the elevator, no words between them, but Adam took her hand, rubbing it tenderly with his thumb.

Melanie's head swam. What were they doing? Was this a one-time thing? These were questions that needed to be asked, but there was no time for answers, at least not this morning. And regardless of the answers, he had to continue with the charade of Julia at least through the gala. How would she handle that emotionally if she and Adam were even entertaining the notion of romance?

Nothing about this insane situation bode well for a genuine, long-lasting relationship anyway. She could see it now, their children asking how she and their father had met. *Well, Daddy had a fake girlfriend because Mommy told him it would get him good publicity, and your grandfather didn't want us to even touch each other, so of course Mommy and Daddy gave in to temptation and had a torrid, secret affair and lied to everyone.*

Adam's phone beeped with a text message and he pulled it from his sweatshirt pocket. He smiled warmly at the screen. "My dad, congratulating me for the *Midnight Hour*."

The elevator dinged and the doors slid open.

"You were amazing," she said, stepping into the lobby as Adam held the elevator door. "I'm sure you'll get a lot of that today."

His phone beeped again. This time he didn't smile when he read the message. Instead, all blood drained from his face. "Hey, Carl," he yelled, panicked, across the lobby to the doorman. "Get Ms. Costello in a cab, right now."

"What's wrong?" She struggled to read his expression, her voice just as frantic as his when she had no idea what was going on.

"You have to go," Adam blurted, lurching for the elevator button. "My dad's on his way." The door slid closed.

Oh my God. No. The doorman rushed Melanie outside, but it was too late. She nearly ran straight into Roger Langford.

"Ms. Costello," Roger said. "Are you?" He peered through the glass door into the lobby of Adam's building. "Were you meeting with Adam?"

Melanie had never been so mortified in her entire life. "Uh, yes. Yes, sir." It felt awful to say it. "There was such a great response to Adam's interview last night. Just want to make the most of it. Make sure all of the media outlets are talking about it. Adam and I were just going over a few things." *Stop talking. Stop digging yourself a hole.*

"That's what I like about you, Ms. Costello. Always thinking, always working hard, never letting an opportunity pass you by."

Now she felt one million times worse. "Thank you, sir."

The doorman finally managed to flag a cab, signaling her with a wave.

Melanie was desperate to make her escape. "I should

go, sir. I need to get into the office." Technically not a lie, but getting through life on technicalities was no way to go.

"Sure, sure." Roger nodded. "Have a good day."

Adam paced in his kitchen. Had Melanie made it into a cab before his dad arrived? He had his answer as soon as his father stepped off the elevator into the apartment.

"I ran into Ms. Costello downstairs." His dad slowly unbuttoned his coat.

"Ah, yes," Adam replied, not wanting to offer any detail in case his story didn't match up with Melanie's. "Dad, please. Have a seat." He pulled out a bar stool just as he received a text. He glanced at his phone long enough to read Melanie's message.

We can't do this. It's not right.

He answered. Don't freak out.

"Hard worker, Ms. Costello." His dad slowly eased onto the high seat, his height making this a good spot for him to sit. "I only came by for a minute, Adam. I just wanted to tell you in person how happy I was with your appearance last night. I received several favorable phone calls from board members this morning. They were very impressed. I was very impressed. You were perfect."

Every word of praise from his father made Adam more conflicted. Now he understood firsthand exactly why Melanie was so uneasy. What if he told his father then and there that he and Melanie were involved? What would he say? Would he be disappointed? Accuse him of going back to his old ways?

The answer didn't matter. Melanie would be furious. If he stood any chance of keeping her, he couldn't jeopardize everything she'd worked so hard for.

If it was Adam's call and his professional butt was on

the line, he might be tempted to throw caution to the wind, risk every personal achievement and dollar in the bank to have the opportunity to be with Melanie like that, every night. It wasn't merely as good as he remembered. It was so much better.

By the time his dad was gone and Adam could reply to Melanie's text with something of substance, he wondered if he'd managed to calm her with his last message. He took care to be reassuring in case he hadn't.

Take a deep breath. Everything is fine. I'm coming to your office.

Her response was too quick for his liking.

Please don't. It will just make things worse.

He fired off a text to his assistant to move his morning meetings. He then turned his phone facedown on the kitchen counter. He wasn't about to get into an extended back-and-forth with Melanie via text message, like a couple of love-struck teenagers. He had to see her. Once he had her in his arms, everything would be fine.

He showered quickly and once downstairs, instructed his driver to get to Melanie's office as fast as possible. Every red light they sat at was torture. Adam's phone kept ringing, but he couldn't concentrate on work and finally had to silence it. Business would have to wait. Nothing was more important than seeing Melanie.

He practically leaped out of the car when they arrived at her office building. The elevator was out of service and he took the stairs two at a time up eight flights, all in a suit and tie. He pushed open the door at Costello PR, the office eerily quiet, except for the chime that announced the arrival of a visitor and his heavy breaths.

"Mel? Are you here?" He straightened his tie and jacket, striding through reception and back to the hallway leading to her office. He craned his neck around the corner. Her door was open. He heard sniffles. *Oh, no. She's crying.* He cleared his throat loudly, not wanting to frighten her. "Mel?"

She peeked out of her office, cheeks red and tear-stained, still as beautiful as could be. "Adam. I told you not to come. I don't want to talk about it. Just go away. We can't do this. I won't do this. It's not right."

"Mel, it was just a close call with my dad this morning. He doesn't know or suspect a thing. It's fine."

She ran her slender fingers through her blond hair, leaning her shoulder against the wall as if it was too difficult to stand. "That's so easy for you to say. You don't have as much to lose as I do. This isn't just my business or my profession. It's my whole life. My entire identity is tied to this stupid office I can't afford. My whole life revolves around keeping the lights on and moving forward. I have nothing else. I can't afford to make a mistake."

His heart twisted in his chest. How he hated that word—*mistake.* "And do you think last night was a mistake?"

"If I get fired from the most important job of my career, then yes."

His mind scrambled, unwilling to believe that she would really be that bad off if she got fired. There had to be a way around it. "What if I pay you the fee that he's promised you? Or let me buy your office space for you. Let me fix it if it all goes south." He stepped closer, longing to touch her, all the while sensing the impenetrable fortress she'd built around herself, and most important, her heart.

"Do you really think I want your money? That I want you to rescue me? I have to do these things for myself. I've been on my own since I was eighteen. I don't know any other way. And don't forget that the entire world knows

I've been working on this project. Every future client is going to ask me about it, they're going to want to know what Roger Langford had to say about the job I did. If he has to tell them that he fired me because I slept with his son, I'm destroyed. I'm done. There's no coming back from that."

"If I came back from my scandal, you could absolutely come back from that."

"Our situations aren't the same. You're Adam Langford. Your family represents the American dream and you're smart and handsome and a self-made man. The world *wants* to love you. I just had to show them the good in you. I'm nobody, Adam. If this comes out, I'll become a footnote, and I can't turn into that. I won't slink back to Virginia with my head held in shame and tell my dad that he was right, that I had no business moving to New York and thinking that I could run my own PR firm. I just don't think you understand the ramifications."

He did understand where she was coming from, but it didn't change the fact that standing here, even with her trying to claw her way away from him, he wanted her in his arms. He wanted her in his life. "I hear everything you're saying, but taking a chance on what's between us is more important than all of that. I think this is about more than your career or my family."

The look that fell on her face was one of utter confusion. "I don't know what you're talking about. There is nothing else."

He dared to inch closer, grasp her elbow. The instant he touched her, he felt exactly how much she'd closed herself off from him. "Think about what set you on this path. Your ex. He's the reason you're in this situation with your finances and your career, but I think he's also the reason you're so afraid to let somebody into your life."

Her eyes swept back and forth across his face. "No.

You're wrong. It's been more than a year, and I've made it work without him."

He nodded in affirmation, seeing that she was struggling with this particular revelation. He knew how she felt. He'd given in to tunnel vision before, focusing on a single goal so hard that he'd forgotten what mattered. "I care about you, Mel. A lot. I understand what it means to be hurt. We've all been hurt. Maybe I haven't gone through exactly what you have, but I understand. I do. And I know that there could be something real between us if you'll just let me in." He gazed into her stormy blue eyes, which were clouded with bewilderment. She needed time. He could see it. As hard as it would be to give her time, he had to. "I want you to think about that. I really want you to think about what that means."

She straightened her stance, sucked in a deep breath. "This isn't just about what you want, Adam. This is about what I want, too."

"Then tell me what you want."

"Right now? I want you to leave and go on with your life and promise me you won't think about me at all once the gala is over."

It felt as though someone had a stranglehold on his heart. Those were not the words of a woman who was ready to think about everything he'd said, everything he'd put on the line. "I can promise a lot of things, but I can't promise that. Not after last night."

"Well, you're going to have to try because I have a job to do."

Sixteen

Friday marked five days without a word from Adam. At least not directly.

Most of his interviews were complete, but there were a few loose strings to be dealt with, and most important, they needed to polish the speech he would give at the gala. They had a back-and-forth about his remarks for Saturday night, but it had all been funneled through his assistant. However much it crushed her, she couldn't blame Adam for shutting her out like that. After all, she'd told him flat out to forget her.

The person Adam had apparently not shut out was Julia. The two of them quickly cropped up in the papers again, holding hands while shopping in SoHo, only two days after Melanie and Adam had made love. By now, the photographers had an uncanny ability to find Julia. Either Julia's publicist was feeding them information or Julia and Adam had figured out how to do it on their own. It certainly wasn't Melanie's doing.

In fact, the whole thing was Melanie's *undoing*. How did she end up right back in the same boat she'd been in weeks ago? Scrutinizing pictures in a newspaper like a crazy woman, looking for absolute confirmation that Adam and Julia were either real or fake. She hated that she was still asking these questions. She hated that she still cared, but she did. She cared so much that it felt as if everything inside her was dying.

The things Adam had said to her that morning in her office played on a continuous loop in her head. *There could be something real between us if you'll just let me in.* She wasn't convinced it was that simple. If anything, it was the impossible, masquerading as simple. Was Adam right? Had Josh damaged her so badly that she'd become incapable of trusting someone? Was her heart really that closed off? She didn't want to believe she'd become that way, but maybe she was used to it. And if she were that way, what would fix it? Therapy? Meditation? Leaping off the curb into the path of an oncoming bus?

Melanie took in a deep breath of resolve, stepping onto the elevator up to Adam's apartment. Today was the day they'd planned to go over his speech and discuss what he would wear for the gala tomorrow night. *You can do this. You'll be fine.* She didn't have much of a plan for dealing with Adam, beyond being professional. Adam, hopefully, would do the same. He'd run through the speech and show her what he planned to wear. She'd give him the thumbs-up and disappear. Then her only remaining hurdle would be the gala, and that involved an open bar, fully stocked with champagne—sweet, merciful champagne.

When the elevator doors slid open, Adam was getting up from one of the bar stools at his massive kitchen island. "You're late." The icy edge to his voice made her feel about two feet tall.

"I am?" Melanie consulted her watch. "It's three minutes after five. You're always late."

"We aren't talking about me, are we? I have things to do tonight."

She sighed. So that was how he'd play this. She didn't want to take the bait, but the way he'd run back to Julia really ate at her. "Hot date with America's sweetheart?"

"Would that make you feel better? If your suspicions proved true?"

Adam's words hurt, even when she couldn't blame him for being angry. She'd been awful to him the last time she'd seen him.

"Let's deal with your suit and the speech, please."

Melanie followed Adam as he stalked back to his bedroom. The instant she was through the doorway, it felt as if something punched a hole in her chest, right where her heart was. The bed caught her eye, pristinely dressed with silky white bedding. It took no effort to remember exactly what it felt like to be with him tangled up in those sheets, the two of them perfectly in sync. There were no issues in bed. It was everything outside the bedroom that was complicated.

If she'd thought this through, she could've moved the wardrobe discussion and speech practice to a less-intimate venue. Too late.

"I picked out three suits if you want to weigh in on it," Adam said, apparently unbothered by the presence of the sumptuously appointed, pillow-soft horizontal surface between them. "I'm leaving the tie to you." He stepped into his walk-in closet, pointing to the valet hooks where the suits were waiting, as well as his vast selection of silk ties.

Melanie already knew she wanted him to wear the dark charcoal-gray suit. He'd worn it the night she first met him and he looked absolutely incredible in it—jacket perfectly tailored to accentuate his sculpted shoulders and trim waist. So she'd have to avert her eyes and bite down on her knuckle every time she saw him tomorrow night. No big deal. She'd endured worse.

She thumbed her way through his ties. The quiet in the closet was suffocating. She had to say something. "Why no tuxedos?"

Adam cast his eyes away when she looked at him. "My mother hates the way my dad looks in black. She says he looks like an undertaker, which, given the circumstances, is probably an image we want to avoid."

"Yes. Of course." *So much for small talk.* She selected a few ties—a steely blue, black with a deep green diagonal stripe, and lavender.

"No way." Adam plucked the light purple tie from her hand and hung it back up. "You and your lavender. It's too girlish."

"It's your tie. Why do you have it if you can't even stand to look at it?"

"It was a gift from my mother. I think of her every time I choose not to wear it."

She deliberated between the other two ties before thrusting one into his hand. "Fine. We'll try the blue. It'll bring out your eyes."

"You care about how my eyes look. Really?"

"Yes, I care. Your eyes are one of your best features."

"If I didn't know better, I'd say you were flirting with me." He twisted his lips. "But I definitely know better."

"Just put on the suit so you can run through your speech and we can both get on with our night. I'll be outside the door."

He let out a frustrated grumble. "Okay. It'll just take me a minute."

Melanie wandered out of the closet and over to the window, looking out at the city. The days were getting longer, only a few months until summer. Where would she be by then? Would she have a few more clients? More money coming in? Logic said that she was on an upward trajectory, thanks to the success of Adam's campaign. So why wasn't she happy? She'd made the choice to focus on her career and it was going to pay off, but it all felt empty. She had no one to share these triumphs with, and as Adam had suggested, that was likely her own doing.

Adam strolled into the room, stopping in front of the full-length mirror on the wall. "Thoughts?"

Melanie steadied herself, leaning against the window casing. He was so handsome, it hurt to take a breath, producing a sharp pain in her chest. Her exhale came out as an embarrassingly choppy rush of air.

"That will work." She straightened, trying to play it off as a triviality when all she felt was a profound tingle from head to toe. Not getting to kiss him while he was wearing that suit was torture. Even worse was knowing that she wouldn't get to watch him take it off.

"What are you wearing to the party?" he asked.

"A dress."

"I assumed as much. Care to elaborate?"

"I don't know." She *hadn't* figured it out and it wasn't in the budget to buy anything new. She'd probably just go with one of her reliable little black dresses she'd worn to this sort of event hundreds of times. "Why does it matter?"

"I'm curious." Adam adjusted the cuff on his shirt. "Are you bringing a date?" His eyes didn't stray from his reflection in the mirror.

Melanie closed her eyes for a moment. This was supposed to be her chance to level the playing field tomorrow night, but she was now far less enthusiastic about the prospect. "I'm going with my neighbor, Owen. He's a doctor." She had zero romantic interest in Owen, and she'd made it clear this was just as friends, but Adam didn't need to know that. She simply refused to attend the party without a date, knowing that she'd have to smile and pretend to be happy while Julia was on Adam's arm.

"Let me guess. Ear, nose and throat."

"Gynecologist, if you must know."

Adam laughed. "You can't be serious."

"Why would I joke about that? Especially knowing what you'd probably say?"

"This is your event. I take it that you asked him out?"

What is he implying? That I can't get a date? "I invited him, but Owen has asked me out plenty of times."

"And have you gone? Out with Owen?"

"We've gone to the movies and out to dinner." She stopped short of clarifying the true context of the outings. They were not dates. There was popcorn and sitting together in the dark, but there was no hand-holding. There was dinner, but it was a slice of pizza at the Famous Ray's near their building. No romance, just friends, at Melanie's request.

"I see. Well, I look forward to meeting your doctor neighbor. I'm sure we'll have a lot to talk about."

"Because you're both so familiar with the female form?"

He delivered a look that shot ribbons of electricity through her body. "We're both big fans of Melanie Costello's form, apparently."

His words ushered in waves of heat, followed by a rush of confusion. Was he jealous? She couldn't imagine Adam envying another man. But what about the look in his eyes and the possessive rumble of his voice? Was he saying that he hadn't given up? And what would she do about that if it were the truth?

"You should probably practice your speech, so I can hear it out loud," she said, breaking the spell of silence.

"Right here?"

Melanie shrugged. "Sure." She trekked across the room to sit, even though she'd been inches from the bed, a perfectly acceptable perch if she hadn't been so afraid of what Adam might think.

"I almost wish I had a podium. Feels strange to stand here and deliver a speech." He straightened his jacket, seeming both confident and vulnerable standing before her. She stifled a sigh. That was the Adam she adored, the Adam who would never be hers.

Adam started his speech, but Melanie noticed something wrong right away. Everything that came out of his mouth was confident and optimistic, but his shoulders had tensed, his voice held a distinct edge of agitation. It was as if he was speaking someone else's words, but he'd written most of the speech. She'd made only a few minor changes and suggestions.

I'm excited for this new challenge.

I've been waiting my entire life for this opportunity.

I appreciate the confidence of the board of directors.

He was saying one thing while meaning another, which couldn't be good. After all, Adam had told her countless times. He was no good at faking anything.

Adam pinched the bridge of his nose when he finished his speech. He didn't even want to hear Melanie's appraisal. He'd seen the bewildered look on her face when he spoke.

"Everything okay?" she asked.

"Um. Sure." Her question caught him off guard to say the least. She didn't shy away from criticism when warranted, and he knew he hadn't done well. "Why?"

"It just didn't seem like you. At all."

"I'm fine." The words sat on his lips—nothing was fine. Everything was very much not okay, and it was about more than LangTel. It was more than worry about his dad. It was about her. The two of them in his apartment, being barely civil and making a grand point to not touch each other, hell, trying to not *look* too much at each other, was utterly and completely wrong.

But things had changed. Every other time she'd said no to him, it had been because they were working together. It was never because there was another man in the picture. The more egotistical parts of him had presumed that there was no other love interest because she wanted to be with him. Apparently he was wrong.

Now she had a date, a man she'd chosen, a doctor, no less. Adam never compared himself with other men, but this was pretty clear-cut. She'd shut down Adam three times. She'd chosen Owen. Maybe she wasn't closed off to the idea of love. Perhaps she was closed off only to the idea of him.

"Are you sure?" Melanie asked. "You seem like something's bothering you. Tell me what's going on."

Here she was, right before him, the woman he couldn't chase out of his mind if he wanted to. She wanted to listen. She wanted to talk. This could very well be their last chance to be together like this, just talking. After the gala, he would go his way and she would go hers.

He sucked in a deep breath and blew it out slowly. "I don't want to run LangTel." Just getting that much off his chest was a relief of epic proportions.

Melanie's mouth went slack. "What? But your dad. The succession plan." She looked around the room, blinking as if she couldn't comprehend what he'd said, which was a big part of the problem. It only made sense to Adam and Anna. Nobody else seemed to get it. "You love a challenge and it's a huge corporation, your family's name is on it. Why wouldn't you want that opportunity?"

He shook his head, dropping to the bench at the foot of his bed. "I know it sounds crazy, but every Langford man before me has been a self-made man. My dad. My grandfather. My great-grandfather. I can't stand the thought of not doing the same thing, blazing my own trail. I want something that I built myself, from the ground up. Is that so wrong?"

She smirked. "Adam, you said it yourself. You made your first million out of your dorm room. You're already a self-made man. Check that off your list and move on to the next big challenge. I have no doubt that you'll kick some serious butt running LangTel. With your mind for technology, you could do some incredibly innovative things."

"You're sweet, but it's not quite as simple as that. At least not for me it isn't."

"But haven't you and your dad been talking about this since you were a little boy?"

Indeed, Adam had been made keenly aware of what had been preordained for him. One of his most vivid childhood memories was of the day his dad brought him into LangTel on a Saturday afternoon, sat him down in the big leather executive chair in his father's corner office. Adam was seven. His dad had talked about things Adam didn't fully understand, told him that the chair and the desk and the whole damn thing would be his one day.

That day was fast approaching and Adam wanted nothing more than to slam on the brakes and make this runaway train come to a complete stop. The future his dad wanted for him wasn't what he wanted for himself.

"Yes, people have been talking about it since I can remember. In the end, I just can't say no to him, especially now that he's dying. If I'd been smart, I'd have said something about this years ago. I just didn't think I'd be confronted with it until he was ready to retire, and I always figured there was a chance I might feel differently by then."

Melanie's eyes grew wide. She hopped forward to the edge of her seat. "But Anna. She wants to do it. She told me when we met about planning the gala. Adam, that's it. It's perfect."

Adam smiled wide. She was so adorable, wanting to help, wanting to fix things for him and for his sister. Hell, she wanted to fix things for the entire Langford family. "Our dad refuses to entertain the subject. He's so old-fashioned, it's ridiculous."

Melanie appeared crestfallen. "Damn. I figured sibling rivalry was the bigger issue." She sighed deeply, their eyes connected, and he sank into them as if they were the only respite he would ever want. "Oh my God, Adam. The scandal. That was your out." She rubbed her temple, seeming even more concerned than she'd been a minute ago. "You could've said no to the PR campaign and just let the board of directors force you out. It would've solved everything."

He almost wanted to laugh. He'd considered that, but then his dad had hired a public relations whiz named Melanie Costello. The moment he saw her picture on her company's website, his heart had wormed its way into his throat. He finally knew the identity of his Cinderella. So he'd sucked it up and agreed to the PR campaign, even though it would likely seal his fate. He had to see his mystery woman again, see if the lightning in a bottle was real. And it was. It just wasn't meant to last.

He couldn't tell her that now—she'd moved on. He had no choice but to accept it. "I thought about that. But it would've made a mess of the family name, and that would have been no way to say goodbye my dad. It really wouldn't have solved everything, but it might have fixed that one problem." He couldn't have lived with himself if he'd taken that route anyway. It would've destroyed his relationship with his dad. Luckily, Melanie had saved him from making that choice. She just didn't know it.

"You know, the day I met with Anna, I felt a little jealous of your family," Melanie said.

"It's not all wine and roses, believe me."

"I know that, but you're still close, you really care about each other. I just don't have that. My sisters think I'm an oddball, my dad is impossible, and my mom is— Well, I never really knew her." She shook her head. "I know your relationship with your dad is tumultuous, but at least you have him. He's still here. You can still talk to him. You just have to find a way to get him to understand. You won't feel right about things if he passes away and you haven't tried one more time."

He'd tried and failed at it more times in the past few months than he could remember. Was that even possible? "How ironic is it that my dad and I are so close and he's the one person I never push to see my side of things? The idea of letting him down is still unfathomable."

Jack lumbered into the room, making a pit stop at Adam's knee, then beelining to Melanie. How that dog loved her. Adam toyed with telling Melanie that Jack had taken to standing next to the bed at night, resting his head on the pillow where she'd slept. Even Jack knew that she belonged there.

Melanie ruffled Jack's ears and smiled at him. "I'm no expert, but it's better to come out with things and live with the consequences. I did that with my dad. It didn't go over well, but at least I said my piece."

She was so smart, so intuitive about people, although she seemed more interested in helping others than examining her own problems. "I like hearing about your family." *It makes me feel closer to you.* He'd wanted to say that last part so badly, but it would sound too much as if he'd fallen desperately in love with a woman he couldn't have. And he had. He loved Melanie with every fiber of his being.

"I should probably go." She stood, straightening her dress and collecting her purse. "And you should get out of that suit so you don't get it all wrinkly before tomorrow."

He rose to his feet to say his goodbye, finding her only a few feet from him. His arms ached to hold her, never let go. He wanted to kiss her for days, escape from the entire world with her. He wanted to cherish and adore her the way she deserved to be. She'd shown him the opportunity in tomorrow, the day he'd been dreading, reminded him that he determined his own destiny. Of course, that pertained to business. There was no controlling it when it came to love, now that there was another man in the picture.

Seventeen

Melanie had rendered herself dateless right after she left Adam's. As difficult as it would be to see him with Julia at the gala, taking Owen as her human security blanket wasn't right. So, she stopped by his apartment, apologized profusely and owned up to everything. He deserved better and she needed to get her head screwed on straight.

She hardly slept at all that night, haunted by images of Adam, the way he'd looked at her after he'd tried on the suit, the gravel in his voice when it seemed as if he might be jealous. Other memories swooped in and out of her consciousness—the mountain house, dancing at Flaherty's, the night when she'd finally allowed herself the pleasure of the sexiest man she'd ever known. She could still feel his tender lips on hers, remember his warm and welcoming smell, conjure the safe sensation of his arms around her. Knowing that her chance with Adam was behind her left a void—one that made the one left by Josh look like a chip on a china teacup.

In the morning, sleep-deprived and feeling duly horrible, she knew she had to keep herself busy on gala day or it'd mean hours of rehashing what she'd gone over countless times. She was going to miss the hell out of Adam and there was no getting around it. She tried on twenty different dresses, threw in a load of laundry, smeared on a facial mask, took a bath, painted her nails ruby red, and spent entirely too much time messing with her hair and makeup. At least she would look good when she said goodbye.

Just when she'd narrowed her choice of dresses down to two, a push notification arrived on her phone. She picked it up and checked it—big mistake. It felt as though her breath was being dragged out of her as she looked at the tabloid photo of Julia leaving Adam's apartment building early that morning. So that was what Adam had on his social schedule last night. Julia had been on her way over.

She plopped down on her bed, still in her bathrobe. She stared at the picture, struggling to make sense of the emotion seething inside her. Logic said that this should make her sad, another sign from the universe that she and Adam weren't meant to be. But there was no melancholy. She didn't even feel bitter. She was flat-out pissed off—not at Adam, but at herself. The most incredible man she'd ever met, the only man she wanted, was about to walk away and she was going to let him. Everything holding her back would expire at midnight, and then where would she be? A few bucks ahead and brokenhearted, that's where.

Julia wasn't what he wanted. She knew it. Even if he hadn't told her as much, her heart still knew better than to accept that. Her heart knew exactly the way it felt when she and Adam were together—complete, fulfilled, as if it didn't make sense to be anywhere else. And when they were apart, she was lost, not just without a map or compass, but without a destination.

In the moments when Melanie had been able to see past

the obstacles between herself and Adam, their chemistry was more real than anything she'd dreamed possible. The rest of the time, even when they were at odds, she'd been unable to deny his pull on her. She'd only learned to pretend it wasn't there.

She couldn't pretend anymore. She couldn't let him go. That would mean giving in to circumstances, and she didn't do that. She fought her way out of everything. She fought to survive after Josh left, but she'd never fought *for* him. He didn't deserve that much. But Adam wasn't Josh. Adam valued her drive and determination. He was caring and thoughtful. He wanted to see her succeed. More than that, he could set her on fire with a single look, and no other man had that effect on her. Adam was worth fighting for, even if he might say that she'd hurt him too many times. She would fight for the man she couldn't allow to walk away. It was time to start listening to her heart again.

Melanie tapped out a text to Adam.

Can we talk before the party? In person. Alone.

Her pulse thumped wildly in her throat. Everything she wanted to say was bottled up inside her. She merely had to let it out. But was she too late?

The instant she sent the message, her phone rang, Adam popping up on caller ID. "That was quick," she muttered to herself. "Hey. I just sent you a text."

"It just came through," he said. "That's funny."

Her heart thundered. "Funny?"

"The timing. I'm standing outside your building. Can you buzz me up? The intercom isn't working."

Outside my building? But why? Panic coursed through her. Her apartment was a mess and her room looked as if a tornado had leveled a department store—dresses and shoes everywhere. "I'm not even dressed."

"Doesn't matter. I need to talk to you."

With no time for straightening up or putting on clothes, much less thinking, she rushed out of her bedroom, pressed the buzzer, unlatched the chain and opened her door.

She stepped out into the hall and watched as he ascended the stairs. He made it nearly impossible to breathe. He was temptation on two legs, in a perfect-fitting suit and five o'clock shadow. Deliberating over whether the front or the back was his best side had been so stupid. The sum total of Adam was the best. "Is something wrong?"

"You might say that. I'm sorry I didn't call. I was worried you might not let me come over." He stood inches away, still making her feel as if she couldn't breathe. "I love the dress. Not quite what I pictured, but I appreciate the cleavage."

Melanie looked down. Her silk robe gaped in the front. Heat flooded her face, and she quickly covered up, inviting him in. "What's wrong? Is there a problem with tonight?"

"I could ask you the same thing. Why did you need to talk to me before the party?"

Now that she was confronted with him—his endlessly magnetic being—it was difficult to start. She only knew that she had to. "I saw the photo in the paper. I don't care if Julia spent the night at your apartment. I don't believe that you want to be with her."

He nodded carefully, killing her with every second of silence. "I'm glad you finally believe me. I came over to tell you that she won't be at the gala tonight."

Wait. Her brain sputtered. Was this just about work? "What?"

"Don't freak out. I know you've worked hard on the party, but I couldn't pretend anymore. That was the reason for the photos of her outside my apartment. Her publicist is fabricating a breakup, at my request. I had to put an end to it now. Not just for my sake. For your sake, too."

Was this him just being fed up with the charade? Or was there more? "I broke my date with the doctor. It wasn't right to take him."

"And why is that exactly?"

She held her breath, a deluge of thoughts crowding her consciousness. He deserved to know how she felt, the mile-long list of reasons she needed him. "Because I'm in love with you. And I don't want to be with some other man, even for a minute. I don't want to watch you walk away tonight." She erased the physical divide between them with a few steps. Just feeling the rhythm of his breaths calmed her, even when she wasn't sure how he felt about what she was saying. The expression on his face was one of shock, but was it horror? "You're my only thought before I go to sleep. You're the first thing I think about when I wake up. When something happens in my day, good or bad, I have this undeniable urge to call you and tell you about it. The only reason I don't do it is because of my job. But I need more than my career. I need you." Their eyes connected and she saw her first sign that he might be on board—he smiled.

"You do?"

"I do. And you were right. I let everything that happened with my ex turn me into somebody who doesn't allow herself to feel. I don't want to be that person anymore. It's making me miserable."

"I hate the thought of you unhappy." He nodded, taking her hand and rubbing it with his thumb. "I had to talk to you before the party because I didn't want you to disappear tonight like Cinderella. I had to see the look on your face when I finally said I love you." He shook his head in admonishment, but he was fighting a smile. "Of course you had to beat me to it."

Melanie's heart back-flipped, making her pulse kick into hyperdrive. "I'm sorry. It's just that I've hurt you so many times, I thought you deserved the truth, even when I wasn't sure what you'd say."

He cracked his half smile, the one that made her feel as if her heart was an ice-cream cone in the summer sun. He reached for her other hand. "I love you and I want to be with you, but I need to know that you're in this for real, for the long haul. I can't handle it if you get skittish and run off again."

A single tear rolled down her cheek. The man who'd once had a revolving cast of women wanted to know if *she* was capable of sticking around. "I only ever ran because I was scared of how badly it would hurt if it didn't work. I'm not scared anymore."

"I mean it, Melanie. The long haul." He reached into his jacket pocket and pulled out a small, navy blue box. "I want you to be my wife. I want to spend my life with you."

Melanie's hand flew to her mouth. She knew that box—it was from Harry Winston. She gasped when he opened it and revealed a stunning emerald-cut platinum engagement ring. She was almost scared to touch it, worried it might disappear—she'd only dared to fantasize about a moment like this with Adam. She'd never dreamed it might actually be true. "It's so beautiful."

"Do you want to try it on?"

She nodded eagerly.

He plucked it from the box and slid it onto her finger. The diamond sparkled like an entire constellation.

"Oh my God, Adam. I love it. But how'd you get a Harry Winston ring so quickly?"

"I made it worth their while to tend to my needs. And I believe there's a bigger question on the table at the moment."

She stopped staring at her hand, instead looking into the face she hoped she could wake up to every morning, forever. "You want to get married?"

"I figured that a signed document was the way to go with you." He grinned from ear to ear. "I'm hedging my bets here."

A breathy laugh escaped her. Was this really happening? Her entire future had done a one-eighty in a matter of minutes. "I never want to let you go. I want nothing more than to be your wife."

He tugged her to him possessively. "Come here." He wrapped one arm firmly around her waist, swept her bangs from her forehead with his free hand. "I can't believe you said yes to something. No argument or negotiation or anything."

She loved it when he took charge, held her in a way that said she was his. "Not just a little something either. A big something."

He cupped the side of her face, rubbed her jaw with his thumb, sending goose bumps across her chest, over her shoulders and down her arms. Then he kissed her—soft and heavenly, practically begging for her to lean into him. She threaded her arms inside his jacket, craving his warmth and touch. Every second of holding on to this incredible man washed away the misery of the past year. Adam was hers.

Now that Melanie was his, kissing her, having her in his arms, was so much more satisfying than Adam could've imagined. Pulled against his body, her heat radiated into him, spiking his body temperature. The suit wasn't helping. Her mouth was sweet, her tongue swirling in a deliciously naughty way, every second of it driving him insane. She was at least partially undressed beneath her robe. He'd seen the gorgeous swell of her breasts when he'd arrived at her door.

He pulled the tie at her waist, unwrapping the most precious gift he'd ever have, pushing the silky fabric from her shoulders to the floor. His hands slid down her back, cupping and squeezing the velvety skin of her bottom. *No panties. Perfect.*

Melanie laughed, her lips vibrating against his. It was so damned sexy. "Adam, honey, there's no time. We're supposed to be at the party by six thirty."

Her arms weren't merely buried inside his jacket. She'd dipped one of her hands below the waistband of his pants. It only made him that much more determined to have her, body and soul. Now.

"There's no way that you say you'll marry me and I don't take off your clothes and make you lose all sense of direction." He nuzzled her neck, taking in her intoxicatingly sweet fragrance.

"My hair. My makeup."

"I've seen your bed head. It's perfect."

She scoffed, but the look on her face, the flush of pure pink blanketing her cheeks, said she wanted him as badly as he wanted her. "I still need to figure out what I'm wearing. We have like twenty minutes. Tops."

"I'm at my best under pressure."

She reached down and palmed the front of his trousers, biting her lip. "So I feel."

He growled into her ear, nipped at her lobe. Her touch made him feel as if he might not last twenty seconds if he wasn't careful. The lower half of his body was buzzing with the prospect of claiming her. "Either we do it in the hall, or you take me back to your bedroom."

She grabbed his hand and rushed down the corridor. He loved watching her move like that—feminine curves in hurried motion. Even better, he eyed her beautiful bottom as he removed his jacket, tie and shirt while she gathered a pile of clothes from her bed and tossed them onto a chair. He stepped behind her as she threw back the quilt. She turned. Her bare breasts brushed his chest.

"Pants. You're still wearing pants." Melanie unbuckled his belt, unbuttoned his trousers. "Be careful. There's no time for ironing."

He fished the condom from his pocket, handed it to her and slung his pants over the footboard of her bed. He stepped out of his boxers.

Melanie raised an eyebrow and perched on the bed as she tore open the foil pouch. "Do you always walk around with a condom?"

"I brought a ring, Buttermilk. Of course I brought one."

He sucked in a sharp breath when she held him in her slender fingers and rolled on the condom. He kissed her, tasting her sweetness, lowering her down onto the bed. He stretched out next to her, pressing his lips to her shoulder, the graceful contour of her clavicle. Her skin tightened when he flicked her nipple with his tongue. He reached between her legs, moved his fingers in a steady circle at her center. She moaned in appreciation. He dipped lower with his hand, finding her more ready than he could have hoped for.

"Make love to me, Adam," she muttered. "I need to feel you."

It wasn't just their schedule that had him eager to oblige. The lusty purr of her voice fueled the blood flow between his legs. He'd never felt so primed.

He settled between her legs, gazing at her wide blue eyes and sexy smile as he eased inside her. She was impossibly warm, her body responding to his with subtle squeezes. He grappled with the wealth of pleasure—her beauty, the way it felt to be inside her, the fact that they'd finally worked through their problems—it would've been so easy to surrender to the physical sensations and close his eyes, but he couldn't stop looking at her. He'd waited too long.

She locked her legs around him. He wanted to take his

time, but there was so little, and he already sensed that she needed more. She arched her back, lifting her hips to meet him. Her head rolled to the side, her eyes closed. Her supple lips went slack, breaths becoming shallow. He kissed her neck, thrusting deeper, wanting her to know every inch of him. He knew her peak was about to rattle them both—she was already gathering around him in strong, steady pulses. She dug her fingers into his back, her breaths short and fast.

His entire body was as taut as a rubber band stretched to its limit. Her internal muscles continued to squeeze him, faster now. The instant she let go, he gave in to it, too. Swells of bliss crashed over him—again and again, subtly fading into contentment. He collapsed at her side, breathing heavily. She curled into him and peppered his face with sweet, delicate kisses.

"That was amazing, but I can't wait until after the gala when we can just do that all night long," he said.

"And don't forget that tomorrow is Sunday. We don't have to get dressed at all tomorrow if we don't want to."

He clasped a hand behind her neck and kissed the top of her head. "I love your beautiful brain."

"And I love you."

Better words had never been spoken. "I love you."

Melanie popped up onto her elbow, glancing over her shoulder at the clock. "I hate to say this, but we need to bust a move. The car will be here to pick me up in fifteen minutes." She pecked him quickly on the lips, then hopped off the bed and began rifling through the clothes she'd dumped on the chair.

He plucked his boxers from the floor, thinking about what she'd said—her car. His limo and driver were still downstairs waiting. Practicality aside, going to the party separately was ridiculous when he'd had his fill of absurdity over the past few weeks. "You taking a separate car makes no sense."

Melanie stepped into a silky black dress while he put on his pants and shirt. "Sure it does. We'll both be single tonight and when you're ready, we'll tell your parents. If you want, we can argue at the party. Just to make it realistic." She held the top of her dress to her chest, turning her back to him. "Can you help me with this?"

He tied the bow of her open-back dress. Not knowing what she'd say to the proposal, he hadn't thought out logistics before he'd come to her apartment. Tonight was going to be difficult enough. He couldn't stomach the thought of more pretending. "No way. We're going to the party together. As a couple."

Melanie whipped around, her eyes ablaze with their usual panic when she didn't like one of his ideas. "Adam, no. That's insane. The entire world is expecting you to get out of a limo with Julia tonight. It's bad enough that she isn't going to be there. It'll be ten times more scandalous if I'm on your arm."

"I don't care." He buttoned his shirt and tucked it in. "I don't want to wait anymore. I won't wait. I love you and you love me, and if that's not good enough for the rest of the world, then too bad."

She stepped into a pair of black heels. God he loved her legs. He couldn't wait for tonight when they could be wrapped around him again.

"It's very easy for you to have a cavalier attitude," she said, putting on earrings. "Your dad isn't going to rip your head off first. He'll rip off mine."

Adam shook his head. "I won't let him do anything of the sort. This is all on me. You held up your end of the deal."

"That's sweet, but you didn't sign a contract. I did." She hurried over to the mirror above her bureau and checked her hair, then began chucking cosmetics into a small black handbag.

He came up behind her and clutched her shoulders, making eye contact with her in the mirror. This was the first time he'd seen them together, as a couple. It was all he ever needed to see. "Enough pretending and worrying about what everyone else thinks. It all ends tonight."

Eighteen

Melanie had done some daring things in her life, but this might top them all. On what was possibly the biggest night of either of their careers, she and Adam were about to out themselves as a couple in front of the media and his family. Daring or not, love made it seem like a perfectly acceptable risk.

A hailstorm of camera flashes broke out the instant Adam's driver opened the limo door, followed by a deluge of shouting voices.

"Julia. Adam. Over here."

Of course, Melanie wasn't the woman they were expecting. She followed Adam out of the car, embarrassment threatening to envelop her, but she refused to do anything but hold her head high. Adam had been dead serious about it at her apartment. They'd allowed everyone else's expectations to get in the way of their love, and there would be no more of that. She could do this. She *had* to do this if she wanted to be with Adam, and she wanted that more than anything.

An audible gasp rang out from the crowd as Melanie stepped onto the red carpet. Again, an assault of shouts rang out.

"Adam. Who are you with?"

"Where's Julia?"

Adam firmly squeezed her hand, reminding her that he was there for her to lean on if needed. She half expected him to rush her up the red carpet and past the press, but he didn't. He led her ahead several steps and stopped, collected as could be. "Calm down, everybody. I'd like to introduce you all to Melanie Costello. She's in charge of my public relations."

"Where's Julia?"

That question had played a central role in Melanie's imagined worst-case scenario. The camera flashes became sporadic. The roar of the crowd dulled.

"You'll have to ask her that. We're no longer together, but it was an amicable split."

The litany of flashing lights returned to full speed, but Melanie didn't shy away. She was too busy beaming at her future husband. Adam had learned to deal with the media beautifully.

"Is Melanie your new girlfriend?" a female photographer asked.

"Let's just say that an announcement will be made later this evening." Adam leaned over and placed a kiss on her temple.

Melanie couldn't believe this was really happening. It was all like a dream when being with Adam was already surreal. She'd spent a year wishing she hadn't been so stupid as to sneak out of his apartment, and the past month wishing he could be hers. And now he was.

Melanie and Adam resumed their march up the red

carpet as other guests arrived behind them. The crowd ahead thinned, making it clear their course was about to bring them face-to-face with Roger and Evelyn Langford.

Adam pulled her closer, whispering in her ear, "It's okay. Let me do the talking. For once."

Melanie smiled, but her stomach was a restless sea. Roger could say anything he wanted in front of a ballroom of the wealthy and powerful. He could destroy her career with one well-worded sentence if he wanted to. Even though Melanie would eventually become Adam's wife, she wasn't about to throw away the company she had built. She would have what she'd once thought was unattainable—her career *and* Adam. Unless his father decided to make it all come crashing down.

"Dad. Mom," Adam said, when they reached the entrance to the grand ballroom.

Roger's jaw was set, as if he was biting down on a bullet. "We need to talk. Now." The anger in his voice was thinly disguised by a smile.

"You're right. We need to talk." Adam looked around the room. There were an awful lot of eyes on them. "Privately."

"There's a smaller ballroom next to this one." Melanie pointed to the near corner of the room. "It's empty. The hotel had said we could use it tonight if needed."

She led the way, her hand firmly held in Adam's, her heart pounding away in her throat. The entire crowd whispered as they walked past. She was keenly aware of Mr. and Mrs. Langford behind them, fearing what they must be thinking. This was not the way she wanted this meeting with her future in-laws to happen.

As soon as the door was closed behind them, Roger set his sights on Melanie. "You signed a contract." He pointed to Melanie's and Adam's joined hands. "And you've very clearly violated it. That morning I went by Adam's apartment. You weren't just dropping by to discuss work with Adam. You were there because you'd spent the night." Roger shook his head in dismay. "Poor Julia. She had no idea my son would break her heart."

Adam didn't let go of Melanie's hand, bringing her along as he moved closer to his father. "Dad, please don't speak to Melanie like that. And besides, it isn't good for you to get so riled up. Take a deep breath and listen to me." Adam's voice was calm and measured, but there was no mistaking his determination.

Evelyn Langford, in a midnight blue cocktail dress and lavish diamond necklace, gripped her husband's arm. "Darling. At least allow Adam to explain."

Roger folded his arms across his chest. "Come out with it then. And it'd better be good."

Adam's shoulders rose as he took a deep breath. "Dad, the Julia thing was a ruse and you knew it, but you refused to believe me. I was never anything less than completely honest with you about it." He squeezed Melanie's hand.

Adam's father appeared crestfallen, but Evelyn nodded in agreement. "You have to understand, Adam. Your father became very attached to the idea of you finding a wife and doing so while he was still here to see it."

Anna swept into the room, decked out in a black strapless dress. "There you are. Everyone's wondering where you went."

"We were discussing the things your brother has decided to do to make tonight more stressful," Roger said.

Adam kept a firm grip on Melanie's hand. "I take full responsibility if there's any fallout from tonight, but if that's the price of being with Melanie, then that's the price I'll pay. I love her too much to hide it anymore."

Anna's eyes lit up. "I had a feeling something was going on."

"You knew?" Roger asked.

Anna shrugged. "I had a hunch after spending time with Melanie. I could just tell from the way she talked about him. And it's not surprising that he'd be smitten. She's smart, beautiful and a great businesswoman."

It was such a relief to feel as though someone in the Langford family beyond Adam was in Melanie's corner.

"Dad, I love Melanie. I've asked her to be my wife and she said yes."

"You're getting married? After knowing each other for a month?" Roger's eyes were no longer filled with anger, but rather astonishment.

"You were excited to think I might marry Julia and it's not like she and I had much history."

"I suppose." Roger shook his head.

Adam turned back to Melanie. "Now what?" he mouthed.

Melanie took his elbow and pulled him close, delivering the message directly into his ear. "Speak from your heart. You hit a home run every time you do."

Adam kissed her on the cheek then faced his father again. "Dad, do you want to know the one thing in my life that I have never questioned? Not even once?"

"That you'd run LangTel someday?"

"No. That you and Mom loved each other. I can see it in the way you look at each other, hear it in your voices. I have that with Melanie. She understands me and cares about me. She'll be a real partner, and that's more than what I need. It's the only thing I want."

Melanie warmed from head to toe, unable to suppress her smile.

Evelyn cleared her throat. "Darling, do I have to remind you that you and I were engaged after two months?"

Roger had no answer for that, only a sigh.

"Love is love, Dad," Adam said. "I wasn't about to consult a calendar when I asked Melanie to marry me. The only thing I thought about was what my heart wanted."

"Don't forget that I was pregnant with Aiden when we got married," Evelyn said to Roger. "These things don't always look like a picture postcard. And it didn't matter that it happened that way. It didn't change the fact that we were a couple of kids, madly in love, and all we wanted was to be together."

Roger turned and looked at her sweetly. "I remember that day like it was yesterday. Best damn day of my life." The corners of his mouth turned up, but it was clear that she'd brought up something far more meaningful than a simple happy memory. It was about everything between them.

A tear rolled down Evelyn's cheek. "See? And you and I did just fine. Thirty-one incredible years of marriage. No one could ever want more than that."

"We did better than fine, Ev," Roger said. "It was perfect."

Now Melanie was fighting tears, witnessing for the first time the power of the love that bound Roger and Evelyn Langford. They were both so strong, so resolute, even when they knew very well they were about to lose each other forever.

"Dad, I just want you to be happy for me, be happy for us," Adam said. "Melanie's the most amazing woman I've ever met, and she's going to be part of this family."

"That's the most important thing, Dad," Anna said. "We need to welcome Melanie into our family. An engagement trumps whatever happens tonight."

"I know you want Adam to have love in his life and to get married," Evelyn said, her tears slowing. "And you've been singing Melanie's praises since the day you hired her. I don't really see what the problem is now that you know the truth." She turned quickly to Adam and Melanie. "Can we see about hurrying up the wedding so your father can be there for it?"

Adam's eyes connected with Melanie's and he cracked his half smile. They would have a lot to talk about once they were finally alone. "Sure," he said. "But there's one more thing Dad needs to hear."

Adam stepped closer to his father, resting his hand on his shoulder. Everything Melanie had said to him last night rang loud and clear in his head. His dad was still here. There was still time, and that meant it was time for the truth. "I can't run LangTel. I love you and you know I'll do anything for you, but I can't live your dream. More important, it's Anna's dream to run the company, and I can't sit by and watch her lose the chance."

His father didn't even feign surprise. He was at least aware of Adam's wishes, even if he'd dismissed them as ludicrous. "You really were serious about that."

"I should've forced the issue, but I wanted to make you happy. I love you, Dad, and I always want to make you proud." Adam couldn't remember the last time he'd cried, but after witnessing the powerful exchange between his parents and now seeing the look on his dad's face, his eyes misted. He embraced his father. There would be only so many more opportunities to do that. He didn't want to pass this one up. It was too precious. "LangTel will still be a family company if Anna runs it. We'll all still have the lives you want for us. She can still meet the perfect guy and get married."

Anna coughed. "Hey. No promises on finding the perfect guy."

Adam laughed, thankful his sister was willing to lighten the mood. "I'll be there whenever Anna needs me, but I have a feeling she won't need me at all. It really will work out. I know it will. I won't let anything go wrong. I promise."

His father sighed heavily. "I wish it were as simple as that. I can't pull a fast one on the board and give them a different succession plan. Even in my role as founder, I can't do that. You understand that as well as anyone, Adam."

Adam had to find a way to fix this, for Anna and for himself. "But I could do it myself, as CEO. The company bylaws leave the nomination to me. I looked it up."

"Well, sure, son, that's what I put in place, but you still need the approval of the board of directors. You know that."

"And that's what I'll do. Once things are stable and I have the full confidence of the board, I want to name Anna as CEO. It shouldn't take longer than a year." Adam knew full well the responsibility that scenario bore, but he had no choice. It was the only way for everyone to eventually get what they wanted. "I want your blessing to do that. I think Anna and I would both feel better knowing that you were okay with it."

"Yes," Anna said. "I need to know that you approve."

Roger looked back and forth between Adam and his sister for what felt like an excruciatingly long time. Whatever his dad had to say, Adam had the distinct impression that there would be no more discussion. This was it.

"You have my blessing," Roger said. "With everyone in this room as witness, you have my blessing."

Anna rushed ahead to hug Roger. Adam followed, embracing them both.

"Speaking of blessings," Evelyn interjected, "Melanie hasn't been welcomed properly, darling."

Melanie smiled sweetly as Evelyn hugged her, Roger watching the exchange. This was the moment Adam had envisioned for the two of them, now that she was going to be his wife and his father was accustomed to the idea.

"I'm sorry if we got off to a rough start this evening," Roger said as Evelyn took his hand again. "I apologize for that. I always liked you, Ms. Costello. You're smart and you know your stuff. I admire a woman who knows her stuff."

"Thank you, sir. I appreciate that."

"I'd like you to call me Roger, please. You've done your job and you've done it well, but you're no longer working for me."

Adam put his arm around Melanie. What a relief it was to hear his dad say that. No more contract. No more worrying about whether his dad might decide to crush her career.

"Please, call me Melanie."

Roger glanced at his wife. "Looks like we're going to get a Langford wedding after all, Evelyn. And as near as I can tell, a hell of a daughter-in-law."

"I'd say we're pretty lucky," Evelyn said, gazing up into Roger's eyes.

"We are indeed," Roger said. "And I'd love nothing more than to sit around and talk about it, but I'm afraid that there's a ballroom full of people waiting for me."

Adam nodded eagerly. "It's time."

They all made their way into the grand space, Adam's parents leading them, followed by Anna. Melanie and Adam, hand in hand, brought up the rear. Adam hadn't gotten *exactly* what he wanted with the LangTel situation, but he did have exactly what he wanted for the rest of his life—Melanie.

Roger took the stairs up to the podium slowly, Evelyn at his side. Melanie and Adam took their places at the head table with Anna. Before a roomful of hundreds of wealthy and powerful New Yorkers and a cavalcade of press, Adam's father began his speech.

"I want to thank everyone for joining us on what will be an important night in the history of LangTel. I'd like to formally announce that pending the board of directors' final approval, my son, Adam, will be taking the helm as CEO."

The crowd clapped enthusiastically.

"This changeover is going to happen as soon as possible," Roger continued. "Because I also must tell everyone that my doctors have declared my cancer terminal."

A marked hush fell on the room.

"But tonight is not about proclaiming a death sentence, it's about setting LangTel on a course for the future," Roger said, his voice booming in the space. "It is one of my final wishes that the board move Adam into this new role swiftly. Adam has demonstrated that he is an upstanding man and an excellent business leader. I couldn't be any more proud of him."

Melanie squeezed Adam's hand under the table. How different his father's proclamation would've sounded if Melanie hadn't convinced him to try one more time to change things, if he didn't have his father's blessing to let Anna take his place.

"I'd like to invite Adam up to the stage to make his remarks, and I believe he has some very happy news of a personal nature to share with everyone." Roger stepped away from the podium and embraced Evelyn.

Adam leaned over to Melanie, speaking loudly, so his voice could rise above the audience applause. "You're coming with me."

"Are you sure? It's your night."

"My parents are standing on that stage together. You and I are doing the same thing." He grabbed her hand and got up from the table, leading her up onto the stage. She stood with his parents as he took his place behind the podium.

Looking out at that sea of faces, he couldn't believe how different this moment was from the one he'd imagined. "I'll be quick because I know everyone would much rather dine on filet mignon than listen to me." The crowd laughed, setting Adam more at ease. "I'd like to thank my father for his confidence in me. I'm excited for this new

challenge and I won't let my father or LangTel down."
Now he could believe the words, unlike the time he'd prac-
ticed this speech for Melanie. With great joy, he tacked
on a sentiment that hadn't originally been in the speech.
"And as to the happy news my father mentioned, I'd like
to announce my engagement to Melanie Costello. We're
looking forward to planning a big Langford wedding and
spending our lives together." Everyone clapped and Adam
waved Melanie over, putting his hand around her waist.
"With that, I'd like to thank everyone for coming. Please,
enjoy the evening ahead."

Several board members were waiting for them once
Adam and Melanie stepped down from the stage. Either it
was the somber news of his father's prognosis, the fantastic job Melanie had done on the PR campaign, or renewed
confidence in Adam's abilities, but regardless, Adam received nothing but well-wishes from everyone he spoke
to. It was such a relief.

After dinner, Adam took Melanie's hand and led her to
a relatively quiet corner. "How long until we get to leave
and I get to peel that dress off you?" He was mentally exhausted, but he was sure he'd be able to muster all kinds
of energy once he had her alone and naked.

She rolled her eyes adorably. "I think we should stay
until midnight. Then we can go."

Adam's entire body warmed to the idea, and to the beautiful creature on his arm. "I'm guessing this was a little
more than you signed up for."

She laughed and straightened his tie. "This is a cake-
walk compared to my family. Believe me."

He took her hand, loving the feeling of the ring on her
finger, knowing that it meant their future together was
sealed. "The next year is going to be great, but it's also
going to be hell. We're probably going to lose my dad and

I'll be trying to convince the board of directors that another change in CEO is a good idea."

Melanie grinned sweetly. "And we have a wedding to plan, too. We'll get through it all. I know we will. Together."

"Tonight wouldn't have been possible without you. Seriously. And we've got to put Costello Public Relations on the map. You need an influx of cash so we can hire some staff for you. Let you focus on what you're so good at."

"And what is that exactly?"

"Your mastery of the world of public relations. You're the only person I know who could convince the world that I have a good side."

"I've seen you naked, Adam Langford." She nuzzled his neck, sending a jolt of electricity through his body. "Trust me, you have more than one good side."

* * * * *

'15_ST15

MILLS & BOON®

It's Got to be Perfect

IT'S GOT
TO BE
Perfect

UNCORRECTED
PROOF COPY

HALEY HILL

* cover in development

When Ellie Rigby throws her three-carat engagement ring into the gutter, she is certain of only one thing. She has yet to know true love!

Fed up with disastrous internet dates and conflicting advice from her friends, Ellie decides to take matters into her own hands. Starting a dating agency, Ellie becomes an expert in love. Well, that is until a match with one of her clients, charming, infuriating Nick, has her questioning everything she's ever thought about love…

Order yours today at
www.millsandboon.co.uk